GIVE ME DEATH

Also by John Fullerton

JOHN FULLERTON

GIVE ME DEATH

MACMILLAN

First published 2004 by Macmillan
an imprint of Pan Macmillan Ltd
Pan Macmillan, 20 New Wharf Road, London N1 9RR
Basingstoke and Oxford
Associated companies throughout the world
www.panmacmillan.com

ISBN 1 4050 3389 4 (HB)
ISBN 1 4050 3390 8 (TPB)

1 3 5 7 9 8 6 4 2

A CIP catalogue record for this book is available from
the British Library.

Typeset by SetSystems Ltd, Saffron Walden, Essex
Printed and bound in Great Britain by
Mackays of Chatham plc, Chatham, Kent

I know not what cause others may take; but as for me,
give me liberty, or give me death!

Patrick Henry, 1775

Give Me Death is dedicated to the memory of Sanaa Mheidly, the first woman volunteer to lay down her life in an attack on occupation forces at a location known as Baater Jezzine in south Lebanon in April, 1985

AUTHOR'S NOTE

Give Me Death was inspired by actual events and some personal experience. I was Reuters bureau chief in Beirut during Lebanon's civil war and I did share a bottle of Scotch with a man who had trained suicide bombers. But this is a work of fiction; all portrayals of diplomats, intelligence and security officers, medical workers, UN officials, militiamen, soldiers, politicians and resistance fighters – whether Christian or Muslim, Western or Arab – are imaginary.

PROLOGUE

Remember.

You will never see it with your own eyes.

You, and all your generation, will never walk the streets, smell the orange blossom, pray at the graves of your forefathers, laze in the shade of its trees. Never will you see your children run across the grass, eat the pomegranates grown in its orchards, drink from its wells, sip wine from its vineyards or dip their bread in the oil from the village press.

Remember always.

This green land made you. This earth gave you life. It is your flesh and blood. Wherever you live, and however long, whatever name you carry and whatever the colour of your passport or the eyes of your children, only this is truly home.

Your grandparents have told you the stories and you have seen the pictures. You know how they were driven from their homes. How they were forced to flee. How they came back, how their enemy's law said they could return.

Always remember, daughter, every day of your life.

How they stood at the army checkpoint, the high court order in their hands.

How the enemy planes bombed their homes, the homes of their fathers and their fathers before them. Right in front of their eyes their homes burned, blasted by the bombs and rockets. Our home. Your home.

It was Christmas Eve, 1950, long before you were born.

Your father was but a child, your mother an infant.

The soldiers used their rifle butts on our heads and shoulders. They beat us and spat at us. One beat your grandfather to the ground with his rifle and kicked him with his army boot. He carried the bruise for months. These were young men. Had they not mothers and fathers of their own? Did they not remember their own people's suffering and exile? They pushed the muzzles of their rifles against the faces of our men and pretended to pull the triggers. They scoffed at the tears of our women and children with their handcarts and hoes, baskets and beds, their threadbare clothing, their holed shoes.

Today your home is no man's land.

It does not exist. Even the ruins are unofficial.

You will know our people's villages by the cactus that grows despite our enemies' efforts to erase all trace – there are scores of such places.

Home is forbidden to you and all our kind, we followers of Christ.

We are the dispossessed, the homeless and stateless, without rights, scattered by the wind across foreign lands.

Carry the hurt in your heart.

Teach your children the secret love of the land.

Teach them not to show their sorrow.

Teach them to hate the Lie.

And remember.

ONE

It was a small mistake, but it could kill her.

Reem realized what had happened when they took her upstairs from the arrivals hall and made her wait outside the security office.

Such a small matter.

When it was her turn the *moukhabarat* officer stared at her for a few moments. And when the secret policeman did speak, it was to ask five questions.

'Name?'

Reem told him.

'Where've you come from?'

'Larnaca.'

'Where are you going?'

'Home.'

'Where is home?'

'Beirut.'

'Address?'

'Daouk building, Rue Soixante-huit, Verdun.'

'You're lying.'

He seemed bored. He did not put any feeling into it. He was not hostile. He did not have to be. No doubt he said the same thing to everyone. More specific accusations and threats would come later. He glanced at her passport, but it did not interest him. It was as if he had already made up his mind. It occurred to Reem it could have been an informer, that they could have been waiting for her ever since she checked in, but she knew it was the way she looked.

All it had needed was a few minutes in front of the mirror.

She had been foolish.

They put her in the unmarked van with the others. There was another young woman off the same flight, weeping, and the odd little man Reem thought was a Yemeni who had sat two rows behind her in economy. Odd because he was always smiling.

The wailing of the other woman nearly drove her crazy. Reem spoke to her softly, and hugged her. It will be all right, you'll see. Not that Reem believed it. But it was important to listen to the van's engine, for gear changes, and to sit near the rear door to try to glimpse where they were headed.

If they turned right, away from the coast for the road that threaded its way among the mountains to the east, it would look very bad. If they continued north and into the city, then she had a chance.

Maybe a beating.

If she was lucky.

. . .

All it would have taken was a dab of lipstick, a touch of kohl, the faux gold earrings, a few strokes of the hairbrush and the little black jacket. If only she had slipped on the heels and picked up the black purse that looked Gucci but wasn't.

Instead, in her white blouse, blue jeans and trainers and with her hair pulled back and held with a simple plastic grip, Reem looked like a student.

Or a courier.

That was it. A damn courier.

If they thought that, about being a courier, she would probably be okay. Her first level of cover would suffice.

Her only tactic now was to stall, play for time.

Reem thought the Ustaz would realize something was wrong when she failed to come through the barrier with the other passengers. He would check. That might take a few minutes, but it would not be long before the Teacher found out she had been questioned and was in the Black Maria.

He would not hang around. He would head back into town, use his influence. He had lots of *wasita*, even with the Syrians.

It might take an hour to call in a few favours. Maybe several.

He would work the phone. Make a dozen calls, perhaps pay one or two visits in person to people in west Beirut.

Lie low, wait, Reem told herself.

The alternative was too awful to consider.

But she must consider it. It was this: that they knew she was coming all along, knew that she was being met, knew that the Ustaz was right there in the crowd. Maybe they had picked him up already. Then her cover would not stand up and she would have to fall back to the second level of defence, and when that broke, there was only the truth.

Even so, all was not lost. What was the truth? She would hold onto the names and places for as long as she could. Reem knew little that could be of any use. The Ustaz had made sure of that, and Reem was grateful for it. She would buy him his forty-eight hours. Squatting in the darkness, in the heat of the truck, listening to the sobs of her fellow passenger, she promised herself she would buy him two days. Only then would she try to save herself.

She had screwed up.

That was what hurt the most – not what the Syrians would do to her.

It was simple. Cyprus Airways had said it was their last flight, that they were going to shut Beirut down, and no one knew how long for. Reem could be stranded in Larnaca for a week. Maybe longer. So she had hurried – and this was the result.

The unmarked truck rumbled north.

Reem could smell the sea.

Thank you, Jesus.

*

The prisoners were taken up one at a time in the lift. Reem went last.

There were two thugs with her. One chewed gum and stared into space. He did not look at the prisoners. He was short and dark and scruffily dressed and seemed to her to be none too bright. He probably enjoyed his work. Pondlife. His companion was younger, taller and very much aware of Reem. He looked embarrassed. The sensitive type. Reem made a mental note. When the time came, it was a weakness she would exploit.

They got out at the sixth floor.

The door was open. The short guard struck her between the shoulder blades, a mighty shove that propelled her inside, into the room of lamentation.

Reem knew where she was. The area was called White Sands. Ramleh al-Baidah. She recognized it when they got out of the truck. The sand on the beach was white, too. Before the war she had gone swimming there with her friend Zubaida. It was a public beach, and it did not take them long in the water to discover why. There was a sewage pipe, and the water was filthy. Reem must have had a dozen hot showers when she got home, scrubbing herself until her skin bled.

The apartment blocks were pre-war, too. Sixties and early seventies. Very expensive. They had fine views across the bay, with the beach and the coastal highway at their feet. Close to the restaurants and nightclubs of Raouche, they were popular among Saudis and Kuwaitis and their ilk, holiday homes for the summer months. Now they were mostly empty, grey shells. Reem looked up at the building she was about to enter. It had a desolate air. The concrete walls were stained; most of the windows were shut, the curtains or blinds drawn tightly, even on a warm spring evening. The balconies were empty. There were no potted plants, no sunshades, no clothes lines.

'Inside.' The thug waved his Tokarev.

That was when Reem heard the roll of artillery fire.

Muffled drumbeats.

Up north. Around Jounieh.

They climbed the steps and entered the grubby lobby.

If anyone had witnessed their arrival, Reem didn't see them.

Reem managed to keep her balance. She skidded across the wooden floor and came to a halt against the wall. The other prisoners were crouched on the floor, handcuffed to the radiators. There were five or six, all male. The second thing she noticed was the broken furniture and torn newspapers scattered about the parquet floor. It was obvious that what was left of a coffee table and a number of chairs had been used to beat the captives.

There were three other men in the room. Reem assumed they were the interrogators. Two of them were in shirtsleeves, both smoking. One held a chair leg in his right hand. He was sweating and breathing heavily, as if he had been interrupted while administering a thrashing.

Thank God, Reem thought, the set-up is typically Syrian. Rough and ready, improvised.

It was the third man who caught Reem's attention.

He had on shiny black loafers with little gold buckles and well pressed black trousers. He wore a three-quarter coat Reem realized wasn't a coat at all but a dressing gown. It had a paisley pattern of reds and greens. He was in his thirties, around five ten with fair hair, a reddish complexion and what the French call *les yeux pers*, grey-green eyes.

It seemed to Reem that he had been woken to welcome the new arrivals.

The Yemeni was struck with the chair leg. Once. The second time it was a backhander with the same instrument. He put his hands up to protect his face, and for his trouble was sucker-punched in the kidneys by interrogator number two. He was forced to his knees and fastened to a radiator alongside the others.

The blows were accompanied by curses.

'Ibn kelb!'

The Yemeni smiled no longer.

The chief interrogator gestured with his chin.

He means us, Reem thought.

The two guards pushed both women into an adjoining room.

They slammed the door shut.

The girl let out a howl and collapsed on the rickety bed.

They heard everything.

That was the whole point of it. They were being softened up. The Syrians had traditional ideas when it came to women. Women were soft, weak creatures. It followed that an hour or so of listening to men begging for mercy and crying while being beaten would help loosen their tongues. They would confess to anything.

'Listen,' Reem said to her companion. 'Stop blubbering for just a moment and listen.' The girl lifted her tear-stained face. 'We must pretend to sleep. We must be calm. We must play the innocent.'

'But we are innocent.'

More tears, a low moan.

Reem pulled her close, shaking the girl's shoulders.

'Of course we are. Listen to me. We know that. We have to convince them.'

It seemed to work up to a point.

By lying next to each other on the bedsprings – there was no mattress – and holding hands, they almost managed it. At least, Reem's companion stopped her snivelling. Reem shut her eyes. A small point of pain had moved from the back of her skull to sit right behind her left eye. She could not shut out the racket in the living room, but she got her mind off it. She thought, as she always did in moments of stress, about her mother and father, her brother and sisters.

She remembered.

They did not have to wait long.

It was the chief thug, the smooth fellow who looked almost foreign.

'What? You sleep?'

He was appalled, as if they had committed some terrible breach of protocol.

'In here – move.'

Reem took her time. She got up off the bed slowly, with dignity. She tidied her hair as best she could, pulled her blouse into shape.

'Hurry, you.'

Reem ignored him. She noticed he was not wearing his dressing gown any more, but a suit. He looked as if he were on his way to a cocktail reception. His hair looked wet, slicked down on his scalp.

Reem looked across at the neighbouring building. A man was standing at a mirror by an open window, wearing a string vest. The lower half of his face was covered in shaving cream. He was shaving very carefully with a cut-throat razor.

Someone screamed in the living room behind Reem.

The cry was cut short.

The neighbour must have heard that, Reem thought.

He did not turn. He did not even pause.

The razor blade moved steadily across the man's cheek, leaving a path through the foam.

A gunman grabbed Reem by the arm and pulled her away.

It was morning, Reem realized.

It was their turn.

TWO

Nick did not feel any blow. Only a weight pressing him down.

Tiger's eye danced; a thousand points of light, the flares of his synapses, blinding with the brilliance of crushing pain.

Consciousness went away and came back again.

The ball he recognized as the porthole, weeping tears of basilisk black sea water.

His own iris squinted back at him.

Baffled.

Upside down.

So this was how it was. How it ended before it had scarcely begun.

All because the BA flight to Larnaca was delayed by a French air traffic controllers' strike, and because he would not wait.

It had to do with gravity, with buoyancy, or the lack of it, the two working against each other. He tried to swim, but was held fast. His arms flapped, heavy against the tide, in a futile effort to float.

Nick was more curious than afraid, a spectator of his own demise, inquisitive how these things are done, how we leave this world for whatever's next.

But so unfair.

At twenty-seven, and his first assignment abroad.

Would he drown or would he burn?

Impaled on his own broken ribs.

Would he hear them crack?

Speared, then suffocated.

Nick could have waited for the next flight.

And the others?

The girl was nowhere to be seen. George too was gone.

Were they brother and sister?

Lovers?

Sylvie was a lawyer's daughter. She had told Nick so when she served him bitter coffee in a cardboard cup. Long white dress, more appropriate for a wedding than a sea voyage, down to her little feet. Oddly overdressed for a stewardess, even in first class (and Nick was the only first-class passenger, the only foreigner foolhardy enough to travel). No, she said, she was no hostess. She was doing her patriotic duty. She did not put it quite that way. Serving her country were the actual words the ingénue had used, lifting up her chin with pride as she said it, and Nick had bitten his tongue, resisting the urge to ask which half, pretty lady.

Glossy black hair all the way down to her waist.

Nick already knew the answer.

When he had asked for something stronger she had looked sorrowful.

Only coffee. She seemed to take it very personally.

A slur on her half-country's honour.

He drank it all just to please. It was instant. It was disgusting. It wasn't even hot.

George was the pilot. Nick had a fleeting impression of olive skin, white teeth, curly black hair. An amateur yachtsman, he said. He too spoke French. The playboy turned pirate knew every reef, cove, riptide. A good man to have on a trip like this, Nick ventured, trying to sound appreciative. It would take him but a short time in his new post to learn it was a national compulsion to impress the outsider. There being so few outsiders, any outsider would do.

In time Nick would grow indifferent to this desire to be liked, even by people who might try to kill him.

Both gone, anyhow.

Nick twisted in the safety harness, hanging toward the cabin roof; no, it was the deck. Carpet up close, so close he could see each grey bouclé knot like picking out individual trees in a forest canopy. Despite the howls in tourist class, he could hear the nearer bass rumble of the Norse crew, muttering up forward in the reddish glow of the bridge.

George had said they were paid $2,000 each for this run.

He said they were Norwegians; big, broad, blond, with huge hands, in summer whites from which protruded red hair and leathery skin smoked and salted from Skagerrak to Sardinia.

Nick could not see them any more, either.

He wobbled, suspended where his feet should be.

Trussed, as if on a gibbet.

Still alive, but not kicking.

Things tumbled in slow motion, rolling around his head.

Cup, shoe, bottle, spoon.

What a way to start and end a career.

So short.

Another lurch, a sideways slip, a roll.

The water rose and receded.

Nick swung. He struggled. At last he could breathe.

More detonations. Like a buzz, a metallic screech, setting teeth on edge.

Buoyancy prevailed.

Nick spun dizzily.

His immediate world was put to rights again.

He was back in his seat.

Upright.

Alive, to his great surprise.

Oblivion could wait. Sour, coffee-flavoured vomit warmed the front of his sodden shirt. He shivered. He clenched his teeth to try to stop them chattering. Nick's thoughts were with the children in tourist.

The entire ordeal had lasted less than half a minute.

He was lucky.

Nick did not have to be there. He could have waited for the Beirut flights to resume in a day or two. What had happened would have happened anyway, with or without him. He could have spent the evening sitting by the sea with a plate of squid and a bottle of retsina, watching the tourists. It was his sense of apprehension that had compelled him to take the Larnaca–Jounieh ferry. It was not his fault that British Airways had missed the connecting Beirut flight. At the outset of his first real assignment after completing the graduate training scheme at the United Nations headquarters in Paris, then Geneva, Nick had wanted to demonstrate commitment. He did not want to seem reluctant. He did not want to show the trepidation he felt in travelling to a war zone. He was scared. Frightened of being afraid, like most young men facing their first battle. So he had taken the initiative. He did not even think to call Geneva to ask his employers. He took a cab for three Cyprus pounds from the airport to the port – it was a ten-minute trip, no more – and found a crowd of people around the ticket office in the harbour area, and jostled his way to the front with the best of them.

Nick had told himself he was saving his employers the cost of a couple of nights in a hotel room. Maybe more. Maybe an entire week.

And here he was.

Aboard a Phalangist boat.

To Nick the term Phalangist already had a sinister ring to it. He had read the history books, and knew in general terms how the paramilitary organization had begun in the 1930s as a sports body modelled on Franco's blackshirts. Or was it Mussolini's? He could not remember, but it hardly mattered. He had seen pictures of the first Phalangists, outlandish in polished boots, baggy golfing trousers pushed into puttees, Sam Browne-style belts, black shirts and solar topis, strutting through Beirut. He had read how the so-called sportsmen transformed themselves into a militaristic political party championing Maronite dominance of Lebanon, and

13

more recently how they had thrown in their lot with the Israelis and Americans against those who considered themselves Arab, both conservative Muslims and the left.

George had corrected him. Not a boat, Nick. A surface effect ship.

She looked fast; a double row of V8 engines in the stern, a trimaran that sat on the water like a huge dragonfly using surface tension, hardly drawing any water at all, even less at high speed. White all over, the hull was raked back, the passengers' luggage lashed under nets on the exterior like a belt of armour. George was very proud of her.

Her name was in black on the cut-away stern: *Eulalia*.

She of the sweet voice. One of the names of Apollo.

The passengers embarked at sunset, the jetty pointing westwards to the dying sun, their preparations watched by curious sailors lining the rail of an elderly French corvette tied up opposite.

Nick and his fellow travellers turned a lazy arc in the dead calm, the Norsemen setting their course east-south-east.

After the lukewarm coffee, the passengers were offered the opportunity to watch a James Bond movie, *You Only Live Twice*.

The Norsemen stopped the video just before the climax and ordered the vessel blacked out. Nick wondered if they knew when they had agreed the contract that they were being hired to lay on a risky demonstration of Phalangist determination, a brazen act of defiance in the face of a Syrian-backed blockade of Lebanon's Maronite enclave. If they had not known it then, they must have done so by now.

They sat in complete darkness, rocking on the unseen sea.

George whispered on his way past that they were waiting for the right moment to make the last few thousand metres at high speed.

Just after midnight Nick saw the guns fire. He saw the flashes before he heard them.

A flicker, orange and red.

14

Nick leaned forward. He cupped his hands around his face to cut out the reflections and pressed his nose against the Plexiglass.

He was unable to read the implications of the ripple of artillery fire, the dull detonations of what he was told later were the D-30s firing from the reverse slopes of the mountains, a backlit prop to Lebanon's slow agony.

The shells made a throaty shuffle like a death rattle in the night sky.

All at once it became very personal.

How could they miss?

They did not.

An invisible hand seized the ship.

Turned it on its side and pressed it down, bow first.

As easy as killing a kitten in a bathtub.

Fuck.

Would they fire a second salvo?

They would.

They would have radar. Maybe OPs as well, sitting up there on the peaks, using nightsights, calling in the grid references. They would see the coast road for miles in either direction, and several miles out to sea.

The fright squirmed in Nick's throat, throttling the traveller's sense of detachment. He knew fear had a nasty habit of bringing about the state of affairs he was so desirious of avoiding. A man or woman afraid of drowning would almost certainly panic on entering deep water – and drown as a consequence. Nick told himself he must be calm. He could do nothing. Yes, he could have released the safety belt before the shells struck. He could have jumped out of his seat. He could have leapt down the gangway to the tourist deck and struggled to open the forward hatch in full view of a couple of hundred passengers.

And then? Jumped overboard?

The crew would have stopped him. He would only have made a spectacle of himself. A Briton losing his nerve was one thing, a

Briton seen to do so by an entire ship of fools quite another. If he was going to die, it had to be with a modicum of dignity.

In silence. Without protest.

He stayed where he was in his first-class seat with his first-class safety belt and his new UN passport.

The water lapped at his ankles.

Our Father.

Who Art in Heaven.

Hallowed be thy

Name.

The ship leaped forward.

Eulalia's V8s thundered.

Nick clutched the armrests, his face turned away from the sheets of spray dousing the porthole. He shut his eyes.

Thy

Kingdom

Come.

Was there more?

The guns fired again.

Flash then bang.

Thy Will be done.

THREE

Some people did go back.

Those people scattered across the Territories, and others still living inside the Green Line of pre-1967, they went back when they could, when the soldiers and checkpoints and curfews permitted, when the crossfire between the enemy's tanks and the inadequate small arms of the *shebab* lessened or petered out in another futile truce or round of peace talks.

Peace. There was no peace.

They could not live there. They made day trips; they were not even allowed to camp overnight. But over the years they had rebuilt the church, restored the village graveyard and replaced the headstones. They held services there on Sundays, and at Christmas some came from as far afield as San Diego and Montreal, Perth and the Bay of Islands, from Manchester and Marseille. They came on tourist visas, holding foreign passports, the congregation spilling out into the churchyard.

Most were seeing their homes for the first time.

It made no difference as to how they were treated. It made no difference if they travelled first or economy, if they had Canadian passports or bore the Irish surnames of their foreign husbands. They could be both wealthy and elderly, but they were recognized at once for what they were the moment the passengers left the aircraft. They were taken aside at the bottom of the steps, segregated from the others, ordered to climb into a closed van and taken away. They were body-searched, fingerprinted. They were insulted, humiliated. It was deliberate, all of it, in every insufferable detail.

It was the routine of hatred, the ritual right of the strong over the weak.

It was because they were what they were. Because they came from where they came from, because the enemy could not overlook any opportunity to belittle them, to deny them respect, to punish them for their impertinence in coming back at all, in dreaming that this was their land.

And at the end of their lives, some returned to be buried in the family plots, flown out in metal caskets by surviving relatives who could afford it and had the patience for the bureaucratic hassles that stood in the way of seeking a final refuge in earth they could call their own.

It was a homecoming of a kind, Reem supposed.

She knew she would never see it in any case, alive or dead.

They twisted her arms behind her.

Two of them stood behind her, one on either side. Each man held a wrist with one hand, and pushed down on her shoulder with the other so that she bent forward. Then they raised her arms behind, turning the wrists inward as they did so. Her arms were levers, her shoulders and elbows the pivots. They were well practised.

Reem felt the pain shoot up her arms like electricity and flare in the base of her skull, but she had to some extent already discounted the pain. She had been waiting for it. Her mind was on the questions they would ask, and on how she would answer.

But there were no questions.

Not yet.

It took her by surprise.

Did they know?

The pressure steadily increased.

She knew something had to give. It would be her knees. They would buckle.

They wanted her on the floor, kneeling.

Reem moved before it happened.

She took a step back, releasing the tension on her arms.

She ducked, twisted sharply to the right and came up snarling and spitting, pulling her arms in to her sides like a boxer.

'Bastards – call yourself Arabs?'

Her captors froze.

Reem bared her teeth. She pulled her right hand free and raised it, a claw, ready to strike downwards.

'Is this how you treat your Arab brothers? Is this how you treat Arab women? Call yourselves men? How dare you . . .'

Reem lunged forward and spat into the face of the tall young man who had shared the lift up to the sixth floor.

When his companion stepped in close, Reem turned back to her left and the fingers of her right hand raked his face, from just below his hairline down either side of his nose and snagged on his lips. Reem missed her target – the eyes. But she felt the skin give, felt tissue accumulate under her nails, saw blood spurt from a torn mouth.

'Shame on you. Shame, shame, shame . . .'

Four men stood around her, uncertain, keeping out of range of her talons and her teeth.

The guard's face bled from four irregular clawmarks.

'Get her down on the floor, you bloody idiots.'

It was the blond. He had heard the ruckus and stood in the doorway, watching, hands in pockets.

His words broke the trance. Someone kicked her feet from under her. An elbow smashed into her back, a fist stunned her on one ear. A boot was in the small of her back, pinning her down while other hands tied wrists and feet. All she could see was the torn newspaper used to soak up the prisoners' blood inches from her nose, and the tips of those shiny black loafers.

Reem breathed in the stench of shit, piss, fear.

They wrenched her back, straining shoulders and spine.

The Yemeni was still there across the other side of the room, chained to the same radiator grill. His eyes were closed. Blood caked his shirt.

They were stretching her like a bow.

Hands lashed her roughly to a chair. They bent her against it, sending sharp stabs of pain through the small of her back to her ribs.

Reem breathed fast, trying to gain control of the pain.

'Bastards.'

She felt her ribs bend.

Her backbone grated on itself.

The head man spoke softly.

'You're PLO.'

It was a statement.

Reem shook her head from side to side.

'We know you are PLO.'

His mouth was near her left ear.

'No. No. No.'

The pain was constant. Burning. As if they held a torch to her back. She ground her teeth, fighting the urge to cry out.

'Tell us. You're Fatah. You were seen.'

Rather than scream, Reem grunted, breathed in short, sharp intakes of air and out through her teeth to stop herself from crying out. How she would have loved to scream, to wail, to beg.

'You were seen,' the blond said. 'You were seen at the PLO offices in Nicosia. He –' the blond pointed at the comatose Yemeni – 'he saw you there. Two days ago. He is another. He gave you up to save himself. Answer me. You are PLO.'

Reem moaned. It was a low, throaty sound. She was not going to answer. She could not. She sounded to herself like an animal panting. She could smell their sweat as they racked her. Their body odour, their dirty feet. A rancid man smell.

'You are PLO. Tell us. Then you can go home.'

Home was a long way away.

It wasn't in their power to send her home.

'Tell us and you can go.'

Liar.

Reem knew his nickname. It had been mentioned more than once while she had pretended to sleep in the other room. His men had whispered to one another when he was out of earshot.

Prince of the Hill they called him. Not his real name, of course, but in a small world like west Beirut, it would not be difficult. She promised herself that she would, if she came out of this in one piece, have the small, pleasurable satisfaction of getting her own back.

Somewhere in the flat, behind a door, in another room, she heard the insistent ring of a telephone.

Reem didn't care. Pain burst in her head. Eventually her muscles would give, they had to, and her arms would be dislocated, sprung from her shoulder sockets. She could not hold on much longer.

Bastards.

They were going to break her. She would be no use to anyone.

That voice again.

'You're PLO.'

Reem forced herself to go limp, to sag on the rack they had improvised. Her head lolled to one side. Her eyes rolled back in their sockets. She dribbled.

It was a pathetic act, but she had run out of ideas.

They wanted to punish, not interrogate. They thought they already had all the answers. They wanted to hurt her. They were succeeding.

While the notion of vengeance was sweet fantasy, Reem did not really hate the Prince of the Hill. She was fully aware that if it was not the Syrians, it could have been the Palestinians. They had run this part of town too, and in their day they had not pulled their punches, either. It could have been the Israelis – God forbid – or their Phalangist vassals. It could have been any of several factions, Muslim or leftist, that made up that loose and turbulent coalition known as the National Movement.

None could claim to have the moral high ground at this late stage.

Some were just less bad than others.

No, she did not hate. She pitied them.

Reem knew the Syrians' natural instinct had always been to support the National Movement. The notion of taking religion and ethnicity out of politics, of removing the privileges of the Maronite landowning oligarchy, of replacing it with one man, one vote – in a word, democracy – was hardly revolutionary.

At the very moment that the Movement had seemed assured of victory, Syria turned her coat. It was not hard for Reem to see why. It was realpolitik. If the Movement had achieved military victory, the Christian right-wingers in the form of the Phalangists and their Lebanese Forces militia allies, egged on by Israel, might have done what they had long threatened to do – partition the country and establish a separate Maronite statelet, a dagger at the throat of Damascus and the Arab world generally.

And if this had not happened, and the Movement managed against all the odds to turn success on the battlefield into a leftist, nationalist Lebanon, it was hardly better. It would have been a democratic challenge to Syria's ruling Baath Party, a rival for the affections and assistance of the socialist bloc.

Reem understood that for Syria there could be no victors, no vanquished in its tiny neighbour.

It must keep the balance of power, and that necessarily meant intercepting PLO couriers working for Yasser Arafat. It meant not antagonizing Israel to the extent of suffering yet another invasion by the Jewish state's army.

'Untie her. Get her up.'

It was not her stage performance but the telephone call.

'You're lucky.'

The Prince of the Hill stood close to Reem, looking into her face.

'Next time you will not be so fortunate.'

Reem lunged forward, but her gaolers grabbed her arms. She twisted and turned, trying to free herself

'Call yourselves nationalists? Is this how you fight our enemies? By beating and torturing your fellow Arabs? Is this how Lebanon's glorious allies behave?'

The Prince's face paled.

'Get her out of here. Now. Before I change my mind. Take her home, Malik.'

He pulled keys from a pocket and flung them to the tall gunman.

'Take my car.'

'Yes, chief.'

Reem saw them open the door. The lift was right there. They were waiting for her. Was it a trick? She took one cautious step, then another. Her back was on fire all the way up her spine. Someone offered his hand, but she shook him off.

'Keep your filthy hands off me . . .'

She would show them.

They watched her. Yes, she would walk unaided. She did not need their help. Reem shuffled past the unfortunates crouched on the floor. She did not look at them. She left behind her the ammoniac stink of body fluids. She felt sore all over. It hurt to breathe. Every muscle ached. Her head pounded. The lift stood open. She told herself that once inside she could somehow lean against the wall and rest.

She would never accept their help. Never.

This time she did black out, but they caught her before she hit the floor and carried her into the lift and then out to the car.

*

The city was dark. There were very few street lights. Everything was shut, the shop fronts boarded up for the night. Reem came to on the back seat of the Mercedes. She tried to sit upright, but the pain caught her unawares. Malik must have heard her move.

He slowed, turning slightly and with one hand stretched back over the passenger seat, offered her a cigarette.

Reem didn't hesitate. She took one. He put the pack down beside him and handed her his lighter.

She drew the smoke into her lungs with a sense of luxurious pleasure.

Carefully, very carefully, she moved slowly back until she lay sprawled across the seat, her head just high enough to see where they were going.

There was nothing out there but rats and cats and gunmen.

Malik had the radio on. He turned up the volume, apparently for her benefit.

It was a Western music station, one of those new twenty-four-hour FM stations, broadcasting news every fifteen minutes, alternating in Arabic, French and English.

A ferry bound for Jounieh had been hit by artillery fire, the newsreader said, in French this time. There were no immediate reports of casualties, but it was believed the vessel had managed to dock.

Army and Lebanese Forces artillery had returned fire.

They were almost there.

Reem did not want Malik, however sympathetic he might seem, to stop right outside her door.

They were two blocks away.

Reem didn't think she could walk unaided any further than that.

'Here,' she said. 'Stop right here.'

Malik did so, pulling into the kerb.

He turned right around in his seat this time. 'Look,' he said. 'I'm sorry, okay? We did not want to hurt you. Please believe me. It's our duty.'

She got the door open, slid out her feet, tested her weight on the ground, then leaned forward and pulled herself upright. Slowly.

Sorry?

Reem shut the car door behind her. She did not look back. She did not say anything. She started walking slowly, conscious of Malik watching her. It was the stagger of a drunk. In Reem's case it was pain, not intoxication.

There really was nothing to say. The ferry, the artillery, her ordeal at the hands of the *moukhabarat* – what would be the point of saying anything?

It was all in a night's work.

FOUR

Sunlight bathed the shabby hotel room in gold.

Nick leaned out of the window, elbows planted on the sill.

Opposite, a fat man stripped to the waist and standing on a rooftop exercised his pigeons by waving a long pole to prevent the birds from landing. The birds flew round and round in tight circles. Most did not seem to mind the mandatory exercise, but a couple of laggards, fatter than the rest, repeatedly tried to land, apparently fed up with the business of circling for circling's sake.

The sky was pale, the air cool. It carried with it the tang of sea, coffee and freshly cut flowers. The cries of children rose from a school playground six floors down, punctuated by the hooting of car horns as the rush hour began.

Nick had woken to church bells competing with the calls to prayer, following a dissonant fault line across the city. He experienced the delicious sensation of being alone in a strange city, a capital at war with itself. No one knew where he was. His employers did not know. How could they? His family did not. To all intents and purposes he had vanished. Nick had been shot at. He had nearly drowned. The intention had been to kill him and his fellow passengers. He had kept his nerve. He told himself he had survived not once but twice. Nothing would be the same ever again; quite how or what difference it could possibly make he did not know. But he told himself he had crossed a threshold, passed another test.

Had it all been a dream? It was so peaceful out there. So unwarlike. It certainly had a dreamlike feel to it, but Nick had only to glance at the floor to see his clothing, flung down where he had stripped off and fallen into bed. The shirt and pants were still wet. He had been led to his room by an ancient hotel porter bearing a hurricane lamp, and then, locking the door behind him, he had pulled the bedclothes over his head in a vain effort to shut out the menacing sight and sound of a city at war, the eerie white light of parachute flares washing walls and ceiling, the staccato stutter of automatic weapons, the thump of mortar bombs and crash of rocket-propelled grenades.

It was no dream.

Nick had made friends with pretty Sylvie and handsome George, perhaps not so much friends as yet but acquaintances forged under fire, and possibly a useful contact in Sylvie's father, the mysterious lawyer in a linen suit with a wide, mobile mouth that always seemed to be on the point of making a cruel joke at someone's expense. A figure of authority, who drove a black S-class Mercedes with tinted windows.

It was a start, a good start. Nick had slept heavily, blindly, finally deaf to the sounds of civil war. The vague, unsettling sense of apprehension had evaporated by morning. He felt refreshed and eager to start work when the telephone rang. Nick turned from the window, sat on the edge of the bed in his shorts and picked up the receiver.

He expected reception or the duty manager, asking if he was checking out. Or housekeeping wanting to know if they could do up the room.

The voice was male. The words took shape at the back of the throat and were bitten off almost before they escaped the speaker's lips.

'Mr Lorimer? Nicholas Lorimer?'

'Speaking.'

'Major Peregrine Dacre, British embassy. Welcome to Lebanon, Mr Lorimer.'

What was that name again?

'I trust I didn't wake you.'

'Not at all. I was about to go down to breakast.'

'We always make a point of checking the passenger manifests, Mr Lorimer, and I found your name. Or rather it was brought to my attention. No doubt you're aware of Foreign Office advice to British travellers with regard to Lebanon?'

'I am, yes.'

It was not to go there if the journey could possibly be avoided.

'I wish to add a footnote, if I may.'

Nick was going to say 'certainly' or 'of course', but the major did not wait.

'Both sides have got their hands on 240-millimetre mortars. You may not be familiar with this weapon. It's often referred to as a bunker-buster, and with good cause. It's enormous. It's Russian. It was used in World War Two to destroy Nazi bunkers deep underground. One of its bombs weighs in at nearly 300 pounds and can go through several floors of a building before detonating, and I am sorry to say it has already done so. More than once.'

Nick said nothing.

'The Syrians have three batteries in the western sector, Mr Lorimer – that's eighteen of the monsters – and they are using them to try to locate and destroy one of the 240-millimetre mortars the Lebanese Forces militia have acquired from either their Israeli or Iraqi friends.

'This particular weapon has been deployed very close to your hotel. I'd advise you to change your location as soon as possible. Now, if you can.'

Something irritable and stubborn uncoiled in Nick's insides.

'I'll move as soon as I've had breakfast.'

Nick would be leaving anyway, heading west, but he was both hungry and thirsty. He needed a shower and a shave and a change of clothing.

'I wouldn't wait, Mr Lorimer. They usually start up around ten hundred hours after their morning coffee, but there are always exceptions and I'd hate you to be it.'

They being the militiamen on both sides. On all sides.

Nick glanced at his watch. It was just after eight.

'I appreciate it, major. How did you know I was here – at the Alexandre?'

There was the briefest pause.

'A certain gentleman you met last night at the port told me you'd had a close run and that he'd dropped you off there. He also said you refused his offer of alternative accommodation.'

Something told Nick he should not mention the lawyer by name.

'The lawyer told you?'

'He's not what I call a lawyer, Mr Lorimer. He's a very special kind of animal, but he does give me the nod when he runs across one of ours. As a favour. He said you had a rough passage.'

One of ours?

'It wasn't that bad,' Nick said.

Dacre chuckled. 'Two dead, four wounded sounds bad enough to me. Let us know where you decide to stay. You must come over and have dinner. There are only three of us left. We always like to see new faces. There's the ambassador – you'll like him – the political counsellor, Andrew, and myself. You'd be doing us a favour.'

'I'd like that. Thank you.'

Nick could be polite, too.

'Thursday?'

'Well—'

He did not expect the invitation to be anything other than the usual English double-speak, and certainly not to be pinned down now. What was today? Friday? Saturday? Nick grappled with the day and the date and failed.

'Shall we say nineteen hours at the embassy?'

'Sounds good.'

'Do you know Rabiyeh? We're up above it on the hill among the pines.'

'I'll find it.'

'Good man. You're going over to the western sector today?'

'How did you know?'

'You UN fellows tend to congregate over there. The museum seems the best bet this morning, but as you will discover, Nicholas, these things can change in a matter of minutes.' The voice seemed to recede. 'Thursday, then. I look forward to it.'

Dacre knew a great deal. He knew Nick's name. He knew when and how he had arrived in Lebanon. He knew where he was staying. He knew who his employers were. It was almost as if he wanted Nick to know he knew these things. Nick was not ungrateful. Of course not. And what was all that about a museum changing in minutes?

Nick did not get a chance to ask.

Dacre had rung off.

Nick showered in a dribble of lukewarm water, dressed and packed in less than fifteen minutes.

In the lopsided veneer wardrobe he found a plastic laundry bag and stuffed his wet clothes into it. Just holding them up for a moment, feeling the clammy stiffness of the cloth between his fingers, breathing in the foul stench of sea water, sweat, vomit and fuel oil, brought it all back.

He left his trainers. He did not touch them.

Docking had been rapid. Hands had reached out in the darkness and helped passengers scoot and slither across the gangplank thrown down to bridge the oily water. Others tore off the netting and grabbed the luggage, hurling the suitcases onto trolleys.

Nick grabbed his own holdall and backpack from a porter.

Their eyes met briefly when Nick pressed a five-dollar note into his leathery palm.

It crossed Nick's mind that the porter was risking his neck to feed his family. There had to be easier ways to survive, but fishing – he did look like a fisherman – was not one of them. The sea was too polluted, militiamen destroyed what remained of the

30

fish by throwing grenades into the water, and Israeli gunboats harassed the few who did try to put to sea.

'Thank you,' Nick said.

'Too much boom-boom,' said the porter. 'Boom-boom,' he repeated, gesturing at the darkened port city and the flickering light from burning houses.

The flames illuminated the man's terror.

Too much boom-boom.

A bright light made Nick turn his head to the right. He thought later he must have taken a step back. That was what saved him. The flash was followed immediately by what seemed to be a giant hammer striking the quayside with tremendous force, right next to him.

He felt the shockwave through his feet, his legs, jarring his teeth.

Dust and smoke filled his nose and mouth.

He was stunned. He turned back, unsteady, still holding his bags.

The porter was no longer there.

Nick looked around. He felt numb. Stupid. Blood roared in his ears. Oh, Nick thought, there he is. The man was face down in the water. There was something wrong with him. It was his head. It had been caved in.

Someone took Nick's arm – a lanky youth in an ill-fitting helmet and an orange jacket with a red cross front and back.

The hand propelled Nick forward, indicating he should follow the crowd into the relative safety of the arrivals hall. It was a concrete structure, more bunker than hall, brightly lit and very crowded.

'Don't worry, mister,' said the Red Cross volunteer. 'Don't you worry.'

Looking back, he thought that the Red Cross worker must have been concerned that Nick might take it upon himself to leap into the gap between the wharf and the damaged ship to try to help the porter.

He shuffled forward in line. It was then that the deafening

roar lessened, the mist before his eyes cleared, and he looked down at himself. He was aware of a warm wetness through his denims.

His jeans were soaked with sea water, his own vomit and the porter's brains.

The man's cranial pan had split open. The delicate, diaphanous sack that had contained a lifetime's hopes, dreams and thoughts had broken open, emptying the wet warm sludge in Nick's lap, spilling down his thighs and onto his trainers.

As Nick passed through immigration and customs – positions manned by unshaven, unsmiling gunmen with pistols in the waistbands of their green fatigues – he was struck by irrelevant regret that he would not be able to wear those trainers again. That was a shame because they were almost new.

He found himself dumbly shaking the lawyer's hand, and George was making the introductions. Then he was ushered past the gunmen and pressed to step over and around stretchers on the concrete floor and walk in single file through a chicane of high sandbags out into the night. There the lawyer's car waited; Nick slung his bags into the boot and sat next to Sylvie's father in the front.

'Welcome, welcome. Call me Antoine, Nicholas. My real name is Antun, but here everyone uses the French version.'

A broad smile, American-accented English.

Christ!

The place was an inferno, and this person called Antoine was doing his utmost to be courteous, hospitable, charming – and here was Nick, someone's brains all over his trainers.

The gunmen had all stood to attention. This Antoine – or Antun – generated a sense of awe in those around him, even among the other passengers. They nudged one another, shuffled their feet and stared.

Everyone else had to scuttle on foot uphill along the causeway;

Antun or Antoine and his passengers rolled past the pedestrians without a word.

No one in the car said anything. No one mentioned the red blankets covering the figures on the stretchers, or why they were still waiting for ambulances. No one mentioned the burning houses, the porter, or Nick's trousers and the distressing state of the trainers that were almost new.

Antoine drove fast along the coast road. There were forest fires in the hills, sparked by the artillery duels, and the Mercedes' headlights caught a blizzard of feathery flakes. Only they were grey and black ash, not white snow.

He switched on the windscreen wipers.

He said very little. Nick would recall him pointing out – somewhat wistfully – that the city's Almaza brewery was on fire.

Antoine went on to explain that there were two Lebanese beer outfits. One firm imported beer from France and bottled it locally. Almaza brewed its own product in the country.

Who gave a toss about beer when the entire country seemed to be going up in smoke? Was everyone else acting crazy, or was it Nick who could not quite come to terms with this mayhem?

Nick watched bursts of sparks and thirty-foot flames lick the walls of the brewery. He could smell the hops roasting.

'Such a waste,' Antoine said.

Nick told himself to put it behind him, not to dwell on it any more, to deal with the present and immediate future. What mattered was the next ten minutes, not the whole day or the entire week. Take it a step at a time. Don't look back. He made one final check of the hotel room and the adjoining bathroom to make sure he had left behind nothing worth keeping, and pulled the door shut behind him. He went down to breakfast. He felt almost overwhelmed by hunger.

It had been a difficult start.

Surely it could not get worse.

FIVE

The dream was the same.

She was going down in the lift. She would go out of her flat, cross over to the metal doors, press the button and wait, listening to the ancient machine cranking and wheezing up, a mechanical asthmatic telling the entire block she was on the move.

Reem would step inside, the doors would close and she would descend slowly.

The little round lights illuminated each floor as she went down.

She woke up as she reached the first floor.

Reem lived on the fifth, but in her dream she never saw the doors open at the ground floor, revealing the foyer, the metal security grill at the entrance, the street beyond.

She had no idea why.

This time when the lift took her down to the first floor and she woke up, it was three in the afternoon. She had slept for eleven hours. She was relieved to find it was her own bed, not the dreary room at the *moukhabarat* headquarters. Here there were no cries of pain, no curses. This was the flat where she had lived most of her life. Once this room had been shared with her sisters, and just down the corridor was her parents' bedroom, the one small bathroom where her father used to spend ages shaving, and the narrow rectangular reception and tiny kitchen. Despite the thin walls, the noisy plumbing, the damp and the awful things that had happened there, it was the closest thing Reem had to a real home, to feeling safe.

It was her life raft.

Light filtered in through the curtains, along with the street noise of cars, of shopkeepers shouting to one another, the shrieks of children returning from school. And gunfire, a sound she had known since the age of seven. Reem got up slowly, feeling stiff all over. It was her back that was the worst. It was very tender, and any sudden movement sent sharp pains shooting into her neck. She managed to pull on a towelling robe, gritting her teeth as she got her arms into it. She shuffled into the kitchen. She fried herself an egg in olive oil with a little black paper and salt, eating it straight out of the pan with bread, and washed it down with a Turkish coffee.

Followed by cheese and an apple.

Reem opened the sliding doors at the end of the reception room and stepped out onto the balcony. It was very narrow, barely wide enough for one person. She carried a yellow hand towel. She tied it to the railing, one end loose.

She went back inside.

She was back. She was available. She wanted a meeting.

Yellow for routine, red for emergency, blue for blown.

He must know what had happened. He had got her out of there, of that she had no doubt. It was the telephone call. The Ustaz needed no warning from her. He knew if he was in danger. He did not need to hear it from her. There was no need to panic.

In the bathroom cabinet she found a painkiller and washed it down with mineral water. She ran herself a shallow bath. Reem told herself the hot water would help soothe the stiffness. Then she would go back to bed.

Sleep. Wait.

She used the old Bakelite telephone in the hall to call the research institute where she worked.

Dalia answered.

'It's me,' Reem said. 'I'm sorry. I was delayed, and didn't get home until the early hours of this morning.'

Dalia's voice oozed concern.

'*Habibti*, we were worried about you. Are you okay?'

'I'm fine. I'll be in tomorrow, I promise.'

'Zubaida sends her love.'

'Please tell her I'm okay and I'll see you both tomorrow.'

'We'll celebrate with one of Zubaida's chocolate cakes.'

'I'm so sorry I failed to turn up and left it to you.'

'Don't worry, my dear – the Institute of Palestinian Peace Studies will survive another day without peace.'

They both laughed.

'I'm glad to hear it,' Reem said.

'How was Cyprus?'

'Very hot.'

'We want to hear all about it.' Dalia lowered her voice. 'Especially about those Greek men.'

'You will, don't worry – but I'm sorry to have to tell you I didn't meet Adonis.'

'Shame on you. Do you need anything?'

'No. Not at all. But my bath is running. I must go.'

'You lucky thing – we haven't had any water in our part of town for two weeks. Enjoy it while you can. See you tomorrow. Zubaida will be so relieved to know you're back safe and sound.'

'Me too, Dalia. I missed you both.'

'Bye, darling.'

They were her closest friends. They had been to the same local school. They had grown up together in the same neighbourhood, sharing some of the miseries and joys of adolescence. Dalia and Zubaida were almost family, and helped Reem make up for the lack of one. They were her cover along with the institute. They had no idea of what she truly was, or what she did out of office hours.

Sometimes the deception felt like betrayal. The secret life felt attractive because it imparted a sense of hidden power, an arcane knowledge. Reem knew the weakness inherent in that attraction was the paradox it created. To be fully savoured, enjoyment of a secret life required an outlet, needed to be confessed, needed to be shared. And yet, the moment the words were spoken or whispered out loud – You know, don't you, what I really do is such-and-such – then the magic would evaporate, the spell of clandestine power would be broken. Worse, much worse, the entire construction of cover, of security, would be smashed.

Reem's own ambition would be shattered.

And all because someone could not help trying to make himself or herself more impressive, more likeable, by blurting out the truth. And how tawdry, how commonplace, how petty the truth could sound in plain, everyday language.

So Reem hugged her secret to herself. She kept her friends and basked in the love and comradeship they gave one another, so vital to women in a male-dominated, traditional society, so precious to those who choose to tread the lonely path of the clandestine life, and Reem tried not to think too much about how she used her friends to make herself feel normal, even happy.

She dressed.

Choosing dark colours, she spent time on her eyes, on her mouth.

Reem would not make the same mistake twice.

Only two kinds of women went out alone at night: married women visiting friends or relatives, and prostitutes. Reem was neither, so the look had to be just right. She had to look married. Older, then, and smarter – but by no means flashy. She could not show too much leg. The skirt could not be too short or tight, while the earrings, necklace and ring – a ring that could be a wedding band – had to be modest.

It was no student that looked back at her in the hall mirror.

Handbag. Keys. A wrap for her shoulders and upper arms that could be used as a headscarf. Reem the respectable matron.

*

An ensemble from Prague was performing a selection of Mozart and Gluck in the American university's memorial hall.

They began with the serene 'Parto, ma tu, ben mio'.

Choral music was not Reem's idea of the perfect evening, especially with a back that felt as if it had been raked with red-hot irons. But she managed to sit upright, hands clasped in her lap. During the interval Reem and the man on her immediate left smiled and nodded at each other.

They made small talk.

'Enjoying it?'

'Very much.'

'Me too.'

'My favourite was "Voi che sapete che cosa e amor".'

'From *Figaro*. It's beautiful.'

When it was over, they walked together in silence towards Bliss Street.

Once the crowd had dispersed and they were more or less alone, Reem said: 'Is this a date, professor?'

'I think it must be, don't you?'

They walked along the pavement. There was no sound of firing. Video shops, juice bars and food stalls were doing a brisk trade among students, most of them in jeans and T-shirts.

If anyone had taken any notice of the couple, Reem thought, they would have said father and daughter. She was taller. She had long hair, black or very nearly. He was stocky, broad-shouldered with a goatee, grey hair swept back from his fore-head. He wore tortoiseshell spectacles, a lightweight jacket over an open-necked shirt.

No one would call him handsome, Reem thought.

Interesting, perhaps.

His black eyes had humour, and a disconcerting habit of seeming to penetrate whatever they looked at.

Was he attractive? Certainly.

If anyone had stopped Reem and asked her who her escort was, she would have said he was her Uncle Faiz, but she sometimes addressed him directly as Professor – it was one of the roles she knew he liked to play, using the cover of an academic.

They came from the same village, then and now, but there were no blood ties.

'I said it must be a date and asked if you thought so too.'

'The answer is I don't know. You're far too old for me.'

'It's scandalous. People are bound to talk.'

'Your students will.'

'Students will be students.'

'If this is a date, Uncle Faiz, can I choose where we eat?'

'I thought we were going to have coffee.'

'You're mean.'

'Professors don't get paid much. How about an ice cream?'

'Librarians even less.'

'It's a tough life.'

'You're paid in dollars.'

'You should be watching your figure.'

'I watch it all the time. As a matter of fact I haven't eaten for a century, and if you're a gentleman, you won't refuse me.'

The Ustaz shook his head.

'You're so stubborn. And what is your choice?'

The banter stopped with the coffee.

Reem had chosen a little place named Myrtom House, styled after a Tyrolean restaurant. It had been owned by a Swiss couple who decamped to Monaco once the kidnappings began and left the place to the staff. Reem chose it not for the food but the tranquility, and the little booths with their high-backed seats that offered a degree of privacy. In the event it was less than a third full, it being only 8.30 and far too early for most Beirutis.

The Ustaz had toyed with his pasta, content to watch Reem eat a salad, followed by a chocolate dessert, the house speciality.

'Thank you for getting me out of there.'

He shrugged.

'They didn't ask me anything. Just the same accusation, over and over.'

'How do you feel?'

'Better. I slept a lot today. But my back – it hurts like hell.'

'I'm sorry.'

The Ustaz took a sip from his glass of the house red.

'Why should you be? It was my fault.'

'Not entirely.'

'If only I'd listened to you and taken more time with my appearance.'

'Reem—'

'It was stupid.'

'Listen.'

'What?'

He leaned across the table. He put his hand briefly on top of hers and took it away again. It happened so fast she thought she must have imagined it.

'It wasn't just the make-up or the clothes.'

It took a moment to sink in.

'You mean . . .'

She looked around, but no one was watching them.

'You mean to tell me—'

Reem's face darkened with anger.

'They were a little overenthusiastic . . .'

'You hired them.'

She felt the rage rise in her chest.

'I called in a favour.'

'Those other people—'

'Oh, it was real enough. The prisoners, the beatings. All that was real.'

'And the girl? The one who was crying all the time?'

There was an uncomfortable pause.

Reem nodded. 'She was my minder. You put her in there with

me. To report back. To spy.' Reem's voice rose, and the Ustaz put a finger to his lips.

'No, damn you, I will not be quiet.'

She was half out of her seat.

The Ustaz shook his head. 'You passed with flying colours. You improvised brilliantly. You took them by storm. I think they were in awe of you. It was a magnificent performance.'

She cursed him inwardly.

Yila'an abouk.

'Don't try to wriggle your way out of this with your flattery.'

If there hadn't been a table between them she told herself she would have struck him. If there was still coffee in her cup she would have thrown it in his face. Her temper was always her weakness, and now it seemed unstoppable.

He put out his hand again, a gesture of restraint.

'Don't you dare touch me.'

What infuriated her most was the fact that his eyes were smiling. He seemed amused, not bothered.

'Reem. Listen. The reason I'm here tonight is to tell you that your training is over. You are no longer on probation. You passed. Your secret life begins. I have an assignment. Your first real assignment.'

The tide building in Reem's throat subsided.

The Ustaz chose the moment to excuse himself. He went to the bathroom and took the opportunity to look around the other booths. When he returned a couple of minutes later, Reem had calmed down.

'That's better,' he said.

'What is?'

'You're smiling again.'

She had done well. The lesson had been an important one. They had not asked her for information. She could not fall back on her cover stories. It was a shock. It was meant to be. A final test. Most people's resistance would have crumbled at that point.

But not Reem's. She had come out of her corner fighting. She had handled it superbly.

That was when the Ustaz told her about her first real mission. The target was a new arrival in Lebanon. A foreigner. British. Working for the United Nations, or at least that was what he told people he was doing.

His name was Nicholas Lorimer.

SIX

Looking down through the green canopy of umbrella pines, Nick could see only the surface of the sea; an improbable blue, faintly wrinkled like skin. Turning his head, he saw the sweep of the bay, a Picasso crayon sketch of a Mediterranean coastline.

A warm day, the air filled with the chorus of cicadas, the scent of wild flowers and herbs.

Too perfect.

It was never-never land.

A fantasy.

And a world away from the dingy labyrinth of west Beirut, with its narrow alleys crowded with washing and webs of illicit telephone and power lines hanging in great bunches off lopsided street lights that never worked, a confusion of one-way streets cut by the broad avenue of Hamra and the Corniche running from Raouche to Ain El Mreisse. The sector was split into a patchwork quilt of militia fiefdoms, every wall plastered with huge images of Nasser, Khomeini, Arafat, Jumblatt, Assad and many, many more.

Kalashnikovs, combat jackets and beards everywhere.

Here it was all mountain, sea and sky.

None of the sense of claustrophobia in that urban rabbit warren, of a densely packed population living one day to the next with their backs to the sea and facing an enemy armed, equipped and on occasion led by foreign powers, where bodies were picked up off the street and buried before first light to avoid attracting yet more hostile fire.

Up here there were no snipers, no gunfire, no bursts of automatic rounds, no deafening crash of rocket-propelled grenades.

After only five days Nick already felt a veteran.

'How good of you to come.'

The white-haired ambassador gave Nick's right hand a firm shake. Sir Henry Long, formerly of the Trucial Oman Scouts, was dressed in cricketing flannels, a striped tie used as a belt. In his left hand he carried a gigantic net, and by the puce and perspiring faces of his close protection team drawn from the Royal Military Police, it was clear Sir Henry had just come indoors after galloping about the mountainside, pursuing his favourite quarry, the local butterflies.

'Lemon and ice, Nick?'

'Thank you.'

Dacre handed him a gin and tonic.

They drank, the diplomats raising their glasses in a silent toast to their guest.

Wilson, the political counsellor, said: 'Good to have you on board, chum.'

Nick declined Wilson's offer of a cigarette. Wilson was a rumpled figure and not much older than Nick, but considerably fatter. He had nodded a greeting without stirring from his armchair.

Nick was careful to admire the hole in the ambassador's office window, made by a fragment from a mortar bomb. He made respectful noises about the ambassador's library and agreed with Sir Henry on the soothing effect of Simenon's Maigret novels in times of crisis. He tried to show appreciation when shown Sir Henry's collections of butterflies from as far afield as Brunei and Belize.

Nick knew he was on parade. He was being assessed. He was, he realized, the major's latest acquisition, and before being hauled off to supper, he was being inspected.

For what?

It was only once seated at a table on the veranda of the major's rented villa, carved into the hillside in the luxury suburb of Rabiyeh – like the embassy, in the Phalangist-held territory of Mount Lebanon – that the purpose of the evening began to dawn on him.

Night had fallen.

Below lay the glittering necklace of Jounieh Bay.

Nick had crossed at Hadath at around four in the afternoon.

It was the first time that he had attempted to cross back into the eastern sector since his arrival in west Beirut. Then he had crossed by car, sat comfortably on the back seat of a taxi, moving smoothly through the checkpoints on either side.

This time it had been different.

They were not letting cars through, not at the museum or Barbir crossings. He tried them all, ending up at Hadath, near Bourj and at the far end of the Green Line divide that snaked through the city. So he had got out of the cab, dragged his bag off the back seat and set off on foot. The driver, Ali, tried to stop him, running up behind Nick and struggling to wrest the case from him.

'No, no, Mister Nicholas. Not good. Too much sniper.'

Ali was right. When the first shots rang out, Nick steeled himself. Every instinct told him he should run, duck, hide. But he told himself it was too late to turn back. Nick had started walking and he forced himself to put one foot in front of the other, to stay upright, not to cringe. It would have been a severe loss of face to turn back now, especially with Ali there, watching. So Nick hurried along the dusty track that ran between breeze blocks and empty containers towards exposed ground. Out there people were running, jogging, sagging under their suitcases and baskets, bunching up, as if running together in a herd provided some form of protection.

Nick forced himself to slow down.

The others ran faster when three more rounds smacked over-head.

Close. Too close.

Like a whiplash.

The last bullet kissed the air somewhere near Nick's ear. Then came the bang of the weapon being fired, somewhere on the battlefront, from a sniper hole in one of the eyeless mansions, once grandiose and now overgrown with scrub and long grass.

Bark from a splintered gum tree rained down on Nick's head.

The bastard's playing with me, Nick thought to himself.

Curiously, he seemed to be slowing down, his legs and arms moving heavily, as if underwater. It didn't help that he was trudging through thick sand. It was also the effect of adrenaline, speeding up his reflexes and making the world around him, including his own legs, seem sluggish.

When he reached safety on the far side, Nick felt the endor-phins kick in. He felt great. Exhilarated. Full of bonhomie, he smiled inanely at the taxi driver, not bothering to haggle over the price.

Glad to be alive.

Some people – hundreds, if not thousands – made the journey twice a day, to and from work. It gave a whole new meaning to commuting.

And how different the eastern sector was.

After less than a week it seemed like a foreign country. The cars were all intact, shiny. The buildings didn't suffer from the pox – the millions and millions of craters, small and large, that defaced every structure on the western side. The streets looked clean, the shop windows full of expensive goods.

Here there was only one leader's face, beaming down in short-sleeved shirt. Neat haircut. Athletic good looks, all signs of middle age airbrushed out. Perfect teeth like a toothpaste ad. He looked robust, healthy, like a tennis pro.

The face of the new Lebanon.

A Christian, pro-Western Lebanon. Definitely not an Arab Lebanon. Definitely not a Muslim Lebanon, either. A muscular, autocratic, Phalangist Lebanon armed by Israel and the United States, a Lebanon that would drive out the Palestinians, the leftists, the Arab nationalists, the Shi'ite mullahs who took their inspiration from revolutionary Iran – all the 'terrorists', in other words.

Scum.

Welcome to east Beirut and its Phalangist warriors, scourge of Islam and the left.

Nick looked up at the smile.

It couldn't be.

He looked again.

But it was.

The lawyer.

In big letters were printed the words el-Hami.

The Protector.

A play on the word *mohami*, lawyer in Arabic.

It was Antun.

Or Antoine.

It must have been the gin, followed by a glass of Ksara blanc de blancs and one of Château Musar, but Nick found himself describing the afternoon's adventure to Major Dacre, telling it as a joke against himself.

'And how's the work going, Nick?'

'Don't ask, Perry.'

They were on first-name terms by the main course – filet mignon – and the second glass of red. By the third glass, they were calling each other by their nicknames.

'That bad, Nick?'

'Worse.'

Nick described his arrival in the office in Talat al-Khaya'at. His amazement at the number of staff – twenty-nine in all – their

47

curiosity, their warm welcome, the show of respect, the first round of coffee and sweets, the five older men, veterans of the United Nations and the organization's long, uneven and ultimately frustrating efforts to help cushion the impact of successive Arab–Israeli wars and the waves of refugees crossing the border, then driven north to the capital by further incursions.

How worried they were about their new boss, an Englishman young enough to be one of their several children. Worried about their futures, his plans for them, sure he had some secret agenda, anxious too about their UN pensions, worth less every day with the rapid erosion in the value of the Lebanese pound.

It had taken a couple of days and the frank advice of the office cynic, Khaled, to set Nick straight on a few issues.

Nick was simply not expected to succeed in his mission.

The task he had been set made Sisyphean toil seem easy.

Dacre recharged their glasses.

'How do you mean?'

'I'm a token, a symbol if you like, of the international community's concern about the fate of missing Lebanese. But no one expects me to actually do anything about it.'

'No?'

'There has to be a military equivalent. A dumping ground, a unit for all the walking wounded, the jam-stealers and bottle-washers, the misfits and the old soldiers who refuse to do the decent thing and conveniently fade away.'

'I don't think so, Nick. We don't have penal battalions in the British army. The Russians and Germans used to. We have enough trouble finding and keeping our recruits without that.'

'Well, that's what my outfit is, Perry. The United Nations Office for Missing Persons (Lebanon). UNOMP (L). There was a cull of staff, you see, and several smaller agencies had their local operations shut down. Too dangerous. The United Nations wanted to draw in its horns, lower its exposure. Geneva was worried about the risks our staff ran in their day-to-day lives out here. So I get what's left, a ragamuffin bunch hanging on to their non-jobs and drawing their pay as long as they can until the next cull. Which won't be long, I'm sure.'

'What will you do in the meantime?'

'Khaled says I should enjoy myself.'

'Are you? Enjoying yourself?'

'Oh, yes.'

'What is there to enjoy over there?'

'There are some very good restaurants, and for someone paid in foreign currency they're dirt cheap. There are some good night-clubs, too.'

'The Backstreet is very popular, I hear.'

'Oh, yes. And there are the bars.'

'Khaled sounds an enterprising sort. What about the work?'

'Waste of time.'

'Really?'

'Well, I do try.'

Nick accepted a cigar from Dacre, who took one himself and passed Nick a silver cigar cutter and a large box of matches.

'So you don't believe Khaled?'

'I've decided to try to prove him wrong. But he does have a point. We can't move around much. People don't want to talk to us. There's not much in the way of official records, police or security, and officials aren't very helpful for the very simple reason they stay away from their offices for much of the time. I can't say I blame them. They're paid peanuts. Just getting to and from work is dangerous. Government barely functions on the west side. I can't even bring myself to insist on my staff coming to work when the firing is heavy.'

Dacre sat back in his chair and sucked on his cigar and looked at Nick as if trying to make up his mind about his guest.

'Have you seen el-Hami this time?'

'I saw his portrait this afternoon as I came over. I had no idea.'

Dacre took the cigar out of his mouth and smiled.

'Some things change so quickly. Others never change at all.'

'Meaning?'

'Meaning he has all the qualifications. He's from a landed family. Gentry. A lawyer. Politics is in his blood. He has his hands on the government's security apparatus, or at least the presidential security organs on this side, and he has friends in all the right places. He's the coming man, Nicholas. Maybe the next president. Fortunately for us he has a London tailor, his guns are Purdeys, his dogs are Labradors and his favourite horse is an Anglo-Arab thoroughbred. He's even appointed himself MFH in a drag-hunt he and his chums run in the mountains every year, the height of the social calendar, or so I'm told.'

'What friends in the right places?'

'The Americans like him.'

'That's all he needs, I suppose.'

'And the Israelis, too.'

'And what about HMG?'

'We don't count for much these days, Nick – but he has taken a shine to the ambassador.'

'That must be a considerable relief, to us and everyone else. In our part of the city they call him el-Harami – the Thief. They make it a play on words. They say *'Hami-ha, harami-ha.'*

Lawyer-thief.

Dacre threw his head back and laughed. He was not at all what Nick had expected. He was by no means POPO – pissed off and passed over. He was young. Early thirties, fit, casual in polo shirt and chinos. Clever. A gunner, and the gunners always seemed brighter than members of other corps, with the possible exception of the Green Jackets.

They left the table, and went over to the low stone wall at the edge of the balcony and looked down at the lights. Jounieh was so well illuminated it was hard to believe there really was a war at all.

Nick said something about having seen Iraqi BTR-60 armoured personnel carriers on his way over – a gift from Baghdad for the right-wing Lebanese Forces militia. Baghdad, Tel Aviv and the Protector of Maronistan made strange allies, Nick added.

Iraq was Syria's rival, Dacre said. They were ruled by rival wings of the Baath Party. Israel would do just about anything – including shelling civilian targets – if it succeeded in causing mayhem in the Arab world and undermined the Palestinian resistance. Backing the right-wing Maronites was another opportunity to get one up on Lebanon, Syria and the Palestinians. The Iraqi materiel was coming in with Israeli help, and the Israelis had helped the Iraqis and Iranians with machine tools and servicing the two countries' air forces – organized under cover of Yugoslav and Turkish industrial consortia.

El-Hami's Phalangists and the Lebanese Forces militia were the beneficiaries.

Nick knew all this perfectly well. It was in the papers. He was being patronized, but he said nothing.

'You could help us, Nick. You really could. If you do have time on your hands – when you're not living it up with Khaled at the Backstreet.'

Dacre had brought out two balloon glasses with generous measures of brandy.

'Your health, Nick. Here's to a successful Beirut tour.'

'Thanks. Cheers.'

They drank.

'You were saying . . .?'

Dacre was playing him, playing it long, pretending to have forgotten.

Dacre said, 'Most of the trouble over here – assassinations, car bombings – is said to be the work of one man.' Dacre paused, swilling the brandy around in the glass which he cupped in the palm of his left hand. Nick noticed he wore a gold wedding band, but he hadn't said anything about a wife or family. 'They call him the Ustaz.'

'Teacher.'

'No one knows anything about him. He's top of the Protector's wanted list. He's on the FBI list, too. No one knows what he is. A Muslim? A Christian? A leftist? Is he Palestinian? Who backs him? Who pays him? The only thing we do know is that he's based in the western sector, and his operations have his signature.'

'Signature?'

'His modus operandi.'

'Such as?'

'Such as using a small-calibre target pistol for a head shot. Such as never claiming responsibility for an attack. Such as using Russian C-4 in his car bomb attacks, and using a telephone signal to detonate his devices.'

'C-4?'

'Plastic explosive.'

Nick was losing the thread. He was getting drunk. It was rather pleasant. It was good to relax, to be among his own kind, to hear his own language, to know he did not have to return to that shithole west Beirut – at least not tonight. As Dacre and his embassy colleagues knew it would be. He made a final effort to focus on the subject, not to slur his words.

'Perhaps the Ustaz is different people, Perry. Or several. Perhaps Ustaz is simply a generic term for a group, a movement, a faction of something bigger – or simply a collective term for everything your friend the Protector and his backers in Washington don't happen to like.'

'It's certainly possible.'

'Why would we want to know?'

'We?'

'The British. We don't have a role out here in the Middle East, other than to sit up and wag our tails at whatever the Americans are doing, or failing to do. We messed up here a long time ago. The Balfour declaration, the Sykes–Picot accord, lying to everybody, creating countries out of nothing and putting fake kings on fake thrones.'

Nick told himself he was talking too much. He should shut up.

'We still keep an eye on terrorist groups,' Dacre said.

'Is that what he is? A terrorist?'

'Last week the assistant military attaché at the French embassy was shot dead as he walked to his car. The captain was shot twice in the head with a .22 bullet at close range. We think it was the Ustaz.'

'Hardly a terrorist act. The target was military.'

Dacre sucked on his cigar.

Nick said, 'Was there a claim?'

'He never claims his hits.'

'So . . .'

'Will you help us, Nick?'

They wanted him to spy. That was clear. That was what the evening was about. It had been planned that way. They wanted someone in the western sector. What was the expression?

One of us.

The other shoe had finally dropped. In return for doing what they asked of him, Nick would enjoy their fellowship, a sense of belonging. He would not be entirely alone among foreigners. He could drink himself silly. He could let his hair down at HMG's expense. He could whinge about his work, and no one would care.

One of us.

Nick's thoughts – increasingly jumbled and unfocused – were interrupted by the arrival of Sir Henry with Wilson in tow, both in black tie and tuxedo.

'Thought we'd join you for a postprandial drink,' Sir Henry said, and proceeded to help himself from a bottle of Armagnac on the drinks tray.

'Bloody boring do over at the Swedish ambassador's,' Wilson said, nodding at Nick and pouring himself a large measure of Lagavulin.

Nick thought it possible he was imagining it, but he thought something – a questioning look, a nod in return – passed between Dacre and Wilson.

Nick could not be sure of anything very much, not after all the gin, wine and brandy he had consumed. He was drunk, and the cigar made him feel ill. His head was spinning. But he was pretty sure of one thing. He had not said yes or no to the major's invitation to spy for his country.

Not yet.

SEVEN

There were showers in the afternoon, but they cleared after an hour.

Reem walked home from the institute, careful to avoid the enormous puddles that had formed in the shell craters. The city, for all its wounds, looked cleansed, refreshed.

Decline in a city under siege is a gradual and almost imperceptible process and Reem knew she no longer noticed the symptoms.

Nobody does, she thought. We are all part of it.

Our clothes become progressively shabbier, our hollow faces show the strain, the constant worry. We cannot sit still, we cannot be alone, we cannot bear silence, we cannot queue in a shop, or wait for someone else to finish speaking. Our pleasures being few, we take what we can as fast as we can, like gluttons. We are driven like sheep to our inevitable end, as if we feel impelled to rush to oblivion.

Reem did not rush. She took her time. She never chose the most direct route. That would have taken her a matter of a few minutes straight up the hill since she worked practically in sight of her own front foor. Window-shopping, especially around Hamra, the Tivoli area and the side streets near the Piccadilly cinema, was one of her few diversions, so she took a circuitous path. She had little money, but like any young woman anywhere, she enjoyed looking and trying things on. Lingering served a double purpose. It allowed her to vary her route. And window-shopping gave her a chance to watch the street – 'mirroring', the Ustaz called it.

Watching for the danger signs.

Combining business with pleasure.

Reem looked for the same face twice, only with a change of hat or coat and coming from a different direction, perhaps crossing the street at a diagonal, hurrying to get closer. Reem had practised it often enough in training, identifying each member of a five-strong surveillance team without giving any indication that she was aware of being tailed.

It was more than training. It was an instinct for self-preservation. Some had it, others never would pick it up. It could not be learned. It had to be lived. Just as Reem could always tell whether someone was carrying a concealed weapon by the way he or she moved.

She kept a lookout for beggars and hawkers with barrows of fruit or cigarettes – all too often static surveillance posts, logging people moving in and out of a specific building. Or the same battered Volvo estate lingering at a corner, the rear doors slightly ajar. The Syrian *moukhabarat* had a penchant for Volvo estates.

Sometimes she would enter a shop and while pretending to admire a handbag or waiting to try on a pair of shoes, she would look out, pretending to daydream, knowing whoever was out there would not be able to see her clearly.

Seeing without being seen.

Sometimes there was another way out, and she would commit it to memory in case she ever needed an escape.

Unless fighting made it impossible, Reem never spent less than thirty minutes clearing her back on her way home.

This time she bought onions, lemons, garlic, tomatoes and parsley.

The traders knew her by sight.

She enjoyed the joshing, the hint of flirtation.

They called out to her.

'Light of my eyes, what is your wish?'

It made her feel almost normal. It was a little escape. In these brief interludes Reem could pretend for just a few moments that she was a normal person leading a normal life in a normal city, taking pleasure in the small things of everyday life that so many millions must take for granted in other countries.

How fortunate they were. Yet what was the point of being lucky if you were not conscious of it, did not treasure it? If you had not fought and won it?

Suede ankle boots, rather scuffed and worn at the heel, pressed blue jeans, olive T-shirt and matching lamb's wool V-neck pull-over, kohl for her eyes, lip balm. A few strokes of the hair brush.

There. Almost done.

A single silver bracelet.

Neat yet casual.

Enough money for a service taxi there and back and enough in reserve for a couple of drinks. Keys. Comb. Laminated ID card. All these in the inside pocket of a short black leather jacket.

She was ready.

A last look in the mirror.

There was still half an hour to play with. Reem had made herself a salad, and now she picked out Mozart's Piano Concerto No. 23 and waited for nightfall, sitting in the reception room near the glass doors at the far end, eating slowly.

Reem looked around the room. She had changed nothing.

The family photos stood where her mother and father had placed them. Pictures of both parents, holding hands, smiling at the camera. Their backs to the sea. That was taken at Shikka, in the north.

Reem's two sisters. Her solemn little brother in suit and tie.

The antimacassars her grandmother had embroidered were still in place on the two leather armchairs. Even her father's collection of whiskies, untouched, each bottle turned the way he would have wanted, with the labels showing.

Johnny Walker. Bells. Cutty Sark.

Everything had been dusted that morning, the worn grey

carpet and reddish-pink kilim hoovered. The Ustaz paid the rent – not directly, of course – and he had arranged for the trustworthy Salwa, a Kurdish widow, to come in and clean the place twice a week. War permitting, she also did much of the shopping, washing and ironing.

It was the same in her parents' bedroom – their clothes in the wardrobe, the sheets and pillowcases on the bed: shaken out, laundered, ironed and starched, sprayed with French linen water. But never altered. Sometimes Reem would go in and sit on the bed and talk. Just as if they were still there, and she had taken in their breakfast and stayed with them and told them her stories while they sat up and ate – just to please her.

Just as she used to as a child.

Her father's shaving kit was still where he always kept it in the tiny cupboard above the bathroom handbasin. The same tubes of toothpaste, the bath oil, the lemon-scented soap.

A museum to memory, to loss, to what was and what might have been.

It was at this hour, just before sunset, that the only beam of direct sunlight entered the living room. The street was too narrow, the apartment blocks too tall for it to be otherwise. Reem watched the oblong blade of gold set fire to the kilim and creep across the carpet towards her feet. The guillotine would advance as far as the toes of her boots, and recede.

Just as it had always done.

It was the second movement – the Adagio – that she found the most moving.

Then it was over, the sun had gone and the swift Mediterranean sunset heralded in the dark.

She had his name. She had a description and she had a photocopy of what Reem thought must have been one of the passport photographs the Briton would have supplied to the immigration authorities.

58

It would have been handled by the local UN staff ahead of his arrival, and that was no doubt how the Ustaz had obtained the snap. Someone on the inside, paid to copy it.

Someone who worked with him.

Five eleven, one sixty-eight pounds, light brown hair, blue eyes. Age twenty-seven.

Seven years older than herself.

She knew something of his routine, such as it was. The English had been living and working in the city for barely three weeks.

He lived alone in a large flat on the seventh floor of the al-Nada building in Ain El Mreisse. It had a view of the sea. Three double bedrooms, two bathrooms, three balconies. There was a steel outer door and a CCTV camera on the landing.

Marble floors. French-style shutters.

A lot of flat for one young foreigner.

The English walked to work. Alone. He left his apartment at about 7.30 a.m. and headed up the hill between the French and Swiss embassies. He walked past the MEA office, the Central Bank and the law courts to his office in Sanayeh. It took him no more than twenty minutes.

If the shooting was particularly bad, he was collected by car, either an office driver or by one of the Lebanon Taxi people.

After work he walked home again.

He would emerge from the al-Nada building a couple of hours later, bathed and changed, and head for the first watering hole on Bliss Street.

His nights were long, starting around 7 p.m. and seldom ending before dawn.

First stop was usually Sammy's Bar.

Sammy's had a frosted glass front on Bliss Street.

The long bar ran down the right-hand side.

A Stan Getz jazz samba oozed from hidden speakers.

'There you are.'

Zubaida was perched on a bar stool down the far end, her black purse in front of her on the bar top. She was smoking.

They greeted each other, Lebanese style, three kisses, cheek to cheek, and because they were good friends, a hug.

'My dear, you're late.'

'I am not.'

'I make it seven ten.' Zubaida looked her watch.

'It's seven.'

Reem indicated the clock on the wall.

'My watch must be fast.'

The barman had moved down to serve them.

'What are you drinking?' asked Reem.

'Orange,' Zubaida said. 'But it's out of a bottle.'

Reem turned to the barman. 'I'll have a Coke, please, with ice and lemon.'

There were only three other customers, all male. Reem thought they were professionals. Doctors from the American hospital, perhaps, in their thirties and forties, a bit old for the usual clientele at Sammy's. The men did no more than glance at Reem as she had passed by, and went back to their huddle, laughing and swigging German beer straight from the bottle.

Maybe revisiting their student watering holes, Reem thought.

It was still early. There was plenty of time.

'You've been here before. You must have,' Zubaida said.

'No. Never.' Reem shook her head.

'So why choose this place?'

'Because when we were studying we never came here. We never dared. Now I do,' Reem said with a smile.

Two women – both heavily made-up and wearing very tight-fitting cocktail dresses in shiny material that caught the light – teetered over to the bar on high heels. The three men stopped talking and looked them over carefully. The two women stared back, unabashed, their appraisal equally frank.

Zubaida raised her eyebrows at Reem and winked.

'Out for a good time,' Zubaida said.

'You bet.'

In another twenty minutes Sammy's was packed.

Students mostly, men and boys, women and girls, Christians and Muslims, Druze and Kurds, Armenians and Palestinians. Most arrived in groups. Members of some groups recognized members of other groups. Groups fractured, broke up, re-formed and merged and broke up again. Friends welcomed other friends. There was a lot of kissing and hugging and back-slapping and a great deal of loud laughter. The men drank beer and the women did, too, but most stuck to soft drinks. Reem knew many would buy one drink and make it last all evening because they could barely afford it. They were determined to have fun. Better to have one drink and miss a meal. Fun at all costs. Look good, holding a drink, looking and being looked at. That was what mattered. It was better to tap your feet to the music and flirt now because tomorrow might never come. So the noise increased, the place heaved and the bar top was crowded with bottles and glasses and bowls of nuts and crisps. Everyone was determined, for a few hours, to enjoy themselves.

The sambas were louder, faster.

Couples kissed hungrily in corners.

Cigarette smoke formed a dense cloud near the ceiling.

People were not talking. They were shouting. A few were even dancing. Couples in tight clinches staggered about like exhausted boxers.

The fighting would have to be both loud and close to be heard at all. Which was the whole idea, Reem thought. Time to forget. Time to live.

Zubaida muttered that she was getting hungry and wasn't it time to grab a pizza someplace.

Reem was starting to think it just wasn't her lucky night.

She told herself she would give it another ten minutes and no more.

No, she was not hungry. Not yet.

Zubaida sulked and lit another Marlboro Lite. In any case, it was too noisy to talk. They had to put their mouths to the other's ear and shout to make themselves heard.

Eight twenty-six.

That was when he walked in.

Nicholas Lorimer, in the company of a Lebanese male.

No doubt about it.

Tall, broad-shouldered, blond.

Just look at him.

He pushed his way to the bar, turning his head to his friend and presumably asking what he wanted.

Money to burn.

Smart clothes.

So damn superior.

He takes life for granted, she thought.

Reem swore under her breath.

Being a foreigner, he stood out. It did not take him a moment to attract the barman's attention. He held up two fingers. Two beers. He paid, grabbed the bottles and withdrew from the melee. Both men stood against the wall.

Now.

Reem leaned over, her head close to Zubaida's ear.

'Look after my seat. I won't be a minute.'

She would work something out. She would pass them both on her way to the ladies', and again on the way back. That way, she would have two shots at it.

Reem had given it plenty of thought. One option was to use Zubaida, as she had a zany, chatty side. She could act the giddy extrovert. She could be Reem's tethered goat.

Reem would only have to nudge Zubaida's arm and point out

62

the good-looking guy over there. It would be easy to persuade her friend to ask the barman who the foreigner was, then encourage him to take part in their game by attracting the stranger's attention.

Zubaida would make the running, and Reem would sit back, letting him come to her.

Zubaida was short, curvaceous, with pale skin and very black, lively eyes and luxuriant hair. She had a friendly, cherubic face that smiled easily, warmly. She was naturally approachable. Men looked at her, were charmed by her. She enjoyed the attention, and Reem knew she was expert at launching into a conversation with total strangers. She had a saleswoman's walk-in ability. Zubaida would usually target someone standing or sitting next to the person she wanted to talk to, and draw them in indirectly.

It was all about the rules of the subtle dating game. Respectable women could flirt – discreetly. They could date, too, but within limits.

Eye contact was a big thing in public places, but if it worked with the Lebanese, it could disconcert the foreigner, who was no doubt still getting used to being stared at by everyone.

'I'll be back in a moment,' Reem said. She touched Zubaida's arm. To get to the ladies' room she would have to squeeze past Lorimer.

In her left hand she carried the keys to her flat.

'Excuse me.'

Reem gave Lorimer's elbow a nudge.

He raised his arm to prevent her spilling his beer, and half turned towards her, surprised, twisting his head around and looking down.

'I am so sorry,' Reem said.

She smiled up at him.

Her left hand hung down by her side. She relaxed her fingers and let the keys fall to the floor.

EIGHT

Nick and his friend Khaled had gone to Sammy's Bar for a few beers. Khaled was off somewhere else later. Nick had his own plans, too. He went out most nights except Friday, Sunday and Monday and after nearly a month in west Beirut he no longer needed Khaled to show him the ropes.

'You see, Nick, the word "bar" has bad connotations. Most of the time it does. For the Lebanese, a bar is someplace where you find, you know, hostesses. The kind who do it for cash.'

There were bars like that, mainly in Maroniteland's Kaslik and Jounieh: sleazy clip joints run by eastside pimp-gangsters and staffed by Thai girls and Filipinas, mostly.

'There are women in here on their own,' Nick said, looking around. 'But they don't look like tarts.'

'Yeah, true, but this is special. It's a student hang-out. It's kind of fashionable. That's why you're here, and me too. Still, women won't come in here alone, or if they do, it's because they are meeting someone. They don't always meet someone, see, but they will at least pretend to. They'll wave at someone outside, and look at their watches. They'll strike up a conversation with another woman and the first thing they'll say is that they're meeting someone but she's late. Whatever works. They'll look busy. They won't want to seem alone. Appearances are every-thing.'

Nick liked Khaled immediately. It was instinctive. They were the same age, almost to the day. Khaled was quick-witted, restless, cynical and acid-tongued. He was carelessly honest, too frank for his own good, and his own safety. In a land where telephones were routinely tapped and foreign agencies kept under close watch by any number of spies, it was a kind of reckless bravado.

Khaled liked a good time. He drank. He smoked. He liked girls and seemed perpetually caught up in some painful romantic or sexual crisis he was only too happy to share with the new *ajnabi*.

He talked about everything, including things others would be embarrassed to admit to even thinking about.

Khaled was normal.

Nick was the boss, a fact he was made painfully aware of almost every minute he spent in the office. Anyone who gained the ear of the boss, who socialized with him, who showed him the ropes, who became, in effect, his adviser and sometime jester, would be likely to gain from the relationship. If there were more staff cuts, Khaled's winning ways might give him an advantage over the others. It was obvious, and something not lost on his colleagues.

Khaled's friendship with Nick made him enemies, too.

Nick would never forget that first day. He had dropped his bags inside the door, and at once started shaking hands. Faces, names – at first he could not focus on any of them, let alone recall them. The staff were introduced by rank, by seniority – years of service, then age. The local manager, Elias Khoury, set the tone. He was the undisputed leader. Then they all sat down in a semicircle and drank coffee and made stilted conversation. There was a strict pecking order. No one spoke unless Nick spoke first. Women – there were only three on the staff – did not count. They came last, regardless of length of service or age, and when the introductions had been completed, they retreated to their desks.

Khaled had also hung back. He was the last male to come forward, just before Nick's secretary, the clerical assistant and the office receptionist. He was the youngest, and had the least service on his file.

It was Khaled who had quietly explained – no offence meant – that Nick's job was all but impossible, and that Nick's filing system, his reports procedure, his division of the staff into search teams would all be to no avail.

Nick had listened, accepted that Khaled had a point and, inwardly at least, sworn to prove him wrong.

By the end of the first week they had a trickle of names.

And it was Khaled who gave Nick the guided tour – the personal, escorted tour of Beirut nightlife, and the low-down on Lebanese women.

'So this place is respectable.'

Khaled put his head on one side, considering this.

'Sort of. Sammy's is what you would call – what's the word . . .'

'Bohemian? Trendy?'

'Right. Rich kids, artistic types, university girls who are really independent – they'll come here. In groups, with friends. Or pretending to be. It's not traditional by any means. And yeah, it's a good place to pull. One of the best in fact.'

Khaled drank deeply from his beer, leaning one shoulder against the wall and putting his head back. He wore his hair in spikes, held upright with lashings of gel. It gave him a punk look. To Nick, the noise and merriment seemed frantic. If there had been a bar on the *Titanic* when it struck an iceberg, he thought, it would be something like this – a frenzied effort to escape reality, the smiles too forced, the laughter too insistent as the lifeboats were lowered past the portholes into the icy sea.

'I don't mean pull quite the way you do, Nick. They won't put out on the first date. Some might, but most will want to take more time. A lot more.'

Khaled was proud of his American colloquialisms. Nick had already pulled, and to use Khaled's expression, she had put out. But Mona was very unusual for a Lebanese. For any woman anywhere, come to that. In fact she had pulled him rather than the other way around. She would call him every few days and express an interest in watching a video – her code for sex.

At first Nick had been eager. Mona had always come to his place, usually in the lunch hour or early evening, war permitting. The war was like the weather. People listened constantly to the news, to the sound of firing, waiting for a break in hostilities. Mona and Nick would put on a video cassette, too, but they never watched it. She did not want to eat or drink. She did not want to date. She cared for neither flowers nor chocolates. She did not even want to talk. She preferred his sofa and the floor to his bed.

Right at the start, when he had been in Beirut less than a week, she had told him: 'I am different, Nicholas, and we will grow tired of each other, you will see. It's the novelty value, that's all. For you and for me.'

She was right.

He knew enough about Mona by now to know she took her her pleasure wherever she found it. Currently it was with a UN helicopter pilot, an Italian whose main topic of conversation was cooking. Jealousy was wasted on her. She lived with her parents in a huge flat in Sanayeh, near Nick's office. They were wealthy people. French-speaking Maronites, but of leftist persuasion. To all outward appearances Mona was perfectly respectable, though considered a little old to make a 'good catch'.

The Backstreet was where they had first met. It had been Nick's second night in west Beirut.

They had danced, and she had pressed herself against him, stoking his arousal. When they had sat down again, Mona asked him if he was still in a hotel. He said he was. Like so many foreigners he stayed at the Commodore, where the staff were particularly well tuned to the needs of their foreign guests, to the extent of asking new arrivals if they would like their bar bill added to their laundry charges because, as everyone knows, journalists' laundry bills are paid for by their news organizations.

Yes, he had still been at the Commodore back then.

'Pity,' she had said, and her slim fingers had brushed his crotch. 'Let me know when you do move, won't you.'

Ten days and four video rentals later Nick was already losing interest in her, and Mona in him. Just as she had said they would.

He had no intention of telling Khaled, although it was Khaled who was telling him now about the back alley clinics that specialized in restoring the hymen so a young woman could still make a good match and marry as a 'virgin'.

Someone bumped into Nick, nearly knocking the beer bottle out of his grasp.

He turned.

'I am so sorry,' he heard her say.

She had the most charming smile.

The stranger muttered something about dropping her keys, and they both knelt down simultaneously.

Nick's chin struck her forehead.

'Ouch,' the woman said.

'Shit,' Nick said, wishing instantly he hadn't.

Now face to face, inches apart, they each instinctively put a hand to the area that stung. He tested his chin with his fingers, she put a hand on her forehead.

They both laughed.

'No damage that I can see,' she said, looking at his chin closely and using the fingers of one hand to move a lock of hair out of her eyes. He noticed the long, thin fingers, the brown wrists, lighter where the narrow bone pressed against the skin.

Down among the cigarette ends, the beer bottle tops, the crisp packets, the nuts, the pools of spilled wine and beer, Nick gazed into large, dark eyes, slightly oval and slanted upwards.

They stared at each other for a moment.

Other people had moved back momentarily, giving them space, but the chatter and the laughter quickly resumed. They were forgotten in a forest of legs and feet again, though Khaled was still peering down, asking if he could help. They ignored him.

'My keys,' she said, breaking eye contact, as if suddenly remembering what she was doing there, and started looking around.

Nick found them, picked them up and handed them to her.

'Thank you. It was my fault . . .'

He put out his hand.

'I'm Nick Lorimer.'

She took it.

'Nick?'

'Yes,' he said.

'Pleased to meet you, Nick. I'm Reem.'

They were still crouched down.

'Reem.'

They both stood up, careful to avoid a second collision. Nick found he was still holding her hand, and she had used it to help herself up.

She smiled broadly, tossing her hair back from her face.

'Can I have my hand back, Nick?'

'Sorry.'

Nick felt his face burn with embarrassment.

'Thank you,' she said.

'Pleased to meet you, Reem.'

'Same here.'

She smiled again, less broadly this time, aware of other people around them, and walked away, squeezing through the crowd back to her place next to Zubaida.

'Christ,' Nick said. 'Did you see that?'

'What?'

'Do you know her?' Nick had to shout.

Khaled shook his head. He finished his beer.

'Never seen her before,' he said, adding, 'Time to go.'

'One more,' Nick said, looking for her in the crush of people.

'Not me,' Khaled said. 'The evening's young, too young to get smashed quite yet.'

'What do you make of her?'

'Who?'

'The girl who dropped her keys.'

Khaled shrugged.

'Looks like a student. Maybe a postgrad – who knows?'

Khaled was not interested. Nick told himself that was because his friend had not really looked at her.

'What can you tell about her?'

Khaled followed Nick's gaze, but he was a lot shorter than Nick and could see even less through the crowd.

'She's dark. Maybe Palestinian. Or Shi'ite.'

'Not that it matters,' Nick said.

'What?'

'I said not that it matters what she is.'

The music was louder than ever.

'Let's get out of here,' Khaled said.

But Nick did not leave immediately.

He pulled one of his business cards out of his breast pocket.

'Got a pen?'

Khaled had not.

Reckless with impatience, Nick asked people at the bar. Eventually someone got hold of the barman, and he provided one.

'Stand still, Khaled.'

'What the fuck are you doing, man?'

'Keep still.'

Nick used Khaled's back to write his home number on the reverse of the card.

'Thanks. Won't be a moment.'

He put the pen on the bar and turned away. He threaded his way through the press of people.

'Reem?'

She seemed surprised to see him.

He held out the card, feeling awkward.

She took it, a serious expression on her face, glanced at it and then at Nick.

70

Her friend was watching out of the corner of her eye, half turned away and drinking something through a straw, feigning disinterest.

The card was white with raised blue lettering.

Nick Lorimer, UN coordinator.

That absurd acronym.

'My home number's on the back.'

He realized when he said it that no Lebanese woman – no respectable Lebanese woman – would call him. Of course she would not do so. He was a complete stranger. He was being presumptuous, and probably committing a frightful social gaffe.

God, was she cool.

'Wait.'

He had started to move away, certain he had gone too far this time, but Reem had her head down, fingers searching. She pulled out a scrap of paper, getting up off her bar stool and taking a step towards him as if she did not want to be overheard by her friend. Reem was taller than he remembered. She had a lean, rangy look. Physical. There was something athletic and self-possessed about the way she carried herself, the very opposite of pampered. Certainly not painted. Cosmetics companies and fashion photographers spent enormous sums of money trying to capture that fresh, sporty look.

'Call me.'

The look she gave him was part scorn, part challenge.

He could smell the soap she used, the touch of perfume.

When Nick got back to his place, he found strangers there.

Khaled had gone.

NINE

There was no water that night, nor the following morning.

Not so much as a dribble.

The news was not good, either, but the BBC seemed laconic about it all.

'Exchanges of shelling across the Green Line separating Muslim west and Christian east Beirut continue . . .'

The newsreader's words sounded so passionless. Routine. How distant the cool words on short wave were from the reality, Reem thought, especially for those who lived close to the Green Line, the civilians who endured these so-called exchanges. Was there any life that was not lived in terror, in fear of imminent annihilation? Was it possible? Even in that far off place called London was there any governing principle other than cruel randomness?

There was a standpipe at the end of Reem's street, but it meant waiting in line in the open and risking being hit and then hauling the water up to the flat. There was no generator for the building and if there was no water, it usually meant there was no power. The water had to be carried up by hand, step by step, up the stairwell to the fifth floor.

For drinking there were big plastic bottles of mineral water, but these too had to be carried. The better off would pay a ragged Kurdish, Shi'ite or Palestinian refugee child to deliver to their front doors, but Reem could not afford to waste even a few piastres. So she left the plugs in the bath, sink and washbasin and twisted the taps wide open in the hope there might be a trickle during the time she was away at work.

For weeks at a stretch there had been no more than a small bowl each day for washing herself, her hair and her clothes.

People began to smell sour. Not dirty, not really dirty, but a sourness of old perspiration and clothes worn too long, a stench that permeated taxis and public buildings, elevators and shops.

The stink of a city under siege.

Reem grew used to the lack of water like everyone else. It was no longer a hardship, just an inconvenience. Life and death were just large inconveniences, and between the large acts were the smaller inconveniences of the daily struggle to live a little longer. The horizon shrank to the next meal, the next cigarette.

The phones went, too.

She would not be able to tell if Nick had tried to call.

By 11 a.m. the firing was general and involved weapons of all calibres.

'It's the Shouf,' said Dalia.

Druze fighters were driving the thugs of the Sunni Muslim Mourabitoun militia from their trenches on the edge of Beirut.

Another war within a war.

The three friends gathered for morning coffee in the library where they worked. Dalia had brought *baklawa*, those rich, syrupy and, to Reem, quite irresistible Lebanese pastries. It did not help that they were conveniently bite-sized. It was so easy to have just one more. And another.

'Thank God we're on the fourth floor,' said Zubaida, helping herself to her third pastry, then delicately dabbing at the corner of her mouth with a paper napkin.

Reem agreed. The ground, first and second storeys were too low. They caught the small arms fire, the ricochets, the shell splinters. The sixth and seventh were at risk from mortar bombs that plunged vertically, and from the big howitzers – French 155s sold to Israel and passed on to the Phalangists and then to the Lebanese Forces militia. These monsters fired their enormous shells at a high parabola, and they would break through the roofs and breeze block walls as if they were paper, exploding inside.

The fourth was as good as it got.

Books in Arabic, English and French stood in ranks, shelf upon shelf. Light came from a rectangular panel of thick glass set high up in one wall. The women sat in the centre on easy chairs set around a coffee table. There was no one else. No browsers, no researchers. No one could remember a time when someone had actually come in off the street and borrowed a book.

Reem let her friends' talk swirl around her. She was not really listening. She had an appointment with the Ustaz, but the way things were going, it seemed unlikely that either would make the rendezvous. There would be no diversions to Hamra, either, no mirroring in the windows of shoe shops, not today. She was faced, not for the first time, with the dilemma of survival. To wait at work, if necessary sleeping on the floor, until the fighting petered out, or to take her life in her hands and run the gauntlet, dashing from one doorway to the next, sprinting up the street.

Reem could not contact him.

The Ustaz shunned cellphones and landlines alike. Everything electronic could be, and was, monitored.

If they missed this one they had a fallback for the next day.

'. . . so tall, and those blue eyes,' she heard Zubaida saying.

They were both looking at her.

'You never told me,' Dalia cried. 'How could you? I'm really hurt. I thought I was your friend. God, how exciting. Why didn't you tell me?' She bit her lip, part serious, part play-acting.

Reem realized they were talking about the Englishman.

Lorimer.

'He gave you his card? Oh, do let me see.'

Reem, to cover her own embarrassment, bent and picked up her purse which lay at her feet. She peered inside and fished it out.

What harm could it do?

'There,' said Zubaida. 'What did I tell you?'

Dalia snatched it from Reem's hands.

'Tell me, tell me,' she said, wriggling on her chair with excitement.

'I don't know what all the fuss is about,' Reem said. A furrow appeared between her eyebrows, the first sign of temper. 'Just because he's a foreigner—'

'Not just any foreigner,' Zubaida said, nudging Dalia. 'Not just any foreigner, darling, but a handsome devil. So tall. I hear he's the boss of his own office with a big staff. Oh, yes. He's young, but he's on expatriate terms. His own driver, a big flat in Ain El Mreisse.' Zubaida paused. 'And unmarried.'

'You're so lucky in love,' Dalia said, pouting. 'You're always so lucky.'

'He's got such a sweet smile,' Zubaida said. 'Just like a little boy.'

Reem knew if she tried to shut them up, to change the subject, it would only encourage them. It was almost with relief that she felt the building quiver, followed by another explosion.

'Oh my God,' Dalia said, clutching Zubaida's arm. 'It's another car bomb.'

The local radio stations were quick off the mark with the first details. Explosive had been packed into a saloon, along with an anti-tank mine. The vehicle, probably with a full tank of petrol, was parked alongside others outside a popular fast-food outlet in a shopping area in the western sector and not more than two miles from where Reem and her friends worked. Initial radio reports said eleven people had been killed and twenty-three injured. It was the third random attack in as many weeks. If indiscriminate exchanges of fire between east and west, between right and left, Christian and Muslim, had not ranged across the city that day, the casualties would have been far higher.

'Murdering bastards,' said Zubaida, turning the radio off. 'There wasn't even a target.'

'Oh, but there was,' Reem said. 'The target is always the same.

We're the target – just for being here. If we live in the west we must be guilty. All of us.'

'People like us,' Dalia said.

The firing along the Green Line ceased shortly afterwards. The power returned. Now they could see the grisly aftermath on television.

It was as if the carnage of the morning's car bomb had brought everyone temporarily to their senses and the war was suspended, at least for an hour or two.

'I think we should call it a day and go home while we can,' Reem said.

'Good idea.' Zubaida stood at once and gathered up the plates.

Reem told herself she could still make the rendezvous if she hurried.

'Do you like him?'

The Ustaz watched Reem's expression when she replied.

'Like? We only exchanged a few words.'

'You have good instincts about people.'

'He's attractive. Intelligent. Perhaps not very mature.'

The truth was that she had wanted to detest the Englishman.

All the English.

'Untried?'

'Yes,' Reem said, turning to look at the Ustaz. 'Untested – from a country where people are not killing one another every day. The English do their killing abroad.'

'I am sure he will get in touch. If not, you will have to arrange another coincidental meeting. What will you do if he asks you out?'

Reem did not share his confidence. For someone like Lorimer there were always lots of Lebanese women. He was an object of curiosity. They would like his looks. Those blue eyes. The fair hair and red cheeks. Yes, and the smile Zubaida so admired. He was a boss. He must be well paid. In short, he would be a great catch. The Englishman meant a way out of this shithole. A new passport, another life, a comfortable life, a safe life.

Who could blame them?

Reem did.

'I'll accept, of course – under certain conditions.'

'Conditions?'

'I'm a respectable woman, and we're not engaged. For the sake of my reputation we have to meet discreetly, in places where neither of us is likely to be recognized by our friends.'

'You will say you prefer the eastern sector.'

'Precisely – away from our usual haunts.'

There was more to it. Reem needed to learn more of the eastern sector's layout and alternative routes. Crossing back and forth with a UN official would also help win the confidence of the *shebab* on the crossings.

The Ustaz paused by a wooden bench donated by alumni.

He had his hair cropped short and his clothing marked him down as a poor workman. Dusty. He wore boots, not shoes. An open-necked denim shirt, khaki combats. Not a university man at all. Reem wondered idly what he had been doing, what letter drop he must have serviced in some poor neighbourhood, what pay-off he might have delivered, and where, right in the midst of the earlier bombardment.

Wood shavings were stuck to his trousers and a strong smell of turpentine hung about him.

'Shall we sit here for a moment?'

It would soon be dusk. They sat next to each other, not too close, and looked across a lawn – threadbare, brown and choked with weeds – to what had been a rose garden. It was now over-grown, uncared for. Behind it, the dilapidated tennis courts, the office of the absent university president, the deserted cafeteria and a backdrop of umbrella pines.

Reem could glimpse the sea beyond.

With no one around, the campus was perfect for a meeting, there being no fewer than five entrances and exits. They had arrived separately and would leave separately, the Ustaz usually the last to leave.

'You mustn't hurry things,' the Ustaz said.

'We need the access.'

'We do, but without raising his suspicions. This is an intelligence-gathering operation and to do it well takes patience. A certain care.'

It was a gentle rebuke. Reem was too impatient for her own good.

'And you think this Englishman has it, professor? The access?'

'I know he does.'

'Is it the daughter?'

'Sylvie? I don't know. I suspect she is partial to Lorimer and probably rather more than he likes her. I think he would prefer the company of George and invitations to parties on George's boat.'

'You don't mean he's . . .'

She meant homosexual.

'You misunderstand me. My information is that he's more interested in parties and sailing and enjoying the relative peace in the eastern sector than he is in Sylvie's charms.'

'If I appear on the scene it could make things difficult.'

The Ustaz shrugged. 'I don't see why. If Lorimer wants to make it clear to Sylvie that he has other interests in that department, he could do worse than take you with him next time.'

'That could backfire on him and on us.'

'It's all speculation until you get there.'

'Why would he go there at all?'

'Lorimer needs to get all the contacts he can for his work. If he has friends in high places that could be useful if he has to evacuate his people from the western sector. And he likes to socialize with the British at their embassy. It's an escape.'

'Self-interest.'

'The Protector could well be the country's next president in a matter of weeks.'

'A powerful friend to have.'

'And one we hope the Englishman would like to show off to you.'

Reem turned. 'I have one request.'

'Of course.'

'I am grateful, Uncle Faiz. Really. But if . . .'

For once Reem was temporarily stumped for words.

'If what?'

Reem tried another tack

'What will you do with the information?'

'That depends on what it is.'

'I want—'

'Yes?'

'If you are going to mount an operation . . .'

Reem paused.

'I want to be part of it.'

There. She had said it.

'We'll see. It's somewhat premature. This is simply a mission to gather intelligence about one man. No decision has been taken.'

The Ustaz had shown no surprise. He did not appear to disapprove.

Had he expected her request?

'I mean, I don't just want to be a part of the team. I want to do it—'

'Do it?'

The Ustaz had got up and was standing in front of her, watching for anyone approaching.

Reem took a breath and said what had long been on her mind.

'I want to be the one who pulls the trigger.'

Was it so hard for him to understand?

She had never been so sure of anything.

As she walked across the grass on her way out, Reem glanced up at the university around her. For so many people, people who knew nothing of exile or loss, whose identity was secure in family, community and faith, this had been a place of endless opportunities, a step up to success, to status, independence and wealth – or merely an affluent husband.

Reem had not said no to these things. It was simply that the possibilities had never occurred to her for the simple reason that they did not exist. They could never exist. Not for her.

Not after what had happened.

Memory was strangely selective. The very spur to her life, the path she had consciously chosen – and there was never any illusion in Reem's mind as to how it must end – was partially eclipsed, an involuntary darkening of those events too terrible to remember and at the same time maintain anything resembling a normal grasp of reality.

It was like scar tissue. It grew slowly over the wounds, a defence mechanism dulling recall so she could manage to put one foot in front of another, take the trouble to dress, to eat, to act like a human being. To function.

But she could pick at it, worry at it, feel its outline, the ridge of flesh that marked the past. It was the constant itch of self-imposed duty.

As she walked out onto Bliss Street and looked for a service taxi, she felt the giddiness she associated with her recurring dream. She looked down at her hands. They seemed to swell as she looked at them, and it was accompanied by a metallic taste on her tongue.

She knew she would have the dream again that night.

The dream of entering the lift, the doors clanging shut, the bright illuminated buttons, the throat-tightening descent and never reaching the ground floor.

When Reem got home she found a note pushed under her door.

It was an unintelligible scrawl, but she recognized the signature.

There was no doubt whose it was.

TEN

He drove her across the Green Line himself.

Nick gave the office driver the afternoon off, and collected Reem after work. He waited for her at the end of the street, on her instructions. She would not say if it was her street, or merely where she worked. Loose talk could ruin an unmarried woman's reputation, especially if she was seen openly with a man. So Nick did not press it.

While he waited he looked at the pictures of the martyrs. They were small, rectangular, white posters with black-and-white mug-shots. They were pasted up in ranks, scores of them together. When he first arrived in west Beirut, Nick had paid them scant attention. He had not understood. There were so many of them, slapped on very nearly every wall. The faces stared out blankly, passively. There were women, too. They were Palestinians and Lebanese, Shia and Sunni, Greek Orthodox and Syriac, commu-nist and fundamentalist, Maronite and Druze.

Battalions of the dead.

The troops and militiamen waved Nick and Reem through. They did not have to stop. No one asked them for their papers. The white Land-Rover Defender with its blue UN plates and a foreigner at the wheel had the effect Nick had anticipated.

'Do you like it over in the east?'

She shrugged, and said nothing. Reem held her chin up, and flicked her hair away from her face. She looked happy. Whether it was because it was her nature, or because Nick was asking her out on their first date, or because she liked the eastern sector and wanted to escape the west for a few hours, he could not tell.

They drove up through Ashrafiyeh with its patisseries and boutiques.

'No shooting,' Nick said. He was working hard at not looking at her too much, at those sun-browned arms, those long legs and the way she filled her top.

'Thank God,' Reem said. She sounded as if she meant it.

She did not look at him, either, but at the shops, the clothes, the furniture, the people. Staring like a tourist, he thought.

As they climbed up Mount Lebanon, the air cooled.

Nick stopped the car on the verge below Ain Saadeh and they got out.

Beirut lay at their feet. A plateau of blue-grey rock crystal protruded out into a glittering Mediterranean. The sea stretched immobile to the horizon. To their extreme left was the airport, to their right Jounieh.

In between were at least five languages, innumerable intelligence agencies, official and unofficial armies, hundreds of thousands of refugees, interrogation chambers, countless whores, arms dumps and war profiteers, and amid all that and despite it, a million and a half people tried to live, make love, rear children, stay alive.

Nick asked Reem if she could point out where she lived. She pointed to where the university was, then Hamra, finally Verdun. They stood so close he could smell her hair, her skin. He squinted along the line of her arm like a rifleman taking aim. And what was the tall building? The Murr tower, Reem said, blackened by fire and torn by munitions, a skyscraper now for snipers in the upper floors and rumoured to be one of many unofficial militia prisons in the basement.

And there was what was left of Sabra and Shatila.

And Bourj al-Barajneh.

Could he see?

Yes.

Where so many Palestinian civilians had been shot in cold blood.

And what was that?

At first he thought it was the sunlight catching a sunroof, a windscreen.

Tiny flashes of light through the heat haze.

'Shooting – see?'

At the southern end – the suburbs.

A muffled thump. Not unlike a cork pulled from a bottle.

Palestinians and Shi'ite Lebanese, yet another war within a war.

Nick saw a smudge of oily smoke rise from a field, drift away slowly.

'This is how God must see us,' Reem said, moving a little away from him. 'How insignificant we are . . .'

He did not hear the rest of her words. Reem had turned away from the city, her face averted so he could not see her expression.

Nick followed her back to the Land-Rover, marvelling at the way the sun caught her hair.

People were dying down there, he thought, gunmen were killing one another, anyone, in fact, who got in their way, and here he was thinking how badly he wanted this woman. He did not even know her. He knew nothing about her. Surreptitiously Nick looked at her moving, really looked this time, taking in her swimmer's shoulders, the deep waist, the delicacy of movement, the way her small feet and ankles carried her, the sensuous swing of hips, the roundness of her buttocks pressing against denim.

Her clothes were clean and pressed, but they were threadbare.

She was poor, he realized, and painfully thin.

Christ, what a sick, insensitive shit I must be.

He drove through the Christian mountain resort of Broumana, full of half-finished apartment blocks, hotels and timeshare developments for the Maronite Lebanese diaspora.

Nick breathed in the smell of sun on the earth, the bitter-sweet wild herbs, rocket and oregano and mint.

'My poor country,' Reem said as they walked over to the restaurant. 'Poor, poor Lebanon.'

Nick measured his step to hers. 'So you are Lebanese.'

'What did you think?'

'I don't know. Someone said they thought you might be Palestinian.'

'What someone?'

'A friend of mine. Khaled. I was with him that night you bumped into me.'

'What did he say, your friend?'

'He said you looked Palestinian. Or maybe a Shi'ite Muslim.'

'Because I'm dark.' She made it a statement of fact.

The exchange was cut short by someone opening the glass doors and welcoming them into a vast dining area with long white tables packed with families.

Reem asked, 'May we sit outside?'

'Certainly, madam.'

Windows and doors ran down the eastern side of the dining room, opening onto a narrow balcony overlooking vineyards and, on a hill opposite, a monastery.

There was enough room for a single row of tables out there.

When they were seated, she said, 'I didn't mean to be rude. I'm sorry.'

'You weren't rude.'

'It's a touchy subject. Not the colour of my skin, but the issue of identity. It's what this war is about. Maybe all wars are about identity. Not about what America calls defending freedom.'

'I understand.'

'Do you, Nick?'

He ordered mineral water for both of them, a half-bottle of red wine for himself, and freshly squeezed orange juice for Reem.

'It's difficult to explain,' Reem said when the waiter had gone. 'Imagine you are living on the front line in a war, and you come home on leave and you find everyone having a good time, making money, enjoying themselves. How would you feel?'

'Angry. Upset. Yes, it would be very upsetting.'

'And if they were your enemies and your enemy's friends?'

'Terrible.'

'Terrible – yes.'

'I shouldn't have asked you over this side.'

'That's not what I meant. Please. It's not what I meant at all. It's wonderful to take a break. Really. Just don't expect me to like these people, to approve of them.'

'I'm sorry.'

'You've nothing to be sorry for. I'm going to have a good time and so are you. Okay? You believe me? Nick?'

'Yes.' He smiled at her. 'Of course I do.'

'That's better. We have a saying in Arabic: Kiss the hand you cannot bite and pray God breaks it.'

She had spoken as if to a child, jollying him along.

Their drinks arrived, breaking the awkwardness between them, and they started ordering food. Nick asked Reem to decide on the *meza* for them both. The air was cool, but the sun warmed their faces. He watched her concentrating on the menu, biting her lower lip. For the main course Reem chose *kibbeh* – the house speciality – and Nick followed suit.

Reem wanted a *tabouli* salad.

'Why bring me here, Nick?'

The waiter brought salted pistachios, olives and strips of raw carrot dipped in lemon juice to accompany their aperitifs.

'To the Coq Rouge? First, it's traditional family cooking – from the north, I'm told. Real cooking. Then there's the setting. It faces away from Beirut, and I couldn't be sure what would be happening, so I wanted somewhere that seemed a long way away from the war.'

'It's a good choice.'

She put out a hand and touched his wrist with her cool fingertips.

'Thank you, Nick.'

She cracked open the salted pistachios.

'Tell me about yourself, Nick. Tell me about your home. What it's like.'

'It's boring, really.'

'Tell me. I want to know everything.'

'Everything?'

She nodded.

'Go on.'

Nick told her he came from a family of do-gooders. How his grandfather had joined the Durham Light Infantry at seventeen and was commissioned in the trenches. To his amazement, Grandad had survived the Great War, and the shock or the guilt or both had propelled him into the Methodist ministry and eventually to China as a missionary. There he met Nick's grandmother, a midwife from Dawlish.

Reem listened intently, but she interrupted several times, questioning him: What was the Great War? What was the Durham Light Infantry? What were Methodists? And a midwife? Dawlish? What was that?

Nick's father was a Fabian socialist and a leading light in the Campaign for Nuclear Disarmament and Amnesty International long before these organizations became household names; his mother had been a Socialist Workers Party activist in her student days. She had form – convictions for public disorder offences on Strathclyde picket lines and for breaking into a nuclear submarine base at Rosyth in Scotland – and had done time – a month.

They were both teachers, respectable members of the community in Elgin Crescent, Sheffield, by the time Nick had arrived. Solidly middle class, their turbulent days of activism behind them. But Mao, Che, Nasser, Castro and Aneurin Bevan were still heroes in their three-bed terrace, and Nick grew up to the sounds of Shostakovich and the words of his father's complete works of George Orwell.

Nick went to grammar school. A university scholarship followed.

Reem urged him on. No brothers? Sisters?

Nick's elder sister, Pamela, had read theology at Oxford and took a first without even breaking sweat, then spoiled it all by running off to Palma and marrying a hashish smuggler and Magaluf bar owner named Kevin.

'At thirty-three, she has had a nose job, three kids and is lady of a Tuscan manor – actually three restored barns – with pool, tennis court and three-car garage. Our parents have forgiven her and go out there for a holiday every year. She's still married to Kevin.'

'She sounds fun.' Reem laughed.

For Nick it had been a toss-up between Spanish and Arabic, between Nicaragua and Lebanon. Arabic and Lebanon won.

'I didn't even know where Lebanon was, not really.'

Reem smiled.

Nick resisted the urge to lean across the table, take her in his arms and kiss her. It was her strange blend of vulnerability and strength, something he could not quite grasp. She was soft, yet hard. She was friendly yet reserved. She was outgoing, but guarded.

They both wanted coffee, poured out of a huge brass pot into tiny cups.

'I've done all the talking,' Nick said. 'Now it's your turn.'

She told him she was a librarian and archivist.

The job did not pay well, but it was sufficient for rent, food and clothes.

'You come from Beirut – orginally?'

Reem shook her head. 'No.'

Something in her look told Nick she really did not want to talk about it.

'And your parents?'

'They're dead.'

'I'm sorry.'

'It's okay. It's a while ago.'

Reem looked away, across the vineyards, already in shadow as the sun dived to the western horizon. The sky was pale, varnished in the soft mountain light.

It clearly was not okay. Nick backed off.

He asked if she smoked. She didn't, but he could go right ahead.

Nick lit up.

'So what do you do in this library or whatever it is?'

'We do nothing, Nick. We drink coffee and sit around gossiping. I collect my wages every Thursday. But there's no work if that's what you mean. We're just going through the motions, dusting the books and waiting until somebody remembers to tell us we're fired.'

'Your English is perfect.'

'You're being nice.'

'No, it is.'

'I studied English – not French – at school, and I did a course in Cyprus.'

They turned to the subject of music. They found they shared a love of Bach and Mozart. Her favourite singer was the late Egyptian diva Um Kalthoum, and her favourite politician the nationalist Gamal Abdel Nasser. Both Egyptian, and both dead. They discussed books and the new Algerian music known as Rai. They talked about the Lebanese author Amin Maalouf and the Egyptian Naguib Mahfouz. Reem began to relax. They both did. She became animated, laughing a good deal, telling jokes. Enjoying herself.

As Nick paid the bill, they saw they were the last to leave the restaurant.

'You're Christian,' he said as they walked to the Land-Rover through the long shadows of the pines.

'Yes, Nick. I'm Christian. Can't you tell?'

She was teasing him, looking at him over her shoulder.

'Maronite? Greek Orthodox?'

'Does it matter?'

'Not at all.'

'You don't give up.'

'I'm sorry. I don't mean to pry.'

'I'm Melchite – Greek Catholic.'

She looked at Nick directly, a serious expression on her face.

'You're a practising Christian?'

'No – are you?'

'No.'

'Not a real Methodist?'

''Fraid not. Does it matter?'

Reem giggled. 'No.'

'You are from the north, then.'

'No.' She shook her head. 'The south.'

She talked while they retraced their journey, winding down the mountain into the warm haze embracing the city. There were two villages, she said.

The villages were Iqrith and Kufr Bira'am.

One Maronite, the other Melchite. Both Lebanese, and both on the wrong side of the 1948 border of the newly established state of Israel.

Reem had never seen her real home. Never would.

She described what had happened, how the villagers could never settle there again. How they saw their homes bombed. How the soldiers laughed at their Israeli high court order. How they had rebuilt the church, planted flowers in the graveyard, buried their dead there.

'Westerners speak out against things they know nothing about. They talk about the Middle East as a conflict between Muslims and Jews. So many Westerners don't even seem to know that there are 150,000 Palestinians in Jerusalem, and many are Christian. Who do they think lives in east Jerusalem, in Bethlehem and in Nazareth? Christians.'

'You're not Palestinian, though.'

'We're all Palestinians, Nick. We're African Americans and we're American Indians and we're Namibians and black South Africans and Chinese Muslims and Karens and Afghans.'

She fell silent, as if aware she had said too much. Nick looked across at her. She had curled up on her seat. She was in her student garb of faded blue jeans, old trainers and a green T-shirt, and had pulled on a navy blue sleeveless jacket. If they had belonged to a student, he thought, it must have been a while ago. In many ways she was so pliant. She was feminine. Yet there was an anger, a single-mindedness to her. It was a lack of doubt, he told himself, a lack of uncertainty, a lack of self-consciousness. In all likelihood she did not think of herself as poor. What made her so sure in a world so unsure of itself?

'Go on,' he told her.

'No.'

'My fault,' he said.

'What for?'

'For encouraging you to talk about things that upset you.'

'It's not your fault.' She smiled at him. 'Well, no, it is your fault. You are British, after all. The source of all our troubles.'

Nick tried to laugh it off, but it hurt a little. Hell, the Mandate and Britain's role as midwife to Zionism was a long time ago. He was not even born then.

'Hey,' Reem said, sitting up straight and punching him lightly on the shoulder. 'Don't take it so seriously. I'm only teasing.'

Nick wanted to ask about what had happened to her parents, her family, but he decided to postpone the discussion.

'What about you, Nick?'

'What about me?'

'Aren't you frightened?'

He turned his head to look at her.

'Of what?'

Reem waved her hand. 'All of it. The place. The people. The strangeness of it all. The wealth and poverty, all mixed up together. Have you ever seen so many Mercedes cars? Or Range

Rovers? These wrecks of buildings. The snipers. The mortar bombs. The war. The way people stare at you. People carrying guns. The shooting night and day. The crossings. The way people on this side will try to kill you in the west, and yet here you are, in the east, eating lunch. The sheer unpredictability of it. And now the kidnapping of foreigners.'

'Yes.'

'Yes?'

'Yes, I'm scared.'

'Of what?'

He was slowing for the crossing. On the other side a massive portrait of a scowling Ayatollah Khomeini prepared to welcome them home.

'Oh. Everything. All of it. Just as you said.'

Reem smiled at him. 'But not of me.'

'You too.'

'Why me?'

'I'm afraid of saying the wrong thing, of upsetting you, of somehow making a mess of things. At the same time I want to know everything about you.'

'Why? Is knowledge tantamount to possession, Nick? Is that how Western men pursue their women? For possession?'

'I hope not.'

'I don't want to be possessed, Nick.'

'I'm glad to hear it.'

Did he mean that? He wasn't sure.

'Not many men would have the courage to admit fear. Not to a woman.'

'Maybe to their own mothers.'

Reem smiled. 'I didn't mean their mothers.'

'I know you didn't.'

They were flagged down. A gunman walked around the Land-Rover and strolled back again to the driver's side, a cigarette in the corner of his mouth and cradling an AK-47 in his arms.

'United Nations?'

'That's right,' Nick said, smiling.

'Go ahead,' the man said in Arabic. '*Ahlan*.' Nick saw he was looking at Reem, trying to figure out what she was. But he did not ask. His natural sense of courtesy had outweighed his sense of duty.

Nick manoeuvred the large vehicle through a chicane of concrete anti-tank traps topped with slices of railway line.

'You did that well,' Reem said once they were clear.

'Did what well?'

'You were calm. You spoke nicely. You weren't too proud or too humble. You showed respect without condescension. That's good, Nick. You make me feel safe.'

'I do?' He felt pleased, but why did he have the strange feeling that Reem of all people needed him not at all when it came to safety, and that it was said to put him at his ease, to sustain his fragile male pride?

'This beats running across,' Reem said.

'You run across?'

'When they shoot.'

'That's crazy. I did it once – and that was enough.'

'It must seem that way to you, Nick. Give it a little more time and you'll be as crazy as the rest of us.'

'I enjoyed today,' Nick said with feeling. 'Very much.'

'So did I. Thank you.'

It was said coolly.

'Can we do it again? Would you do it again?'

'You're asking me?'

'Yes.'

A moment's hesitation seemed like an age to Nick.

'I'd like that. Yes.'

He tightened his hands on the wheel lest she see that he was shaking with tension – and with relief. God, why did it matter so much?

Was it loneliness?

The effect she was having on him physically?

Or was it just Mona's defection to an Italian pilot?

'Then shall we say Saturday?'

'Call me first, Nick, please.'

'Sure. If the phones work.'

'Stop here, please, Nick.'

It was Verdun, but which street he was not quite sure.

The one-way system never ceased to confuse him.

'Is this where you live?'

Reem nodded.

'Reem . . .'

He got out, went round and opened the passenger door.

'Have you ever met the Protector?'

'No.'

'Would you like to?'

She gathered up her bag and jumped out.

'I don't think so, Nick. Why? Should I?'

'I've been invited to his forty-fifth birthday party on Saturday.'

Reem seemed to consider this.

'Saturday,' Nick said. 'It might be amusing. All the top brass over there. Antoine will be the country's next president, they say.'

'Antoine,' Reem said, as if tasting the name, rolling it around her mouth like a wine taster. 'Antoine.' Reem looked at Nick, and for the briefest moment he saw her dark eyes flatten with anger.

'Look, we really don't have to go. I wasn't thinking. There's no reason—'

'No. I'd like to.'

'Sure? I know they're not your kind of people.'

'I'd like to. Yes. Really. But call me – if, as you say, the phones work . . .'

'Of course.'

There was no kiss. Not even a handshake. They were standing on the street, in public. There were people at the windows, on the balconies. People walked past. They would see everything. Neighbours. Neighbours meant gossip. You idiot, Nick told himself. How self-centred, how selfish. What did he really expect?

'Saturday – or perhaps Friday.'

Somewhere on the Green Line an automatic weapon chattered away. A burst of three rounds, then four.

Five days. Five. A bloody lifetime. Could he live that long without seeing her again? Perhaps if he had suggested meeting for coffee first . . .'

But she was gone, striding off down the dark street.

ELEVEN

There was no shooting, and few city lights burned.

A little before midnight Reem walked down to the Corniche to escape both the humidity and the oppressive roar of private generators. She was as silent and insubstantial as her own shadow, listening to the rats scrabble out of her way on the broken paving. A stiff wind whistled off the sea and caressed her cheeks, whipping her hair back so it stung her neck. It blew from the north-west, straight uphill. It blew away the smell of chocolate and coffee and newly baked bread. It blew away the smell of Turkish tobacco and cats, it blew away the scent of jasmine and the stink of rotting refuse. Best of all, it carried off the stench of the dead, the dead no one would ever find under the enormous heaps of rubble after more than a decade of inter-necine war.

There was a storm out there somewhere.

Reem faced out to sea, pressed against the railings, munching an apple, leaning into the wind. Blind to the world, the world blind to her, she heard feet come and go behind her, voices faint, hesitant, ready to run at the first sound of outgoing or incoming. As a child she had known the Corniche crowded with people, with holidaymakers, with water-sellers and ice cream vans, with piles of watermelons as big as cannonballs, the smell of grilled maize cobs, of stalls selling coffee and tamarind juice and renting out the narghiles, the sweet, blue smoke from the water pipes, her mother holding her hand sticky from sweets, the heat on her head, proud of her beribboned pigtails, her pink frock, the impossibly blue and placid sea and its briny smell, a promise of mysteries to come, of far off places, of dreams.

He stood next to her, quite silent, his hands gripping the top rail.

She could not see his face, but she was sure the Ustaz was staring out to sea, savouring the moment before hearing her report.

She had been taught report-writing, the business of listing each fact on paper, the detailed sourcing. But nothing was ever written down. Everything had to be memorized. Paper could not be trusted.

All she could see was the white of broken water as waves smashed relentlessly against the rocks below her, then the clawing of the water receding, as if trying to cling to the pebbles, to hold onto the shore, reluctant to be drawn back on itself for another suicidal assault.

Like us. We will never give up.

She flung the apple core into the night.

Headlights swept the Corniche. A militia patrol, Syrian troops, smugglers, whatever – their blond beams lit the explosions of white froth, and Reem felt the thunder in the stones beneath her slippered feet, the percussion beating in the hollow iron at her hips.

She had always known what the end would be.

She never tried to explain it to the Ustaz. As expected, he had shown irritation on her initial approach, not because he had not liked her or approved of her, but because knowing him at all for what he was had showed up a chink in his armour of secrecy. How could this slip of a schoolgirl, this indigent orphan, this presumptuous urchin – for that was what Reem was when she volunteered herself, imposed herself – know who he was and what he did when much of the world sought him, wanted to identify him and tried and failed to kill him?

He had begun with a scathing refusal, a sneering rejection, and when blunt obscenity had also failed to drive her away, he had tried to humiliate her into leaving. She tore her nails scrubbing the floor of his miserable room. She washed his shirts. She made his coffee and brought him breakfast. She dusted and ironed. She never complained. Not once. And he never acknowledged her, not then. He could have leaned over and kicked her with his boot, and she would have uttered not a sound of complaint.

She knew even then what she wanted.

Reem would pay the price.

Eventually he did address her. He was brusque. She could be a courier. But first she needed a trade, he said. She needed to improve her English. He would pay for her studies, and he did. He had her trained as a librarian and then had her spirited east, to the Bekaa, under a blanket on the back seat of a car, for training of a different kind.

Reem had first caught sight of him in a mirror, in black tie and standing in the lobby of the Commodore, his image splintered by the glass, by the spiky fronds of the pot palms. She herself worked then as hotel chambermaid, already learning so much of human frailty and human exigencies by the state of a pair of unwashed sheets or a pillowcase, by the make-up on a dressing table, the toiletries on a bathroom shelf, a towel discarded on a chair, the angry words and muffled cries of pain behind a locked door; all these the forensic tools in tracing the human condition.

She had always known her path, even then, and now she was on her way, moving towards her dark apotheosis, or more likely, she thought with grim satisfaction, her aphelion.

Her dark star.

Kept even from the Ustaz in the beginning.

'Reem . . .'

She turned to the sound of his voice.

She liked Nick. That made it so much harder. It was preferable to dislike someone in order to use him, but she could not bring herself to do so. She had tried. There were a thousand reasons for dislike. Any one of them would have done, from halitosis to reactionary views, from stupidity to clumsiness. But none applied to him. He was kind. He was courteous. He was undoubtedly intelligent. He listened. He did not smell. He made no effort to force himself on her. His table manners were refined, so much so he did not even know to eat with his fingers. He tried hard not to cause offence, to avoid trampling on her feelings. He was still a man, somehow, despite all this politesse, this gentility, this self-restraint and attentiveness. The tyranny of man over woman was so much easier to bear if dressed in the clothing of good manners, and she liked him for that alone.

Reem knew he found her attractive.

She had felt his physical presence, and she had responded without being able to help it. The blond hairs on his forearms when his hands gripped the wheel; the muscled shoulders under his shirt when he leaned forward at the table; the way he watched her when she spoke, giving her all his attention; the strong pointed chin, the nose that looked as if it had been broken, its ridge line crushed in some childhood sport; all this added to the impression of noble pugilist. His child-man's smile; the line of his throat, how the Adam's apple moved when he spoke – she wanted to touch, to feel his skin. Above all, it was his candidness, particularly his confession of fear.

His innocence.

Were all foreigners like Nick?

She did not trust herself. How could she? Nothing had prepared her for such feelings. But Reem had made up her mind that she would enjoy the weekend, come what may. She told herself she would keep the guilt over Nick and the lies she must tell in abeyance, and the double purpose of her journey buried deep in her mind. Deceit had long been her currency. As long as she could remember she had anticipated the costs both to herself and to others of the double life and what it would entail. He would take her over to the east in his big white car once again, this time on Friday at lunchtime. They would drive through the villages of Mount Lebanon. They would lunch at her favourite village of Hasroon on the way to the cedars. He would drop her off at Kornet Shewan where she had said she had friends (she had lied; she knew no one in that village). She would make her own way by bus through Phalangist and then Syrian lines to Aunt Sohad's home in Koura, and there, for a night and half a day, she would forget what she was, what she was becoming, for this was home, or as close to her real home and to her own mother that she could ever be.

A few hours of pretence, of languishing in her comfort zone, without fear of discovery.

No questions, no criticism.

Followed by the very antithesis of safety on the Saturday afternoon: the Protector's birthday reception. Like David, she would face her lions in their den. Look the enemy in the face, and smile, and not tremble.

But she would not think of that now.

Reem woke.

She turned her head to the left. The hands of her bedside clock showed it was a few minutes after three in the morning.

Voices raised in the corridor, light rising and falling, brightening and dimming through the curtains, spreading and receding on the ceiling.

Then her awareness of the sound. Not thunder. Louder. Right overhead.

She was out of bed and upright in a moment, struggling into a coat, fully awake, feet searching for slippers, finding flip-flops, grabbing keys and purse.

Reem ran for the door.

As she ran she counted the rounds.

One. Close.

Barbir.

Two. Closer.

Mar Elias.

It was the way children counted off the seconds – each representing a mile – between the lightning flash and the sound of thunder. This time the flash and bang were instantaneous and the building slithered under her, rocked again, and Reem put a hand out, palm against the wallpaper, steadying herself.

She heard a row of windows collapse, a loud popping sound followed by the cascade of glass into the street.

The light was a continuous surge, flooding the rooms.

Three.

Holy Mother of God.

Her ears popped with the abrupt change in pressure.

Bastards. They had straddled Reem's block.

It didn't end there.

The artillery barrage was constant, individual incoming too numerous to tell apart from the next salvo.

Outgoing, too.

Flashes from the muzzles of howitzers hidden behind walls, in garden plots, vomited projectiles at a smoke-filled sky.

She had the door open, stumbled out, pulling it shut, turning to lock it – aware of the absurdity of doing so – and ran for the stairwell.

They were all there.

The Itanis from the top floor, all eight of them, the kids in a row, sixteen dark eyes watching her.

The Armenians from across the landing.

The old couple from downstairs, holding each other, arthritic fingers clutching rosaries.

Praying.

The radios were turned high, at least six stations gabbling away simultaneously.

'A meeting of the Security Cabinet ... truce ... army to take over ... Prime Minister Karami ... Baabda presidential palace...'

Snatches of news fragmented by the noise of shellfire.

Someone passed her a bottle of mineral water.

Reem sat with her neighbours on the filthy steps and tried not to think about the cockroaches running over her legs.

The detonations continued, a wall of sound and destruction advancing and retreating, the enemy stalking them, seeking them out, walking his mortar bombs and his shells back and forth, raking the streets Reem knew so well.

Raining steel, a wind of fire.

Rue Makhoul, Sharia Habib Srour, Talat al-Khaya'at, Madame Curie.

Manara.

Little blue plaques in French and Arabic.

Her own: Rue 68.

Someone was brewing coffee, making a fire on the steps.

She knew what morning would bring. A sea of glass and tumbled masonry blocking the street, shops razed, power lines down, water pipes broken. The Red Cross people digging out the bodies, the endless fires.

Shoes and broken china, books and toys.

Glass ornaments twisted by heat into strange shapes.

It was so damn cold on the stairs.

The Itanis shared their bread and olives.

That was where Nick found Reem two hours later, as the sky in the east turned aniline pink.

Crouched in the stairwell, hugging her knees, eating olives out of a plastic bag, spitting the pips back into the cellophane to deny them to the roaches.

She looked up at him as he climbed up to her.

Reem showed no surprise.

She sounded apologetic to be found *déshabillé*, sucking the oil from her fingers, one by one, wearing a man's coat – her father's – over her nightdress, plastic flip-flops on her feet.

It was a serious security breach – Lorimer was never supposed to know where she lived. But Reem did not say so.

'I'm so hungry,' was all she said.

Then: 'How did you find me?'

TWELVE

She did not invite him in while she dressed. He waited down-stairs, in the deserted lobby. By her manner Reem let him know that he had, to some extent, compromised her in front of the neighbours simply by appearing in her building. It was kind of him, certainly. He had meant well. She was touched. It was also foolish. Nick could have been killed. Had he thought of that?

The truth of it was that he had thought of her, not himself. But there was no way he could tell her that without sounding drearily pompous.

It was a spur of the moment thing, he said. Unplanned. Khaled had called him close to midnight. A family had reported the abduction of the husband and father by unidentified gunmen at around eight, and Khaled had collected Nick in his battered Fiat and they had visited the family – not far from Reem, in Qasqas.

Three children, the mother distraught, convinced she would never see her man again. How would they eat without his wages? Nick had put his hand in his pocket, but Khaled had held his wrist and shaken his head.

'No. Maybe later. Not now. It would be an insult, chief.'

It was awful. Nick did not mean the frightened children or their inconsolable mother. That was bad enough, but not that. It was his helplessness. What could he do? Make things better? How? By muttering banalities, false reassurances that he would report the case to the United Nations in Geneva, to the Inter-national Committee of the Red Cross, make sure it received some attention in the local media? He did all that, every day, but what good would any of that really do? None. None at all. Would it bring the father back to his children? Would it put food on their table while they applied the bastinado – the *faraka* – to the poor fellow in some city cellar? Nick felt an intruder, a voyeur, exploiting the family's tragedy to justify his salary, his expense account. What use was he to anyone? He could barely look the woman in the eye. He had felt guilty and wholly inadequate.

As a do-gooder he fell pathetically short.

Perhaps that had been the point of the exercise from Khaled's point of view.

'I think Khaled wanted me to see for myself,' Nick told Reem. 'Show the boss how bad it is. How the whole thing stinks. Show Lorimer what we Lebanese have to live with, how we work, what we have to do and see how he likes it. And appreciate how useless these high-minded foreigners and their precious organizations are . . . how condescending, how irrelevant.'

They had finished the interview, he said. The woman – a Sunni Muslim wearing the *hejab* – had insisted on making coffee for the uninvited callers and they had finished and were getting to their feet, making their excuses when the artillery strike began.

So along with everyone else, including the kidnapped technician's family, they had taken shelter in the corridor.

It was Khaled who had found out where Reem lived.

'He told you then?'

'Yes. When the shooting stopped and he gave me a lift home. Just as I was getting out he said, "Oh, by the way, the woman you met at Sammy's Bar . . ."'

'Go on.'

'He said your name was Reem Najjar and you lived in the Daouk building, Rue Soixante-huit, that you worked in a library at the bottom of your road and that he knew because he had a friend there. Seems everyone gets to know everyone else sooner or later.'

Nick did not say so, but it was the first time he had heard Reem's surname. She had never told him, and he for some reason had never asked. It was odd to feel that one knew someone, felt attracted to them, wanted to be with them, yet knew so little – objectively speaking – about them.

'Who was the friend?'

'He didn't say.'

'Did you ask?'

'No. Does it matter?'

Reem did not reply. Nick had the impression that it did matter to her, very much. She seemed upset, perhaps even offended, at his turning up at all on her doorstep. Well, not her doorstep exactly, but clambering over the legs of her neighbours in her fetid stairwell.

Nick said he had pretended to go into his al-Nada building, but he had waited instead just inside the foyer by the lifts until he was sure Khaled had left, then he had set out on foot to find her.

The firing had lessened by then, he said.

'I just wanted to make sure you were all right,' he said. 'It sounded pretty bad in your area.'

'It was,' Reem said. 'But, as you see, I'm fine.'

'Okay. Good. I'm glad.'

She waited for him to do something, or say something. Nick felt awkward, shifting his weight from one foot to the other. He told himself he was not going to apologize. He had nothing to apologize for.

'You'd better go,' she said at last.

'Yes,' he said, nodding. 'Yes. I had.'

He was waiting for her to ask him into her home. He wanted to meet her family, join them perhaps for breakfast. He wanted to make their friendship official and public. He wanted to be the official boyfriend. He wanted to go out with Reem – openly. Was that so unfair? Was he really asking too much? What he really wanted was acceptance. But how could he be accepted when he played the foreigner so well? Perhaps it would be unfair to Reem and her reputation if nothing came of it. Then she would be spoiled goods. It was absurd, but that was how it was. But the invitation was in any case not forthcoming, and, feeling not a little foolish, Nick trudged home again, not bothering to vary his route this time – what kidnappers would be out now, for God's sake – along streets strewn with masonry and broken glass, the bitter taste of fire in his nose and throat, of smouldering wood and rubber, paint and plaster.

His feelings were hurt just a little. He did not blame Reem. He put it down to their differences. Differences in experience, in expectations. He had acted spontaneously, had failed to realize he was being too familiar, that there were costs involved – costs for Reem, not himself. He must be patient, see things their way, adapt to the mores of Beirutis if he wanted the relationship to continue, to deepen.

The call came through to the office on Thursday afternoon just before Nick packed up for the day.

It was Dacre.

'Ah, Nick. When are we going to have the pleasure of your company?'

The days had crawled by and with the prospect of seeing Reem the very next afternoon – they had agreed to travel to the east together after lunch on Friday – Nick was feeling upbeat, too. He had expected Dacre or Wilson to get in touch before now. Indeed, he had been dreading it in one sense. In another he had looked forward to it. He had been sure they would pursue the issue of his working on their behalf – their eyes and ears in the western sector as they had put it. Now it no longer seemed to matter. He had decided he would think of something if either of them did bring it up. It was surely unlikely and not worth worrying about. It could not have been that important after all. In any case, they had probably forgotten, or found more promising material to do their spying for them. But Nick had rather been hoping for an evening of food and drink, and it had not been forthcoming until now. He was both a little disappointed and relieved.

'I'm coming across tomorrow, as a matter of fact.'

'For the great man's birthday on Saturday?'

'That's right.'

'It'll go on all day, you know. Party workers in the morning, military and security types for lunch, diplomats and journalists in the afternoon, the heavy mob in the evening, from the patriarch to the prime minister. It probably won't break up until dawn on Sunday. God knows how he does it – the man's inexhaustible.'

'So I hear.'

The papers were full of the Protector's talents, including his appetite for work, his physical stamina. Only west Beirut's independent *an-Nahar* and the pro-Syrian *as-Safir* had mentioned how he had brought down a rival Maronite warlord in the north by killing him in church, stabbing him by the font, then marching in the funeral cortège, right behind the coffin. No one had dared challenge him, then. Few dared to do so now, not with America and Israel behind him. No one mentioned the massacres at Sabra and Shatila or Karantina.

'Can you fit in a drink tomorrow evening? It would be good to see you and I'd rather like a chat.'

A chat.

Nick hesitated. Reem was doing her own thing, visiting people in the north, she had said. So he would be at a loose end until Saturday. He had given no thought to where he would stay. On the one hand he did not want to admit it, on the other he was a touch resentful he was not being asked to dinner.

'Nick – you there?'

'I was thinking about it. I'm sorry.'

'Where will you be staying?'

'I haven't really thought that far ahead.'

'Well, that's settled, then. You'll stay with me. I've masses of room.'

Nick had no excuse to hand.

'Come up to the embassy around six. I've got to show up at a Lebanese do at seven thirty, but I shouldn't be more than an hour . . .'

'Okay.'

'You've had quite a heavy week. That artillery exchange on – when was it – Tuesday and Wednesday, must have been pretty horrific.'

'It was, but it was no exchange. The western sector is no match for the east when it comes to firepower . . .'

'We can talk about that tomorrow evening.'

Meaning the phones were watched. Or listened to. Whatever.

'Major—'

'Perry, please.'

'Perry, I will try to make it as close to six as I can, but don't be surprised if I'm late. What with the crossings and the security situation generally.'

Nick had no intention of telling Dacre about Reem.

'If I'm not there, someone else will be. Chris – you remember Chris, don't you, the Royal Military Police staff sergeant – he'll be here. He'll take care of you.'

Nick did not know Chris. Or perhaps he had forgotten.

Only then did Nick realize that Reem and Dacre would meet at the Kaslik yacht club. Of course. From what the major had said, they would be at el-Hami's birthday party at roughly the same time, on the Saturday afternoon. It was not only for diplomats and journalists but UN and NGO officials, too. It did not really matter, only Nick would have preferred to keep his love life to himself. It was nobody's business but his own.

The question was whether Reem minded.

It began well enough.

They had agreed to meet at the Wimpy Bar in the Piccadilly area, and he caught sight of her through the window as he drew up. She gathered up her belongings and ran out, gave him a big grin, fleetingly brushed his cheek with hers (he felt her hair, smelled its fragrance) and tossed her overnight bag on the rear seat.

'Can I drive this time?'

The question took him unawares.

'Sure. I didn't know you did.'

'Oh, yes.'

They changed places.

'This is fun,' she said.

Nick knew he should not let her, but he did not have the heart to say so. She looked so happy. Confident, too. He knew the rules. Non-UN personnel were on no account allowed to drive UN vehicles. It was largely for insurance reasons. It also involved the sensitive issue of staff security.

'I have my Lebanese licence,' Reem said, glancing in the side mirror and pulling out into the traffic. 'And I have an international one, too. From Cyprus.'

'You do?'

'I went to Larnaca for an English language course. I told you, didn't I? The institute paid. It was just before we met. So I spent my free time polishing my driving skills as well. It seemed like a good idea.'

'You don't seem to have any trouble driving this beast.'

'It's easy. It's got power-assisted steering and it's a four-wheel drive. I'd like to try it out in the mountains one day.'

'I was afraid you'd say that.'

'Oh, yeah? You English.'

There was a queue of cars as they approached Mathaf.

Reem exchanged words with the driver of a taxi heading in the opposite direction.

'Doesn't look good, Nick. He's just been turned back. No vehicles. Only pedestrians are being allowed over. It's the army – they've taken over the crossing, apparently.'

'Oh, hell.'

Reem shrugged. 'Let's see what happens. Maybe the UN is an exception.'

Nick said, 'I think I'd better take over. They're less likely to stop a foreigner – at least someone as obviously foreign as I am.'

They changed places once more. Reem squeezed past. Nick was tempted to put his hands around her waist, to pull her down on his lap. Her scent, and her close proximity, made him feel light-headed.

'Look.'

Reem indicated with her chin.

'Shit,' Nick said.

Lebanese soldiers in French-style berets – black ribbons at the back – were stopping all vehicles. The troops carried American M-16 rifles.

A ranger unit, light infantry modelled on the US formation of the same name.

Ahead of them a Cadillac with CD plates had been halted, and was preparing to turn around. A man had stuck his head out of a rear window and was arguing passionately with a squat soldier in a camouflage uniform. The soldier was unmoved by the harangue. He had his orders.

'It's the Egyptian political secretary,' Nick said. 'He's not very happy – he was probably planning a dirty weekend with his mistress.'

They watched the argument for a moment or two.

'Now what?'

'We walk,' Reem said, reaching over the back of the seat for her bag.

Was she serious? One look at her expression told him she was.

'What about the Land-Rover?'

'We can call your office. Get them to collect it. I'll have a word with that captain over there.' She meant the short fellow who had stoically withstood the tongue-lashing from the Egyptian. 'Don't worry so much, Nick. Have faith.'

Faith? Faith had nothing to do with it.

He had done this once. Once was enough.

But he did not argue.

Crack-bang.

Whoever was shooting was firing single rounds.

'They're trying to scare us,' Reem said.

'They don't have to try. I'm already persuaded.'

She turned and looked at Nick over her shoulder.

'You want to turn back?'

He shook his head. No. But he did. He really did. He wanted it more than almost anything. Only he could on no account admit it to Reem. Nick was sweating, and it wasn't just the hot sun. Once they left the wall of sandbags it would be open ground for about 150 metres, maybe 200, before they could reach cover again.

His mouth was dry.

'Ready?'

There was no one else out there.

Reem took his right hand in her left.

Nick nodded, feeling his heart thumping at his ribcage.

Crack-bang.

Fuck.

This was not a good idea.

'Let's go,' Reem said.

She gave his hand a tug.

Nick was struck dumb. He was petrified. But he was more frightened still of showing his fear.

'*Yalla* – now.'

She was off.

They were running side by side, holding hands.

Crack-bang.

The time between the crack of the bullet passing them and the bang of the weapon firing was a microsecond. So very close, Nick thought. The bastard or bastards can see the colour of our eyes.

Nick was sucking air into his lungs.

They were in the open.

He saw a blur of camouflage-pattern smock as he ran, legs pumping hard, the soldiers' mouths open. Shouting. He couldn't hear them. Their faces were turned towards the pair of runners.

Were they shouting a warning?

Ordering them to turn back?

Too late now.

Reem was smiling. She seemed to enjoy it. How could she?

Crack-crack.

He saw the rounds smack the dirt just ahead, throwing up sand.

Playing with us, firing low.

They can kill us any time they want.

Reem's hand tightened.

Never again. Never.

Not even for you, Reem.

Nick no longer felt his legs. They seemed to work independently of his stupefied mind.

The top half of him was flying, but his weekend bag was bumping into his legs, slowing the bottom half down. He seemed to be wearing wooden clogs on his feet, not trainers.

The eastern sector lay ahead.

THIRTEEN

Aunt Sohad gave Reem a hug, wrapping her arms around her.

From the wide balcony that ran along the front of their home, a village house faced in yellow stone and roofed with terracotta tiles, they had seen Reem's service taxi roll to a halt. They recognized the passenger as she paid off the driver. She crossed the lane over to the gates and walked up a drive shaded by two huge umbrella pines from whose trunks a score of cicadas rasped noisily in concert.

Sohad and her two girls, Maha and Hana, as well as their Ethiopian maid hurried down to welcome her, the girls arriving first and planting wet kisses on Reem's cheeks.

Sohad was close behind, arms wide.

'*Habibti . . .*'

They would not let her carry her own bag. They would probably have carried her too if they could have managed it.

'Home at last, dearest. Welcome.'

Sohad's daughters took Reem's hands and skipped excitedly on either side up to the front doors, pulling her along with them.

For lunch there was *moutabal* and *hommous* as well as *tabouli* and Reem's favourite main dish, *fatteh*, a dish popular in Syria and Jordan. For Reem it was an irresistible palette of vivid Mediterranean flavours: garlic, grilled aubergine, chickpeas and yoghurt.

Best of all, no prying.

No questions.

No lectures.

No fussing.

They sat out at the back under the vines, in dappled sunlight.

Auntie Sohad's bull of a husband was absent, to the unspoken relief of all those present, including Sohad herself. He was away in Tripoli, attending to business. He had his own haulage company, and traded in cement. The wealthier he became, the busier he was. No one was more pleased than Kerim's wife and daughters.

Reem felt they were happy to enjoy the fruit of his labours, happier still to do so without the presence of the man who made it possible.

When he was around, his loud voice and peremptory manner could be heard throughout the house, issuing orders to wife and daughters, servants and hangers-on, and the reception rooms were full of strangers. Food and drink were in constant demand for the crowds of business associates.

Today lunch was rounded off with coffee and chocolates.

There was talk of friends, of the village, of Sheikh so-and-so and his errant offspring, of a recent marriage at the neighbouring village, and the two girls talked of their school and the eccentric behaviour of their teachers. They talked about their favourite films, of Michael Jackson's latest chart hit, 'Beat It'.

Teenage talk.

There was no mention of politics.

Beirut and the war seemed a world away.

And afterwards, an afternoon nap, Sohad dozing in her favourite armchair, the front doors open wide to catch the breeze.

Familiar rooms, familiar smells, familiar birdsong outside the tall, yellow-shuttered windows. The sound of a tap running, slippers on the tiled floor, a door closing, the thump of a cupboard drawer; Reem could plot people and their movements simply by the trails of sound.

She lay on her back on Sohad's huge four-poster and looked up at the high ceiling. There was plenty of time. The party was

not until the following afternoon. There was no hurry to decide
what to wear.

She thought of Nick.

How they had run together.

Reem turned onto her right side, drawing up her legs and
tucking her right hand under her cheek. She slipped into sleep,
thinking about him.

That evening, out on the stoop, they kept their voices low so as
not to disturb Maha and Hana who had gone to bed.

Reem asked, 'You lived right next door?'

'Yes, where your Armenian neighbours are now. We rented
the flat when we came back from west Africa.'

'So you were there, too . . .'

'When they died?'

Sohad nodded. 'Yes, child. We were there.'

'You remember it? All of it?'

'How could I forget?'

'I remember very little,' Reem said.

'Perhaps that's the way it should be, sweetheart. You were a
tiny thing.'

'I should remember. I want to. I'm no longer a child.'

Sohad regarded her best friend's daughter. Her late best
friend's daughter, and Reem thought she could almost see what
Sohad was thinking – how much should she say? What harm
could it do now – all those years gone by?

Maha and Hana were in bed, hopefully asleep.

Sohad and Reem sat on the swing-seat on the porch. The iron
gates at the bottom of the drive were shut. Reem could smell
jasmine and the mosquito repellent – twists of chemical that
burned slowly beneath their feet, wisps of bitter blue smoke
keeping the insects at bay.

Sohad had already read Reem's cup.

The coffee grounds were swirled around the sides of the cup, which was then upended on its saucer and allowed to drain. Then the reader – Sohad in this instance – would decipher the shapes and squiggles.

Dragons and elephants, banknotes and grimaces. Friends and enemies, lovers and ghosts, angels and a fortune in gold.

She, Reem, would travel. She would indeed find fortune.

She would achieve so much. She would realize her ambition.

Oh, sure.

'No handsome stranger?'

They cracked up laughing.

'Tell me,' Reem said, serious again. 'Please.'

'What do you remember?'

Reem frowned, waved off a mosquito.

'It's confusing.'

Sohad waited.

'There are only bits. Images. Like parts of photographs, scenes from a movie that aren't part of a sequence. Jumbled up. Censored. You know?'

'Go on.'

'Memory plays games. I remember the screams. My mother's screams.' Reem stared away into the night, screwing up her eyes as if trying to picture it. 'I remember their crying. My sisters.'

'You don't have to, dearest—'

'I want to.'

They were silent for a moment.

'I saw the gunman,' Reem said. 'I recognized him. I heard the shooting. Single shots. Bam-bam-bam-bam. Like that.'

'Where were you?'

'On the stairs. I think it was the stairs.'

'Then?'

In the distance a jackal howled, followed at once by a fusillade of yelps and barks.

Reem said, 'I saw someone on the stairs above me. There was a grill. I was looking through it. I don't know what the grill was,

116

exactly. I saw a boy. He was crawling up the stairs. He had his back to me. He had on a striped T-shirt. I could see his back, a hand, the dirty soles of his bare feet. I didn't know why, but I wanted so much to talk to him, but I couldn't. It didn't seem to dawn on me at first who he was. Then he turned and looked at me. He just turned his head. I saw one eye, looking at me. It was a solemn expression. Sad. His look said, "Where are you? What's happening? I'm hurt." Then I saw then he was bleeding. It was Michael—'

Reem stopped speaking. She took a deep breath.

'Stop now,' Sohad said.

She took Reem's hand in her own.

Reem shook her head, biting down on her emotions.

'He put out a hand. I put one arm, then the other, through the bars. I wanted to help, but I couldn't reach him. I didn't know it then, but my brother was dying. He was still trying to climb up the stairs. There was blood all down the steps. So much of it. I didn't know what death was, then. I didn't understand a thing.'

'*Habibti* . . .'

'No.'

Reem took several deep breaths.

'My brother was nine.'

'Yes.'

'He got away. The killer. The bastard shot them all one by one and he got away.'

'Palestinians shot his son.'

'I know that,' Reem said, anger and contempt in her voice. 'His son was a thief.'

Tears rolled down her cheeks and she wiped them away with the back of her hand.

God, why had she started talking about this?

Sohad said, 'He tried to bribe the Palestinians to put his son's picture up on the walls with the martyrs. They wouldn't. They refused. They had caught the boy stealing a cash box from a printer's and they took him into one of those ruined houses –

some place in Barbir hit by shells and gutted by fire – and they executed him. He had been warned before.'

Reem said, 'His father was the local butcher. I saw who it was. My mother sometimes bought our meat from him when she couldn't be bothered to go further down the street. He used to cheat with the weights, and he would keep a little fat in the pouch of his white apron and if the customer wasn't watching closely enough, he'd adulterate the meat. He was a crook, too. When his son was shot he got out his Kalashnikov and came into our building and he killed my family.' Reem looked down at her hands in her lap. 'We weren't Palestinians, but he thought we were. We were defenceless. We were the next best thing. Leftists. From the south. Murdering women and an unarmed man was easy for him. A soft target. And the bastard got away with it. The coward ran away. They never found him.'

'You were with us,' Sohad said gently. 'You were playing. That's what you meant by the grill. To stop our children – they were toddlers then – from falling off the balcony we had a big grill put up. That's where you were. Out on the balcony. You know how small those balconies at the back are.'

'And?'

'We heard the shooting. It was very loud. Close. We were scared. Kerim peeked out of the window. He saw the gunman. He said you were alone out there. I went out through the kitchen and grabbed you and carried you inside and slammed the door before the filthy bastard could kill you, too.'

'You saved me.'

Sohad squeezed Reem's hand.

'Dearest. I wish I could have saved all of you. Your mother was my very best friend. You know, don't you, that your father tried to protect your mother with his body. They found him lying across them, trying to shield them from the bullets. He was a brave man. At least he did not live long enough to see them die.'

'No, I didn't know.'

Reem and Auntie Sohad hugged each other then, and both

wept, Christian and Muslim, the one for a mother she barely remembered and the other for the sister she had always wanted.

Later that night Reem dreamed her dream.

She left her home and walked over to the lift and pressed the button and waited in the darkness for it to clank up to her floor. She got in, and watched the lights flicker as the lift began its shaky descent. Only this time it stopped at every floor, even the ground, where it had never stopped before, at least not in the dream. Then the doors opened and there was the foyer and the grill that protected the entrance and the street beyond.

At that point Reem woke up.

The grill. It was similar to the barrier on Sohad's balcony through which Reem had seen her brother's murder.

'Michael,' she said aloud.

Next morning she borrowed a backless white cotton dress with an embroidered bodice and full skirt. It belonged to Maha and fitted perfectly. It was just right, everyone agreed, for an afternoon function. And then just in case the afternoon overlapped with the evening, Hana insisted on Reem borrowing a little black number, a sheath of black silk and sequins, and heels to go with it. Gorgeous, Reem said it was, and Hana and Maha laughed with delight to see tomboy Reem relinquish denim and T-shirt and allow herself to be transformed into a dark angel.

'No one is going to recognize you,' Maha said.

'Not as a white swan or a black swan,' Hana agreed.

'From ugly duckling, you mean,' Reem said.

There was much trying on of shoes and trying out of lip gloss, and finally, after lunch, the girls took Reem off to their favourite Koura hairdresser. Sohad insisted he was inexpensive by Beirut standards, and yet so much better than anyone left in the capital, in the western sector that is.

They did not ask Reem who or where or why.

Just that she have a good time and come back safely.

She borrowed a little camera from Hana, a point-and-shoot affair with automatic focus and exposure.

'I'll bring back a few snaps from the party.'

'Have a wonderful time, *habibti*.'

'Don't wait up for me.'

'Don't worry. We'll leave the gate open.'

Nick was saying something about the Kaslik club looking like Cap d'Antibes.

Reem knew nothing about the French Riviera, but could see what he must mean; the white masts of the million-dollar yachts jostling for space in the marina, the villas and chalets masked by magnolia and bougainvillea, the brick walkways, the open-air restaurants, the date palms, the huge swimming pools, the pool-side bars.

And the people.

God help us, the people.

'Old money and new money,' Nick said.

Old money dressed conservatively, women in dark colours, men in suits and ties, and was mainly elderly. Ms New Money was preternaturally slim and thanks to surgery seemingly age-less. She flaunted herself with fake blonde hair, heavy make-up, bold Versace and little strings of gold and pearl anklets, and wobbled precariously on gravity-defying heels, her partner in black (Armani, naturally) with gold glinting from an open-neck polo shirt, a gold Rolex on his wrist.

Old or new, they brayed at one another in French.

It was warm, but Reem had gooseflesh at the mere sound of it.

Here they were, the people who insisted on speaking French and aping the mannerisms of her country's former colonial masters, people who called themselves Phoenician or simply Leba-nese – but who never admitted to being Arab.

They surged around an enormous buffet as waiters in white jackets circulated with champagne, replenishing glasses and calling people monsieur and madame.

The latest Police hit 'Every Breath You Take' was losing the battle to be heard over hundreds of people all talking at once at the tops of their voices.

Reem saw the Protector almost immediately.

He stood alone, legs apart, gripping a half-empty champagne flute.

Black trousers, black loafers, blue button-down shirt open at the collar, white cotton jacket.

His minders – of whom there were half a dozen in a loose half-circle – were steering the newcomers towards him, releasing people singly or in couples to make the final approach. An aide took the invitations one by one, read off each name aloud as the guests stepped forward.

The minders all wore navy. They had their hair cut very short and wore shades. They carried radio receivers in their ears. The microphones, Reem thought, must be in their lapels.

Armed too, no doubt.

Israeli-trained.

No chance of getting to him directly, not after the bag search and the frisking at the entrance and then the second electronic check halfway through the tunnel to the club's recreation area. The gunmen had examined Reem's camera – and handed it back without a word. It was just as she thought: women, well dressed women, Christian women, were above suspicion – or below it, depending on one's point of view.

El-Hami's greeting to each newcomer was a bob of the head, a handshake, a smile and a word of welcome.

The minders kept the guests moving along at a brisk pace.

'They've thought of absolutely everything.'

Reem turned towards the voice. So did Nick.

'How are you, young Nick? Aren't you going to introduce us?'

He stood behind and between them. He was short, plump, his

hair dark with sweat was plastered to his scalp and his shirt was hanging out of his trousers. He looked very hot.

He did not wait for Nick to respond.

'Wilson. Andrew Wilson. I'm with the embassy. You're a dark one, Nick, hiding away your friend here, keeping her all to yourself.'

Reem thought Nick looked awkward and not a little irritated.

She came to the rescue. 'How do you mean they've thought of everything, Mr Wilson?'

'My God,' Wilson said, leering at Reem's décolletage. 'What a relief not to have to speak my schoolboy French. I meant security, miss. Take a look at the roof. See what I mean? They've got marksmen all over the place. Closed-circuit television cameras, too. Our boy's taking no chances.'

Reem's eyes followed a wave of Wilson's arm, encompassing CCTV in the date palms to the outline of a man and a rifle on the roof behind her.

'Our boy?'

'The white man's last great hope. Your next president.'

Not mine, she thought. Never mine.

Wilson was drunk. He was rocking on his heels and his face was very red. He had stepped forward, turned and faced them. He leaned towards Reem and raised a forefinger and wagged it at her.

'You know where this laddie started his career, don't you,' Wilson said. 'Karantina, seventy-six. He was just a simple foot soldier. Right near the port. You must know it. A plot of land owned by Maronite monks.' Wilson stepped sideways into a waiter's path and snatched another glass of champagne, depositing his empty glass in its place, and moved back again.

Wilson said, 'There were refugees. Armenians. Kurds. Palestinians. The usual riff-raff our boy and his kind love to hate.' Wilson took a swig of champagne. 'Where was I? Yes. The Pals got some of their boys in with arms and ammunition. They put up a stiff fight. Bloody heroic, actually, and doomed. Lebanon is wall-to-wall heroes – only they're all under the ground. They turned the Sleep Comfort factory into a strongpoint. Sleep Comfort. Some sleep. They refused to surrender because they knew the end would be the same whatever they did, right, miss? A very long sleep.' Wilson put his head back and emptied the glass.

'Afterwards they allowed the press to take pictures. You'd be too young to remember, miss, but maybe you saw the pictures in *L'Orient Le Jour*. The Phalangists drank champagne standing and sitting on the bodies. Pictures of boys and girls, terrified, holding their hands up while the grinning Phalangist gunmen paraded them at gunpoint. Kids whose parents had just been butchered in front of them.'

Wilson watched Reem, expecting a reaction. He was rocking back and forth like a trawler's mast in a force-twelve gale.

Reem looked at nothing, expressionless.

Wilson said, 'It reminded me of pictures of Jewish kids being rounded up by the Nazis. But our boy didn't care. He blamed the press. He and his people were proud of what they did. Oh, yes. A victory, they called it. They still are proud. You know our birthday boy has a photograph of himself opening a bottle of bubbly at Karantina in seventy-six against a background of bodies of civilians. It's on his office wall. You can see it for yourself. I did. And you know where that is, don't you. His headquarters? At Karantina, of course . . .'

Wilson sniggered into his glass.

'Six years later el-Hami was the Phalangist battalion commander in Sabra and Shatila who called Elie Hobeika on the radio. Hobeika, in overall charge, was watching from a command post on a nearby building along with his ally from down south, Ariel Sharon. Our boy asked Hobeika what he should do with the women and kids, and Hobeika shouted at him that he knew perfectly well what to do and not ask such a bloody stupid question again. I tell you, our boy's going to make one hell of a president. A real force for reconciliation.'

Wilson pulled himself to attention and lifted his glass in mock salute.

'To the Protector . . .'

'I think we'll join the queue,' Nick said, taking Reem's hand and drawing her away.

Once they were out of earshot, Nick turned to her.

'He thought you were a Maronite from this side. A Phalangist hardliner. I hope the ambassador doesn't see him in his present state. You see, Wilson loathes these people almost as much as you do.'

That was impossible, Reem thought.

Waiting in the queue, Reem had plenty of time to look around.

There had to be at least thirty security men on duty.

There were men watching the beach, watching the seaward approaches. She counted four.

Wilson was right. The Protector had left nothing to chance.

A landward approach would be equally futile. The road dipped to the coastal shelf, and all vehicles had to turn sharply to pass through an arch that was well guarded, then across the car park before taking a U-turn and drawing up alongside the entrance. Yet more young men with hard faces, earpieces and 9 mm Berettas under their summer jackets opened doors and checked invitations.

Nine.

Male and female guests were briefly separated for a rapid frisking while their bags and purses were searched, also by hand.

Four more. A baker's dozen.

Visitors then walked past a hulk of modern statuary and down a broad flight of stairs. Just before heading out into the gardens there was an electronic scanning device of the kind used at airports to check bags. Two people, a man and a woman, wielded hand-held scanners for the guests.

On the mezzanine gallery above, the entire process was watched by three men with pump-action shotguns.

Eighteen.

Mentally, Reem began preparing her report.

And the marksmen on the roof outside.

Twenty, maybe?

Thirty?

Question: did he ever stay in the club overnight?

Reem turned to Nick. 'Do you think what Wilson said about Karantina was right?'

'About his role in the massacre?'

'I meant having an office there. And the pictures on his wall.'

'I don't know about the pictures.'

'Can we go?'

'To Karantina?'

Nick looked at her, surprised.

'Why not?'

'I suppose so,' he said doubtfully.

It was their turn.

Nick handed over his invitation.

'Mr Nicholas Lorimer and Miss Reem Najjar.'

Nick went first.

She saw Nick shake the Protector's hand.

Then she found herself walking forward.

Christ's sake, he's not royalty.

The enemy.

He stood four-square like a tank, a powerful man, his broad chest and heavy arms more appropriate to a prizefighter than a politician. The long head with hair combed straight back swung towards her, then bowed slightly, and his eyes met hers, as if to say, 'And what do we have here?'

Appraising.

How could he remember so many faces?

He couldn't possibly.

Stop worrying.

His voice was a deep rumble.

The Protector did not offer his hand. He was waiting for her to do so first.

'Miss Najjar. Welcome. Thank you for coming . . .'

The enemy made a half bow.

Reem kept moving like a sleepwalker.

She realized afterwards she had not given him her hand.

She had not uttered a single word.

Nick was waiting for her.

'Now,' Reem said, 'I think I will have that glass of champagne.'

FOURTEEN

Reem insisted on taking snaps, seeking a different backdrop each time.

Sylvie and George had come up to them, hand in hand, and after the usual greetings and introductions, Reem produced the little camera and took their picture, just the two of them, with the sea behind. She took two more, and still dissatisfied, wanted them to stand together this time, arms around each other, with the tennis courts and headland as backdrop.

They offered to take a picture of Nick and Reem together. Reem accepted, but asked everyone to turn around because she said she wanted the main club building in the picture.

'Would you be a darling, and take another in front of the club?'

So they trooped out front, and had their picture taken again, twice, this time with the inclusion of two unsmiling Phalangist bodyguards on el-Hami's payroll.

Nick took three of Reem alone, and two of Reem with Sylvie and George, each time with a different background.

Between them, they used up a roll of thirty-six colour negatives.

For her part, Sylvie made a fuss of Reem, complimenting her on her dress and hair.

'You must both stay this evening,' Sylvie said, and taking Reem aside, told her she was very welcome to make use of one of the family chalets if she needed to change. 'Our place is just up there,' she said, pointing to a first-floor balcony. 'No one will mind. My father isn't staying . . .'

To Nick's surprise, Reem readily agreed.

The women left together. Sylvie was going to show Reem her place, and how to find it. She could have a spare key for the evening. George slapped Nick on the back and suggested a beer at one of the pool bars. He said he did not care for champagne. It gave him a headache.

The two men had little to say to each other. They drank their cold beers in the shade, and watched the parade of people.

George asked, 'Where'd you find her?'

'Reem? We literally bumped into one another.'

'You've been here, what – four weeks? You haven't lost any time, have you?'

He sounded envious.

Nick had plenty to think about. The previous evening, once Dacre had poured their drinks on his veranda, he had made his excuses and vanished indoors for a few minutes, returning with a white file. He tossed it onto the table.

'Take a look,' Dacre said, pulling out a chair and sitting down. 'If there isn't enough light we can go inside.'

Nick opened the folder. There were three sheets of paper, stapled together. All three carried two red stripes intersecting in the centre – a saltire, with each stripe running diagonally from corner to corner. All three pages were marked SECRET. The top sheet or cover was headed Distribution, followed by a single acronym, UKUSZCA

At first it made no sense.

The second sheet contained printed text, broken down into five paragraphs.

The third page gave the source: Liaison.

There was a comment section at the bottom, but it was blank.

'Take a look at the photograph,' Dacre said.

There was a six-by-eight print in the folder that Nick had almost missed.

He slid it out onto the tablecloth.

Head and shoulders, the man facing the camera.

'Recognize him?'

Nick stared at the image.

'It's taken from the Interior Ministry's registration archives in west Beirut – where the Lebanese register for their compulsory ID cards.'

'I know what it is,' Nick said.

He had put the photograph aside and was reading the five paragraphs.

'It's not a good likeness,' Dacre said. 'It's out of focus because it's been enlarged, and it was taken several years ago with East German film, when he was around seventeen, but I'm sure you know him.'

'Why are you showing me this?'

'I thought you should know.'

It was no answer.

'But why?'

'He's a friend of yours, isn't he, Nick? From what you've said yourself you spend a good deal of time together in working hours and off duty.'

'What are you saying? That he's dangerous? That I'm at risk?'

'Nick, I shouldn't be showing you this. But I think you really ought to know who you're dealing with.'

Khaled looked out from the glossy photographic paper, a younger, thinner, serious Khaled, with longer, wilder hair and a beard.

Nick read the five paragraphs again.

He put the report and the photograph back into the folder and pushed it back to Dacre.

'He's still my friend,' Nick said.

'Of course,' Dacre replied. 'I wouldn't expect you to react in any other way. It does you credit.'

*

So Khaled was Khaled Mrabat, a Palestinian.

Not Lebanese.

According to the intelligence report, Khaled's elder brother, Joseph, had commanded a Fatah unit near Sidon in '78 when the Israelis launched a big incursion as far as the Litani River. The operation was to 'punish' Lebanese civilians for the presence of the Palestinians rather than take on the Palestinian fighters concentrated around Sidon and Tyre. Many Lebanese villages were shelled and bombed, sending the wretched Shi'ite residents streaming north towards the capital – not for the first or the last time. Without orders or any word from their absentee senior commanders, Joseph's boys put up a fight, and Joseph, aged twenty-two, was wounded in the legs and captured.

Israeli soldiers tied him to a telephone pole and their commander, a lieutenant in the Golani Brigade, shot him twice with a pistol at point-blank range, once in the forehead and once in the cheek, just below his right eye.

The body was found and identified by his father two days later.

The soldiers looted Joseph's house, dragged his wife and two children out of the basement and beat Joseph's father senseless. Several soldiers gang-raped the wife.

Joseph's woman was named Khadijeh. She was twenty.

The invaders turned the local school into an interrogation centre, and a large compass was used as a spike, driven into the captives' ears in an effort to get them to talk.

Khaled got away. He made a run for it. He disappeared for months, but was eventually picked up in the southern town of Jezzine by pro-Israeli militiamen, given an impromptu beating and handed over to Israel's security organization, Shin Beth, on suspicion of being an arms runner, although no weapons or ammunition were found.

Accused of membership of the PLO, Khaled was sentenced to eleven months in the Israeli-run Khiam gaol because he was only fifteen. Normally the sentence was one year. The Israeli military court took less than three minutes to reach its decision. No defence was allowed, and Khaled was not allowed to speak on his own behalf, other than to enter a plea of guilty.

Now here he was, with a Lebanese identity card, working for the United Nations in Beirut.

Dacre tapped the file. 'Did you know about any of this?'

'No.' Nick, deadpan, sipped his gin and tonic.

'What's young Khaled up to? It says in there he's a member of a communist organization. OLCA.'

'Surviving. Having a good time when he can. There must be thousands of young Palestinians and Lebanese who have fought the Israelis – in seventy-six, seventy-eight and eighty-two. It changes nothing as far as I am concerned, either as his friend or his boss. As for having Lebanese ID, I'm sure there are many Palestinians who've managed to pull it off one way or another so they can work and not rot away in some refugee camp. Have you seen those camps? There are people there who were driven out of their homes as early as forty-eight. They will die there. So will their children if the likes of Ariel Sharon get their way.'

'Nick, the report suggests he is still active.'

'It's hardly an earth-shattering revelation. I'd be a fucking red, too, in his shoes.'

Dacre jumped up and began pacing.

'Our information is that the Ustaz is planning a big operation on this side of town. Our best guess is that the target is the presidential hopeful you will be meeting tomorrow. El-Hami. We need all the help we can get to try to find out what it is he's planning.'

'And you seriously think Khaled is involved?'

'I don't know, Nick. I really don't know. Perhaps you can tell us. He must have said something. It's not just Khaled. It's people like him. People with a cause, a grievance, people who might be playing a relatively minor role – you must rub up against these types every day of the week.'

'It would be hard not to.'

'You'll help?'

'You want me to spy.'

'I want you to keep your eyes and ears open. I want you to tell me the moment something out of the ordinary comes to your attention. Are you willing to help us, Nick?'

It did not occur to Nick until much later that evening – while eating pizzas with Reem, Sylvie and George – what UKUSZCA stood for. It was surely obvious; the five-member intelligence club that shared communications intercepts from a global surveil-lance network – the United States, the United Kingdom, Canada, Australia and New Zealand. The victors of World War Two, *sans* France and the Soviets. In Britain it meant GCHQ, those huge golf balls at Fylingdales and the domes on top of Mount Troodos in Cyprus. As for the source – Liaison had to mean the infor-mation had come from one of the non-UK partners. The thought led to another realization – how could he have missed it? Khaled's family name was Saad. It said as much on his Lebanese ID. Nick authorized expense payments to one Khaled Saad every month.

So what was this about Mrabat?

Which name was genuine?

Dacre had insisted the mysterious Ustaz was a professional. He must have had external support and training.

Nick remained unimpressed.

'You're pissing in the dark, Perry. It's guesswork. And if you were this mysterious Ustaz, you would accept help from what-ever quarter it came. So don't give me this KGB-trained hood crap.'

'Is that a no, Nick?'

'I didn't say that.'

'So what are you saying?'

'I'll think about it.'

'If it helps, Nick, we know about your parents and their

background. It's not a problem as far as we're concerned. Your security clearance is AOK.'

'It never occurred to me that it might be a problem. And if it was, it would be your problem, not mine.'

Nick struggled to keep his temper in check.

'How long do you need to make up your mind?'

'I don't know, Perry.'

Nick was not sure he would ever do so.

'Can I have your answer by this time next week?'

And there they left it.

'What's the matter, Nick?'

'Nothing.'

'You look like something's bothering you.'

He was dancing with Reem next to the Olympic-sized pool, its azure water lit from below. The politicians had gone. Even el-Hami had left with his entourage of gunmen. The younger set were enjoying themselves to the sound of the Eurythmics and Michael Jackson. Reem and Nick were doing a gentle soft-shoe shuffle around the tiny dance floor to Irene Cara's 'What A Feeling'. There was no elbow room to do much jumping about. Anyway, it was a warm night.

'I want to talk to you about something.'

'Sure. When?'

'Tomorrow.'

Now she looked troubled. 'I have to go back tomorrow, Nick.'

'It's Sunday. Let's go swimming. We'll go back in the afternoon. I hope we can take a taxi across. I don't fancy a repeat of Friday's run.'

She looked at him, her eyes smiling.

'It would be great to go swimming.'

'I thought we might try Byblos.'

'You mean Jbeil.'

'Same thing.'

'I'd like that very much.'

'There's a great fish restaurant there.'

The number changed to the previous year's hit, 'Love Is a Stranger'.

She let him draw her closer to him and put her arm around his neck, her fingers touching the back of his head.

'Nick.'

He could feel her breasts against his ribs.

'What?'

'Thank you.'

'For what?'

'For today. For tonight.'

She drew his head towards her, shut her eyes.

No one was watching.

And if there was, tough.

FIFTEEN

She swam ahead of him, keeping just out of reach.

Reem waited, letting him catch up, then just as it seemed he could grasp a hand or an ankle, she was off, slipping away, twisting and turning underwater, losing him again, turning back and watching him trying to find her on the surface.

He was strong, but Nick was no match for Reem submerged.

She swam out, then dived, slipped through a gap in the rock barrier fifty metres out, and circled round.

Her head broke the surface and she turned and smiled at him.

'Come on, Nick, what's keeping you . . .'

After five minutes of this tantalizing catch-me-if-you-can she let him grab her, pull her to him so they faced each other on the seaward side of the reef, big flat rocks that projected only a few inches above the surface.

Reem said, 'They can't see us from the shore.'

The fishermen standing on the rocks with their immensely long rods were facing out to sea, too, not in the least interested in a couple of swimmers.

Reem held Nick lightly by his shoulders.

'I know,' he said.

She liked his muscular chest, even more when pressed up against it.

Their kisses had the salty tang of the sea.

Nick pulled down her bikini top.

'Naughty,' she said.

'But very nice.'

His tongue and lips felt hot after the sea water.

Exciting.

Delight and shame wrestled.

It was no contest. Delight won.

What he was doing made her tremble.

She said, 'Fair's fair. If you do one, you have to do the other.'

No, it was too much.

Letting go of Nick, Reem pulled up the straps of her top with her thumbs and slid through the circle of his arms before he could react, dropping down, diving deep, following the contour of the sand sloping up towards the coastline, slipping once more through the rocks.

Breaking the surface again she stood and turned to watch Nick.

He was laughing, shaking his head.

'I can't come out quite yet.'

She knew why.

She walked up to the two plastic sun loungers they had hired from the beach club and picked up a towel.

Nick was still in the water, waist deep.

'Take your time,' she said, grinning at him, drying her arms and back.

They both heard the artillery fire to the south, from the hills above the capital, but neither mentioned it.

At this range, it sounded no more threatening than a distant summer thunderstorm.

Reem wondered whether they would be able to cross that afternoon. If not, it might provide her with the opportunity she needed to fulfil the task – her first real operation – set by the Ustaz.

They walked arm in arm around the little crusader port, and climbed up to the Frankish castle built on foundations of Roman columns. They made their way to the miniature Roman amphi-theatre and Nick stood entranced at the Etruscan reliefs and

Phoenician tombs that had been partially excavated before the war.

One civilization lived and died on the ruins of its forerunners.

Nick offered Reem his hand to climb down the steps of one sub-terranean chamber housing a Phoenician sarcophagus, and she kept hold of it, fingers laced.

'Reem . . .'

She turned.

'Can we go out together? I mean, formally?'

She smiled, but shook her head.

His question was not unexpected. She had given the issue some thought. She did not want to disappoint Nick. She did not want to raise his hopes, either. That he was sincere, enjoyed her company, wanted her, of this she had little doubt. And the truth of it was that she liked Nick, too. It was a lot more than liking. She found him very attractive. He made it possible, just for a few hours at a time, to forget there was a war, that she was using him to achieve her ambition. It was this fear of losing what little she had – these pleasures they enjoyed together, the attention he gave her, this taste of a life she never believed possible – that made her resist what he wanted because she knew it could not work.

'I'm sorry.'

How lame she sounded even to herself.

His face fell.

'Why on earth not?'

They sat side by side on a large stone warmed by the sun and looked out over the unruffled sea.

'This is my place, Nicholas. It's unfortunate, but there it is. It is part of me, and I am part of it. I cannot leave, whatever happens. My life is bound up with Lebanon.' She kicked a grass tussock. 'This is my earth, my dust. You say dust? Or soil? Never mind. To leave, to be somewhere else, constantly on the move, restless, never at peace, thinking about what was happening here – I couldn't do it.'

It was not entirely true. Leaving was a temptation, and a strong one. Given the chance of leaving, few Lebanese could resist it.

'But I'm not asking you to leave.'

She lowered her head, frowning, staring at a line of tiny brown ants marching stoically across the hot earth. 'No? Aren't you? Are you going to quit your job and settle here, then? A Westerner in west Beirut? If you survive the war, and escape the kidnappers, what will you do for a living, Nick? Would you take a local job on a monthly wage in Lebanese lira that won't even buy one of these lunches you take me to?'

'I hadn't thought that far ahead.'

Reem placed her left hand in the palm of his right.

She spoke gently.

'I know, Nick. Of course you haven't. But if we go out formally, as you put it, it means an engagement is imminent. Marriage follows. That's our way. And then? Where do we live? Do you want a family, and if so, where would you raise one? Here? Is that what you want? Are you asking me to marry you, Nicholas? Are you?'

Reem looked up into Nick's eyes. His expression was that of a child who has been told he cannot have another slice of cake.

She was being unfair. Cruel, even. She knew it. She had ambushed him, using his desire to confound his reason, calling his hand. Perhaps he really did love her – although he had not used the word. Wisely so. Perhaps it really was no more than young healthy bodies in the Mediterranean sun.

Perhaps.

But it would never happen.

Reem could not let it happen.

'Nick?'

'Yes?'

'It is not my intention to hurt you. Please. Believe me. We must live for what we have now. You were right not to think too far ahead. Let's enjoy what we have, and see what happens. Let's make no decisions one way or the other. Not yet, anyway.'

On the way back they entered the great hall of the fort, and mounted the single stone staircase. There were no handholds, and the stair had a sheer drop on one side, down onto a rubble of limestone blocks.

They held hands and Reem went slightly ahead. The staircase simply ended. It led nowhere. At the top she turned.

'Lunch,' she said.

He drew her to him again, and this time, without warning, kissed her stomach, just above her belly button. Reem bent, holding onto his shoulders, feeling light-headed, and kissed him hard and long on the mouth.

When they drew apart she felt unsteady on her feet.

'I hate heights.'

They went down together, slowly, wordlessly.

They had lunch under a yellow awning on a concrete platform that projected out among the rocks. They began with a salad of wild rocket and onion with olive oil and lemon juice, a bottle of dry white Ksara, and ordered grilled *sultan brahim* – red mullet. Reem chose the fish herself from a large tank.

They ate the fish with their fingers, dipping the food into bowls of *taratour*, a sauce of crushed seasame seeds, garlic, oil and lemon.

'Yesterday you wanted to say something to me,' Reem said.

Nick nodded, his mouth full.

'What was it?'

The waiter was nowhere in sight. There were two other tables occupied by diners, and they were well out of earshot. Um Kalthoum was in any case making sure no one would overhear.

'I trust you, Reem.'

'You do?'

'What if I were to tell you that I'd been asked to spy?'

'So?' Reem shrugged and picked up her glass.

'So what do you think?'

She sipped the wine.

'Nick,' she said patiently, 'we Arabs assume that most foreigners, especially the Americans and English, are spies. Why should it surprise me?'

She drank more and put her glass down.

'Did you think I was a spy?'

'The thought crossed my mind,' she said, using a strip of bread to pick up a bite-sized chunk of fish and dip it in the *taratour*.

'And if I was, how would you feel?'

'What difference would it make how I felt, Nick?'

She popped the food in her mouth and watched him. Nick's pale skin had caught the sun and turned quite pink.

'I don't really know. I suppose I would want your approval, or at least, not to suffer your disapproval.'

Again she shrugged and looked out to sea, across the rocks, streaming with white water as the waves retreated. Truly, these English were strange.

Nick pressed on. 'Wouldn't you object?'

'It's nothing to do with me.'

'What if I said the British had asked me to report on people in west Beirut?'

'Have they, Nick?'

Now Reem was interested, but she took care not to show it. What was he getting at – had they specifically asked about her?

'Yes,' he said.

'And?'

Reem waited. Nick had put on his sunglasses, for the glare from the sun was strong, even under the awning.

'I said I'd think about it.'

'And have you thought about it?'

'Aren't you going to ask me what they wanted to know?'

'Does it matter? I think I can guess, anyway.'

The waiter came up to take away the plates. He placed finger bowls before them. They both wanted coffee, and Reem asked for a second bottle of mineral water. Nick lit a cigarette.

'So guess,' he said when the waiter had gone.

'They wanted to know about your friends. The people you mix with. Militant Muslims. Palestinians. Leftists.' She had a pretty good notion who it was they were interested in, but she wanted to sound uninterested. Bored, even.

'First of all I was shown a file on a colleague of mine whom they said was still an activist, and then they told me they expected an attack in the eastern sector – on el-Hami.'

'Who is "they"?'

'Dacre – he's the military attaché.'

'Is he their chief spy?'

'Actually they all seem to be in on it. There are only three. And I have a funny feeling that it's the man you met at the party yesterday – Wilson.'

'The drunk who talked a lot.'

Nick nodded. 'Only I think it's an act. I don't know why.'

'Who was this colleague?'

'Khaled. You remember—'

'And this attack?'

'Assassination attempt. By someone they call the Ustaz. It's not the first time. Dacre had mentioned him before. He seems to be quite an obsession over in the east. He's been blamed for the killing of a French military officer among others. I said this Ustaz was probably several people, or a complete myth. They seemed to be convinced he was about to do something to knock Antoine off his perch before he has a chance to become president.'

The coffee arrived.

'You like these people at the embassy, don't you, Nick? You like the chance to be among your own people. It's natural. And I'm sure they look after you very well, no?'

141

'I suppose I do. Sure.'

'You'd like to please by saying yes, by slipping them the odd titbit, just to keep them happy.'

'I'm tempted – but it runs counter to my UN role. If Geneva found out I'd be out on my ear and it would bring the world body into disrepute.'

'Aren't you taking yourself a little too seriously? I'm sure there are a lot of very senior UN people playing spying games, and that there always have been. You're not going to make much difference.'

'You're right of course.'

'What if you said you can't help them. What then?'

'I just wouldn't get invited up there.'

A second rumble of artillery from the south.

'You'd be – what's the word?'

'Ostracized.'

'You'd be ostracized,' Reem said. 'Would that be so terrible?'

'No, not at all.'

Reem filled her water glass and drank, her eyes on Nick. It occurred to her that the situation offered all manner of opportunities. It was not so much a matter of what Nick felt he could or could not do, but how she could influence him to make the right decision. Right for her. Right for the Ustaz. Right for the Cause.

'So what exactly are you going to do, Nicholas?'

'What would you do in my shoes?'

She laughed.

'Me? But I'm not in your shoes, Nick.'

'But if you were.'

He had asked for it. He had insisted. Reem could not know whether the Ustaz would approve her tactics or not. It could not wait. She had to improvise and act as she thought best. That was what he had always taught her to do.

'If I was in your shoes, which are in any case several sizes too big . . .'

142

'Yes?'

'Then I would definitely say yes.'

'You would – really?'

'Yes.'

'Why?'

'You can make stuff up. You can tell them you found out nothing. You can seem forgetful. You can feed them rubbish. How are you supposed to know what they want? People are trained for this sort of thing, Nick. You haven't been trained to spy, have you?'

'Of course I haven't.'

This was clearly not the response he had expected. Reem asked herself if anyone could really be so very naive about the ways of the world. Was it possible? Did he need her approval so badly? Or was it too just an act?

'Then say yes, Nick. Say yes, and let's forget it and enjoy the rest of the afternoon.'

SIXTEEN

'Where is he?'

No one seemed to know. The query was met with sidelong glances, shrugs – and silence.

Nick stormed along the corridor and barged into the local manager's office. He did not knock, just pushed open the door to find the occupant reading *as-Safir*, his feet up on his desk.

'Where is he? Where's Khaled?'

It was Monday. Nick was not in the best of moods. He and Reem had crossed separately, and he had not had the chance to speak to her since the previous evening. She had spent the night at Sylvia's chalet, and said she would be crossing later in the day. Nick had taken a taxi. It was calm. There were no incidents, but he worried about her. Now Khaled had not turned up for work. He had left no message, and they had missed an important meeting with a contact in the Deuxième Bureau.

Nick's intrusion was bad manners by any Middle East standard, but the manager of Nick's UN office cheerfully ignored the boss's lapse, took his feet off the desk, folded his newspaper and put it aside.

The consummate diplomat, he hauled himself to his feet, straightening his jacket, and beamed at Nick as if he, Elias Khoury, was the luckiest person alive ever to be insulted by a Westerner.

'Mr Nicholas,' he said. 'Welcome.' He raised his voice. 'Ramia – two coffees, please.'

'Where is he?'

'Please. Take a seat. Make yourself at home.'

Elias closed the door so that whatever outburst Nick was about to give vent to would not be heard by the entire staff.

Nick did not want to sit. He did not want to make himself at home.

'Where the bloody hell has he got to?'

Nick had never seen Elias out of a suit. He never appeared at work without a carnation in his buttonhole, either. He never appeared flustered, not even during the worst bouts of street fighting, and he was invariably deferential to Nick, putting the palm of his right hand across his heart in a sign of respect, and when playing a particularly humble role, he would pat the top of his own head. A veteran of the Arab Legion in Jordan, he had worked for a Foreign Office propaganda outfit in Cairo in the 1950s as a radio monitor before joining the League of Nations.

He spoke a fractured jumble of languages, starting with execrable French. Or as Khaled would say, rather unkindly, Elias spoke no language known to mankind.

'Mr Nicholas, *je suis toujours à votre service. Toujours.*'

He was at his most placatory, his most appeasing.

It must be serious.

'Cigarette, M'sieu Nick?'

'No. Thanks.'

The older man undid the middle button of his double-breasted jacket and resumed his seat.

'It is most unfortunate,' he began, waving an unlit cigarette in the air.

'What is?'

Nick thought he was about to hear an elliptical tale of Khaled's drunken conduct, or a veiled description of trouble over a girl.

'It appears Khaled was taken from his home last night.'

Nick collapsed into the chair.

'Taken?'

'Seized. Snatched.'

'Who? Amal? Hizbollah?'

Nick thought it might be some internal issue – a petty rivalry, a score to settle among factions. Khaled knew a lot of odd people, and leftists were targets for some of them.

Elias spread his hands and raised his eyebrows. 'Who knows, Mr Nick?'

'We're supposed to be tracing missing people, and one of our staff – a team leader – is himself abducted? What's going on, Elias? You know everything in this town. That's what we pay you for. You have the contacts. You know everyone worth knowing. What the hell has happened?'

'I am making enquiries, Mr Nick. So far, there isn't very much.'

Nick was far from satisfied. 'He didn't turn up for work at eight – that's four hours ago. What have you found out? Did he have any debts? Was he in trouble over a woman, maybe?'

Elias took his time lighting his own cigarette.

'I talked to a neighbour,' Elias said quietly. 'By telephone. He said he saw someone of Khaled's description dragged out of his home at three a.m. There were three men. They were armed. He had never seen them before.'

'He would say that. They probably wore masks.'

'And one more in the car. The driver.'

'Did he get a description? The registration?'

'Sadly, no. It was a very old Mercedes. It had no plates, he said.'

'Damn. An unregistered battle wagon – stolen, probably, and now dumped. What else?'

'Mr Nick—'

'Was this personal, Elias, or wasn't it? Money, a family feud . . .'

'No, Mr Nicholas, I think not.'

The secretary brought in the coffees.

Normally Nick would have asked Ramia how she was, and enquired about her family, but not today.

Elias said, 'Are you sure you won't smoke, Mr Nick?'

'Perhaps I will, after all.'

Elias sat back in his executive leather chair and placed the tips of his well manicured fingers together and watched Nick draw on the Turkish cigarette.

'You like?'

'Thank you, Elias. What can you tell me?'

'You were friends with Khaled, no?'

'We still are, I hope. So what? What difference does it make?'

'You know about his past, then?'

'I heard some gossip.'

'Ah.' Elias nodded. 'You know then that he is Palestinian?'

'Someone told me something of the sort.'

'Did you know he'd been in jail?'

'Again, I was told.'

'Khaled had a very bad experience. He was in Khiam – in the south.'

'What has this got to do with what's happened?'

Elias leaned forward and spoke in a stage whisper.

'He was political, Mr Nicholas. *Engagé. Tu compris?*'

'He used to be in the PLO, if that's what you mean.'

'*Oui, c'est vrai.* Fatah, but that was in the past. A long time ago. I speak of now. Your friend is an activist. A communist.'

Nick remembered what Dacre had said.

And how he, Nick, had responded.

'Not the Lebanese Communist Party, *bien sûr* . . .'

'Who then?'

Without thinking, Nick stubbed out the cigarette and immediately regretted doing so.

'I mean the Organization for Lebanese Communist Action. They broke from the CP in the sixties . . . The CP stayed loyal to Moscow, but OLCA was more nationalist, a Marxist kind of Arab nationalism . . .'

Nick was thinking hard about the secret file he had seen.

Elias was still talking.

'Have you heard of OLCA, Mr Nick? Khaled was a member of OLCA. *Certainement*. For sure, *mon ami*. I know this – it is fact.' Elias rapped the desk top with his knuckles for emphasis.

Nick snapped out of his daydream. He must act, and do so quickly. He would order a full staff meeting. They would drop everything. Absolutely everything. They must concentrate on finding Khaled. Speed was essential. He must report this to Geneva, but he must act first, then worry about writing reports.

'Was, Elias? What do you mean – "was"?'

There was something incongruous about Elias stepping daintily through a mound of rat-infested rubble with tassled Italian loafers on his feet and wearing a grey suit and Lanvin tie.

He seemed to know where he was going. He showed no hesitation.

It was barely a mile from Nick's apartment – but it was another world in all other respects.

'He lives here?'

'*Oui. Là-bas.*'

Across a patch of waste ground and around the back of an eight-foot mound of rubble of what had been a bombed out school there was a rudimentary ladder – just a plank with strips of wood nailed across it to provide some grip.

'Careful, Mr Nick.'

It led up to a shack, a makeshift place of wood and tar paper that had miraculously escaped the artillery bombardments and was wedged between the kitchens at the rear of two restaurants, the kind of shack that sold coffee and *manaeesh* – sandwiches of hot bread, oil and oregano – to students on their way to the American university.

'Wait – they won't let you in.'

But they did allow Elias inside.

A few moments later, Elias beckoned to Nick.

It was a miserable hovel. There was a rudimentary steel and

glass counter, some stale-looking croissants under glass, a sink, a dripping tap, a gas bottle, a few chairs and tables on a strip of old lino, and beyond it a back room. On one wall were pinned news-paper cutting and pictures of Beirut's leftist artists, musicians and cantatrices, the Rahbanis and other celebrities of a nationalist or leftist persuasion. A young woman in faded jeans led them silently through a curtain of coloured plastic strips.

'Khaled lived here?'

There was a rumpled bed, a single shelf, a stool.

A cupboard, a child's cot.

The woman said something to Elias. Her face was swollen from crying.

'What does she say?'

Elias said, 'She says they took all his papers. They searched. They broke things and made a mess and threatened her. Then they took his papers and him. They had Kalashnikovs. She says it was a mess, but she has cleaned up already.'

'Who were they? Were they Syrians?'

She shook her head when Elias translated.

'Not Syrians. Not the *moukhabarat*. Lebanese. Phalangists. She calls them dogs. Whoring sons of bitches.' Elias shrugged as if to say it was what she said, but he could not vouch for any of it.

'Police? Army?'

'She says no. She says they were *zaaran* – you know?'

'Thugs.'

'*D'accord*. From the east. The people armed by Israel. Mr Nick, this was a meeting place for friends, *tu sais*, people with a common outlook. Poets, musicians. Members of OLCA. There are many such places. What do you say *en Anglais* – hideouts?'

'Yes. Hideouts. And who is she?'

Khaled had never said where he lived, not exactly. Nick had never tried to find out. Khaled had certainly never spoken of a woman he lived with.

Nick felt he knew so little. Here was the home of someone he thought he knew. Someone he drank with. Someone whose secrets he thought he shared. Someone whose company he enjoyed. Christ, Khaled was a friend.

Not was. Is a friend.

The place had no bathroom.

'She? You don't know? She is the cafe owner, Mr Nick. *Elle s'appelle* Aisha. *La femme de* Khaled. His wife, no? She is Kurdish. Their child is being taken care of by his grandmother until this is over. Aisha says she will wait for him. Her boy Sami is two years old. I have seen him. A sweet child. He will miss his father.'

There was the International Committee of the Red Cross. There were the militias, east and west. There was the Foreign Ministry, the Ministry of the Interior, the dreaded Deuxième Bureau – a captive of Syria in the western sector, of Israel and el-Hami's Phalangists in the east – and there were the French military monitors who kept tabs on flare-ups on Beirut's Green Line battlefront. There were Elias's countless and unidentified contacts throughout the western sector.

There was the army, or what there was of it on the western side.

The prime minister's office.

The presidential palace at Baabda.

Nick insisted they all be contacted, then visited in person by a member of staff.

Nothing so far.

And there were the Syrians, Elias insisted.

Syria's people knew much about most things.

The brigadier general commanding the Syrian contingent was not in his office. He was unavailable. Naturally. And naturally, no one knew where he was. Somewhere down south. The southern front-line village of Marjayoun, perhaps, or Sidon. Someone else in his office said he had had to go to Damascus and would not be back until Friday.

No, his secretary insisted, they did not know when he would be back.

Nick smiled. He was so sorry. He was an inconvenience. It was all his fault, or the fault of his UN organization.

He apologized. He would wait.

At first he sat upright on a wooden bench in the corridor of the brigadier's headquarters and practised his Arabic with the help of *an-Nahar* newspaper.

He was ignored. No one paid him the least attention.

Nick smoked while he waited. People walked past and looked at him and away again – they showed no hostility. In fact they showed no interest at all.

Nick thought he heard shouting or crying on another floor, but he could not make it out.

For the first time in several hours he thought about Reem, their weekend in the east, what she had said to him when he had asked for a more open, intimate relationship, their swim, their kisses, dancing by the pool, his blurting out that stuff about spying. God, he had made a fool of himself, but she didn't seem to mind. Her advice to go ahead with it – was she really serious? It was sometimes hard to tell with Reem.

By now she should be back home from the library where she worked.

Somebody was shaking him by the arm.

For a moment he did not know where he was. He had fallen asleep, curled up on the varnished boards, his left arm used as a pillow, in a strange corridor.

He looked at his watch. It was already seven.

'Nicholas Lorimer?'

'That's me.'

The stranger was impeccably turned out, and smelled faintly of aftershave.

They shook hands.

'I am Daoud. Please – come this way. We can talk in my office.'

Daoud was short and slim and mild-mannered. He was blond, with pale grey-green eyes. He wore a crisp white shirt with short sleeves and a striped tie. He looked like a schoolmaster. He sat behind his desk and examined Nick's credentials one by one – his British passport, his residence permit, his blue UN identity card in its plastic cover.

He made a little pile of the documents to one side.

'So. How can I help?'

'A colleague, a member of my staff, has gone missing.'

Daoud opened a drawer and took out a pen and a single sheet of paper.

'Name?'

'Khaled Saad.'

'Nationality?'

'Lebanese.'

Said without hesitation. Nick knew the Syrians would not bother about a missing Palestinian. There were too many of them.

'Affiliation.'

'Sunni Muslim.'

'Registration number?'

Nick had it. He knew it off by heart by now.

'Address?'

'Rue Sarkis, Ain El Mreisse.'

'So – how did this Khaled disappear?'

'He was abducted.'

Daoud listened intently to the story, taking the occasional note. When Nick had finished, Daoud put the pen and paper back in the drawer, closed it and turned to Nick. He leaned on his elbows, clasped his hands together and smiled.

'Cigarette?'

'Thank you.'

Daoud pushed a pack of twenty across the table. Nick did not want another, but it was something to do, a way of connecting with this man.

The Syrian got up and came round the heavy desk to light it. He rested his backside against the desk top, looking down at Nick.

'Why did you bring this matter to us, Mr . . .'

'Lorimer. Because you have some authority here. Because you are helping the army take control of the crossings. Maybe you know something.'

'You are right of course. We do know things. But because we know things does not mean we can always do something about them. That's the trouble with intelligence – you cannot always act on it. You see?'

Nick thought he did.

'We are trying to do the right thing here in Lebanon – for both our countries. We want peace. The Lebanese – most Lebanese – desire peace. Syria needs peace. Israel does not want peace. America does not want it, either. England, too.'

It was more question than statement.

'I'm working for the United Nations.'

Dacre's face suddenly flashed up in Nick's mind.

'I'll make enquiries.' Daoud pushed himself up off the desk and went round it back to his own chair and sat in it, idly pushing the cigarette pack back and forth.

'I'll be in my office most of the night,' Nick said. 'Then you can find me at home.' He took out one of his business cards, but Daoud was not interested.

'We know where to find you.'

That sounded ominous.

'I wish you luck, Mr . . . Lorimer.'

They both stood up under the stern gaze of President Hafez al-Assad.

'Thank you,' Nick said.

They shook hands again.

'Maybe your colleague has something to hide. If he does, you will not be doing him a favour by coming to us. This Khaled will not thank you for it later. Maybe he was a drug smuggler. A criminal. Or a spy.'

'I don't think so.'

'Was he a friend of yours?'

'He still is – I hope.'

'Of course. My English is not that good.'

'It's perfect,' Nick lied.

'You are too kind.'

He's testing me, Nick thought. Trying to see if I'm holding something back.

Nick was certain he would get nowhere with these people. He had wasted four hours, but at least he had made the effort.

Daoud went as far as his office door and opened it for Nick.

'What are your views, Mr Nick?'

'I don't have any,' Nick said. 'Not really.'

'I meant about your friend.'

'He had views, certainly. Perhaps they killed him.'

'Perhaps they did.'

'Khaled was not bad,' Nick said. 'He was kind.'

Daoud smiled. It was a look that said he had not believed anything Nick had said.

'Turn left, then take the stairs. And if you need to speak to me again, Mr Lorimer, just ask for Colonel Daoud. Or the Prince of the Hill. That is my nickname. People around here know me more by my nickname.' He shrugged. 'I really don't know why they call me that. But when you ask for the Prince of the Hill, most people will know who you mean.'

SEVENTEEN

Reem left the colour prints and negatives in their original yellow envelope and snapped on a broad elastic band to hold them in place. She dropped the packet into her shopping bag, an open-topped leather affair. Her purse, sunglasses, lip balm and a tissue packet followed.

The bag was very worn. It would not attract attention.

Reem inspected herself in the mirror one last time, ran her comb through her hair, adjusted her kohl.

Her signal had been answered almost immediately.

It was good to be busy, to think about the task in hand.

Good to think, not feel; to be rational, not sentimental.

She was needed. How many could say that? Truly? Her work was valued. What she had, what she knew – all this the party needed.

Why was it, then, as she sipped her coffee in the twilight of the reception room (today she dared not draw back the curtains for she did not want to draw attention to her presence) that the sound of the sea, the cool sand under her feet, that incredibly blue sky, the sheer beauty of Jbeil's ancient town and not least the taste and feel of Nick's kisses kept intruding?

The harder she pushed it away, the more persistent the memory became.

It seemed so real, even two days later.

The manner in which he held her, and the way she clung to him; the intimacy of it was a novel experience, so much so it had kept her awake at night.

In the crusader fort, on those precarious stone stairs, leaning on his shoulders, his face pressed against her belly.

Even when she did sleep, the images returned in dreams. How she raced him through the reef, led him an otter's dance underwater, watched him covertly while sunbathing next to him, drinking in those calf muscles, the strong shoulders, the flat stomach, the high ribcage.

At that point the dream had darkened, became nightmarish.

El-Hami stood on the road, looking down on them, waving.

Grinning, a grotesque rictus of pain, and, looking closer, Reem saw he was covered in his own blood.

In her dream-turned-nightmare, she asked Nick what el-Hami was saying.

Nick said something in response, but there was a roaring in her ears.

She woke, gasping in the darkness, the taste of death in her mouth.

In daylight the pictures kept returning as if they had a will of their own.

Memory was tactile, had not only a taste but a smell; a scent of sunlight and sea air, Nick's salty lips, his warm body, the wine they had drunk together, the touch of his fingers.

Dear God, she was like a schoolgirl with a crush.

Reem told herself not to be so foolish. All of it would fade with time. Yes, she had enjoyed herself. There was no reason why she should not do so again before her mission was accomplished. Other people took such leisure for granted. In all probability Nick would not give it a thought – in the West there was ample leisure time and the means to enjoy it. For him, it was nothing special. She was just another girl. For Nick, her class enemy, it was just another weekend, another flirtation, another escape.

Nothing special.

Stop it, woman. This is the Arab's inferiority complex talking, the acid of centuries of humiliation eating at the soul.

Stick to what you know.

Keep to your own kind.

All she had to do was look at the photographs of her family, smiling out at her, the Shikka coastline behind them.

Little Michael.

So serious.

Sometimes she felt as if he was there with her still, in the flat, watching over her.

Librarie Liban in Hamra had a lower ground floor and a series of interlocking rooms, each crowded with stacks of books in parallel ranks and against the surrounding walls.

A perfect layout for a brush pass.

The books were mostly in Arabic with perhaps a third in French.

Reem strolled in, paused to remove her sunglasses, dropped them into the shoulder bag and walked slowly down to the lower level. Moving from room to room, she would stop to take a single book from the shelves and leaf through it, reading the blurb and back cover before replacing it. Reem did this slowly, thoughtfully, and each time she pretended to examine a volume she would raise her head and check the movement of people around her.

Cookery. Health. Psychology.

Don't rush it.

Take it nice and slow.

Shifting sunlight and shadow, floating motes of dust, the sound of a kettle whistling in a back room. The smell of Turkish tobacco.

There was one other customer on the lower ground floor, a plump woman wearing a headscarf and with two small children in tow. Reem was always in the view of at least one sales assistant, but the staff were not at all interested in her. They were stacking newly arrived books on the shelves and carrying boxes up and down the stairs.

No security cameras.

Right at the back, in the children's section, she found what she was looking for.

A top shelf of illustrated reference books and children's encyclopedias.

A gap between the fifth and sixth books from the left, the two fat volumes with bright covers.

He was watching her.

Standing sideways, holding up an enormous and very expensive coffee table book on Islamic arms and armour, the Ustaz turned his head slightly.

He was near the window and stairs right at the front. The light fell on his head and shoulders and reflected off the reading glasses perched on the end of his nose. He must have followed her in, but she had not seen him.

He was playing his academic role, dressed in cotton jacket and grey trousers.

The two children were screaming and pulling their mother towards a rack of comics. The mother seemed too exhausted to resist or object.

Reem's left hand went into her bag and withdrew the photographs.

Reem pushed the yellow packet in the gap.

She turned, moved along the shelves.

She did not look back.

Keep moving.

Steady.

Avoid eye contact and no one will remember you.

Out on the pavement the bright sunshine and racket of car horns almost stunned her. She groped in her bag for her shades and put them on. She looked left, then right, as if getting her bearings and trying to decide which way to go. Then she sauntered south, gazing in the shop windows as she went.

Stopping and starting, speeding up, then slowing.

Pretending to look at shoes.

Backing up, hesitating.

For a long look at a really pretty pair of summer sandals.

Cupping her hands to see what was written on the price tag.

Lord, it was thirty bucks.

Everything was priced in dollars now, the Lebanese currency in free fall.

Walking on, stopping again.

Darting across side streets, dodging the shrapnel-riddled cars.

The shattered pavements were populated by shabby men selling lottery tickets, and obstructed by stalls of plastic shoes and cheap toys, the hawkers with their toothless smiles and their barrows of fruit, entire families from the Bekaa out shopping, the money changers and newspaper vendors and bearded fighters swaggering along in combat jackets and carrying Kalashnikovs, the heavy traffic, the service taxis tooting their horns to catch the attention of pedestrians – so much movement, so many eyes, so many knowing looks.

Syrian troops at the intersection with an RPD machine gun on a bipod.

Each and every one an enemy.

Reem kept going through the bluish car fumes and dust.

Watching her back.

Mirroring.

A flare of a match, the interior light yellow as the car door opened, darkness again as it closed, the smell of leather and cigarette smoke. Her knees in tights, the sound of the nylon, her nervousness, straightening her skirt.

The Ustaz, his face briefly outlined.

He had many questions and much to say after she made her report.

They sat on the back seat of a ten-year-old green Mercedes parked on the Corniche. The Ustaz leaned forward and tapped the driver on the shoulder. The man got out without a word or backward glance and leaned against the bonnet, smoking a cigarette. Reem could see the cigarette end rise and fall.

The driver was armed. He carried a pistol in a shoulder holster under his leather jacket. When he moved to get out from behind the wheel and turned to close the door behind him Reem had glimpsed the strap that held it in place across his chest.

There was no moon. The city was quiet. The Lebanese army, with Syrian support, had taken control of the Green Line battle-front and the country seemed to be holding its breath, wondering how long this particular truce would last. A few hours? A week?

Everyone was awaiting news of the new president-elect.

The Protector.

There was a crowd out tonight, making the most of the respite. Men and women strolled past, arm in arm. Young cyclists hung around in groups and other teenagers sped past on roller skates.

Reem could smell the water pipes, the grilled meat, the Lebanese coffee, she heard snatches of west Beiruti conversation, the radios, the sigh of a quiescent summer sea.

The Ustaz had made some small changes to his appearance. He was wearing glasses with heavy frames. He looked straight ahead, watching the lines of slow-moving traffic.

'How is the English?'

'Lorimer? He's fine.'

'He suspects nothing?'

'I don't believe so.'

'There is something I want you to tell him that he can take back to his friends at the British embassy.'

'Certainly.'

'Did you drive yourself around on the east side?'

'I borrowed Lorimer's hire car, a VW Golf.'

'Did you visit your new friend Sylvie that way?'

'Yes.'

'On your own – without the English?'

'Yes, I did.'

160

The Ustaz sat very still, hands flat on his knees, eyes on the offside mirror.

She thought he must have adjusted it so he could monitor the cars.

'You went alone to Karantina on Monday morning?'

'I took Sylvie's father some flowers as a thank you for the use of the chalet. They didn't know quite what to do with me, the flowers or the hire car. Then I took the Golf back as agreed and crossed by taxi.'

'Was he there?'

'El-Hami? Oh, yes. He was very busy. He was polite, said a thank you and went back to work. Sylvie was there, too, of course. She is one of Antoine's aides. She works in the outer office. There must be a dozen personal assistants and typists. They didn't like me taking pictures, but Sylvie came to my rescue. That's why there's only a couple of shots of the gate and an exterior shot of the Protector's office.'

Sylvie would be one of the casualties.

Reem felt a stab of pity.

Her only fault was her loyalty.

But for the grace of God—

The Ustaz broke into her thoughts. 'If there's time I would like you to make one more visit to the east. Perhaps at the weekend with Lorimer. I doubt that you'll be able to use the UN vehicle. The Land-Rover. But you've had enough practice, haven't you?'

'Oh, yes. It won't be a problem.'

A warmth, a quickening of the heart, a sense of pleasurable anticipation arose in Reem – despite herself. Another weekend like the last? It was almost too good to hope for.

Don't. Don't even think it.

It was part of the national disease: short-term horizons.

Don't be a fool.

Nick was the enemy, too, she told herself. He could not escape his country's imperialist instincts any more than he could his own class. His naivety, his ignorance of the struggle, his liberal parentage, none of that could save him from his place in the order of things. Nor should it.

Sentimentality shuts out the truth.

She must not let it blind her now.

'It's a matter of days.'

'*Akeed*. Of course.'

'I must remind you this time – the days leading up to a big operation – is one of extreme danger. As we prepare to move we expose ourselves. Every hand is against us. The Phalangists, the Zionists, their American friends, the British and French, even the Syrians. Understand?'

'Of course.'

'Maximum care must be taken. Tradecraft matters more than ever now – you must keep to the rules. Extra vigilance is required.'

'Yes, Uncle Faiz.'

'If Lorimer tells you anything about Khaled – anything he finds out about his disappearance or his reappearance – I must know about it.'

Reem knew better than to ask why.

'One more thing. It is very important. It's really the reason why I wanted this meeting. You once said that if there was to be a job, if there was going to be an operation against el-Hami, you wanted to pull the trigger. That was the expression you used. Remember?'

Reem wiped her moist palms on her skirt.

Her heart was beating a tattoo, a scaffold drum roll.

'Tell me. Do you still feel that way? Or have you changed your mind?'

'Nothing has changed, Ustaz.'

His tone was patient, gentle.

'It wasn't just in the heat of the moment? Be honest, Reem. With yourself and with me. It's natural to have doubts. We would not be human without them. There is no shame.'

A traffic cop in grey walked past. He glanced down at the car.
'No. Of course not.'

She was afraid. Of course she was. There was nothing wrong
with that. She had often been afraid. Courage consisted of controlling fear, using it. There was no point going into all that with
the Ustaz. He would be worried if she were not nervous. Only
the stupid or those entirely lacking in imagination lacked that
necessary frisson of fright that keeps the nerves and instincts
sharp. In any case, she told herself, there was no way she could
pull out now. It would be shameful.

Cowardly.

The leather seat creaked as he turned in the seat to face her.
He was close enough for her to smell the olive oil soap he used.

He spoke very quietly. 'Look, Reem. You also said to me once
– it was more than once but it was a long time ago now – that
you wanted an Operation of Quality. Do you remember?'

'Yes.'

'Do you still want that, too?'

Reem nodded, but he would not have seen it.

Her throat felt constricted. She swallowed before answering.

'Yes. Very much.'

'I want you to think long and hard about this, Reem.'

He paused.

'Reem?'

'Yes.' It came out as a croak.

'Nobody expects you to be a martyr. You must know that. I
don't expect it of you. The party does not expect it. I don't even
ask it of you. There is no shortage of volunteers. They are queueing
up. We turn ninety-nine per cent away. We only take the best. We
cannot order you to do this. Understood?'

Reem took a deep breath. 'Yes, Uncle Faiz.'

Was she not the best? Had she not earned the right?

'Think very hard. You have a life ahead of you. You are young.
You are attractive. You are intelligent. There is everything to live
for. Everything. You have been to the east. You have led what

must have seemed to you for a day or two to be an almost normal life. You have seen there is another way.'

Everything to live for?

No, she thought. Not for me.

For me and my kind there is everything to die for.

'Promise me you will think very carefully about it. When you first came to me I did my very best to discourage you because you said at the outset you wanted to be a martyr. I was cruel. I humiliated you. I insulted you. I made you do menial work. I made you work without pay for all hours of the day and night. You were too poor then even to eat. Remember? I tried everything I could think of to dissuade you – to drive you away. I told myself you did not know what you were asking. I thought you were a romantic – that you had not thought it through. You were the last surviving member of your family, and as far as I was concerned that was a very good reason to go on living. I knew I could make good use of you in other ways. I was right. Do you remember the arguments we had?'

She could not speak.

'I underestimated you. I apologize. You are very good at what you do. You're a natural. You're one of the best students I have ever had. In many respects you are better than I am – and with time you will surpass me in all aspects. You could take over my job in the organization eventually – if you survive. Your comrades hold you in the highest esteem. Consider carefully, Reem. You are like a daughter to me now. There will be other operations, other opportunities.'

At his mention of the word daughter Reem felt an uncharacteristic impulse to weep, a surge of self-pity quickly suppressed.

She told herself it was nothing but tiredness. She was being weak. It would be a lot better once she got on with the details, the practical side of preparing the attack.

He had turned away again and was watching the cars in the side mirror. 'You took the pictures. You saw how the target was protected. You saw the Kaslik chalet and on Monday morning you went to Karantina. You will have realized from what you saw and from these pictures of yours that whoever executes el-Hami will not survive. This time it will not be a bullet from a high-powered rifle on a rooftop, a pistol shot at close range, or even a grenade thrown from a passing car. Nothing so easy. You have worked that out already. I know you have. You have considered all the angles. I know you too well, Reem. It will be a Quality Operation. There will be many casualties. Many. Civilians, too. So think carefully and tell me your decision. Promise me you will consider it carefully, and that you will speak truthfully.'

The truth?

The truth was all around them all the time.

Her brother was the truth. Her sisters. Her mother.

A father who tried to shield them.

The home she had never seen.

'I promise.'

What else could she do or say?

They agreed arrangements for their next meeting.

The Ustaz lowered the window.

His tone was abrupt. 'Bilal – *yalla*. Let's go. We're finished.'

The driver flung aside his third cigarette.

Bilal opened the driver's door, took one look around him and got back behind the wheel.

If she did not speak up now, Reem thought, there would be no going back.

EIGHTEEN

Nick had never seen a dead body.

Not close up.

Not in the flesh.

A body does not smell in print or on the screen.

Different too, because this was no stranger who had once inhabited the waxy, swollen man-like object on the metal table.

There were two elderly slab men in green plastic aprons preparing the corpses for a bespectacled pathologist. The pathologist talked as he worked. He was in his thirties, irritable from lack of sleep with dark rings around his eyes, and he spoke in rapid bursts of colloquial Arabic as he wielded knife and saw.

At the policeman's nod, one attendant pulled back the sheet, folding it back expertly, all the way, revealing a slack jaw, the dead molten eyes like those of a fish, the massive gunshot wound, the limp penis, the waxy flesh sheathed in matted body hair, the grey-blue patches across chest and thighs, the bloodied feet.

The ends of the fingers and toes were torn. They looked black in the unforgiving glare of the strip lights.

Nick felt frozen in time and space, unable to move, unable to take his eyes away. He wanted to, but for some reason he could not manage it.

A voice said, '*C'est lui?*'

Nick nodded.

'*Oui?*'

'Yes. *Oui.*'

It was him. Once it had been. Not any more.

God help him.

Another voice, deeper, said in English, 'Sign. Here.'

A finger pointed. Nick signed. The words were in Arabic and French and he did not bother to read. The words would not come into focus. He used a Biro that was tied to the clipboard with string.

The clipboard was moved out of his range of vision.

Someone's hand on his arm.

Pulling him back.

Poor devil.

'I don't think you want to stay when he starts work on this one,' said the voice. Gruff, but not unsympathetic.

A policeman's voice.

'Come away, sir.'

He should leave. Now. He had done what was asked of him. One of the slab men approached the body Nick had identified as the remains of his friend and colleague, Khaled Mrabat, alias Saad. The man held a scalpel in his right hand.

'Gas.'

Nick did not move fast enough.

The blade was dropped – inserted – vertically in the abdomen.

Perhaps half an inch. Less.

So sharp, it did not need to be pushed.

There was a hiss of released pressure. The air quivered with the heat from the puncture. Nick stumbled for the door, hand over nose and mouth, almost tripping over the other corpses.

He ran to the edge of the car park and threw up under the evergreen hedge.

The copper looked embarrassed, that was all.

The telephone had woken Nick. It was still dark, and he managed to knock the instrument off the bedside table in his confusion. He almost pulled a muscle scrabbling around on the floor trying to find the bloody thing.

'Monsieur Nicholas?'

It was 4 a.m. according to the bedside clock

'*Je suis désolé*, M'sieu Nick.'

'What?'

'*C'est moi*, Nicholas. Elias, *tu sais. Toujours à votre service.*'

Toujours fucking toujours.

Elias wasted no time. He was outside Nick's block of flats with his own car a quarter of an hour later, and he was not alone. Daoud was with him. Elias, in making the introductions (unaware they had already met), paid his companion the unusual tribute of simultaneously placing his right hand over his heart and patting his own head. Only a senior Syrian *moukhabarat* official could, in Elias's estimation, be worthy of such a paroxysm of deference.

'You know each other?'

Nick smiled and offered his hand. Daoud took it.

'Colonel.'

'Mr Lorimer.' Daoud gave a stiff little nod. 'How are you?'

The secret policeman had brought along an escort. It consisted of an ancient, stub-nosed GAZ-6, a muddy Soviet-built jeep with canvas top and a Syrian army divisional flash of a yellow cobra painted on the bodywork. It was packed with five exhausted-looking teenage Syrian conscripts with grubby faces under their helmets and clutching Kalashnikovs so old the blue had entirely worn off the metal, turning them silver in the reflected light.

Elias drove his own car, a vast Chevrolet with fins.

Daoud sat next to him.

Nick huddled glumly on the back seat.

He could not stop yawning.

The jeep brought up the rear.

Elias looked at him in the rear-view mirror.

'*Préparez-vous*, M'sieu Nick.'

'What? What did you say?'

They turned into the courtyard of the American university hospital and stopped outside the mortuary.

They had to step over and around the bodies. There were so many. Stacked up like firewood outside, awaiting identification.

'A bad night,' Daoud said in English. 'The truce is fucked.'

Nick realized he had slept through it, whatever it was.

The pathologist apologized. Conditions he said, with a slight smile, were far from ideal. They worked round the clock, twenty-four hours a day. He himself had worked three shifts in succession. Some staff simply could not get to work.

Death had taken place more or less twenty-four hours before. Around midnight the previous night, maybe a little later, but before dawn almost certainly. The cause of death was a gunshot wound to the back of the head. A large-calibre round, probably from a pistol, and fired at close range.

It had taken away part of the skull.

The victim had been beaten sometime before he died. He had two broken ribs. He had been tortured. There were burn marks on his feet, his genitals, and his fingernails had been forcibly removed.

Probably in situ.

His wrists were still bound when he was shot.

From the angle of entry he was in all likelihood kneeling when they finished him off. The gunman had stood slightly to one side, and the bullet had entered the victim's skull just behind the ear.

The pathologist spread his pianist's hands and said to Nick, 'Monsieur, if it is any consolation, it was probably a relief by this point.'

Nick said nothing.

He thought, the family must never know.

By the time Khaled's remains were found, rigor mortis had come and gone. Bluebottles, the first of several waves of insects to descend upon any corpse left in the open at this time of year, had started their work.

The victim had put up a fight. There was tissue – not his own – under his nails. The blood in his mouth was of a different group. In this instance O positive. Khaled was AB negative – comparatively rare.

'Maybe he fought back when they took him,' ventured the cop, an elderly inspector in plain clothes. 'Took a bite out of one of his kidnapper's hands, or maybe an ear.'

This O positive blood had stained his clothing, along with his own more copious body fluids.

There was quite a crowd of them. Elias, suave even at this hour; Daoud, in a black leather jacket, fully aware of the fear his presence communicated to all but Nick; the unnamed police inspector, quite powerless save for the role of rubber-stamping the paperwork (quite literally); and Nick himself, conscious of his inadequate Arabic, trying to interpret the coded looks and smiles. They all smoked Elias's expensive Turkish cigarettes unashamedly until none were left. Elias did not seem to mind. On the contrary, he appeared to regard it as a compliment to his good taste. The Syrian soldiers fidgeted uncomfortably in their vehicle. They did not dare shift themselves without Daoud's permission.

One of the attendants emerged from the morgue.

'His effects.'

He handed over a brown paper bag.

Nick signed for them. Daoud watched over his shoulder.

The Syrian said a patrol of his country's troops had found Khaled in a drainage ditch in the Basta area. Curled up on his side in a fetal position, hands still bound, under some leaves and dirt. The spot was close to the Green Line. There were gardens, low walls, some trees, long grass. Good cover, in other words. It was an area frequented by drug users and homosexuals when there was no fighting, he said.

When there were skirmishes, it was infested with snipers.

No one would have raised the alarm in such a place.

Not at night.

It was not an area for law-abiding citizens, even in daylight.

Shouts for help, screams of pain, the sound of the coup de grâce – it was nothing unusual these days anywhere in the city.

The police inspector added – pointlessly – that the going rate for a hit in Beirut was fifty American dollars. His remark was ignored.

Daoud asked if Nick wanted to see the place where the body was found.

He shook his head.

'No thanks.'

'Then my soldiers can go? These are the men who made the discovery. Their shift ended long ago. Maybe you would like to talk to them. Maybe in New York they will expect you to do so.'

'Of course they can go.'

'No questions – for sure?'

Daoud seemed almost disappointed.

'No, it's okay, thanks.'

'Mr Lorimer, I asked you before if you had any views. Remember?'

'He might have been murdered by anyone who hated Palestin- ians or leftists, or Arabs generally,' Nick said. 'That could mean practically everybody. I'm sorry.'

'Or maybe it was personal,' Daoud said. 'Maybe it was some- thing to do with a woman.'

'You don't torture someone if you're jealous of them.'

'You are right. Where were you last night?'

'At home. Am I a suspect now, colonel?'

'Was anyone with you who could corroborate that?'

Nick frowned. 'No, colonel. There wasn't.'

The police inspector took no part in this exchange. He had Daoud's report. That was sufficient.

He dared not say otherwise.

'Please thank the soldiers,' Nick told Daoud. 'Thank them for me on behalf of the United Nations. I'm sorry they have been kept away from their beds for so long.'

'It's nothing,' Daoud said. 'This is their duty.'

Would Nick advise any surviving kin and return Khaled's belongings?

There was not much. A cheap wristwatch, a comb, the equivalent of seven dollars and twenty-three cents at the previous day's rate of exchange, a couple of keys, two Biros and a tube of chewing gum. The most personal item was a nine-carat gold chain with a locket containing a miniature page from the Koran.

No ID card, no driving licence.

'He had a little address book,' Nick said to Daoud. 'Blue. Hardcover. He wrote down contacts and so on – addresses and telephone numbers of people he met during the course of his UN work.'

There was no sign of it.

Reem was at the back of Nick's mind all day.

He was too busy to think clearly about her, although at one point, just after the funeral that evening (most funerals were conducted swiftly and at night so the mourners would not attract enemy fire from the east), Nick did wonder whether she thought about him as much as he did about her.

Probably not.

He needed her, though. He needed to talk. It had been the worst day, the very worst, since his arrival. Running the gauntlet of the Green Line was nothing compared to this. He desperately wanted to talk about it. Ironically, it would have been Khaled when he was alive. His only close friend. Over a couple of beers Nick would have unburdened himself, secure in the knowledge that if he needed to do the same, Khaled could always rely on Nick to give him a sympathetic and uncritical hearing.

But his friend Khaled was dead.

It was hard.

Even harder to accept that Khaled had lived in a shack with a family he had never mentioned. As they had lowered Khaled's remains into the grave and his Kurdish widow tore her hair and screamed and writhed in the arms of her stony-faced relatives, Nick realized for the first time just how much he missed his friend. And how little he knew of him.

That afternoon he and Elias had ordered flowers in person from a Sanayeh florist run by identical twins with identical moustaches, Baptiste and Claude. They bought practically the entire stock because they were buying them for the local staff, regional management and on behalf of the UN Secretary General himself. Nick had paid for some of his own, too, a dozen handsome yellow roses from the Bekaa, out of his own pocket, and he found the time to take them home and stick them in the sink, determined to take them to Reem later.

It was too late to call her at work.

He did not have her home number.

It was Rue 68, and the Daouk building. He knew that much. But Nick was still unsure which floor she lived on. Had she said the fifth or sixth? Had she really said anything at all?

He tried to visualize her in the stairwell that night of the artillery bombardment. He recalled clambering up over the legs of her neighbours, past the women and children, through the cigarette smoke and stepping over the paraphernalia of food and drink and blankets.

Afterwards, once the funeral was over, and he had paid the undertaker, the hire car firm for the hearse, and handed over an envelope of cash to Mrs Saad (or was it Mrabat?) – her husband's UN gratuity, he had called it, tactfully – he walked home, spurning offers of lifts from Elias and other colleagues. Elias had urged him to take a taxi. He agreed he would, but he had no intention of doing so. He wanted some space, some fresh air. He wanted to be alone. But at the northern end of Hamra he felt he was being observed. He thought he saw a battered Volvo turn a corner, but when he looked again, there was nothing there.

He told himself his mind was playing tricks.

The shopkeepers had long since cranked down their shutters.

There was no one about.

173

Just cats and rats.

In the distance, police and ambulance sirens.

Another car bomb, another shooting incident.

Again, that sense of eyes burning into his back.

Nick looked over his shoulder. The street was deserted.

He must be mistaken. He was tired, jumpy, wired from all the day's talk of death, the sight of Khaled's naked body and its torn flesh and imagining too all the pain and humiliation he must have suffered before the end.

Why? What had his tormentors wanted?

He walked down between the Swiss and French embassies towards his building. He could see his flat and two of its balconies up there, straight ahead. To his right moonlight glinted on the helmet of a French marine sentry shifting from foot to foot in a pillbox on top of the embassy wall.

He could have sworn he heard footsteps behind him.

Nick turned once more, but there was no one following.

'You're a mess,' he muttered to himself. 'Nothing a decent kip won't sort out.'

When he had got back to his flat and locked himself securely inside he poured himself a triple Jameson's, went through to the master bedroom, kicked off his shoes and lay against the pillows on his king-size bed, telling himself he would rest for a few minutes. His clothes still stank of the mortuary's ammonia. He promised himself he would wash and change and set out to find Reem. He missed her.

Nick wanted to tell her just that.

Alone and in private.

He fell asleep thinking about her, conjuring up her smile in his mind's eye, and imagining what it would be like to be invited to share her bed.

It was only the next morning, when Nick went down to the area reserved for residents' parking under the building, that he saw his Land-Rover 110 was missing from its usual space against one of the cream retaining walls.

He stood in the parking lot, holding the dozen roses, trying to figure it out. His parking space, number 5A between a red Ferrari and a black 7-series BMW, was empty. He knew he had not used the vehicle at all the previous day. From almost start to finish, he had been a passenger in Elias's Chevy, so unwieldy in Beirut's alleyways. Had it been there the previous afternoon when he returned with the flowers? Was it there the previous night when he got back, exhausted and frightened of his own shadow?

He could not remember.

He had not looked.

Why would anyone want to steal a Land-Rover, a long-wheeled Defender, a white one, so clearly marked as a United Nations vehicle? Three-series BMWs and Golf hatchbacks were the militia favourites, and the usual way to lift them was to put a gun to the head of a motorist at a red light and kick him out onto the street and take his car and his keys. This was far more difficult to accomplish, and the UN vehicle would stand out on Beirut's potholed streets. So why bother? And how would the thieves have got it out of the compound without either the electronic key or the combination number to open the gates?

Perhaps the concierge would know something about it.

It was not just a matter of a stolen car. Car theft was common-place in Beirut. With the Land-Rover's loss, Nick's little bubble of protective foreignness had been punctured. First it was Reem, now it was the car. He had a sense of being exposed, of being vulnerable, of being dragged into the vortex. His UN passport, his youth and his innocence had performed the function of a voodoo amulet against the evils of contamination by this war, but the magic would not insulate him any more, not in his mind or anyone else's.

Nick patted his pockets. He still had his keys.

Pity about the roses. They were already starting to fade.

Something else occurred to him.

175

He should have brought it up at the hospital morgue. The thought was there, or rather the question, but it had been submerged by the sight and stench of what was left of Khaled, the presence of Daoud and the unctuous manners of Elias. If indeed there was no laminated Lebanese ID or driving licence on Khaled when he was found, how had they provisionally identified the remains as Khaled's in the first place?

NINETEEN

Reem could do little more than listen when Nick told her what had happened to Khaled. There was not a great deal she could say, nothing that would help at any rate, and she reasoned that the less she said the better.

He needed her reassurance. Here in Lebanon she felt she was in charge. Of the two of them, she was the dominant partner. She showed him the way. She led. She liked that. She preferred it. Back in England their roles would no doubt have been reversed. There he would lead, play the guide, adopt the manners of the traditional male. In such a strange and unfamiliar place, she would have to play the role of follower, the stranger.

Nick was deeply shocked, and as he told her about his visit to the mortuary, he came close to tears. It was apparent that his grief at Khaled's death was matched by a growing sense of horror at what Khaled must have endured in the hours immediately before he died. She knew it was a delayed reaction. She had seen it before. Nick was badly shaken. He was also troubled by the fact that he knew so little about his friend, and how little Khaled had chosen to tell him about his personal life.

How little of it that was true, that is.

Had those stories been lies? Or was Khaled really a womanizer with a complicated and self-defeating love life? Had he made it all up to entertain Nick during those revels in city clubs and bars? Were the self-doubt, the confusion, the hilarious faux pas, the endless jokes told against himself, all a fiction? Was the relationship, from Khaled's perspective, simply invented to amuse a conceited foreign paymaster and keep him at arm's length? Had Khaled been playing him along, insulating Nick by spinning tall stories about himself, aping Western manners and pretending to enjoy their evenings out drinking? Where had he got the money – had he squandered wages he should have spent on his wife and child in that miserable dump he called home? Was Nick so insensitive that he had failed to realize that the pittance Khaled earned at the United Nations could not sustain such a lifestyle, embracing rounds of drinks at Sammy's Bar and the Backstreet?

And why did he have two names?

All she could say, and it was the truth, was that she did not know anything about Khaled Saad aka Mrabat.

Was the gap so unbridgeable between Lebanese and Westerner? Nick was unsure, but Reem could see the whole thing had depressed him and damaged his self-confidence, sharpening his sense of otherness. Her response was not entirely sympathetic. Despite herself she was secretly pleased to see that at last this rather complacent Westerner was beginning to know what it felt like to lose someone special in some violent episode.

Reem said nothing about Colonel Daoud, the Prince of the Hill, or what she herself had suffered at his hands in her final exercise as a resistance probationer.

Compared to Khaled's ordeal, what had happened to her in training had been child's play.

The Ustaz had asked to be informed whenever she had news of Khaled, but here she was on the east side with Nick for what was probably their last time together. She had no way of contacting her 'Uncle Faiz'. She could not use the telephone. Short of returning to the western sector, news of Khaled's death would have to wait until her return.

She had never met Khaled. Until the Ustaz had mentioned the matter, she had never connected him with the party, but now, drinking coffee with Nick in Jounieh on Saturday morning, she began to wonder.

Reem did not want to think about going back.

Each hour they had together was precious. She was determined to make the best of what time was left, even if it involved a lapse in party discipline.

It was her last weekend.

'I almost forgot,' Reem said.

She put down her coffee cup.

Nick turned to look at her.

'There's going to be a big attack.'

Her tone was flat, disinterested.

'What do you mean?'

'There's going to be a military offensive at Souk al-Gharb. You know it?'

'Never heard of it.'

'It's a village, Nick. So far it has changed hands at least three times. It's Maronite – or it was when people still lived there. A few still do. How, I can't imagine. It's in the hills above the highway just to the south of Beirut. A farming area. There's a ridge with several hills along it.' She put one hand palm down on the table between them, then drew it into a fist. 'Like this. A fist of land with five hills or joints, it looks down on the coast road and the southern suburbs, and the village on the slope of the biggest hill is Souk al-Gharb.'

'So why tell me?'

'Because you should take care, Nick. The other side will shell west Beirut to get back at the fighters' families. To hurt their morale. In retaliation, especially against civilians. They always do. A trick el-Hami learned from the Israelis. I think it will be very bad this time. You must sleep in the shelter of your building and maybe warn your staff. Just don't tell anyone it was me who told you.'

'Of course not. Who's going to attack?'

She leaned forward and lowered her voice. 'Our people.'

'Our people?'

God, must he be so slow today?

Reem looked around to make sure no one was in earshot. This was Jounieh, after all. Phalangist and Lebanese Forces territory. They were in a first-floor restaurant. It was part of a big glass and concrete complex called Espace 2000 which housed cinemas and boutiques. Many of the commercial properties were empty with FOR RENT signs. The few people who were wandering around were kids, teenagers who had been to see an early performance of a Hollywood blockbuster starring a long-haired Australian in the role of a renegade Los Angeles undercover cop. Kids could never get enough of guns and killing.

In the upstairs restaurant the duty waiter had been asleep, lying on one of the leather banquettes. He did not seem to be unduly upset at being woken to serve coffees and ice cream.

With a foreigner he could expect a decent tip.

Nick repeated the question.

'What do you mean – our people?'

'Our people in the west. Who else?' How naive could Nick be after – what was it, a month? 'The PSP, Amal, the SNSP, the communists – what we used to call the Movement. They're going to attack Lebanese army and Phalangist positions, try to push them off the ridge.'

'Why?'

'Because we want to spoil el-Hami's little game. As soon as he gets into the presidential palace a few weeks from now, he's going to sign a treaty with Israel and launch an offensive with US air support, maybe with direct help from down south. He will try to advance from Souk al-Gharb down the ridge and effectively cut Beirut off from the south of the country. Chop the highway in two. Complete our isolation. A big victory for America's boy wonder. Isolate the terrorists, the riff-raff of the refugee camps, set them up for the kill.'

'So?'

'So the Movement – hopefully with at least Syrian artillery support – is going to hit first. A pre-emptive attack, I think you

180

call it, sometime in the next week or so and just before he takes over as president. They'll push the Phalangists, the Lebanese Forces militia and Christian-led army battalions off the ridge. A two-pronged assault, with the Syrians pressing from the east with some Saiqa forces. You know what I mean by Saiqa – Palestinian units under Syrian control. They are going to try to cut the enemy off.' Reem frowned, seeking the right word. 'I think you call it a salient. They are going to try to cut the salient, then roll it up.' Reem made snipping movement with her fingers, as if they were scissors, then snatched at something in the air, like catching a fly.

'Right?'

'A salient – yes.'

'So that's what it was I almost forgot to tell you.'

Nick was suspicious. He could not help it.

'How do you know all this?'

'I overhead people talking about it. At work.'

'Who?'

'Does it matter, Nick? Why do you ask? You know where I work, who runs the institute. You're not going to tell your English friends, are you?'

'Does that bother you?'

'What will they do with it?'

'God knows. Signal London, file it away.'

'Or tell el-Hami and his friends in Tel Aviv and Washington? I'm sure your English friends will tell the Americans, no? They tell the Americans everything. And the Americans tell everything they know to the people down south.'

Nick shrugged. 'If you don't want me to say anything, Reem, I won't.'

Liar.

Reem stared out of the window of the cafe, suddenly distant. It was a dangerous game. She was simply obeying orders. Some of what she had told Nick – perhaps most of it – was true, no doubt. Good intelligence was worth a lot to her country's enemies. But the lie would be nestling in there among the facts, like poison.

Kiss the hand you cannot bite and pray God breaks it.

For a moment she pictured el-Hami thrashing around on the floor of his office, foaming at the mouth, clutching at his own throat. Dying in pain, and taking his time. Good. It was a fantasy that gave her much pleasure, but that was all it was, unfortunately, a childish fantasy.

'You must do what you think best, Nick. I tell you because I don't want anything to happen to you.'

Lie for lie.

'That's sweet.'

His expression softened and he reached across the table and squeezed her hand. She did not respond.

God, this was awful. She did care about him, that was true enough. She was drawing him deep into the shadows inhabited by the likes of the Ustaz and herself. What did the Russians say? They had a proverb: It is the pike's job to keep the carp awake. Nick was her carp, a handsome and desirable one at that. You know he will tell them, she told herself. If he were able to stand back and think about it, he might work out why I am telling him. Maybe he is beginning to doubt, to question. But this is a world he knows nothing of. Nothing has prepared him for this. Not all the books in the world could do so.

'I'd like an ice cream,' she said. 'My favourite – it's called Coup Ajami, *mistica* flavour with almonds and honey. It does terrible things to my figure, but never mind that. Ajami – it means Persian in Arabic – has a branch in the western sector, too. You'll have one with me? Do we have time?'

'Of course.'

Mistica. It was probably not a taste he would like.

'Great – I love their ice cream. They make it here in the restaurant. Thank you.' She sounded too grateful, even to her own ears. 'Maybe you'd prefer chocolate, Nick, or strawberry cheesecake.'

Nick gestured to the waiter.

The Lebanese Forces had started levying taxes on businesses throughout the eastern sector. It was illegal, but who could stop them? El-Hami was no doubt all for it, and perhaps took his cut of the illicit revenue. It was no more than an elaborate protection racket, enforced at gunpoint. When the bill eventually came it would have a little Lebanese cedar stamped on it – representing the 12 per cent militia surcharge, courtesy of those bastards and the psychopath they called their leader.

How many bullets would they be paying for with their coffees and ice creams?

'So who did you overhear, Reem?'

He had risen to the bait. Good.

The Ustaz had described this little exercise as a barium meal – people with suspected stomach cancer would be asked to swallow a white, radioactive substance that would show up on the X-ray machine. That way the doctors could see where it ended up, where it emerged. Just like the titbit of raw intelligence.

Nick had taken the medicine just as the Ustaz had said he would, and he and his comrades would be able to follow it all the way down.

It was the vernal equinox, the official start of spring, when days and nights are of equal length. It was getting steadily warmer.

After a great deal of trying things on and throwing them off again, Reem had chosen a yellow, summery frock with a wide skirt and narrow shoulder straps. She had bought it second hand two years before. A real bargain. She had put her hair up because of the heat, but now she undid her hair clip, shaking her hair loose so it fell to her shoulders.

They drove through Ashrafiyeh in Nick's hired Honda, up towards Broumana, a familiar route for them both. As they climbed the hairpin bends up the slopes of Mount Lebanon among the pines, so the air cooled and the stink of the city gave way to the scent of wild flowers.

There were two new checkpoints. One was a joint Lebanese Forces–Phalangist affair, the second a barricade manned by members of a Christian-officered army brigade. On both occasions the checks were perfunctory. One glance at Reem's ID and Nick's UN card was enough. It helped too, that the Honda was so obviously a car hired on the eastern side. There was also more military traffic, Reem noticed, mostly Vietnam-era US-built trucks carrying infantry, and new earthworks, probably artillery positions being readied to provide fire support for whatever was being prepared by el-Hami's forces.

'I've got a place here,' Nick said. 'Just for the summer.'

He sounded a little sheepish, Reem thought. Perhaps he was worried she would be offended that he should have taken a summer rental on enemy territory. It was nothing she had said directly, indeed, their political discussions had been very general, and Reem had kept, or had tried to keep, the strength of her feelings to herself. He should not feel guilty – the eastern sector served as an escape for both of them and for different reasons, and she had encouraged him to bring her over.

'Where, Nick?'

'Ain Saadeh. I thought of renting a villa at the cedars all year round, but I counted no fewer than fourteen checkpoints en route – two armies, three militias and it all takes far too long to get there and back.'

He was thinking for them both.

Ain Saadeh was the next village, just below Broumana, and the place where they had stopped the last time to admire the view, and had picked out the flickering muzzle flashes of a distant exchange of small arms fire.

'Would you like to see it?'

'Yes – I would.'

She had agreed without the slightest hesitation.

For an unwed, unrelated female to accompany a single male,

or any male, but particularly a conspicuously foreign male, into a rented and furnished apartment, back home it would not only set neighbourhood tongues wagging, but it could forever mar the woman's reputation.

But this was the eastern sector. Reem was not known locally. She would be known for something else entirely, not afternoon trysts with foreign men.

To hell with it.

What was there to be afraid of?

It was not that difficult.

One step at a time, she told herself.

Don't spoil it by thinking too far ahead, by looking at your watch.

Don't think at all.

Nick was explaining that, as an expatriate, his life in west Beirut was cheap. He was not paid much by Western standards, but it was hard currency and he managed to put most of it aside. He paid no tax. His accommodation and transport were paid for. He lived entirely on his expense allowance.

'You sound guilty, Nicholas.'

'I am. Who wouldn't be? If you'd seen Khaled's place you would feel the same.'

'I'm pleased for you, Nick. Not envious. Not angry, either. Enjoy it while you can. And I'm sure Khaled lived better than many, and if he could hear us now he would agree with me.'

He smiled at her, grateful for the reassurance.

She asked, 'Why didn't you drive your UN car today?'

'It was stolen.'

'Stolen? Are you sure? Why would anyone do that?'

It was a reminder of what all this was about. About what was intended for her now she had accepted the role the Ustaz had offered her.

'It was parked underneath the flats where I live and the next morning it was gone.'

'When was that?'

'Two days ago.'

'Thursday?'

'Yes – Thursday.'

'Are you sure you didn't park it somewhere else and forget about it?'

'You mean after one of my drunken binges?'

She laughed. 'Something of the sort.'

'I don't think so. At least I hope not. I'd make an awful fool of myself if it turned out I'd left it outside the Backstreet. Very embarrassing.'

Nick had pulled in to the side of the road.

'Is this is it?'

'Yes. Are you sure about this, Reem?'

He looked worried that she would change her mind, either because it was in the east or because of what she thought it would do her reputation, her sense of self-esteem.

She thought to herself that Nick did not know her all that well, or he would have known that she was not someone who changed her mind very easily once it was made up. It was made up now.

'Course I'm sure,' she said. 'I want to see your holiday home. Come on.'

It was a modern building, yet like all summer places for rent, quite spartan.

Blonde wood, cork tiles, beige walls, potted rubber plants.

The duty manager or whatever he was behind the reception desk smiled at Nick and said, '*Bonjour.*'

He did glance at Reem as he gave Nick the key, but he asked no questions.

They went up in the lift.

Nick was looking at her. He had quite a tan now, and his hair was all mussed up, standing on end after the drive. They did not say anything. He led the way and unlocked the door to number 52. He stood aside for her to go in.

It opened into the living room. There were two plain brown sofas, a low coffee table. To the right a kitchenette, to the left a short corridor with the bathroom and bedroom.

Sliding glass doors straight ahead. Nick helped her open them wide and Reem stepped out onto the balcony. It was small. There was enough room for a couple of chairs, that was all.

It was like standing on the edge of a sheer cliff. There was a vertical drop to the road below. Below that the mountain fell away through pine woods and village orchards to the coast. The road vanished in a series of hairpin bends. Reem gripped the top of the railing and bent foreward.

Half the world was the sea, glittering in the hot sun, the other half all sky.

'Tea?'

Reem did not answer but turned and went back inside. There were heavy, rubber-backed green curtains to keep out light and heat.

'It's so bright – can we close them?'

'Sure.'

Without the glare of the sun, it felt like being underwater. The light was reduced to a dim glow. The curtains moved, and Reem could feel the cool air wafting into the room bringing with it the smells of mountain and sea.

Nick said, 'I'll get the tea.'

Reem stayed standing. He has such a frank face, she thought. There was a little indentation on his brow when he frowned with concentration. He was frowning now as he got the cups out of the cupboard over the sink.

'First show me the rest of the place.'

She went ahead of him down the corridor. To the left was the windowless bathroom. Tiny, it was tiled in dark brown, but it did have a bath, and there was water.

'And this is the bedroom.'

A big room, sliding glass doors, a low double bed, a built-in dressing table and mirror.

They were both in the doorway. Reem turned. She faced Nick. He ran his hand through her hair and kissed her. While they were still kissing, she pulled him into the room.

'One moment.'

Using both hands, Reem pulled her dress over her head in a single movement.

They staggered over to the bed, laughing, and fell on it together.

He kissed her all over.

It was so good Reem thought she would die.

Later it was sore, as she had expected it would be.

Then the pain went and it got better quite quickly.

A lot better.

TWENTY

Reem lay against him.

They were both naked.

When Nick woke he found her crying.

She lay on her left side and had her back against his chest, their legs intertwined, his right arm around her, his left buried and quite numb under her.

The top of her head rested under his chin.

She made no sound, but he felt her tears as they ran down her cheek and trickled onto the knuckles of his right hand.

The sun had slid down the sky until there was only a glow below and on either side of the curtain across the open door to the balcony.

It was getting a lot cooler.

He kissed the back of her head and neck.

The smell of her hair, her skin, aroused him yet again.

'Reem?'

Her right hand moved, discovered his leg, felt along his thigh.

'Are you all right?'

She shook her head.

'Tell me.'

Another shake.

Her right hand found and held him.

'I don't want this to end, Nick. Not ever. I want to stay like this. Just like this. Feeling you against me. Holding you – like this.'

He felt a nipple harden against his palm.

'Does it have to end?'

A nod. 'Yes.'

'Why?'

Silence.

'You don't trust me enough to tell me.'

'Trust you?'

She let go of him and rolled over to face him, all in one movement.

With the back of one hand she wiped her cheek and sniffed.

'Reem. Look. I'm not stupid. Naive, sure. Ignorant, certainly. But you don't come over to the eastern sector with me just because you enjoy my company. I am useful to you. I hope I go on being useful. I don't mind being used. You hear me? I don't care what it takes. I really don't care. But I wish you would tell me what you're up to. You owe me that.'

She was looking at his face as he spoke. She was examining his eyes, his mouth, searching like a map reader seeking a special feature like a hill or lake. She still said nothing.

'Do you think I'm a spy, Reem? Do you? Do you think if I knew what you were up to I'd trot over to the embassy and tell my friends all about it?'

'Wouldn't you, Nick? Haven't you already? Isn't that what English patriots do over their gin and tonic? Get drunk together and swap secrets? Aren't you a patriot? Queen and country? Isn't that what you believe in? My country – right or wrong?'

'No.'

'No?'

He tried to kiss her, but she turned her face.

'Tell me what you believe, Nick.'

'I believe you and I could be happy together.'

'Oh.' She was watching him again. 'Happiness.'

She was not making fun of him. It was not sarcasm. She looked solemn, and a little disappointed. Even sad. Was happiness such a dirty word? They had just made love – twice – and he was well

190

aware it was the first time for her. Yet somehow something was missing, something was absent in the way she regarded him.

'You took all those pictures. You made friends with Sylvie, rubbed shoulders with people you consider your enemies, and never once did you voice your own opinion. You were so self-controlled. You were like a complete stranger. Then you went over to Karantina all by yourself on Monday and saw el-Hami. You drove my car all over the place, east and west. It was the first thing you asked of me – if you could drive my UN Land-Rover. Now it's been stolen. A coincidence? What are you up to, Reem?'

'What do you think?'

'Tell me.'

'I can't.' Reem's eyes filled with tears.

'Dammit – why not?'

'You're hurting me!'

He had put both hands on her shoulders and, without even being aware of it, had shaken her.

'I'm sorry. Forgive me . . .'

He released her.

Nick told himself he would strip the bed, remove the sheet with its evidence.

'Damn you, Nicholas Lorimer. Damn you. Trusting you is the worst thing I could do to you. The very worst thing I could do. I must spare you that, don't you understand? Don't you see?'

Nick met Dacre after dark in the Beirut Cellar, which was not a cellar at all, but a place of wrought iron, dark wood and hard benches behind a high wall.

It had the atmosphere of a student pub, tucked up one of those Ashrafiyeh alleys of expensive apartments. It was a quiet road off Rue Sursouk: faded Ottoman palaces hidden by screens of palms and ferns, trees and ornate ironwork, bougainvillea all over the big balconies; the kind of place that seems damp and cool even in broad summer and downright miserable in winter.

Dacre insisted on drinking Almaza beer out of the bottle although he was far too old to be mistaken for an east Beirut student, notwithstanding his yellow T-shirt, baggy khaki shorts and white trainers.

He had been playing tennis and had had no time to change.

'So, Nick – what news from the west?'

Nick gave him what he felt sure Dacre wanted; a concise summary of Reem's report of an impending pre-emptive strike on Souk al-Gharb. Matter of fact, no elaborations.

'And the source?'

'You can say a security source.'

'Can you be more specific?'

'I'm afraid not, no.'

To Nick's relief, Dacre did not press it.

'It dovetails nicely with everything we've been hearing,' Dacre said.

Nick thought, well, the information would fit. It was supposed to, but there was a twist in there somewhere. All you really care about, Major Dacre, is that you and Wilson have your new agent in west Beirut and at last the fellow has come up with something. You want to believe it, so you will.

'Thank you, Nick,' Dacre said. 'Yes. It's useful. A good contribution to the week's harvest. London will be pleased. Thank you again.'

Dacre snapped shut his little notebook and dropped it into his sports bag under the table.

They both chose salad and the pepper steak. In Nick's case, he picked it because he could not be bothered to look further.

'I read about your friend in the papers,' Dacre said after he had given their orders to the waiter. 'Khaled. I'm so sorry.'

Nick nodded.

'I did warn you.'

'I wish you had warned him, not me.'

'Obviously we had no idea . . .'

'Of course not, I'm sorry.'

'Has it occurred to you that you could be next?'

Nick drank his beer to avoid having to answer.

'You were seen around town rather a lot with Khaled. I did tell you the fellow was OLCA, didn't I? Palestinian? Formerly PLO?'

'So?'

'Your girlfriend. Reem. Isn't that her name?'

Nick's steak arrived. Dacre liked his steak well done and would have to wait for his.

'Wilson was at some do,' Dacre said. 'You know Wilson. He's got a nose for champagne, especially if it's free.' He chuckled. 'That's it – el-Hami's birthday. You were there with someone. Wilson said she was – what was the word he used – fragrant. No matter the fragrance, Nick, my sources tell me Reem Najjar's trouble. Seems she's another leftist. An orphan, and from the south. Her people lost their homes during al-Nakba – what Arabs call the Catastrophe, the founding of the state of Israel and the expulsion of hundreds of thousands of Arabs. You certainly can pick 'em, can't you? Troublemakers with a grievance. It must be a special talent.'

The waiter brought the major's steak. It looked to Nick as if it had been burned to a crisp. But that was how he apparently liked it.

'Have you taken sides, Nick?'

'I work for the United Nations, Perry – remember?'

'You wouldn't be the first romantic working for that organization to take up cudgels on behalf of an aggrieved party, Nicholas. We're only human.'

'No, Perry, I haven't taken sides.'

'Perhaps it's time you did, chum.'

Dacre helped himself to a second dollop of Dijon mustard. 'Not like English mustard at all,' he muttered. 'You need so much of this French stuff to get the same effect.'

'Meaning?'

'Your country, Nick. It's the only side either of us should be concerned with.'

'I wasn't aware the British were taking sides in Lebanon.'

'You know perfectly well what I mean.'

'Do I, Perry? I wish the British could see themselves not as they want to be seen but as others truly see them.'

'And how's that?'

He is humouring me, Nick thought. He said, 'As a nation of hypocrites forever meddling in other people's affairs, and lecturing them about how they should behave. Arrogant and condescending.'

Dacre finished his beer and smiled at Nick.

'Aren't you being a little hard on us – and on yourself?'

'What are you trying to say, Perry?'

'Simply that from the point of view of someone like el-Hami, your choice of friends seems, well, to be honest, rather suspect.'

'Balls.'

Nick's face was burning. The fuck. What did he know?

Reem and Nick had parted barely two hours before. Nick could still smell her; her skin and hair, the scent she used. He missed her.

Dacre was concentrating hard on sawing up his steak in a systematic, soldierly manner.

'Don't you UN types get R & R breaks, Nick?'

'Once a month – four days in Cyprus, all paid for.'

This was safer ground.

'You've been here a month now?'

Dacre was speaking with his mouth full, looking up to watch over Nick's shoulder the arrival of other diners.

Nick looked at his watch.

'Five weeks, five days, nine hours and thirty minutes.'

'That bad?'

Nick did not reply. He was not hungry any more. He put his knife and fork together and pushed his plate aside, the steak half eaten. He felt sick. It was not the food. The food was fine. It was himself. It was shame. It was regret. It was guilt. It was having accepted hospitality in return for tittle-tattle. It was not having had the guts to say no at the outset, at his own self-deception. To hell with them.

You're a pathetic idiot, Lorimer, and I don't know why she puts up with you. On the other hand, of course you do, but you won't admit it to yourself.

'Dessert?'

'No thanks.'

'Coffee?'

Nick shook his head.

'I think you should take your break, Nick. It might be wise. Until things cool down. Until el-Hami's settled into Baabda palace and is busy getting a new government organized and has forgotten all about the young woman taking so many photographs of his Karantina headquarters and her British boyfriend. Best you steer clear of the east for a while. For your own safety.'

'It had nothing to do with me. I wasn't even there.'

Coward.

'Well, you introduced her. Showed her off. Took her around. You know perfectly well what I mean. I hear she photographed the family's holiday chalet at Kaslik and then turned up on Monday at Karantina. Take my advice, Nick. Take the R & R. And forget the girl.'

Forget Reem?

The beer had made Nick feel bloated. But it was worse than that. Dacre had somehow managed to make Nick feel ashamed of himself. It was the bile of self-disgust in his gullet, not indigestion. He felt grubby as well as angry. He had behaved like a child. He had been weak where he should have been strong. He should have stood up for himself. And for Reem. He had to get away. Now. Nick wanted time to himself. He needed to think. He thanked Dacre. He said all the right things. He got up from the table, shook the other man's hand and pretended to listen and agree to whatever his host was saying about getting together again later that week.

Of course. Yes. Sounds good. Great.

He did not hear any of it, not really.

There would not be a later. Not this week, not the next.

Nick had made up his mind.

He patted his pockets, found the Honda's keys.

Squeezed out from behind the table.

Keeping the smile on his face.

Not waiting for a baffled Dacre to get the bill.

Hurrying or he really would be sick, right there.

Nick was sweating furiously.

'Thanks, Perry – all the best.'

Only when Nick was sat behind the wheel of the rented car, cooling off with the windows all the way down and watching the other drivers smoking and chatting, standing around their employers' Mercedes and BMWs in the street, did he realize he had completely forgotten to mention the loss of his Land-Rover.

TWENTY-ONE

The streets were stifling.

A dirty brown haze smothered the city.

Heat shimmered above the parked cars crammed onto the pavements and squares of Beirut. Every spare inch seemed to be taken. Reem weaved in and out of the traffic, hurrying on foot through the glittering sea of scorching metal and glass, aware that any one of the parked vehicles massed on either side of the road could be booby-trapped.

It was chance.

Lucky one day, unlucky the next. There was no telling who would live, who would die.

She flagged down a service taxi, a yellow Merc from the mid-sixties, much resprayed and patched, and the driver sent the young man next to him to the rear so Reem would have the seat to herself as the only woman.

'*Ya binti* – there you go, my daughter,' the driver said, waiting for her to pull the door shut before stamping on the accelerator, slapping the horn and pulling back out into the dense traffic. He was a big man, entirely bald with an immense Groucho moustache. The back of his check shirt was black with sweat.

A tiny and very worn Koran dangled from the rear-view mirror along with a string of blue prayer beads. The word 'Allah' in the style Reem recognized as Thuluth adorned the dashboard.

'Where are you going, m'moiselle?'

'Shikka.'

'Certainly.'

It would be her last night in Koura with Auntie Sohad and her daughters Hana and Maha.

After an interval of perhaps thirty minutes, once they had run the gauntlet of the first Lebanese Forces checkpoint, the driver spoke again. 'You are not from these parts, I think.'

She did not want to answer him because of the strangers in the back.

He seemed to know what was bothering her.

'Don't mind them,' he said, glancing up at the mirror to inspect his other three passengers. 'They're harmless enough – and if they have anything to say about it, I'll throw them out on their arses, don't you worry yourself.'

He grinned at her and Reem smiled back.

'That's better. Such a smile and I know summer has arrived early. Now tell me – you're from the south, daughter, right? Jezzine, perhaps?'

'The north.'

'Ah. The north. Is that right?'

He did not believe her. It was not her accent. Reem's Arabic was universal. She could be practically anything. Palestinian, Shi'ite, Maronite – she could not be pigeonholed. She knew she had no accent. She wondered what it was that told him she was lying. In any case, he did not seem to mind. Jezzine was indeed a Christian town so he had got that side of things right.

'So you are going home.'

'Yes.'

'I'm from Akkar,' he said. 'You know?'

Perhaps people from Akkar considered anyone who lived anywhere else a southerner.

'I know of it,' she said. It was in the far north, up near the Syrian border.

On the next corner two women in headscarves chatted, gesturing furiously with their hands, oblivious of their several children pulling at their skirts until one toddler, a chubby little boy with curly hair, broke away and stepped into the street.

The driver was quick. He hit the brakes and swerved, just avoiding an oncoming truck.

They were all thrown forward.

The driver put his head out of the window. 'Look after your children, ladies,' he shouted. 'Take care of them, for God's sake. For all our sakes.'

As they set off again, he shook his head.

'Idiot refugees . . .'

He glanced over at Reem.

'No offence, m'moiselle. I'm a refugee myself. We are all refugees of one kind or another. Christian, Muslim, Palestinian, Maronite, Armenian . . . It makes no difference, no?'

'That's true,' said one man on the back seat.

'May God help them,' his companion mumbled.

A few moments later the driver said to Reem, 'You see that . . .'

He gestured with one callused hand at the dashboard. He did not mean the Koran or the inscription. He meant a small black and white photograph tucked against the windscreen. Reem had not noticed it until now. At first she thought it was the driver himself as a young man, only clean shaven.

Younger than Nick, with a similar expression.

Innocent.

'My son. Walid. My eldest. I have another son and three daughters.'

'Really? You are fortunate. Walid is such a fine-looking boy. Handsome.'

'He was,' the driver said. 'He was.' He stared straight ahead, his lips moving in prayer. No emotion showed on his face. He held the wheel with both hands, arms locked, stretching his back.

'Walid was martyred. He was nineteen.'

Reem was lost for words. Should she commiserate? Should she congratulate a father on the death of his eldest boy?

She felt a sharp pain in her throat as if someone had his hands around her neck and was trying to throttle her.

Dear God, not this. Not now.

The driver leaned slightly over and said in a whisper loud enough to be heard by everyone on board. 'I'm proud of what he did, m'moiselle, God rest his soul. Oh, yes I am. Walid got six of the bastards. Six. With an RPG.' He took his right hand off the wheel and held it up, showing all five fingers, then closed it into a fist again, and released his thumb.

'Six. In the south – near Marjayoun. And I don't give a damn what anyone thinks. What can they do? Lock me up for something my Walid did? Shoot me? It broke his mother's heart. She has never recovered. Me? I am proud, God forgive me. Yes. God rest his soul. He is happy. He has found peace. I know it. Our enemies are not superhuman. It took my own son's life to teach me this simple thing. If only we could each of us account for six, or even three, all of this mess would be over in no time . . . 'God rest his soul.'

His hand swept the air, taking in the pockmarked buildings, the filthy streets, the rubble, the broken pavements, the slogans on the walls, the pictures of the martyred, the poverty.

Reem had stopped listening.

She looked at the picture again.

He was only a boy.

A man-child.

'God bless him,' Reem said quietly. She kept her face averted. She did not want the boy's father to see her tears.

Reem stood in the shade of an overhead bridge, a flyover that siphoned off traffic heading for Shikka. The highway divided here. The left-hand road went to the port city of Tripoli, but Reem was heading off to the right along a road that climbed inland, into the foothills of Koura.

She stood at the side of the road, her bag between her feet.

Reason told her she would never have met Nick were it not for her vocation. She must keep that thought in the forefront of her mind. It would be her life raft. She would certainly not have finagled a meeting with him in Sammy's Bar otherwise. She would never have ventured east with him. She would never have gone swimming, or eaten *sultan brahim* washed down with a bottle of Ksara under a yellow awning. She would never have met el-Hami, or photographed his Kaslik yacht club or his head-quarters. It was duty that had brought them together. Her duty. It was Nick's ability to provide the access she needed, and that was all there was to it. She would certainly not have visited his one-bedroom place in Ain Saadeh and allowed a Westerner to make love to her in his bed.

It had been the most wonderful afternoon of her short life.

No.

Don't think it.

Wrong.

She told herself it was because she had nothing to lose.

Reem had no need to worry about her reputation or a virgin marriage.

She had tasted 'normal' life. She had had fun. She had, for a very short while, known what it was to feel like a woman with a man and without any obligations or guilt.

Another service taxi slowed, a maroon Merc this time, and she bent to talk to the driver, her left hand moving her hair out of her eyes, and climbed in the back, putting her bag on her knees and going through the ritual without even being conscious of what was said. She nodded to the other passengers, a Muslim couple. The wife wore a *hejab* over her hair. Her husband had the look of a farmer. Reem would get out just at the turn-off to her village. Well, not her village, exactly. Not really. Her adopted village.

I can't back out now, she told herself.

What I want, what I feel, doesn't matter.

Reem tried to imagine it: going back to the west, putting out the yellow towel and then – God, how could she – telling the Ustaz that she was calling it off. She could not go through with it. Sorry. She was leaving. It was over for her. He would have to get someone else, one of those many volunteers he had mentioned. Yes, it would cause a delay and she regretted any inconvenience to his plans. But she could no longer do it.

She pictured his face – grave, quietly appalled. Trying not to let his disappointment and disapproval show. Taking his time, choosing his words, trying to sound reasonable.

Had he not always said she could withdraw at any time?

She could never do it to him.

Or to the party.

Had this not been her life's ambition, to die in the service of her people, her country?

To strike a devastating blow at the very heart of the enemy leadership?

What had all these years of sacrifice and struggle been for if not to avenge the deaths of her parents, her sisters and her brother and to wreak havoc on her foes for their theft of her land?

All the hard work, the effort, the bloody-minded refusal to take no for an answer – was that all for nothing?

And the cause?

She had fallen in love. She had slept with a foreigner, an English spy, and wanted more, much more. She wanted all of it. She wanted to leave with him. She wanted him all to herself. She wanted his children. She wanted a life raising kids and washing clothes and cooking food.

Reem wanted peace. She wanted to run, to escape.

No way.

It was absurd.

Pathetic.

The taxi slowed. She reached forward between the front seats with the money, two grubby notes.

It was the last Lebanese Forces checkpoint.

'Keep the change.'

'Go in peace.'

She would walk the rest of the way.

It was only a few hundred metres, and the sun had set.

Reem told herself she had said goodbye to Nick. He had watched her, she knew, until she was out of sight. But she had not turned round or looked over her shoulder. She had kept going. She had not even waved.

Of course she missed him.

She ached for him.

Nick had the natural, unconscious grace of a wild creature, an animal.

His charm was his lack of self-awareness.

He was quite exquisite.

Reem had never known such tenderness in another, had never experienced such a strong urge to return it, to wrap this man in her arms, to take him into her heart.

But it was over, all of it.

Reem told herself she was no coward.

She would not cry. Not another tear.

Reem swore on the graves of her ancestors.

On her village.

On Michael.

Walking towards the checkpoint, she crossed herself.

I swear.

Nicholas Lorimer had served his purpose.

At the checkpoint the Lebanese Forces militiamen watched her approach.

They saw her cross herself.

One of us.

The gunmen of Christ stood aside. They looked at her legs, at her body moving under her clothing. Even their commander, a bespectacled second lieutenant with a gold crucifix at his neck, came out to look. One militiaman winked at his comrade and let out a sigh. At a nod from the lieutenant, he slowly lifted the barrier.

Her enemies let Reem through without a word.

TWENTY-TWO

It was Tuesday morning. Nick received a telephone call while shuffling paper and listening to radio reports of clashes around Souk al-Gharb.

He thought it might be Reem. He hoped it would be. He had had no contact since Saturday, when she had left Ain Saadeh at dusk. She had insisted on leaving alone, taking the lift to the ground floor, then walking around the building and taking the steep stairs down to the road below, and he had waited on the balcony.

It was for the best, she said.

Please don't be upset, Nick.

We have to be discreet.

The last Nick saw of her was her head ducking into the rear of a service taxi.

She had not looked up. She did not turn to wave.

There was so much he had wanted to say, but he had not known how to begin.

The previous day, Monday, he sent flowers to her place of work. So far, there had been no response.

But it was not her. It was the secret police.

'It's for you,' Elias told Nick, standing in the doorway with one hand cupped over the receiver. Elias looked worried. 'It's the Syrian *moukhabarat*,' he added in a whisper. 'They asked for you by name.'

'I'll take it in here, Elias. Would you transfer it, please?'

He got up and shut his door and went back to his chair.

The call was not in itself particularly unusual, although the telephone lines had been working intermittently at best. It was the identity of the caller that surprised Nick.

'Mr Lorimer?'

'Speaking.'

'Daoud here. How are you, Mr Lorimer?'

'Very well, thank you colonel, and yourself?'

'*Nashkur Allah*. Very well, thanks to God. Mr Lorimer, you reported the loss of your United Nations vehicle, did you not?'

There was something odd about these words of piety from the local head of the Syrian secret police. Daoud did not strike Nick as someone who was prepared to leave much to God's will if he could help it.

'I did report it, colonel, yes. To the local authorities. The police and the Lebanese Interior Ministry.'

In other words, he had not told the Syrians.

'It is is my duty to tell you, Mr Lorimer, that it has been seen.'

'Really? When?'

'Yesterday. Monday. It was observed at one of our check-points.'

'Where?'

'Aley. You know Aley. It used to be a place for tourists before the war. In the Shouf, on the road between Damascus and Beirut. Your car was heading east towards the Bekaa. It was around noon.'

'I know Aley. Why didn't your men stop it?'

Nick looked up at the map on the opposite wall. From where he sat he could see the winding road, the town of Aley, and not far away, on the northern flank, the Christian village of Souk al-Gharb. Whoever held Souk al-Gharb posed a direct threat to the route that served as an umbilical cord between west Beirut and the Syrian hinterland. That road had always been an objective of Israeli invaders and their Maronite surrogates, the Phalangists and Lebanese Forces.

What the hell was the Land-Rover doing there?

Something was very wrong.

'They stopped your vehicle, Mr Lorimer, but it was not suspected. Not then. The driver's papers were in order. Our military people had no reason to keep it there. It was not searched. They had received no orders to that effect. It was not reported stolen to them in any case. It is an internal Lebanese affair. We cannot interfere with every stolen vehicle. You understand?'

What rubbish.

'This was a United Nations matter, not local at all. Who was the driver?'

Nick did not sound very appreciative, even to his own ears.

'A woman, but I do not have a name. They did not keep a record of her details. They had no reason to do so. But they remembered. A Christian, they said. Lebanese. But then of course national identity cards can be faked. It's big business nowadays. You wouldn't have any idea who it might have been, would you, Mr Lorimer?'

'No, I'm afraid not. Are you sure?'

'The registration number is the same, Mr Lorimer. There are many Range Rovers in Lebanon, they are so very popular with the *zaaran* and militias. They are smuggled in from the Gulf. But not so many Defenders, I think. It's a type used by your organization and by the British embassy.'

Its boxy shape was unusual, certainly.

'Were there any passengers?'

'Not that I know of.'

Was the Syrian making it up?

Daoud said, 'I have issued orders that if this vehicle appears again at any of our checkpoints it will be held and the occupant or occupants detained for investigation – if that is your wish. But please do not complain if you find that your UN staff find themselves being held up and questioned by Syrian security forces. We are only trying to be of assistance, to you and to the people of Lebanon.'

Like shelling the shit out of people who fail to toe the Damascus line.

'Thank you. I'm grateful to you and to the Syrian authorities.'

Nick pitied anyone held for investigation, even car thieves.

'It is nothing,' Daoud said. 'It is my duty to help the United Nations.'

Nick was puzzled. Was it Reem that the Syrians had seen behind the wheel? Was it really his Land-Rover? If so, had Reem lied when she said she was going to Koura to stay with family friends? Or had she spent the night and then taken the long way round via the north and then the Bekaa Valley to the east and down to Aley just to pick up the Land-Rover? It was a long and tiring journey. And why would she be heading east again? Was it to avoid LF and Phalangist territory? But what about the Syrians? They were as vigilant as the right-wing Christian militias and had their own reasons to apprehend guerrillas, other than those partisans Damascus sanctioned. And regardless of the driver's identity, what was the Land-Rover doing in the Shouf in the first place?

What did she want with his vehicle, anyway?

Unless of course Daoud had concocted the story to make the same point that his British counterpart, Major Dacre, had been at such pains to deliver. Namely, that Nick's liaison with a young woman, Reem Najjar, was known to the various security and intelligence agencies.

Was it just that – a warning?

Nick had just ordered a coffee when it happened.

He knew he would not get it now.

The explosion was not in itself uncommon.

They happened every two or three days.

It was tit-for-tat mass murder. A bombing over here, prompting a bombing there, then another this side, an endless retaliatory spiral of massacre and counter-massacre, civilians invariably the target and the objective to achieve the highest body count.

In Lebanon, Nick reflected, the phrase 'the bomber will always get through' had a special resonance. Despite innumerable check-points, the army's gradual takeover of the crossings on the Green Line, and the special security cabinet's avowals of a new crack-down on militant elements, explosive-rigged cars still seemed to reach their intended targets.

This one was big enough, destructive enough, for broadcasters to interrupt news of the arrival of an emissary from the Arch-bishop of Canterbury in Beirut to try to win the freedom of foreign hostages. No mention of the thousands of missing Leba-nese. Nick had come to regard one American hostage as being worth six west European hostages, and a single west European kidnap victim equivalent in news value and politically (Was it not the same thing?) to ten Lebanese. That made one American life equivalent to what, sixty Lebanese?

Too generous? Perhaps a ratio of a hundred to one sounded about right.

He switched on his office television set, but there were no images of the bombing as yet. The camera crews had yet to arrive on the scene.

This latest blast bore all the early signs of yet another car bomb: the thirty-second roar of the blast and its echo, funnelled by the closely packed buildings, then the cascading sound of collapsing walls and windows, the popping of secondary explosions of car fuel tanks and whatever else the bomb makers might have added to the cocktail to prolong and magnify the effect – an anti-tank mine or two, a half-dozen RPG warheads, an anti-personnel device perhaps, maybe one of those canister bombs of US manu-facture supplied gratis to Israel and still now harvesting death among the fields and groves of the south.

Whatever it was, it rocked the building housing Nick's outfit, and the half-minute roaring sound was followed by the clatter of falling debris.

Close.

UN staff ran for the relative safety of the corridor, knocking over chairs in their haste.

Nick stayed where he was. He listened to the debris tapping at the windows like a hundred hungry fingers. The frames shook violently in the aftershock, and he was thankful for the anti-blast curtains.

When the roar subsided, he and several staffers went out onto the balcony to look.

Pieces of hot metal and oddly shaped bits of molten glass crunched underfoot. He wrinkled his nose at the sharp stench of burning.

'Verdun,' said one.

'No – Barbir,' said another.

'Qasqas,' ventured a third.

Everyone started arguing about where it was. Except Nick. He watched the smoke. At first it was a balloon of dark, venomous muck over to the left. It expanded fast, filling the sky. It boiled into a thick, vertical column above the surrounding buildings, propelled upwards from the point of origin. It moved vertically with great rapidity, volcanic in its power. It changed colour from black to grey and white. The column thinned into a stalk of smoke, grew taller, then flattened at the top to form a cloud. The wind bent the plume of smoke and carried the cloud over the city.

The sun vanished, and the birds in the trees and shrubs surrounding the law courts began their evening chorus although it was only 11.11 a.m.

All this took less than two or three minutes.

Ash lay everywhere.

Verdun, almost certainly.

The city streets rang to the scream of sirens.

Fire engines. Ambulances. Militiamen. Troops.

Civilians ran in different directions. Some ran towards the epicentre of the blast and others away from it. They collided on the pavements. It was a matter of temperament. Some were drawn to danger, perhaps out of a desire to help. Others were frightened, and needed to get away as fast as possible.

Did someone say Verdun?

Jesus Christ Almighty.

Nick ran all the way.

He sprinted flat out.

As he got closer the crowds grew increasingly dense, slowing him down.

He pushed his way through, using his arms as a swimmer, sweeping others aside, gouging a path with his shoulder.

He did not apologize or excuse himself. Nick could not speak. His lungs were doing all they could to drag enough oxygen into his blood to keep his legs moving. He was drenched in sweat as if he had just taken a shower, but he was barely aware of it.

Militiamen and police were battling to hold the crowds back. The fighters used their rifles, their fists, their boots.

Other gunmen jumped on the running boards of the ambulances and fired bursts skywards with their automatic rifles to clear a path for the wounded.

Nick thrust his way through to the front of the mass of humanity, and a militiaman sporting a black beard, jeans and trainers pushed him hard in the chest. He very nearly fell over. Someone helped him stay on his feet by grabbing his arm. He would have been trampled underfoot otherwise. Right next to him another gunman – a skinny PSP fighter wearing a maroon beret – loosed off four or five rounds from his Kalashnikov. To his left half a dozen veiled women wailed and tore their clothes and flung themselves at the militia cordon, trying to reach the site of the attack. The militiamen beat them with their rifles, too, without regard for their gender or their grief.

Nick could not see anything very much.

The crowd was seething with anger, surging against the militia line, falling back and surging forward again. Thousands of voices were raised in anger, in demands for vengeance.

A steady, communal moan of rage and fear.

Smoke and a huge pile of rubble blocked his view.

Nick's throat burned with the fumes.

The institute had fallen in on itself.

The front seemed to have collapsed, leaving the interior exposed. When the smoke cleared for a moment it looked to Nick like a rotten tooth. He could see the stairwell plainly, but it ended somewhere between where the third and fourth floors would have been. Further up, Nick saw a desk protruding into the empty space of what had been an office; someone's jacket hung behind a door, and a telephone dangled in space.

'Let me through,' Nick said. 'Let me through.'

He flashed his United Nations card and to his surprise, it worked. He found himself walking forward, stumbling over the debris.

The dead were laid out in two rows down a side street.

No one stopped him.

The bodies were side by side, as if at attention. There were two military trucks, tailgates lowered, ready to receive the victims' remains.

A sympathetic Amal militia officer lifted up the tarp covering the bodies, just enough to show what was left of their faces.

'Twenty-seven, mister, but there will be more,' he said.

Even so, what was left was barely recognizable.

As Nick moved down the line of human remains, scorched, torn and disfigured, his shoes squelched in their blood.

At least half were women.

He could tell from their clothes, not their bodies, which were too badly mangled and indistinguishable from the men.

'Tell them out there,' the officer said to him in English. 'Tell the world what is happening here. Tell the Americans. Tell them. Please. Tell them we are not the criminals or terrorists. They have done this to us. We have done nothing to deserve this. Except to ask for our rights, our land, okay? Tell them, mister. You see what they do. This was a library they attacked. Nothing else.'

The officer followed Nick, still talking.

Nick no longer listened.

Reem was not there. She was not among the dead.

Maybe she had not turned up for work that morning. Maybe she was not feeling well. Maybe what Colonel Daoud had said was true. Maybe she was in Aley. Maybe she had stopped off somewhere else.

Anything. Anything at all. It did not matter what. Anything but this.

God make her be in Koura still.

Please God make her safe.

Alive.

Unharmed.

It did not matter what she was up to.

The officer gave orders to his men and they started picking the bodies up, carrying them to the trucks, piling them up like logs.

Nick knew he must find the wounded.

He was sure most would be taken to the American University Hospital. It was the biggest and best-equipped facility in the western sector.

He pushed his way back into the crowd, ducking under a militiaman's arm, and thrust his way through once again, ignoring the protests.

Television crews had set up ladders so they could film without obstruction.

At the back of the crowd newsmen were swaggering around in baseball caps with large signs on their chests saying PRESS. They stared at Nick, a frantic Westerner, headed in the wrong direction.

The dead meant nothing to these voyeurs, he thought.

But that was how people here saw him, too.

A voyeur.

Spy.

The enemy.

Once out on the other side, in the clear, Nick started to run at a steady pace.

His blue cotton shirt was soaked, a sopping wet rag that clung to his torso.

The hospital was little more than a mile and a half away.

There was still hope.

TWENTY-THREE

The three librarians gathered for coffee.

Reem stood, bending forward over the Damascene table, the coffee pot in her right hand, about to pour the black liquid into the first of three cups.

Zubaida stood next to her, a plate of *baklawa* in both hands, about to set it down.

Dalia had just sat, pulling her skirt over her knees.

Dalia was laughing.

They were celebrating the news that the president-elect would not take up office for another three weeks, maybe a month. There was to be a round of negotiations among all parties to the conflict first.

Reem looked up. Zubaida was saying something.

'If only he'd never told me that, I'd—'

Her mouth opened, her lips formed the words. But Reem never heard the rest. Behind and above Zubaida she saw the wall clock.

11.09.

Reem saw the panel of brick lights to her left detach itself from the wall and move into the centre.

Odd.

There was no sound. None that she was aware of. Just the white light, like a camera flash. The bricks seemed suspended in the centre of the room like big droplets of water, tumbling.

Bright jewels falling.

Reem could not hear Dalia's words.

*

She staggers rather than walks.

Reem puts one leg in front of the other.

Her good shoulder, her right, is against what was left of the wall of the stairwell.

She shuffles down.

One step at a time. Her left foot leads.

She hears moaning.

Crying.

Keening.

Some steps are missing. There are gaps in the wall.

She feels her way, sliding the left forward, then the right.

The stairs are broken, the steps littered with rubbish.

Her nose, mouth and eyes are full of smoke and dust.

She spits, coughs. Her phlegm is black with dirt. Her right hand is across her body at chest level, and holds her upper left arm, gripping it tight.

Her left arm does not work.

She feels no pain.

Reem keeps slipping on the mess. The foyer has vanished. So has the front door. Through the smoke and dust is a crowd of people.

People in red smocks and helmets.

Running towards her.

Lady.

She stumbles into the open.

They catch her.

Is that you, Michael?

Her brother's face.

Hold on, lady.

We're going to get you out.

Miss, hold on.

There is so much blood.

Mine.

She lies in it, like a bath.

Hold on, lady.

Mikey?

Reem is on her back, confused, unsure how she got there, staring at the sky, at the buildings gliding by.

Floating.

Blue sky.

Is this how it ends, sweet Michael?

She is lifted, carried forward feet first.

Christ.

That hurts.

Shouting.

Gunfire, very close.

Empty cartridge cases, still hot, spin around her.

Eyes heavy.

So tired.

Michael is there.

My little brother.

He is smiling.

Not yet, Michael.

She feels herself being moved.

Lifted again.

Put down.

Pushed.

Lying in the back of a truck.

Please.

The left arm useless.

Michael, sweetheart, is that really you?

Don't sleep.

I can't go yet, Mikey, my love.

Someone ties on a tourniquet.

Uses her blood to smear the time on her forehead.

T and the numbers 11.14.

I'll be with you soon. Very soon.

All of us, together again.

Hold my hand.

Someone is calling.

It is me. So sorry.
Not yet, Michael.
There is so much I still have to do.
Wait for me.

TWENTY-FOUR

'Mama.'

Dr Nessim took Nick by the arm.

'This way.'

'Mama.'

The dying man put an arm out, his eyes unfocused, looking past Nick.

'This way. Watch your feet.'

He had no legs.

Nick could not help himself. He could not help staring.

Dr Nessim said, 'You know something, Mr Nicholas? Everyone calls for his mother. It doesn't matter who he is. Muslim, Christian, Jew, Lebanese, French, Israeli, Syrian, male, female, soldier, civilian, young or old, rich or poor – always it is the same. It does not matter. They call for their mothers. We are all human. We end life as we begin.'

'He is dying?'

'Sure.'

'Can't you do something?'

'For him? No, not really. What can be done has been done.'

A gurney rattled past. The two men stood back for the Red Cross workers. The volunteers were running, leaning forward, grasping the sides of the trolley, propelling the device and its bloodied bundle towards one of four surgical wards.

'This way, Mr Nick.'

They were in the foyer. Packed with people, mostly in white

coats, all of them hurrying and shouting. 'What did you mean –
"not really"?'

Gunmen overtook them.

'It's times like these when we're swamped.' Dr Nessim
shrugged. He was still walking quickly, just ahead of Nick,
shouting over his shoulder to make himself heard. 'We have to
make decisions about people. They arrive. We give them a
cursory inspection. Sometimes it's just the orderly, the nurse or
a junior doctor. If the injured person is too badly hurt . . .'

Dr Nessim's voice trailed off. He looked at Nick helplessly, his
expression seeming to say, Don't ask me to spell it out for you.
But Nick had to understand. He could not bear not to know. He
needed answers. He had to be able to force some order, some
sense, on this cauldron of pain and blood.

The inner courtyard was quieter. It was also full of people, but
they lay in rows on the ground; it was slick with blood. Used
bandages were scattered everywhere like red sponges. First aid
workers wandered among the wounded, carrying bottled water.

'We make the badly injured as comfortable as we can. You see?
We have to leave them. We attend to those with a chance. We
call it reverse triage. The badly wounded, well, they are left to
die out here so that those with a better possibility might live. We
must save our resources for those with a better chance of living.
You understand?'

'And Reem Najjar?'

They were walking rapidly along a corridor. The blood was
sticky underfoot.

'She's out of surgery now.'

Nessim explained. They thought she was dead. The Red Cross
man had felt no pulse. They put her with the others in the
courtyard. Those without hope. To die. Later, maybe, if some
were still alive, they would get more attention.

Nessim had recognized her. He had just driven in with some
blood supplies he had collected from other clinics.

Quite by chance.

Nessim was the hospital's deputy administrator. He too was a Greek Catholic. From the same village. Well, his parents were. Like Reem he had never seen his home. Only in pictures. He smiled, as if to apologize for the fact of loss.

'We Melchites are a small community here and in Palestine, and I recognized her. I meet her sometimes on her way to work or in the local market. She's a librarian, isn't she? I know her parents died some years ago. My wife knew them. Good people. They used to attend the same church.'

Nick nodded.

'I went over to check,' Nessim continued. 'Then I was sure. I searched for a pulse. It was very faint. Miss Najjar was still alive – but only just. She had lost too much blood. Far too much. I picked her up. I ran with her into surgery. Someone had just died on the table and they rolled him off and I put her down. I asked the surgeon to do what he could. He was very tired. He said she was dead and said I was wasting everyone's time. I told him she was alive moments ago and to please try. I insisted. If I had arrived only five minutes later it would have been too late.'

They were at the door.

'They changed her dressings and gave her a massive transfusion – only because I asked for it. We are running short of blood, you see. If she had died it would have been a terrible waste.'

Nessim waited for Nick.

'Here. In here. This is the recovery room.'

TWENTY-FIVE

Time lost all meaning.

There were no hours or minutes. There was no day or night.

Both wakefulness and sleep evaded Reem.

All was pain or non-pain. Pain was a world unlike any other; a monstrous master that crushed Reem in its grasp, stripping her of all thought, all self-respect, all humanity. It was without mercy. It was implacable. It reduced her to a quivering, snivelling thing writhing on the barb that impaled her.

It made her helpless, and she detested it.

There was nothing she could do but hate it. She could not escape. She could not fight it except by hating it. She was good at hate. Now she nursed her hatred, clinging to it in her private ocean of agony.

It kept her afloat, saved her sense of self.

Pain's drug-induced absence brought her periods of glorious nothingness, a sinking, a floating down to immense depths, a dream-filled otherness that she relished, unwilling to surface.

To have this painlessness, to keep it, to prolong it, to enjoy its protection, Reem would have done anything.

Either way, there was no dignity.

She heard voices right above her bed.

Two men.

She could smell them too.

Cologne, sweat, cigarettes, alcohol and ammonia.

Maleness.

Reem knew them both. They spoke in English. The younger, impatient voice she recognized as Nick's. The deeper, slower and heavily accented tone was that of Dr Nessim.

'How is she?'

'We have managed to save the arm. It was the loss of blood that was so severe. She's still very weak. But we saved the arm. Apart from that, there are no serious injuries. She was lucky.'

'That's good. Excellent.'

'She won't know you. She's in too much pain.'

'Can't you do something?'

'Oh, yes. Of course. We do. Up to a point. She does sleep a lot of the time. It's really a state of half-sleeping, half-waking.'

'Is she sleeping now?'

'Maybe she is.'

'Am I the only visitor?'

'No. There is a woman who brings her food and feeds her. Sometimes she sleeps here, on the floor, keeping Miss Najjar company.'

'Who is she?'

'Salwa – I don't know more than that. She's Kurdish.'

'Anyone else?'

'A man. Her uncle, I believe. I've not seen him. He sent her the flowers and food.'

'Can she hear?'

'I think so, yes. Some of those bandages will come off in a day or two. Most of the lesions are very minor – apart from the left arm which sustained a small but deep puncture. It was a shard of glass and it severed a vein.'

'Does she hear us now?'

'I do not know, Mr Lorimer.'

'How long will she be in hospital, doctor?'

'It depends. I don't know. It depends on her recovery.'

'She will recover completely, won't she?'

'She's young. It will all depend on her attitude, how determined she is. But there's no reason why she shouldn't resume a normal life.'

'Is there anything I can do?'

'I don't think so. Just visit her. Patients need company. It can make all the difference to their morale.'

'Is there anything she needs that she isn't getting?'

'You'll have to ask her that yourself.'

She felt her hand being held by different people at different times.

Salwa's hands were small and strong, the skin roughened by manual labour – the washing and cleaning, cooking and ironing, the carrying of water and food from the market – the labour, in short, of the poor.

Honest hands.

Salwa held Reem's hand firmly, palm to palm, her fingers holding Reem's right hand tight, as if preventing her from falling.

Salwa came in the late afternoons and fed her. Usually broth, more recently small spoonfuls of *tabouli*, *moutabal* and *hommous*.

Salwa said little. She helped Reem relieve herself in the bedpan. She gave Reem mineral water, and sometimes fresh juice she had prepared herself. Salwa washed Reem gently, and dried her quickly with a clean towel. She sat on the edge of the bed and combed Reem's hair to distract her from the pain. She brought clean sheets and a pillowcase. She was Reem's personal attendant at a time when the ward staff were too busy for such luxuries. Salwa was practical. Salwa was unsentimental, businesslike. She had lost most of her family in the camps, and her husband who died fighting in defence of Karantina.

She knew what pain was.

The Ustaz usually visited Reem at night.

She never heard him coming until he sat on the end of the bed, or brought in a chair.

It was quieter then, but hardly deserted. Friends and relatives slept in the corridors. They cooked meals and boiled up tea or coffee on the balconies at any hour, and hung out the patients' washing from the windows. But at least most of the radios were turned off, and the chatter had mostly ceased by midnight.

His hands were large, the nails trimmed short.

There were calluses on the palms, and the fingers were long and knobbly and strong – too strong because sometimes while holding Reem's right hand he hurt her without meaning to.

He read to her slowly, hesitatingly in his deep voice with its west Beirut accent.

He was very calm and very patient.

She liked him to read poetry best of all.

Al-Mutanabi was her favourite.

They did not talk. They exchanged thoughts by the pressure of their fingers. She would thank him for his readings by squeezing his hand He brought her the best gift of all: reassurance. He was there for her, even though they both knew she was no use to him.

But she swore to herself she would be.

Nick. She dreaded his visits and yearned for them simultaneously.

He visited twice a day, like clockwork.

Early in the morning; Reem guessed it was around six or seven.

He smelled of shower gel, aftershave and clean laundry.

Late; after work, she thought, on his way home. At these times he smelled, not unpleasantly, of sweat and cigarette smoke. Sometimes alcohol. Wine, most likely, drunk at lunchtime.

She would reach out her right hand and touch his face, feel the outline of his chin – soft like a baby's bum in the mornings, rough as a cheese grater by the evening – as well as his wide mouth, his funny broken nose and his eyes with their strangely long lashes. Her fingers would touch his throat, his shirt, then run down his arms, feeling the springy hair on his forearms and wrist, finally moving to take his hand.

A strong hand, not as big as the Ustaz's, shorter somehow. Broader, blunter.

Softer. A pen-pusher's hands. Someone who worked in an office.

He was horribly cheerful. She was as nervous as a schoolgirl. She wanted him to kiss her on the mouth, and didn't want him to. (He kissed her like a whisper on her one cheek that was not bandaged.) She did want him to because she wanted to know how he felt about her, and she did not want him to because she knew that she not only looked truly awful, but probably smelled as bad.

No amount of Salwa's washing and scrubbing could rid her of the hospital stink.

God, she must be a frightful sight. All those dressings, and the yellow stuff they painted on the minor cuts on her face. And the bruising. Blue and black. Shit, what a colour scheme. A real work of art; a bloodied Kandinsky. She had never felt so unsure of herself, so vulnerable, so needy.

What must he be thinking?

Thank God she could not see herself in any mirror or she would die of shame.

And then those worst of thoughts, in the depth of the night, when she was at her lowest ebb, feeling the darkness all around her, unable to sleep because of the pain, the endless snoring from other beds, the heat, the mosquitoes.

Was there someone else?

Who was he seeing now?

He had slept with her – had his little Arab virgin – and was that all there was to it? Had he got what he wanted, finally? Was he already moving on to someone else? Were these visits just because of his sense of decency, his duty? Did he feel sorry for her? Did he pity her?

Dark thoughts.

But she wanted none of his pity.

It was the waiting for him that got to her. It was always better when he did come to see her. He told her about his work. He told her about his colleagues. He had a self-mocking style and a sense of the ridiculous that made her laugh so much the stitches hurt.

He mentioned that he was to take four days off. Rest and recreation it was called, paid for by his employers. He was delaying it, he said. He didn't want to go anywhere, not now, not yet, not while she was still bedridden. If they made him take it, he said, he would lie to them and spend the time in the hospital. He would camp there like all those people he had to step over on his way to her ward.

Reem was not sure whether to believe him or not.

Nick said he would take his R & R once she was back at home, on her feet.

Would she go with him? To Cyprus?

It would be good for her.

Yes, he knew the unwritten rules. He knew all that. Would she at least think about it? Please?

She squeezed his hand.

Smiled a lopsided smile under the dressings.

Yes. She would think about it.

Did he love her?

She could not ask.

The day most of the bandages came off Reem celebrated by letting Salwa wash her hair.

Dr Nessim had her moved her to a private room with only five other patients, all women, all war wounded, mainly from the south and Beirut's southern suburbs.

When Reem expressed concern about the cost, Nessim said not to worry. It was all taken care of. Her Uncle Faiz had seen to everything.

'Don't worry yourself. You'll be out of here . . .'

Reem's left arm stuck out at an odd angle, resting in a tube of plaster and supported by a contraption suspended from above her bed.

Best of all, the pain had retreated to her arm and shoulder. It no longer racked her entire being. It had lost the battle for possession of her body and mind. Its territory was limited to the site of her main injury. She could think, speak and even read for short periods.

She slept better.

There were still terrible headaches, and her vision would blur if she tried to do too much.

Her lesions itched terribly as they mended. The heat did not help. She became hungry and thirsty. She wanted to get out of bed. She fidgeted. She argued with the woman in the next bed. It was very silly – over the best way to prepare *makloobeh*, a Syrian dish of aubergine, meat and rice.

She was restless.

Her face was a sight. It was still discoloured and swollen.

She told Nick she resembled a heavyweight boxer who had gone eight rounds – and lost. She laughed, and that hurt, too.

He said he didn't care. She was gorgeous all the same, no matter how many bandages she had.

Did she believe it? She wanted to.

That same afternoon Dr Nessim sat beside her and said how much he was impressed by her recovery. Attitude was everything, he said.

The results from her urine and blood tests had come in from the lab.

Were they good?

For a moment or two Nessim seemed lost for an answer.

Well, yes. It all depended on how one looked at them, he said.

Nessim was never judgemental. He was a doctor. A psychiatrist.

He was very gentle when he gave her the news.

227

TWENTY-SIX

It was hot enough to melt the streets. In the hospital, all the doors and windows were wide open.

Nick did not tell her what the papers were reporting.

It would only upset her. Reem would probably hear it eventually from someone else anyway.

About a week after the bombing the independent west Beirut daily *an-Nahar* cited unidentified security sources in reporting that the latest bomb attack in the western sector had been carried out by Israel's proxies, believing the institute was a front for the shadowy Ustaz and his fellow militants.

The story was picked up by other media, and by foreign journalists, and a few days later the institute's governing council issued a statement – from the safety of Tunis – denying any links with guerrillas, terrorists or armed factions of any sort.

As for Reem, she kept her news to herself and did not tell Nick until the third week after the bombing.

Nick brought her some magazines. Women's stuff. *Vogue*, *Marie-Claire*. He thought she would like the pictures. Reading still gave her headaches, and there was nothing in them about the war.

'We don't have to go to Cyprus, you know. We could go anywhere we want.'

'That's sweet.'

'We could go to Italy.'

'Cyprus would be fine.'

'Would it? You've been there.'

'I like it.'

'Maybe it's too close to home.'

'What's wrong with that? I like my home.'

She looked so much better. She smiled at him, but Nick felt a nervousness, an underlying tension.

'What is it?'

'Nothing.'

'You can tell me.'

'I know.'

She smiled too brightly, as if close to tears. She was upset about something.

Nick leaned closer.

'Reem . . .'

'Yes?'

'Tell me.'

'It's nothing.'

'Please.'

'I don't want to, Nick. I like you to visit me. I don't want to drive you away.'

'You'll never do that.'

'You will be upset.'

'I don't think so.'

'I don't want to tell you. It will only worry you.'

'Does it worry you?'

Reem shrugged. 'A little. It worries me that it will worry you.'

'It won't worry me.'

'I'm going to have a child, Nick. A baby. Please don't be upset or angry.'

Nick was more than taken aback. He felt he had been punched in the gut. He felt sick. But he did not show it. He hoped not. It simply had not occurred to him. He opened his mouth and what came out sounded lame, even to him.

'It's okay. It's fine.'

'Really?'

'Really.'

It was anything but.

'Nick . . .'

'I did take precautions. I did everything.'

'I know you did. I don't blame you. These things happen.'

'Let's get married as soon as you get out of here.'

'You mean that?'

'Of course I do.'

'You're wonderful.'

'You too.'

'We're both marvellous.'

He put his arms around her, careful not to hurt the injured arm, and he kissed her properly on the mouth. A lingering kiss.

'We'll get married,' he said when they came up for air. 'Then we'll go away for a while. I'll take some leave. We could go to Italy and Spain. You'd like that, wouldn't you?'

'I'd love it,' Reem said, watching him.

It was a dream. A fantasy.

'You mean it, don't you?'

'Why wouldn't I, Nick?'

He saw the man she called her uncle.

Nick had approached quietly along the corridor. Most of the people who had slept there, camping out, had gone. It was one of those rare and all too brief periods of tranquillity.

Dr Nessim had told Nick about an incident the previous day. Two gunmen had come in, seeking the doctor of one of their friends who had died on the operating table. They had stood over the doctor while he worked, and when the man died they threatened to kill him.

The two gunmen had come back, seeking vengeance. They found the doctor smoking outside, taking a break. They chased him through the wards. Eventually they trapped him. The unfortunate doctor had leapt out of the window, jumping on the stomach of a patient to escape. He was two storeys up. He broke a leg on impact.

The good thing was that the thugs were satisfied. A broken leg, they decided, was sufficient.

Nick looked round the door. There, sitting beside Reem, was a stranger.

He sat very straight and still, hands on his knees, face in shadow. What was he doing? Was he daydreaming? Praying?

Reem's eyes were shut.

The uncle seemed to be very patient, waiting for her to wake.

Was he really her uncle? If he was so attentive, why did she not speak of him more often? Was this perhaps the man the newspapers were talking about – the notorious Ustaz?

What was Nick supposed to do? Telephone the Deuxième Bureau, summon hospital security or call Colonel Daoud? Or perhaps just walk in and introduce himself and say, 'Are you the man they call the Ustaz?'

And what would happen to Reem?

Nick would do none of those things.

He stayed where he was, watching.

Reem's visitor had very short grey hair. Ascetic. Like a priest, Nick thought.

After a minute or two Nick went away again, on tiptoe.

He wondered if Reem, or perhaps Dr Nessim, had told this 'Uncle Faiz' about Reem's pregnancy, and whether the uncle knew the identity of the father.

It was five days later when they spoke again of Reem's pregnancy.

'Do you want to have the baby, Nick?'

'Of course I do.'

'You want to be a father?'

'Very much.'

'You're not just saying that to please me?'

'I want to please you. But I'm not saying that to please you.'

'What kind of world will we be bringing this child into, Nick?'

'A lousy world.'

Reem had her right hand, her good hand, on her stomach.

She said, 'What kind of life will that be?'

'Better than no life.'

'Are you sure?'

'Sure I'm sure.'

'I'm not so sure.'

'Don't talk silly. We'll be very happy, and our child will be happy, too.'

'I don't want to leave, Nick.'

'You don't have to.'

'For the child we have to.'

'We can talk about it later.'

'Do you think it's a boy or a girl?'

'I don't mind.'

'Really? You don't?'

'Really.'

'If this is true then you are too good.'

'Nobody's that good.'

'You are.'

'Can I kiss you?'

'As often as possible.'

Later she said, 'I'm going home on Saturday, Nick.'

It was Thursday. Nick had already told Reem he had a job to do in Sidon. It could not be avoided. Four homes had been raided by the South Lebanon Army and the families' menfolk dragged away into the night. He was taking the office driver and Elias, and it was going to be terribly hot in the south. They would be away a few days. Reem was worried about the checkpoints and the Israeli aircraft and artillery, but Nick said it was quiet. There had been a flare-up around Souk al-Gharb, but nothing like the big battle Reem had told him about. The trip would be only for three days, he said. Four at the most.

'You will come back.'

'Of course.'

'You will take care, won't you?'

'I'll find you,' Nick said.

'Nick?'

He turned at the door.

'I love you, Nicholas.'

'I know,' he said. 'I love you too.'

'Whatever happens,' she said, 'you will believe that, won't you?'

'Of course I will.'

'Promise. Whatever happens.'

'I promise.'

They had to cross to the east, then head up the mountain towards Ain Saadeh and Broumana. It was the same route Nick took to his flat, the same road he had driven Reem for their romantic meetings in Broumana restaurants and cafes, and for that afternoon together in his bed before the bombing. Elias wanted the air conditioner on for Nick's sake, but Nick said no, thanks very much. He wanted the windows open, all of them all the way down, so he could hear what was happening around them. In the ten weeks he had been in Beirut he had developed a sense for trouble, and it involved listening to the first signs of a new skirmish. If there was going to be an artillery duel, Nick wanted to hear the outgoing before the incoming fell around them.

They hired Ali from Lebanon Taxi for the job. A southerner himself, Ali was very reliable, very cool under fire, though he was a fancy dresser and something of a ladies' man, with a wandering eye for the female form. He would take them up to the end of Druze territory in his Volvo estate, then they would hire another car on the other side.

233

They left the road before Ain Saadeh, taking a right-hand turn.

It was a lot cooler at the higher altitude, but it would not last.

The Lebanese Forces had refined their checkpoints. Not only were their militiamen wearing Israeli body armour and Kevlar helmets, but they carried Israeli Galil assault rifles. The checkpoints were the real thing this time, not simply a chain or pole across the road. The militia selected a bend in the road, or a rise, or both. They used *chevaux de frise* and concrete anti-tank obstacles to create a narrow chicane, and posted a machine gunner to command the approaches.

Portakabins were set up some way from the checkpoint, and Ali was ordered to park his Volvo in a lot specifically set aside for the purpose.

The goons ran mirrors under the vehicle. They looked in the wheel arches, under the seats, and in the boot. Ali was told to wait next to his car.

Next to it, not in it.

Elias and Nick were kept waiting in a Portakabin.

They had to stand.

Outside, the Christian gunmen wore fatigues. Inside, they were plainclothes intelligence types, with pistols in their waistbands, short-sleeved shirts and surly in manner.

Elias had no trouble. His Lebanese ID and UN card were handed back to him without a word.

Nick's passport, his driving licence and his UN accreditation were taken away to another room.

It was twenty minutes before they were returned to him.

Once safely back in the car, rolling downhill along a rough country lane among the pines, Elias laughed.

'They don't like you, Mr Nick.'

'Is that right?'

'I'm a Christian and from west Beirut but they take no notice of me. What did you do to upset them, Mr Nick?'

'Nothing.'

'That man they took your documents to wasn't Lebanese.'

Nick said nothing.

'He was foreign. An Israeli.'

'How do you know?'

'He wore one of those things on his head. He copied all your papers.'

'A *yamulka*?'

Elias was on the back seat. He leaned forward. 'That's it. A *yamulka*. He was Israeli *moukhabarat*. He dressed like Shin Beth, too. Short-sleeved shirt, very loose, hanging out of his trousers. Sleeves almost down to his elbows. Pistol underneath shirt, in pants, at the back. We saw many such people in eighty-two and seventy-eight. He copied everything. Any idea why he would do that?'

'None.'

'Maybe they think you are mixed up in something.'

'So?'

'They don't like you, Mr Nick. They can't do much because you have UN papers. But they don't like what they see. They are angry. They would like to detain you. They have this hungry look when they see you. I have seen that look before. They would like to ask you many questions. You have upset them, I think.'

'They've never liked the United Nations, Elias. Never.'

There was a five-mile stretch of no-man's-land. It was rolling country, and a switchback road. It got hotter again. It was no more than a dirt track and they kicked up a huge cloud of dust that swallowed them up. It got in Nick's eyes and ears, and he could taste it.

The windscreen was caked in dust except where the wipers had managed to scrape them clear.

The Syrian checkpoint was casual in comparison with the LF.

This time neither passengers nor Ali had to leave the car. Ali was asked for everyone's papers, and Nick and Elias passed theirs over to him. He then handed them to the Syrian through the window. While one soldier shuffled through the ID cards, two others watched the travellers.

They were not particularly curious.

'*Yalla* – go.'

A slight movement of the right hand, dismissing them.

The soldiers wore red berets.

Paratroopers, Nick thought.

The same corps that had fought so valiantly in the vineyards and orchards south of Beirut when Israel invaded in 1982. The paratroops had been slow to move out of the way, or perhaps they did not receive the order to withdraw until it was too late, but the Israelis had caught up with them. The Syrians fought back hard at close quarters despite being outgunned.

These soldiers did not search the car. They made a note of the registration, that was all. The fact that it was a west Beirut taxi, that Ali was himself Shi'ite, Elias Greek Orthodox and that Nick was a foreigner with UN accreditation was more than sufficient to persuade these boy-soldiers that the Volvo and its occupants posed no threat.

Once the Syrians were out of sight, Elias grabbed the seat in front of him and leaned forward again.

'We're close to Souk al-Gharb here,' he said. 'That's where those Syrians are heading.'

Elias was right. Five minutes later Ali almost ran into the back of a Syrian truck. It was the tail end of a large column of troops and artillery moving up to the Souk al-Gharb front. Nick thought Reem's timing might have been hopelessly off target, but it certainly looked like an offensive was building up in the area as she had predicted.

Ali stopped the Volvo.

They would wait for the dust to settle.

It was another hour to Druze territory, Ali said.

Nick got out, stretched his legs, slapped his clothes and stamped his feet to rid himself of some of the dust. Elias and Nick laughed at each other – their faces were caked with the stuff.

Ali handed round cigarettes and bottled water.

They left the car doors open, and perched on the seats, legs and feet outside.

Ali played a Fairuz tape. She sang the syrupy favourite that never failed to move Nick: 'Ya Watani'.

You my Country.

> Streets and alleys all change
> All my friends have gone away
> All that's been
> Is no more.
> Everybody has grown older,
> Different,
> Except you, my country,
> This little child.

It must have been the dust. Not theirs, especially, but the billowing plumes stirred up by the Syrian military convoy heading up to the front.

They must see it miles off, Nick realized.

Because that was when the first mortar rounds came in.

Crouched in a drainage ditch of dry red soil by the side of the road, his cheek pressed against the roots of a tall tree, Nick remembered he had failed to ask Reem the one thing he wanted to know. Was it true what the papers said – that the institute was a base of some kind for the Ustaz, and did that mean she worked for him? Just like Khaled? Was that who Uncle Faiz really was?

TWENTY-SEVEN

Reem covered her face and wept not out of pain but guilt.

She had hauled herself to her feet and struggled out of the mess of what had been the library. She had lost a great deal of blood. All that was true. Instinct had propelled her down the broken stairs and into the open.

The instinct to survive, Nessim had called it.

To survive – only to die?

It made no sense.

From the perspective of a survivor, it was madness.

She had given no thought to her friends.

How could she have been so selfish?

Zubaida had been plain lucky. A large volume toppled from the top shelf and somehow opened itself as it fell. It knocked her down, but it saved her life. It had acted like a helmet, falling open across her skull. They dug her out of the rubble with a couple of cracked ribs. A huge glass splinter was found embedded in the book itself.

It was a collection of Arabic poetry that had saved Zubaida, the least literary of the three.

Dalia had not made it. She never knew what hit her, they said.

Crushed by a concrete beam.

Poor, dearest Dalia. So innocent. The youngest. She had died with a smile still on her face. Instantly. She would not have felt a thing.

How did the rescuers know? Perhaps the Red Cross workers

said it of everyone who died simply for the sake of the living, a small consolation for Dalia's grieving relatives.

Zubaida brought flowers to Reem's ward, but neither of them could speak. They hugged each other, and cried, and Zubaida, for lack of anything better to do, found something for the flowers and filled it with water and set it by the bed. She had also brought hot food and some decent coffee and they shared both, again without saying anything, Zubaida perched on the end of the bed. What was there to say?

Reem could not tell her, her very best friend, about the new life growing inside her. She just could not. She wanted to. Perhaps one day it might be possible. She could barely face it herself. So many lives taken, cut off, destroyed.

And now this.

Life given, out of wedlock, to a woman, of all women, whose life was no longer hers but devoted to the struggle.

If there was a God, then he was a cruel and arbitrary prankster.

Would the baby be normal after what had happened?

Was the child going to have all its faculties, its normal features?

No reason why not, Nessim assured her.

Was there any chance the hospital was mistaken?

Nessim shook his head.

They would run tests. They would monitor the situation closely. But the important thing was for her to recover, regain her strength, exercise, eat well, sleep and then consider what had to be done.

Coded words for legalizing the situation. Marrying, in other words.

Was that the solution?

Poor Nick.

He had no idea what he had got himself into.

They took the plaster off her arm, changed her dressings and helped her wash herself. She shook her helpers off, insisting she would dress herself, but she had underestimated the difficulties, and the time it would take. All in all, it took an hour. Her arm hurt badly. A good deal of flesh had been torn off the upper left portion, exposing the triceps. A blood vessel had been severed – hence the sudden and heavy loss of blood. It was healing nicely now, but she still had to grit her teeth against the pulsating ache. Eventually Reem walked out of the hospital unaided on Saturday morning, while it was still early, still fresh, dew still on the grass.

They needed the bed, she knew. They were expecting another flood of casualties.

The guns had been going at it all night in the mountains to the south, somewhere in the vicinity of Souk al-Gharb, according to the radios. The Syrians were providing supporting fire for a combined force of Druze, Palestinians, Kurds and Lebanese leftists – an army of the dispossessed – advancing on the ridge. According to the radio stations, el-Hami had been up there the day before for a briefing on the defences held by Lebanese Forces, Phalangist and Christian army units, notably two ranger battalions. Reem knew Nick would have passed that way, and she had lain awake at night, worrying about him at every roll and thud of artillery fire.

Nessim drove her home.

The bright sunlight gave her a headache and the movement, coupled with car fumes, made her feel sick. What a relief it was to walk into the dim foyer of the Daouk building and lean against the wall for a moment, resting while Salwa and Nessim carried in her few belongings and brought down the lift.

She thanked Dr Nessim for his kindness.

She shut her eyes while the lift carried her up to her floor.

Salwa had bought food and prepared breakfast, setting plates and cups on the dining table: *zaatar* and olives, fresh bread and cheese, the coffee already prepared.

Everything had been cleaned and dusted.

The family stared at her out of their frames.

Michael.

Her parents, holding hands at Shikka, smiling.

Her sisters, serious in their high school graduation gowns.

They welcomed her back. Are you all happy to see me back home? I've missed you all, my dears.

I very nearly joined you.

Be patient.

Reem asked Salwa to help her slide open the door to the balcony. She thanked her for the food, invited her – no, insisted – that she stay for breakfast, and when she finally left, Reem went out and tied the yellow towel in place. It took longer with one hand.

She was exhausted. Just getting home had involved enormous effort. She was shocked at how weak and easily tired she had become. Her left arm, pinned across her chest, ached and itched by turns. There was no running water, and no power. All the windows and doors were open to the street to catch any sea breeze, and the curtains and blinds drawn to shield the rooms from the neighbours.

Never mind about the water and power.

Reem double-locked the front door, put up the chain. She disconnected the telephone in the hall and went into the bedroom, kicking off her shoes, painstakingly removing her blouse and skirt, and lay down on her back.

She listened to the familiar sounds of home. The car horns, the cries of the hawkers flogging their fruit and vegetables, the gruff voices of the Daouk twins who ran the grocery on the ground floor, the distant gunfire, the muezzin calling the faithful to prayer.

It was good to be home.

She was going to miss it when the time came.

The Ustaz would respond sooner or later. She could wait.

Reem closed her eyes and slept.

*

The fourth car from the corner, an elderly green Peugeot, showed rinds of red rust along the edges of the door panels. It was very dusty. It carried the red plates of a registered taxi, but the plates themselves were so filthy that the numbers were indecipherable. In short, typical of west Beirut cars, probably the property of a teacher or mid-level civil servant, and second hand at that. Reem walked past twice, making doubly sure. Identification was always in triplicate, in this case a copy of *an-Nahar*, a battered straw hat and a toy dog.

She watched the car from a chemist's shop for several minutes.

Her final approach was from across the street, a diagonal half-run, a glance right and left and right again and opening the back door behind the driver. She pulled it shut behind her.

A stench of stale cigarettes and a cacophony of Egyptian popular music.

Her arm throbbed, unused to the movement.

The driver turned off the tape deck.

He was young, shaggy-haired and aggressive. He pushed into the traffic, moving fast, cutting in whenever he could, mounting the pavement and even the central reservation, smacking the horn continuously.

They moved at speed, south along the Corniche, past the university, the Riviera Hotel, Bain Militaire, the Raouche fish restaurants.

Reem watched the mirrors.

A motorcyclist kept a steady distance behind them of about sixty metres. He made no effort to hide. He carried a passenger. Both were male, both wore T-shirts and both wore helmets that covered their faces. The machine was high off the road, one of those off-road bikes, good for moving in bursts of speed through traffic jams. Good, too, for taking a shot through a car's rear window. Plenty of height for the shooter.

She turned round in her seat, looking past the straw hat, the toy dog and the newspaper through the grimy glass.

'Ours,' the driver said.

Reem's eyes met his.

He winked at her.

'It's okay. They're ours.'

The Ustaz looked straight ahead, across the track. 'It still hurts.'

It was more observation than question. There was a tension in him, a physical alertness. Part of his mind seemed to scan his surroundings, to test even the air they breathed.

'Yes,' she said. 'It does hurt, more so when I'm tired.'

A gecko flitted between her feet, darting into a crack in the stone.

He frowned. 'Any feeling in your fingers?'

'Coming back. Slow, but—'

'You will need two hands.'

'I know I will.'

'They're getting close,' the Ustaz said. 'It's become something of a race.'

'Khaled was one of ours?'

The Ustaz nodded.

So she was right. He had been party, too. He had infiltrated the UN apparatus and had provided the Ustaz with Nick's personal details. Khaled had shadowed Nick from the start, watching him at close hand, assessing his usefulness, drinking with him, sharing intimacies. Nick was never a spy, not really, or the Ustaz would never have given Reem's relationship with the Briton his blessing.

Khaled had been the stalking horse.

Now he was dead, and she had very nearly been, too.

Dalia was another – innocent – casualty.

One of how many – seventeen dead and twenty-four wounded?

The toll had been reported as much higher, but had been scaled back when those reported missing and feared dead had turned up unscathed.

The Ustaz said, 'If it had been half an hour earlier they would have got me, too. Which was the aim of the exercise. I was the target, Reem. Maybe you too. Maybe el-Hami hoped he could get us both at the same time.'

'How long do we have?'

The Ustaz raised his eyebrows. 'God knows. He'll try again. He has to.'

'I'm holding you up, aren't I? I'm putting you all in greater danger with this delay. The longer you wait, the more dangerous it is for all of us. I'm jeopardizing the operation. Perhaps I should stand aside, let someone take the job.'

Say yes. Please.

Decide. Give me a way out.

For the child.

'No.'

No was not what she wanted to hear.

'Tell me the truth, Uncle Faiz.'

'I never lie to you, Reem. If I can't tell you the truth for whatever reason, then I don't say anything. You know that by now. I'm prepared to give it two weeks. At the end of that he'll be more difficult to reach. He will be president and will have the full protection of the state. He will move less, and spend more time in the bunkers under Baabda presidential palace. It will become that much harder to accomplish.'

She said, 'I don't know if I'll be ready in two weeks.'

'Rest. Get better. Eat properly. Sleep. Get your strength back. Do your physiotherapy. Let me do your thinking and worrying for you.' He turned towards her. 'Are you sure – absolutely certain – you still want this?'

Reem had never been more unsure of anything. She did worry, of course she did, all the time. She was not worried whether she would not be ready, but that she would be.

But she nodded, looking down at her feet, not meeting his eyes.

She meant no, and she said yes.

Perhaps she would feel differently when she was fully rested.

He said, 'You have choices.'

'I know.'

Instinctively her right hand went to her belly.

'If you're in any doubt . . .'

Doubt?

She doubted everything. The bombing had shaken her resolve. She had new reasons to want to continue living. Three, to be precise. One was Nick, the second the unasked-for spark of life in her womb. The third was that she had been so close to death, a hairline from oblivion. Looking it in the face she realized for the first time how much every fibre in her being wanted to live, and how powerful that urge was. Despite herself.

Reem said nothing to the Ustaz about her pregnancy.

Like her Uncle Faiz, she could not lie effectively without him seeing through her attempts at dissembling. They knew each other too well.

But she could stay silent.

The driver had taken her to the wreck of the national sports stadium and left her there. It looked like a fortress wrecked by besiegers, its outer walls holed and sliced through by artillery fire.

There were two checkpoints, one PSP and one Amal, en route.

Once at the sports ground, the driver had stopped long enough to let Reem out, then reversed, turned around, and sped back towards the capital, the taxi's tyres spinning, kicking up dust. Reem walked through what was left of the main gate to the athletics track just as the motorcycle drew up behind her. She did not look back at it.

The Ustaz sat alone on the crumbling terraces, about halfway up, on the far side. She waited for him to come down to her. She did not have the strength or stamina to climb up to him.

They sat on massive blocks of masonry pleasantly warm from the afternoon sun's lingering rays. The motorcyclist and his passenger left the bike outside and approached across the track on foot and then separated. They had taken off their helmets. They took their places high up at opposite ends.

'Who are they?'

'Our guardian angels. Our protection. From now on they will always be around until this thing is over.'

The sun was going down, the light turning gold on the athletics track, now a sea of rubble.

One heavily built man was running around the section left intact and mostly clear of broken chairs, bricks and concrete. He ran backwards and forwards, skirting the debris. He wore a baggy sweatshirt and pants.

'Is he someone you know?'

'Your escort,' the Ustaz said. 'He needs the exercise, as you can see. He will take you home when we're finished. His name is Otman.'

'I want to thank you. For all your help at the hospital. The food, the private room.'

'Nothing. My duty.'

He still did not look at her.

'Nicholas Lorimer has gone south,' Reem said. 'Something about four kidnappings by the South Lebanon Army.'

'What will you do about him?'

'Do?'

For a nasty moment Reem had the idea that the Ustaz knew about their afternoon of love-making.

Surely not, not in the east.

But he meant in the longer term, ahead of the operation.

'Do I have to decide now?'

'How long will Lorimer be away?'

'A few days. Back on Monday, he said. Maybe Tuesday.'

The runner had stopped directly below them. He started doing press-ups – rather half-heartedly, Reem thought.

'I think you do have to decide,' the Ustaz said. Now he turned to her, looking at her properly. 'The sooner the better – for both of you. How do you feel about that?'

Reem thought the answer must be written all over her face.

She could not help it.

'He must have an idea – more than an idea – of what you're up to.'

'Why should he?'

'Your driving his Land-Rover and then the hired car, your enthusiasm for the eastern sector, the photographs you took of el-Hami at Kaslik and Karantina. First Khaled dies. Then there's an attack on your library, with the newspapers suggesting the target was the man they call the Ustaz. He must have figured it out by now.'

The Ustaz was right, of course.

Reem just didn't want to admit it.

'He hasn't said anything.'

'I wonder why, Reem. My guess is he doesn't want to face it, not until he is forced to do so. Maybe he thinks he can win you over. Has he asked you to marry him?'

She did not answer, but she knew her silence was affirmation.

'Let's walk a little,' he said gently. 'Do you mind?'

The Ustaz helped her up. She leaned on his arm.

'I'd like to,' she said. 'They tell me walking is good for me.'

Reem knew the Ustaz needed to move because he was worried about explosives. About snipers. About directional microphones. He would have had both the road and the stadium thoroughly cleared before their arrival, but he could not allow himself to become too confident.

She told him she would go north, lie low, bury herself in village life.

For two weeks or so of convalescence.

He approved.

'When we meet again,' the Ustaz told her, 'I will show you the weapon we have fashioned for you, the one you will use when the day comes. It is very special. You will see. Then you will make your final decision. Not before.'

TWENTY-EIGHT

Nick pressed himself down.

Four mortar rounds fired in swift succession, exploding up and down the road, smashed into the trees and undergrowth on either side.

Leaves and twigs rained down.

It felt very personal.

The car, he thought, must be a target.

'Come on.'

He waited for a break in the firing, then ran along the ditch, bent over, to put distance between himself and the taxi.

Nick could smell the explosive, the flinty stench of smouldering undergrowth.

Neither Elias nor Ali followed his example. They too were in the ditch, but right below the car, its doors still wide open. They were reluctant to leave the Volvo, as if it might in some way provide them with shelter or a means of escape. But if there were spotters calling in the mortar bombs, Nick thought, then they were in the wrong place. Whoever was out there, shooting at the road, might make the taxi the aiming point.

He beckoned to them, but they took no notice.

He heard the next outgoing – a popping sound as the mortar crews tugged the lanyards on their weapons, the firing pins striking the mortar bombs and the projectiles shooting up out of each tube in swift succession – and gave up trying.

He lay flat.

The next salvo fell much closer.

Each detonation blotted out all sensation, all thought. It was like a massive hammer striking granite. The ground jumped and shuddered under the blow. Smoke, oily and dark grey, rose lazily from the point of impact. It was not like an artillery shellburst at all. The crash of the detonation was a dull thud. The cloud of smoke and dirt was dense, oily, squat – expanding lazily like a fat mushroom.

The killing ground of a mortar bomb is circular. There is no hiding from it. It plummets vertically. Walls, ditches, trees are no protection. These were 82 mm rounds, with a killing radius of 150 metres or so.

The next one was well within that.

It was the third of another salvo of four. The mortar crews walked the rounds down the road towards Nick and his companions, from the direction in which they had been headed, left to right. The first on their side of the road, the second on the far side, among the eucalyptus trees, the third right slap bang in the centre of the road, sending up a huge cloud of reddish-brown dust and acrid grey smoke.

The fourth burst in the ditch alongside the three men.

Jesus. They must have seen us.

Nick saw the impact. He was curled up against the red earth, clawing into it. If he could have buried himself in it, he would have. His face was turned to the right, his eyes open. He saw the flash of light, felt the blast wave, watched the ditch evaporate and both saw and heard something black and jagged sweep over his head with a high-pitched whizzing noise. He was struck by flying debris; stones, earth, bark, wood splinters.

He cowered down, eyes squeezed shut.

Silence.

He counted. One. Two.

Three.

The reply was not long in coming. The mortar crews somewhere in the hills behind him had not gone unnoticed.

Nick reached ten when artillery opened up. Nick assumed

it was the other side, trying to locate the mortars and silence them.

First, the outgoing. A series of heavy barks.

The shells tumbled end over end. As they closed in they made a sound overhead somewhere between a rattle, a shuffle and someone loudly clearing his throat.

They seemed very low, as if just the above the trees.

The shells burst perhaps 400 metres to their rear.

Several enormous explosions, so close they formed an inseparable roar.

Nick cringed. He could not help himself. He put his hands over his ears. He bit down so hard that his jaw ached.

He knew artillery shells throw forward, the smoke curling away in the direction of the fire. They were safe where they were if they stayed down – unless the gunners shortened their range, walked the barrage back.

They were between the two sides.

He raised his head very slightly and turned, looking back, over to his left.

Ali was lying on his back, smoking a cigarette. He seemed quite unconcerned. He gave Nick an insouciant wave, and grinned, showing his white teeth. He made a gesture, a circular flick of the right hand, thumb and forefinger extended. Meaning, 'How goes it, Nick? Enjoying yourself?'

After twelve minutes or so, the firing stopped.

Except for a long burst from a machine-gun somewhere up ahead, a 12.7 mm, Nick guessed, and then closer the sharp double crack of a Kalashnikov rifle on single fire.

They waited another five minutes in the ditch, the hands on Nick's watch crawling round with agonizing slowness.

In his mind's eye, Nick saw Reem's face. Her walk. Her smile. He reminded himself he was a father, or was soon to become one.

She was going to have a child. His.

All it took was an afternoon and a moment's passion, and three lives would be forever altered.

For a couple of hours he had been truly, gloriously happy, the war forgotten, the United Nations forgotten, the futile and frustrating job forgotten.

What the hell did he think he was doing out here, getting shot at?

How could he be so bloody stupid? He missed her. He had a reason to live now. He wanted above all to be with her again in the calm of his Ain Saadeh bedroom. She would be back as her old self soon enough. The wound would mend. Did he love her? Yes, sure he did. Could he doubt it?

But was it enough, though? They were so very different. There was so much he did not know.

They would marry. There was no point in thinking about it. It was never a matter of whether he wanted to, or whether he was ready. It just had to be.

Uncle Faiz would have to agree – even if he was the elusive Ustaz.

What was the alternative? A backstreet abortion?

Out of the question.

Trouble was, he really did know so little about her.

Once back in the car, Nick accepted a cigarette from Ali.

It was one thing to have radical views. He could handle that. But that strange behaviour at Kaslik and Karantina was another thing entirely – the snapshots, her fascination for his vehicle. What did it all add up to? An activist, certainly, but was she the kind of person the likes of Dacre would want to know about, the kind el-Hami would like to get his hands on?

What was she up to?

What had she been trying to achieve? Whatever it was, her enemies had reached out to Khaled and then her.

*

They were all covered in red dust, but he was the filthiest, smeared with it from head to toe. It was in his hair, his ears, all over his face. Both his trousers and T-shirt seemed to have been dyed in terracotta. His hands were ingrained with dirt, his fingernails black from digging into the ground. He had never been so frightened, not even on the ferry from Larnaca.

Elias offered him a light, cupping his lighter with both hands. Nick nodded his thanks as he ducked his head towards the flame. He tried to hide the fact that both his hands were still shaking.

They crossed the bridge on foot at noon. The sunlight was particularly harsh. The heat had drained the world of all colour. Ali stood among the Druze fighters and watched his passengers walk away south across the causeway, Nick leading. His shirt stuck to his back. His hair was stiff with a mixture of dirt and sweat.

Thorns snagged his trousers. Cicadas and crickets rasped loudly in the spiky grass. Grasshoppers sprang out of his way. White butterflies danced around him.

Both men were out in the open, visible to both sides.

Easy targets.

They trudged towards a checkpoint, a tin hut and a gate manned by sullen members of the South Lebanon Army, Israel's militia proxies, officered largely by Maronite rightists and its ranks filled mostly by reluctant Shi'ite Muslims. The militia's commanding officer was a renegade Lebanese army officer, who would face charges of desertion and possibly treason if he ever made the mistake of pitching up in west Beirut.

Above the hut a ragged Lebanese national flag drooped from a pole.

A black Mercedes awaited them, a vast S-class saloon fit for a cabinet minister, which Elias observed had probably been stolen in Beirut to order and shipped south by the car-stealing mafia that organized such matters. It had no plates. The driver was a tall young man in a striped T-shirt, prematurely balding, who introduced himself as Michael. He was supposed to be the UN driver for the area, but the first thing Nick noted as he settled in the leather front seat was a 9 mm Beretta in the open glovebox.

'For my personal protection,' Michael said.

It was his own car, he told them.

They passed a Shi'ite village a few minutes later, and Michael sneered at the sight.

'Dirty people,' he said, turning to Nick. 'Very dirty people.'

Nick said, 'I'd be dirty too if I was that poor.'

There it was. The bigotry that lay at the heart of the conflict was right there in the contempt written across Michael's face, the huge air-conditioned car with its leather seats, the automatic pistol, Michael's clean jeans, his Ray-Bans and cowboy boots, the dismal houses around the stagnant pond.

No electricity, no running water. No store. No school.

Dirty?

Children, goats and chickens meandered around in the mud.

Women in black – mourning for their war dead – washed clothes in the same grey, frothy ooze, slapping the clothes on rocks.

Nick's liberal instincts boiled to the surface, but he kept his tone light.

'Isn't it true that if a village inside the occupation zone doesn't give up its menfolk for service in the SLA, then they don't get power, water or a village school?'

Elias tapped Nick's shoulder. Meaning, leave it.

Nick took no notice. 'Isn't it also true that in those villages that refuse to set up a council of Israeli-appointed members to run things, the same thing happens? They're effectively boycotted and have a dusk-to-dawn curfew imposed on them – unable to trade, to send their kids to school, to sell produce in the local market, to travel to Israel or indeed to Beirut, for work? Isn't it also true that the SLA is the only real source of employment?'

Silence.

They bought chicken and garlic sandwiches at a roadside stall.

Michael would not look at Nick. His mouth was full. He pretended not to hear.

'Of all the communities, the Shi'ites received the least investment, whether from their own landowners or the state. They welcomed the Palestinians as liberators, but by the time of the Israeli incusions in the 1970s and the invasion of 1982, they were fed up with the predations of corrupt commanders in the PLO's "state within a state".'

Elias was handing out fizzy orange drink in cardboard cups.

He shook his head at Nick. 'Drop it, Nick.'

Nick was not going to drop it.

'Thanks to the likes of Ariel Sharon, the Israelis squandered the opportunity to gain allies in their conquest of Arab land. Instead, the Shi'ites were arrested, tortured and kicked around. Many were locked up without trial. One day, with a little help, they'll boot the SLA and Israel out of here.'

Michael gave no sign of having heard a single word. He wiped his hands on a paper napkin, threw it aside and sauntered back to the car.

Elias shook his head. 'Michael is a Phalangist with connections.'

'Fuck his connections.'

He had made a stand, but at what cost to himself and others? It was childish. Stupid. Why did he feel compelled to do it? He didn't really know.

They were on their way to the village where the abductions had taken place when they came across half a dozen armed men standing by the side of the road. Hardly unusual, almost commonplace. As they approached, one gunman stepped into the road in front of them and raised his hand. He carried an automatic rifle under one arm like a member of the English landed gentry out on a day's rough shooting.

Michael slowed.

'Who are they?'

They wore no badges. Elias, sitting in the back, leaned forward and peered between the front seats through the dusty wind-screen. He shrugged. He did not know. The gunmen on either side of the road had unslung their AK-47s. They pointed their weapons at the Mercedes. They wore brown fatigues. Some were bearded. They looked as if they were living rough. To Nick they could have been SLA, Amal – pretty well anyone.

Nick said, 'Keep going, Michael. Go round him.'

But Michael ignored Nick and stopped. He lowered his window.

There was a swift, urgent exchange.

'We have to get out,' Elias said. He seemed resigned to it. Elias seemed to think that if a man had a gun and was pointing it at him, it was foolhardy to try to argue. Michael had already opened the driver's door and started to climb out. Was Nick imagining it, or did Michael know these people? A gunman leaned in, looked around, and found the pistol.

'Out, out,' the leader said, gesturing with his rifle. Nick noticed he had a gold chain around his neck.

The leader pushed Michael's Beretta into his own waistband.

Elias obeyed. Nick followed, reluctantly.

They stood at the side of the road. Two gunmen searched the vehicle. The rest crowded round while their chief – a young man, unshaven, with an Armalite rifle slung from one shoulder – examined their documents.

He looked at Nick. It was a frankly curious stare. His skin was darkened and roughened by the sun and constant exposure to the weather. His hair was dark brown and very curly. His eyes were a light grey, startling in such a weathered complexion of walnut.

They were about the same age, Nick thought.

'English,' Nick said. 'United Nations.'

Elias was looking worried.

255

'No,' the leader said at last in heavily accented English. 'English, yes. United Nations . . .' He spat, turning his head to one side. 'No United Nations. Spy. English spy.'

The young man barked out an order.

The muzzle of a Kalashnikov rifle was jammed into the small of Nick's back and he was driven forward. He could not help himself.

His arms were grabbed, and he was forced to put his hands on his head.

'Walk.'

The leader tossed aside the UN cards and Nick's passport. Out of the corner of his eye, Nick saw them land in the field.

Elias was alongside. They were trudging across a ploughed field. The soil was very dry and stony. The commander led, the rest followed, but Nick was prevented from looking back to see what had happened to Michael.

'What the hell is happening, Elias?'

Immediately someone struck Nick a glancing blow in the ribs, using a rifle butt. Nick stumbled, but managed to right himself and keep going.

'Shut the fuck up,' said one gunman.

They were out of sight of the road.

Elias and Nick were pushed into the ditch at the side of the field.

The second ditch in a day.

The gunmen stood around them in a half-circle, looking down at them.

The commander said, 'Lie down.'

Elias began to lower himself to the ground, but Nick stopped him, putting a hand out and grabbing his arm.

'No, Elias,' Nick said. 'Don't.'

'I said lie down.' The commander was shouting. He cocked his rifle and pointed it at Nick's face, the muzzle an inch from his nose.

Nick shouted back.

'No.'

He squared his shoulders and straightened himself up. He had this strange feeling that if they sat, squatted or lay down in any form whatsoever – if they gave the slightest sign that they were willing to submit, to abase themselves – they would be shot outright, in the back. If he was wrong, he told himself, and if they were going to shoot him anyway, he would die standing up, on his feet, looking the bastards in the face.

'Go ahead,' Nick said. 'Shoot.'

He hardly believed they were his words. Elias had fallen to his knees. He was sobbing out prayers for his wife and his three children.

Nick raised his chin.

Go on, cunts. Do it.

Michael's remark about the 'dirty' villagers had unleashed something in Nick. It was like a stopper pulled out of a bottle containing weeks of pent-up anger and frustration.

Elias had shut his eyes, his lips moving.

The commander jumped down into the trench. Nick could smell him, a nauseatingly sweet stench of body odour, cologne and cigarettes. He felt the Armalite's cold muzzle nudge his right ear, then settle against the bone just behind it.

Nick's heart beat so fast he felt sure it was going to break right out of his chest. Sweat dripped off the end of his nose. It ran cold down his neck. Droplets hung in his eyelashes. When he blinked the salty water stung his eyes.

He understood then that fear and pain are not the same.

He understood, too, that fear will make a man kill.

He needed a drink of water.

He needed to pee.

Nick turned his head. Whatever happened, he was determined to keep his eyes on the commander's angry face.

TWENTY-NINE

They made a great fuss of her.

Though she would never have admitted it, Reem enjoyed every moment. Aunt Sohad and her daughters gave her the best room and the most comfortable bed. They would not take no for an answer. They insisted. They commanded. They refused to listen to Reem's protests. They ran a hot bath for her. They gave her the only mosquito net said to have no tears or holes. They brought her more food and drink than she could possibly have consumed. They set up a chaise longue on the terrace for her. Best of all they sat with her, kept her company. Secretly, Reem was delighted to be the centre of such solicitous care. She felt loved, needed, and the attention they gave her seemed to satisfy a thirst, a need, that she was scarcely aware of back in Beirut.

After two or three days the intensity of the household's concern began to wear off, to everyone's relief, including Reem's. The hot days of early summer developed into a pleasantly normal routine. Reem was not aware of it, not to start with, but there were obvious improvements almost at once, a clear acceleration in her recovery. Her colour returned. Her skin's healthy look was restored. Her hair regained its gloss. She smiled more. The pain lessened. She ate and slept better. She gained weight. She had dreams, not nightmares.

Reem began to relax.

The days slipped by all too quickly, merging into one another. Could not all life be like this?

It could. Possibly it was. Until the neighbourhood *abadai* put on a uniform and was given a rifle and decided he could push people around in the name of this dogma or that, with a foreign power or a local dictator to back him up with a few dollars and a box of ammunition every week.

At the edge of the village there was the evidence. Two houses had been demolished by the Phalangists in the early stages of the war because their owners or residents resolutely opposed them.

One householder was bulldozed alive inside his home.

The day began with Reem walking a quarter of a mile to the village baker to fetch the flat loaves dressed in hot oil and *zaatar*. She could smell the oregano as she walked, a borrowed straw hat on the back of her head to protect her from the sun. She would stand in the queue at the stone building, enjoying the village slang and laughter, breathing in the smells. When she returned they would all sit out front on the porch, drinking coffee and eating a breakfast of dates, cream cheese, honey, figs and the crusty bread Reem had carried back in a plastic bag, the still warm *manaeesh* that she adored.

While the gates stood open, the house was open to all: the man who owned the garage on the corner and acted as a land agent would come over with the latest gossip of who was buying what plot of land; another neighbour, the village taxi driver Ya'oub, might drive Reem to the local shops to have her hair done or visit the dressmaker; or it might be the headmistress of the local school, an institution famed throughout the north for the number of scholarships its students won to university. Everyone would sit out on the terrace, drinking coffee and smoking. Social distinctions did not matter, neither class nor creed. A doctor in Arabic literature would have a lively conversation with the local handyman, a shepherd might argue with the local dentist. What united them was community, language.

Reem would draw her legs up under her and lean on her right elbow among the cushions, breathing in the warm air and the animated talk.

But as she got better, so her thoughts turned to the Ustaz and her task.

The stronger Reem was, the weaker her doubts.

That did not mean Nick was forgotten.

One particularly humid afternoon, Ya'oub took Reem into the town of Koura to the telecommunications building, where she made a telephone call to Beirut. Ya'oub had waited outside in his car. He said later she was gone a full half-hour, and that she made only one call. He did not know who it was she had called, but he insisted that she had spoken for no less than twenty-eight minutes to Beirut. He had it on the best authority.

He had driven Reem back home again, he said, deep in thought.

Not cheerful. Silent.

The truth was more prosaic. Reem had called Nick's United Nations office in Beirut. She called his direct line. It rang for ages. No one answered. She tried the number twice, without result. She called the same office again, using the general number, and had a long and confused conversation with the telex operator, an Armenian. From this she gathered that Nick was still in the south, and no, they had not heard anything, and did not know when he would be back, and no, sorry, m'mselle, there was no manager or responsible person she could speak to. They were at lunch.

She called his flat.

No one picked up. She left a brief message, but not her name.

'Nick. Are you okay?'

At least when he got home he would know she had thought of him, had called him. That she cared.

Ya'oub was right when he said Reem was preoccupied. Nick had been due back on Monday, Tuesday at the latest. It was now Saturday. Still, she told herself, there was no reason to panic. There was in all probability a very good reason for the delay. If

Nick's UN colleagues knew nothing – even a lowly telex operator
– it was surely good news.

When the sun moved over the roof and brought its direct heat to
bear on the front garden and the terrace, the occupants moved to
the rear, with a vine trellis overhead. They could look out at the
orchard of fig, watermelon, olive, lemon and date palm.

The Israelis were invariably the uninvited guests at noon – a
pair of F-16s would show themselves as glints of light and weave
parallel vapour trails in the cloudless sky, followed by two sonic
booms as the aircraft broke the sound barrier, turning out to sea,
leaving their daily calling card to all Lebanese, Syrians and
Palestinians.

'To show us,' Sohad said.

After lunch out there on a long trestle table covered with a
blue checked cloth – anyone who dropped in would be pressed
to accept their hospitality – Aunt Sohad would drink coffee and
retire to her bedroom for a siesta. If the curmudgeonly husband
Kerim was there too, for once, he would sit in his favourite
armchair in the main reception room, catching the air that came
in the open front doors and flowed around the high-ceilinged
room and out the high windows at the back. Within minutes he
too would be asleep, his snores rustling the newspaper that lay
open across his belly.

Reem, too, would sleep. She would creep in under her mosquito net and lie on the top of the bed, and dream.

The beauty of the house was its simplicity.

It was built of enormous blocks of yellow stone. The double
front doors were very tall. They opened onto the tiled reception
room. Its ceiling was two storeys high to help keep it as cool as
possible in these summer months. The bedrooms led straight off
the reception room. They too had tall, white-painted wooden
doors. There were four bedrooms, three of them en suite. At the
rear was a simple kitchen and bathroom extension. The windows

were tall, and had yellow shutters that were pulled shut as the sun turned through the sky.

Screening the terrace were tall rose bushes, habitat for tiny, bright-green tree frogs. A paved drive ran down to the high wrought-iron gates. Luxuriant grass grew on either side of the drive, and tall pines provided shade and a home for cicadas and crickets.

Potted plants of red and pink flowers lined the marble porch.

Bougainvillea tumbled its purple extravagance over fences and walls.

Aunt Sohad was up every morning at dawn, watering her garden and the orchard from the water tank on the roof that was regularly replenished by an electric pump connected to a communal well.

Kerim complained the house and its environs were primitive – particularly, no doubt, for a man of his stature. He was always talking about building a modern villa in its place. Aunt Sohad paid all this scant attention. The house and the land on which it stood were hers. Unusually, he had no say in the matter, and she poured scorn on his notions of how to live.

'Build your villa,' she told him. 'Go ahead. Build your concrete Christmas cake. By all means waste your money. Throw it away. Go on. But you won't do it here on my land. And don't expect me to live in your palace, because I never will.'

While the deadlock continued, Kerim preferred his bachelor penthouse in Tripoli and the company of his narghile-smoking business cronies. Which suited everyone concerned, not least Aunt Sohad.

Was this what all marriages were like? Reem wondered.

All romance and attentiveness for a few weeks, then the hard labour of bearing and rearing children, then the yawning gulf of indifference, a shrinking of affection?

Arab men always looked at other women, too.

Were Westerners the same? Did they play around, and consider it their right to do so? Was Nick like that? Was it like that for everybody?

She could not remember how her parents had lived together, no matter how hard she tried. Had they been happy? She had been too young. It was as if she had blotted out the past. Or perhaps the crime that had ended her family's lives so violently was such a catastrophic event that it had left precious little room for other memories.

Her bandages came off.

A German-trained doctor who ran a village clinic for local people was impressed.

'You're a lucky young woman,' he said. 'You've mended well, and there's no sign of any secondary infection.'

He refused payment.

Her left hand had come back to life. Reem could move the fingers. She could pick up a fork and lift food to her mouth. She could make her own bed.

She even played badminton with Maha and Hana on the front lawn, using her right hand, but even so her left arm ached.

It looked pretty awful. She would have to wear clothes with sleeves down to her elbow to hide the worst of it, or use a wrap.

When Aunt Sohad drove Reem and her daughters to the northern town of Zhgorta for lunch on the Sunday, Reem asked if she could try her hand at the wheel of the family car.

Her left arm felt stiff, and her left wrist hurt in manoeuvring around the mountain bends in the road. But she could do it.

'I didn't know you could drive, Reem,' said Aunt Sohad. 'Where did you learn?'

'Cyprus,' Reem said. 'I took my test during my English-language course.'

*

'Let me read your cup.'

Aunt Sohad and Reem were alone on the terrace. They sat next to each other on the comfortable swing seat.

Hana and Maha had gone to bed and were already asleep.

It was close to midnight. Reem had helped Aunt Sohad close the gates at the entrance to the drive.

They waited for the coffee grounds to settle in the saucer under the upended cup.

After a few minutes Aunt Sohad picked it up.

'Oh,' she said, turning the cup in her hands. 'Oh.'

'What is it?'

'I see a young man. Fair. Maybe a foreigner.' She looked up and winked at Reem. 'He likes you, Reem. But you have your back turned. You are pulled two ways.' Aunt Sohad paused, turning the cup again, peering into it, frowning. 'You have to decide which path to take. Head says one thing, heart another. The one is a long journey; the other is short. There is someone else. Older. In the shadows so I cannot make out his or her face. He or she is very serious, almost frightening. He watches. He says nothing. He is waiting. He will not interfere, but he waits for you.'

Aunt Sohad put the cup down.

'He protects you, the dark one, but I don't like him.'

Reem said, 'What else?'

'An animal. It has four legs but I can't make it out.'

'Go on.'

'It's silly. Take no notice.'

'You look upset, Aunt Sohad. What else did you see?'

'Nothing, child. It is not to be taken seriously. Come. It's late. Time we were both asleep.'

Lying in bed, Reem heard Aunt Sohad's radio.

It was the voice of the Egyptian cantatrice Asmahan. Reem

mouthed the lyrics silently to herself, lulling herself to sleep with a love song.

'Come quickly and help me
See what has happened to me
Because of your love.'

By Sunday she knew what she wanted to say to Nick.

It was a matter of how and when. She had to choose the right moment. It was not something to be said over the telephone. Or even in a letter.

Reem had to tell him face to face. In private. She rehearsed it again and again in her mind. She would tell him she loved him. She had missed him. She wanted to be with him. There had never been anyone else before Nick, and there would be no one else afterwards.

All that was true.

She dreamed about him.

But she would not marry him.

She could never leave Lebanon, and he could not stay.

You think you can, Nick, but it would be so wrong. You have your life ahead of you. There is so much you can do. You have so much to give the world. Don't squander it. You'll see I'm right. This place has no future, not for you.

And the child?

She was so sorry. It was a mistake. She was not pregnant after all. She had sought confirmation at her local clinic in Koura and the result had come back negative.

So very sorry, Nick.

But it is for the best. Really it is.

I am not going to have children. I have made up my mind. Not now. Not while there is a war. Not when everything is so uncertain, when we live from one moment to the next. I simply cannot think of relationships and raising a family.

She hated lying to him.

265

But it was for his sake.
It was the kindest way. It was the only way she knew of.
Would he believe her?
There was still no word from him.

THIRTY

The vehicle plunged off the road and bounced across the field straight towards them, trailing dust.

It stopped short, skidding to a halt, and briefly vanished in its own cloud of murk. When it reappeared, Nick identified a Willys Jeep, the original article, with a canvas roof, two whip aerials, a small tattered Lebanese flag and three men in uniform, two in front and another sitting in the back in a helmet and holding a rifle across his knees.

The chief thug turned away from his prisoners and trudged over to the new arrivals. A burly officer in fatigues, wearing a black beret and shades, sat in the front passenger seat. He nodded at Elias and Nick and appeared to ask a question. Something, Nick thought, along the lines of 'Who the hell are those people?' The chief goon answered at length. The officer listened. He took off his sunglasses and looked long and hard at the prisoners while the goon talked.

The officer cut the gunman short by raising a hand. The gesture was unmistakable. Stop. Enough. He replaced his shades. He gave an order. It was brief, even abrupt.

It was too far off for Nick to hear what was said.

The jeep leapt backwards, reversing fast, its wheels kicking up another storm. The driver turned it in a wide arc as its passengers held on with both hands. It lurched and rocked its way back the way it had come.

The militiaman sauntered back, each footstep kicking up a little puff of dust. He was in no hurry. He looked down, as if deep in thought.

Nick held his breath.

'*Yalla.*'

Let's go.

The commander waved his arm. He did not look at Nick or Elias.

His men shouldered their weapons and turned away.

Nick and Elias watched them go. Nick could scarcely believe it. He wanted to, but he thought it might be a trick.

When he was a dozen paces away, the commander turned round and called out.

'You – you can go. Don't come back, English. Next time . . .'

He drew a finger across his throat.

Point taken.

The gunmen moved on in extended order across the stubble, their curly-headed chief in the centre. Neither Elias nor Nick moved until they were out of sight.

Nick helped Elias out of the ditch. They started walking back the way they had come.

There was no sign of Michael or his Mercedes.

'We were in the wrong place at the wrong time, Mr Nick. That's all.'

'Maybe. But it was my fault for winding Michael up. I'm sorry. You were right, Elias. I should have listened. The bastard probably tipped them off. Told them to teach me a lesson, take me down a peg or two.'

'I don't think so.' Elias was trying to shake the dust off the lapels of his lightweight summer suit.

'Then what happened to him? He made no effort to stop them taking us away.'

'I think he knew he had to keep his mouth shut. Stay out of

trouble. They probably told him to leave, to forget what he'd seen and heard unless he wanted the same treatment.'

'I thought you said he had connections. What's the point of connections unless they're useful? The first thing you do when we get back to the office is take him off our list. No more payments. No more expenses. Not another penny of UN money. Okay?'

Elias shrugged.

'Okay?'

Elias was not happy. He said, 'You're the boss.'

'You think I'm being unfair?'

'You won't get anyone else down here with his access, his freedom of movement.'

'He's fired.'

'Okay.'

'Let's have another beer, then I'm going to shower and change and we'll have dinner. Tomorrow I'm going back to that village.'

'Did you hear what they said?'

'You don't have to come, Elias.'

They had found their papers and then walked for an hour. A farmer offered them a lift in the back of his battered Datsun pickup to the nearest village – not unlike the place Michael had described as 'dirty'. They finally reached Jezzine, a pretty Christian town set among jagged peaks, and found a hotel that was open. They seemed to be the only guests, although the bar and dining room were crowded at mealtimes with men in suits and jackets – local businessmen and town councillors, Elias said. The town lay just outside the Israeli occupation zone, but was still under its influence. On their way into town they saw Israeli armoured personnel carriers parked in the main square, next to the church.

In the hotel, everyone seemed to be listening to the radio. Voices from transistor sets dominated the public rooms and could be heard through the thin walls separating the bedrooms. The news was impossible to escape. Several stations were reporting the inter-party negotiations had broken down and el-Hami had issued a bellicose statement saying he would take the presidency come what may.

Next week, he said.

Sitting in the bar, covered with dirt, their hair matted, Nick and Elias had attracted a good deal of curious looks from customers and staff.

'How are you going to get there – to the village?'

'I'll hire a taxi. I'll go very early – long before those thugs have woken up. I'll be back in time to join you for breakfast.'

'And if you're caught?'

'I won't be.'

'Who will interpret?'

'I'll find someone.'

'Don't.'

'Something is going on there and it's my job to find out what it is.'

'Don't, Mr Nick. Please. If you go, I'll have to go, too.'

'I didn't ask you, Elias. I don't expect you to. You have a family. I'd rather you didn't come, frankly. I'd feel responsible.'

Later, lying on a lumpy mattress under a sheet and looking at the half-moon out of the window, Nick wondered if he was doing the right thing, after all. Perhaps he was being foolish. Stubborn. Geneva would not expect it of him. They would be horrified if they learned of the risks he was planning to take. What would Reem say? She ran risks herself. She was in no position to criticize. She was a participant, not an observer.

Nick's bag had been in the Mercedes with his spare set of clean clothes, his toilet kit, a paperback, his Walkman and three of his favourite cassettes. He had cleaned himself as best he could with the tiny bar of soap in the hotel bathroom, and he had shaken out his clothes and aired them by putting them on the window ledge. He had washed his underpants and socks in the handbasin and hung them on the radiator.

The evening meal of *shish taouk* and a bottle of white wine had helped him unwind.

He asked reception for a wake-up call.

Nick told himself he would sleep on it.

He would decide in the morning.

He was woken at six sharp. Nick lay in bed for a few minutes, then rolled out. He showered quickly, dressed, and went down to reception. He was about to ask the desk clerk to find him a taxi when he heard his name. He turned to see two men approaching.

'No breakfast, Mr Lorimer?'

They had been waiting. They got up out of their chairs in the foyer and came up to him. The first, a stocky man in his shirt-sleeves with dark, Mediterranean features, showed his ID.

He was Ersal, a UN liaison officer in the south. A Turkish national.

His tall, blond colleague introduced himself as Captain Olson, a Norwegian army officer and UNIFIL peacekeeper in a camou-flage uniform, Glock pistol in a holster at his waist.

They shook hands.

'We heard you had a spot of bother yesterday,' Ersal said. 'If you're still interested in that village, we thought we'd come with you. Captain Olson has brought some of his people along so I don't think we'll have any problems on the way.'

Over coffee in the otherwise deserted dining room, Ersal explained.

Nick's tormentor of the previous day was notorious. A ren-egade Druze, he was an intelligence officer in the SLA. His favourite activity was harassing the Norwegian peacekeeping battalion in the area, shooting up their patrols, sniping at their sentries, driving his car at Norwegian troops on foot, and – it was rumoured but never proven – trying to abduct Lebanese who lived in the battalion area.

'Actually,' Ersal said, 'I quite admire him. He's a one-man army. He gives us more trouble than the rest of the SLA put together. He has an excellent informer network, and seems to know everyone.'

'You'll forgive me if I don't share your high opinion of him.'

Both Ersal and Olson laughed.

'He was going to shoot the two of us.'

Ersal's expression changed. He looked very serious. 'Oh, yes. He might well have. He would have used the occasion as a training exercise by getting one of his recruits to do it. That's how he works. But that was his commanding officer in the Jeep who called a halt to his game. You were a foreigner, a Westerner and a UN official. That adds up to a lot of heat if you'd been whacked. Olson called the major and told him your blood would be on his hands if anything happened to you. It was your driver who went straight to the Norwegian battalion headquarters and got things moving. Then he went on to the UNIFIL headquarters at Naqoura. Michael. Isn't that his name?'

Nick nodded.

He felt ashamed. He had misjudged the man. Michael might be unpleasant, a religious bigot, and his personal politics might be anathema, his possession of a pistol inappropriate for anyone claiming to work for the United Nations, but he was certainly not a party to what had happened.

On the contrary.

He had done the only sensible thing he could in the circumstances, which was a lot more than Nick could say about himself.

It was no village. There were half a dozen double-storey homes along a road. That was all. It was a recent housing development, and it was incomplete. Some buildings still lacked plaster and paint. The gardens were patches of bare earth and weed.

It had been that way for more than a decade, Olson said.

There was no shop. No school. No bus stop. There was a single overhead power line that drooped between lopsided poles.

There were no men here. Only women and children.

'You see? Up there? That's where they fired from.'

Fatima said she was thirty-seven, but she looked twice that. She wore black. She made coffee for her visitors and then carried out of the house framed photographs of her family members who had died. She showed them where the tank shell had gouged out part of a wall and balcony.

She too looked up the ridge, about 400 metres away. Nick had to look carefully to spot it. Just a row of sandbags above the skyline marked the outpost.

'They had a tank there. It had been there for about a week. We were sitting down to dinner . . .'

Fatima pointed to each child in turn.

The tank fired twice. It was more than enough.

Ali, fourteen, died outright as he sat at the table on the porch. His sister, Rima, seventeen, died on the way to hospital. And the youngest, Hussein – his body was pierced by no fewer than forty-seven flechettes.

Fatima had the post-mortem X-ray and brought it out of the house to show the visitors. The outline of the five-year-old was clear. So were his kidneys, lungs, liver and heart – all shot through with the steel darts, an anti-personnel weapon used by the occupation forces in the West Bank and Gaza as well as south Lebanon.

That was some weeks ago, when the weather was just warm enough to eat outside.

And the people next door, Ersal wanted to know, what had happened to them?

'They came in the night. Six SLA men. They took everyone of military age. The father, his brother-in-law and his two sons, aged sixteen and twenty-two.'

'Where are they now?'

'Khiam prison.'

Olson was scribbling in his notebook. The International Committee of the Red Cross would be asked to check the names.

'You know this for sure?'

Fatima did not know. It was conjecture. But that was where most of their menfolk were detained – without charge, without trial, subject to beatings, electrical torture. Indefinitely.

'And the mother,' Nick asked. 'Where is she?'

Fatima shrugged. She and her daughters had gone to stay with relatives.

'When did this happen?' Captain Olson was still writing.

'Last Friday.'

'Eight days ago?'

She nodded.

'Time?'

'When they always come for us. In the dark, before dawn.'

Nick said, 'Why do you think they killed your family and took your neighbours away?'

He offered Fatima a cigarette and took one himself.

'Because they don't want us here,' she said. 'The SLA threatened us, and when we did not move, they shot our children. We still did not move, so they took all the men. To punish us. To punish us for trying to keep what is ours. Because they want our land. They want all our land.'

At the flyblown UN peacekeeping headquarters in Naqoura, down on the coast and just to the north of the Israeli frontier, Ersal ushered Nick and Elias into the white Portakabin that served as his office. He pulled out a file and checked the names of the family members wounded by SLA/Israeli fire.

It all checked out.

Olson had taken his men back to their Norwegian base.

'One thing she didn't mention,' Ersal said, passing round Coca-Colas and cigarettes, 'was that the previous day a young woman drove her car through both SLA and Israeli checkpoints and blew herself up right outside an Israeli military headquarters near here. Six Israeli soldiers were killed, seventeen injured. Five Lebanese died, three of them SLA officers. Here – I've got her picture in the file.'

'So you're saying the attack on the village house was revenge.'

'Yeah – something like that,' Ersal said. 'Unofficial vengeance directed at a civilian target, and picked at random. It seemed like it at the time, but all the family ever got was a frosty apology from the Israelis – which we had to convey to the lady you met today.'

Nick took the photograph of the suicide bomber, a six-by-four glossy, copied from a newspaper.

The likeness was striking.

So young.

Those eyes. So like Reem's.

'What was she like?'

'They say she was only a kid, really. Nineteen. A university student. Top grades all the way through school. A Christian. Greek Orthodox. Good family. Professional people. There's this notion in the West that suicide bombers are all poor, uneducated Muslims. It simply isn't true.'

Nick put the Coke down. He felt light-headed, slightly nauseous.

'You okay?' Elias was looking at him, an expression of concern on his face.

Ersal said, 'At the time I remember people saying it was the first major suicide attack organized by the man they call the Ustaz. If he exists. No one I know has ever seen him. Rumour has it he recruits suicide bombers, pays for their studies, trains them up and selects only the best of the crop. He uses Christians and Muslims – from nationalist and leftist circles. There used to be posters offering $100,000 for information leading to his arrest or death. Most have since been pulled down.'

Elias had taken the young woman's photograph and was looking at it.

'Such a waste,' he said, handing the picture back to Ersal.

Nick said, 'Is that what you think, too?'

Ersal sighed. 'That's a tough one, Nick. Personally? Let's say I think it's a strategic error. It only justifies everything the other side does – it gives them carte blanche to attack civilian targets, to destroy civil institutions. It would be that much harder for them to justify their war on Lebanese and Palestinian civilians if it wasn't for the excuse of suicide attacks. But there's another side to it, equally important. Emotion.'

Elias said, 'Emotion – meaning what?'

'Put it this way. The occupier has everything. He controls the skies. He has so-called smart bombs. He has a superpower that backs him up whatever he does. He is ruthless. He will use a helicopter gunship and a US-made Hellfire anti-tank missile to hit a clearly marked ambulance full of children. Western media show no interest. To them, you are a terrorist. You have nothing. You have only your brain, your bare hands, and a few chemicals you can buy in a shop. And your anger. You try to show everyone the enemy is not superhuman. He bleeds just like your kith and kin. That's what I mean by emotion. It's a matter of self-respect. It's a matter of dignity. You can't just lie down and let them fuck you over and over. So you do what you can. I don't approve of it, I don't like it, I can't excuse it – but I understand it. I even sympathize with it. That's my personal opinion.'

Ersal reached for another cigarette.

Elias turned to Nick and said, 'We have a word for it when we hear a suicide attack has taken place. From a child to a grand-mother, the immediate, instinctive response is the same. *Bistehlu*. They enemy has earned it. They brought it on themselves. They deserve it. *Bistehlu*.'

Nick got to his feet, edged past Elias, trying not to step on his feet.

It was like a panic attack. His face felt hot. He was sweating, and his heart was jumping all over the place.

'Going to get some air. Won't be a moment.'

276

'You okay?' Ersal asked.

'Sure. Don't worry – I'm fine.'

He was not fine. Nothing about him felt fine. Outside the sky was full of stars, so bright Nick could clearly make out the makeshift UN buildings, the sandbagged shelters, the big radio aerials, the barbed wire, the waves turning white as they broke on the shingle beach.

Nick flung his cigarette away.

It was obvious. Of course it was. He had known – for how long? Two weeks? Three? He just hadn't wanted to face it. Reem did not have to say anything. He had read the signs, but he had refused to believe them. He had not wanted to believe them. But he must.

He had to get back to Beirut.

THIRTY-ONE

Reem slid the photographs out of their frames.

She sat on the sofa in the sitting room and held up each print, turning it to catch the light. She pressed her lips to each figure, wiping the glossy paper with her sleeve before putting all the pictures away in a brown envelope. It was a ritual, and very private. There would be no other ceremony, certainly none that mattered as much as this. She carried the envelope into her bedroom and put it flat in the bottom of her overnight bag that lay open on her bed. It was the same cabin bag she had taken to Cyprus, still new-looking and paid for out of the expenses provided by the Ustaz.

Back in the living room, she placed the empty picture frames face down where they stood.

Goodbye.

Mama and Papa. Selena and May. The youngest, Michael.

She emptied her father's bottles into the sink.

I won't be long.

Reem carried out one last inspection. She was systematic, taking it a room at a time. Starting high with shelves and cupboards and working down to the parquet floor. No bills, no bank statements, no expired savings books, no receipts. She opened and shut drawers. No university records, no pay slips. No library cards. No letters, no diaries. Nothing under mattresses or hidden in pots or under a pillow. No car keys, no stray notes left in the pages of the books on the shelves.

Nothing to give anyone a name, a link with her or her family.

No trace. No carrion for the vultures that would descend on this place – afterwards.

I am the last to leave.

She packed three changes of clothing. Her prettiest dress, the yellow floral print with the flared skirt and tight bodice. Reem thought of it as her going-away dress. The one Nick had admired. Flat-heeled pink shoes; pretty yet sensible, and good for driving. A pair of navy slacks, two pairs of blue jeans, three blouses with sleeves, a favourite silk scarf (it took up no room, after all, and she could use it as a wrap to hide her scars); her make-up – the very minimum – and enough underwear. A pair of blue pyjamas. Another pair of pumps, black this time.

She had made sure there were no name tags.

Salwa would take whatever furniture she wanted.

The pretty English tea service – it probably was not worth anything – would go to Aunt Sohad.

It was Reem's way of saying thank you.

The family pictures, the clothes, the make-up, her little bits of faux bijoux, the real gold crucifix – all of it would go with her on her journey. Nothing of her life – nothing meaningful – would remain.

She looked round one last time. No expression. No tears.

Reem moved backwards to the front door, like a good infantry-man watching his rear.

She pulled the door shut. Locked it.

Reem crossed the landing. She pushed the button, and for the last time, she told herself, she listened to the old American-made lift shake and judder its way up to her floor.

The green metal door groaned open.

It was time.

She took a service taxi to the bus station, and after thirty-five minutes her battered blue bus, belching exhaust fumes, left for the Khalde crossroads south of the city. At Khalde she sat in the rear of another service taxi, headed east this time for Shtoura up in the hills, along the Damascus road. There was a great deal of military traffic en route. It slowed them down, not least because of the tailbacks at the checkpoints, which seemed more numerous than ever. The Syrians were making people get out of their cars and open their boots and their baggage for inspection. Men of military age were frisked. Standing at the side of the road during one such episode, Reem noted that units of Saiqa fighters, members of the Syrian Social Nationalist Party, and PSP gunmen were also on the move.

With the talks in disarray, the combatants in the Lebanese conflict all seemed to be shaping up for a major battle just in time for el-Hami's elevation to the presidency.

Just as the Ustaz had said, even if the timing was out.

At Shtoura they were waiting for her. It was cooler in the hill resort. People were eating lunch under the trees, soothed by the sound of the river that ran through the centre of town.

One man took her bag from her and tossed it in the boot of a four-wheel drive. Another opened the rear door for her.

No one said a word.

She dozed on the back seat for much of the way. From time to time she was aware of men's voices, a blur of uniforms, the outline of a rifle, a face peering in at the car. At some point one of the two men left, and only the driver remained.

It was nearly dusk by the time they descended to the Bekaa Valley.

The driver insisted Reem cover herself with a blanket while he drove through Baalbek. It was already hot, and the blanket was stifling. She had only a glimpse of the city's Roman ruins, the horse-drawn carriages waiting for the tourists who would never come, the posters of Khomeini, the banner across the main street pledging death and destruction to Israel, the tattered pre-war placards advertising the summer Baalbek festivals and, parked in neat rows in a ploughed field on the outskirts, Syrian BMP-1 armoured vehicles and artillery, the guns dug in and their long barrels in camouflage paint pointing like accusing fingers at the dying sun.

Pointing west.

There were no festivals nowadays.

How shabby and run down Baalbek had become.

No one asked her anything. No one asked her for her papers.

In the darkness she was sitting up again, the blanket flung aside, the vehicle rolling down a muddy dirt track between rows of conifers. It had rained sometime in the previous day or so. Everything looked so richly watered, so abundant. To her left was a low drystone wall. The driver slowed, and turned left, bumped over a cattle grid through an open farm gate set in the wall. They stopped in a field of lush grass. The only spectators were black and white cows, quietly chewing. The driver got out and walked back and closed the gate. When he opened his door, Reem breathed in the smell of damp grass and fresh cow droppings, farm smells delightful to any jaded city dweller. Ahead of them, on the far side of the field, she could make out a low white building, presumably the farmhouse.

The driver stopped the car before a low wooden footbridge, but he kept the engine running. He turned in his seat, smiled and nodded.

Neither of them said a word. Reem got out, hauled her bag out of the boot, slung it over her shoulder and set off for the bridge. She did not look back. She heard the car reverse and turn.

Reem seemed quite alone. Her footsteps on the wooden bridge sounded as loud as gunshots.

She followed a gravel path around the corner of the building. Whoever owned or had hired this place had made sure that any visitor's approach would be heard whether they wanted to be or not. The place looked deserted. It exuded a secretive, hidden air as if it was seldom occupied, but she noticed that a wooden stairway ran up the side of the building to a landing on the first floor. As she contemplated climbing up, a door opened. It was a stable door, in two halves. Whoever it was opened the top first, and looked out.

'Welcome. Come on up.'

He drew the bolt from the bottom half of the door and swung both halves open wide and stepped out onto the landing.

It was very dark.

The figure lit a cigarette and flung the match away.

She knew the voice.

'Whisky?'

He did not wait for an answer, but placed the tumbler before her.

'Thank you.'

'Help yourself to water.'

He drank his straight. Sipping it quickly, pouring himself another, watching her dilute hers so heavily from the jug it was almost colourless, filling the glass to the brim, leaving a taste that was as pleasant to Reem as bitter medicine. Still, she quickly felt the warmth rise in her limbs and face. It was a comforting and comfortable sensation. She drank out of companionship, to avoid emphasizing any distance between herself and the Ustaz, but it really was not that bad.

'How do you feel?'

'Better.'

She knew it was the start of her quarantine. No radio or television, no newspapers. No news. No telephone within several miles; no letters, no visitors that had not been vetted, no outings, no drives into town. No shopping.

She was isolated, her only contact with the outside world was the Ustaz.

There were plenty of books, of course; mostly Arabic, mainly poetry, literature and politics.

Reem passed along the shelves, prowling around the room,

glass of watered-down whisky in hand while the Ustaz sat back in his chair and drank, his eyes on her back.

She said, 'These yours?'

'Some of them.'

'I think I can guess which.'

No response.

'I don't think it's this Frunze Military Academy treatise on combined arms operations, printed in Moscow in 1974, or Yuri Andropov's autobiography.'

There were several seminal works known to her: George Antonius's *The Arab Awakening*, and the very works that had set her off on her journey at the age of twelve or thirteen, if only in her own mind, for her heart had long been ready, Zeine N. Zeine's *The Emergence of Arab Nationalism* and *The Struggle for Arab Independence*.

There was a pile of tattered *National Geographics*.

'Well,' Reem said, 'I can tell which are yours.'

'Yes?'

'The Egyptian Sayyid Qutb,' she said. 'Executed in 1976 – and here's another one that looks like yours, by the Iranian, Jalal al-e Ahmad.'

'Qutb was hanged in 1966 not 1976.'

'I stand corrected, professor. But isn't it strange how much our Arab intellectuals and writers borrowed from the West this century – from fascism, from communism, from national socialism?'

'Not really.'

'Could we not have done better ourselves?'

It was pride talking.

She came back to the table and dribbled more whisky into her glass.

'So?'

'Arabs, mainly Christian Arabs, borrowed whatever was new and fashionable in the way of ideology and harnessed it to their own national ambitions – especially in the 1930s and 1940s. It was a response to Jewish nationalism. Zionism. These ideologies were material, industrial, rational – everything we are not.'

'And the Muslims?'

'It seems to me that radical Islam is a knee-jerk defence, a reaction to the import of these secular "isms" into our culture. It's like an immune system reacting to foreign bodies.'

It was so dark now in the room she could no longer see his face.

'Are we foreign bodies, Ustaz?'

'What do you think?'

'I think you shouldn't answer a question with another question. It's a cheap trick. But I will tell you what I don't think. I don't believe in any "ism", foreign or otherwise.'

There was a long silence. Reem watched the stars through the open door.

'So why are you doing this, Reem?'

'Isn't it a little late to be questioning my motives?'

'And what was it you said about cheap tricks and answering a question with another question?'

They sat out on the steps before going to bed, listening to a nightingale and, in the distance, jackals howling in the foothills of Mount Hermon.

The Ustaz smoked his last cigarette of the day.

There were so many questions. How many had slept in the little room that would be her home for the next few days? Were the bars on the dormer window in the converted loft to keep her in or others out? How many others had slept on the army cot and used the same thin blanket? Had they all gone through with it? Had they been successful?

She had already broken the rules. God knows what the Ustaz would do if he knew. Twice. Three times, if she included the failure to confess her misdemeanours. She had left two messages for Nick, one on his office voicemail, the other on his home telephone.

She knew all telephone lines were tapped, or could be, and she assumed that practically everyone who was anyone in the intelligence racket got a feed of whatever it was they wanted. The Americans, the Israelis, the Syrians, the Soviets.

Probably the Iranians, Iraqis and Saudis, too.

Oh yes, and the Egyptians.

Whoever knew the right people, had sufficient influence and could pay in hard currency.

Reem knew the Deuxième Bureau and the *moukhabarat* used word recognition systems. She took it for granted that Nick's telephone lines would be monitored simply because he was British and a UN official.

Using cellphones was out of the question – all mobile calls were scooped up by US signal intelligence, Washington having stepped up electronic surveillance ever since the first American nationals had been seized for ransom. So Reem had used the public telephones in the main west Beirut exchange. She left no name in her messages, nothing to identify her as the caller.

She could not explain anything to Nick.

There was nothing she could tell him.

Just that she cared. That she missed him.

That she was sorry.

That he should not wait for her, or go looking.

That he should do the sensible thing and forget her, go home and live a full and happy life.

That she hoped he would not be angry but would understand.

Eventually.

THIRTY-TWO

He heard the message on his office voicemail. It was the first of three messages, but Nick did not bother with the other two.

'Nick. Are you there? Hope you're okay and that everything went well and you're back safe. I miss you. Nick, I'm sorry. Truly sorry. It's not going to work out. I wish I could tell you face to face, but you're not back and by the time you are, I'll be away. I can't ever leave Lebanon, Nick. You can't stay. It's too dangerous. I'm sorry it has to end this way. I did want to see you one last time. You made me happy, you really did, and I'll never forget it. I asked you once to always remember that I loved you whatever happened. I meant it then. I still mean it.'

He ran out into the corridor, crashed through the fire doors and leaped down the stairs, taking them four at a time. He did not say a word on the way out. Elias had looked up, surprise on his face.

They had planned to have a drink together.

'Nick—'

But he was gone, hurling himself down the stairs and out to the street.

He stepped out in front of a service taxi, tossed a handful of greasy bills across the seat and was outside his flat in six minutes.

Inside his front door, dropping his bag and reaching for the telephone in nine.

He pressed the button. It was the only message on his machine.

'Nick. I'm going away for a while. I just wanted to say goodbye. I left a message on your office voicemail. Hope you don't mind, Nick. I wish you a long and happy life. I wish you everything you want for yourself. Forgive me. I hope that one day you will, and that eventually you will understand why I am doing what I'm doing. Nick, I am not expecting. The tests came back negative. It was a mistake. Do not come after me. Do not try to find me, I beg you. I think of you every day, of our time together. God bless you.'

He played it again. He gazed at the telephone, but unseeing. He had to act. He could not just leave it there, shake his head, pretend nothing had happened, just shrug it off as something that happens and then is over. This was not just the end of a casual undergraduate fling at university. Nick simply could not do what he might have done at another time and place. He could not shower and change and go out and get drunk and find some other girl to console him while his hurt pride healed.

This was not about being dropped. It was not about male self-esteem.

He turned, opened the door again, stepped out, patted his pockets to make sure he had his wallet and keys, pulled it shut, locked it, and called up the lift.

Nick started to think hard on the way down.

He was a foreigner, a Westerner, in an Arab capital at war with itself.

Where every lowlife had a gun and a hit cost less than lunch.

Where would he start?

He needed help, but where would he get it?

Who was there he could he trust?

No one.

There was Major Dacre; little trust to be had there. Dacre and Wilson had used him as their bait in west Beirut. Their decoy. There was Daoud. No way. Only where their interests might converge, and Nick could not see that they did. Daoud was always a couple of steps ahead of him, anyhow. Elias? Elias was a senior colleague; wise, experienced, tactful, honest and he knew the local scene. That was the positive side. But Elias had his pension to think about, and wanted to maintain his status as the senior local staffer in the office.

Elias would not be much help.

Too docile, too comformist.

Afraid for his family. Who wouldn't be?

There was Khaled – but Khaled was dead.

It was Khaled who had made a fool of him. Not that Nick had not deserved it. But Khaled had pretended not to know Reem, then had given Nick her approximate address – sufficient to find her, anyway. Khaled had been a part of it, whatever it was.

He had been deceived by almost everyone.

He went to the American university hospital.

'Dr Nessim, please.'

The plump woman with messy hair in a nurse's white uniform behind the reception desk looked up. She seemed to take in Nick's sweaty face, his hair standing on end, his filthy clothes and, above all, the frantic expression.

'Dr Nessim?'

She looked down. She had lost interest, dismissed him as a crazy private client.

'Dr Nessim not here.'

She did not look at Nick.

'Got a number for him?'

'Come back tomorrow.'

'This is an emergency. I need to contact him now.'

'No. Tomorrow.'

Cow.

If it had been anywhere else, Nick would have yelled 'Fuck you.' But this was Beirut. People who did that lost face big time.

It was not polite. It was worse – it was shameful. It reflected badly on the culprit. Men died for a good deal less.

He saw a corridor marked PSYCHIATRIC SECTION. He ran down it. He punched at each door as he passed. Most were locked. If any were open he would skid to a stop, peer in at the surprised occupant, asking the same thing each time.

'Dr Nessim?'

They all shook their heads at the mad *ajnabi*.

Thirty minutes on and Nick was standing outside the accident and emergency section in the dark, feeling hopeless and stupid and very, very tired. He had searched the entire wing. He had run up and down stairs and endless corridors. He had banged on every door and stopped everyone he had met.

For the most part they had not understood a word he said.

Those who had something to say he failed to comprehend.

Nothing; nothing to show for his efforts.

He had tried orthopaedics.

There was no one he recognized, and no one recognized him. They did not remember Reem. After all, there had been so many that day. One of the worst in many weeks.

Her old room was empty, the beds all made up with fresh linen and ready for the next round of slaughter, the next slabs of broken flesh off the Lebanon chopping block. He found a crumpled cigarette packet and a last cigarette in his pocket. He lit it with shaking fingers.

The courtyard where the badly wounded were left to die was empty, the bloodstains washed away, expunged.

Now what the hell do I do?

He reacted instinctively when he saw a white-coated figure approach a small hatchback in the parking lot. The figure unlocked the vehicle and prepared to get in, first throwing his bag on the back seat.

'Dr Nessim? Is that you, Dr Nessim?'

Nick forced his stiff legs into a shambling run towards the car.

It was not Nessim.

But it was a colleague of his, an Armenian psychoanalyst named Katurian, younger than Nessim, of slighter build and darker.

Nick introduced himself. He told Katurian a family friend and former patient of Nessim's, Reem Najjar, was in danger. Nessim had saved her life. He was the only person Nick knew he could turn to for help in trying to find her before it was too late.

'I'll take you there, but I'm not sure Nessim can help you.'

'I'm not sure either.'

Katurian smiled. 'Well, we can try.'

'He knew her family. I think she said he came from the same village.'

'Get in. It's on my way.'

For several minutes neither man said anything.

'What's your interest, Mr Lorimer? Purely professional or . . .'

'She is – or was – my girlfriend. At least I thought so.'

'How do you know she's in trouble?'

'She left messages for me. I've been away in the south for a few days and when I got back today there were two messages. She was saying goodbye.'

'She was ending the relationship?'

'It was more final than that.'

'I don't follow.'

They were nearing Verdun.

'You see that, doctor – the ruins?'

'You mean the institute?'

'Yes. She worked there.'

'I'm still not entirely sure I understand.'

Nick told him about Khaled. How they used to go drinking

together, how he was warned off his colleague. Next thing he was found murdered.

It was such a relief to talk, just let it out, even to a stranger, someone he'd accosted in a parking lot. Perhaps it felt good precisely because this was a stranger. No matter if it made no sense. He had to trust someone.

'And the girl?'

'Again, Reem seemed to be some kind of activist. Then her workplace was attacked. You remember. There were suggestions somebody called the Ustaz was based there and he was the target.'

'When was that?'

Nick told him.

'And now she's disappeared?'

Katurian seemed sympathetic but uneasy, unsure if Nick himself wasn't the patient who needed help.

They had drawn to a stop.

'This is it,' Katurian said, peering up out of his window at the building to see if the lights were on. 'Nessim lives on the third floor.'

It was a solid 1930s block of blue stucco with art deco ironwork.

Nick had left out el-Hami's birthday at Kaslik, the missing Land-Rover, Reem's interest in driving, the Karantina visit, the photographs. It was too confusing, too unreal. No one would believe him.

'Do you mind if I tag along?' Katurian asked. 'I'm still not sure what this is all about, but you've got me interested.'

'You look like shit, Mr Nick,' Nessim said.

'Thanks.'

'You two better come in.'

The Nessims made them welcome in their two-bedroomed flat,

crammed with dark-wood furniture and Damascene inlay. Mrs Nessim made a fuss of the visitors, insisting on serving up the remains of a delicious family supper and making them a pot of coffee, then left them to talk. Dr Nessim's three children were already asleep.

Nick told Nessim what he had already said to Katurian.

'What is she, Nick? She's not Muslim. She's one of us. Christian. So is she SNSP, Baathist, Nasserist, PSP, PLO – what?'

'I don't know. I was told both she and my friend Khaled were OLCA.'

Katurian and Nessim exchanged glances across the dining table.

'I hate this war,' Nick said. 'I still can't figure out why people are still fighting.'

Katurian pushed his coffee cup aside. He asked, 'Did OLCA ever carry out a suicide mission?'

'Not that I know of,' Nessim said. 'But there's always a first time.'

'The gods have smiled upon you Mr Lorimer,' Katurian said. 'If you'd approached anyone else in the car park tonight you and my friend here would have been in the shit. You were just lucky that Nessim and I grew up together, went to the same school and studied medicine together. You must be lucky. Anyhow, your secret is safe with us.'

Nessim said, 'You know what they call these operations?'

'Yes,' Nick said. 'They use a euphemism for a kamikaze attack. According to the papers, they call it an Operation of Quality.'

Katurian said, 'The press says the Ustaz finances them by taking contracts.'

'Contracts?'

'He kills for cash, apparently. Provided they are generally in line with his thinking, he'll accept anything. He'll do it for the Syrians, the Soviets – whoever. There's a lot of competition, but they say he's the best. Takes all the difficult jobs. We receive some of his successes in our mortuary, right, Nessim?'

'There's one more thing,' Nessim said.

He looked hard at Nick.

'Did Reem tell you she was pregnant?'

There was no point trying to dodge the truth.

'Yes, she did. I was the father. I asked her to marry me. I said if she wouldn't come abroad with me, I'd settle in Lebanon.'

Neither Nessim nor Katurian looked in the least surprised.

'And she said?'

'I thought she was pleased. I thought she agreed. But maybe I wasn't paying close enough attention because she left a message on my phone saying it was all a mistake, and that her subsequent tests had proved negative.'

'And how did you feel about that?'

'I loved her. I still do.'

'And now? I hate to ask you, Nicholas, but I feel a certain responsibility. She has no living relatives left, and I did know her family. We come from the same village. Maybe she told you.'

'It's because she means something to you that I looked for you. There's no one else I can confide in.'

Nessim got up and returned with three glasses and a bottle of Cypriot brandy. He poured out three generous measures. They raised their glasses without a word and drank.

'So you would have been happy to be a father?'

'Yes, I would.'

He spoke with greater certainty than he felt.

Katurian offered Nick a cigarette. He took it and Katurian lit it for him.

'You said she had no family,' Nick said. 'If that's true, then who was the character hanging around Reem in the hospital? I heard her call him Uncle Faiz.'

'I've no idea,' Nessim said.

'He was older. Old enough to be her father. Fifties or early sixties. Hair cut very short. Trim build. Simple clothes. Quiet. Just sat there by her bed not saying much. He was there most evenings.'

Nessim shrugged. 'Sorry. I don't know.'

Nick drained his glass.

Nessim said, 'I'm sorry to say this, Nicholas, but Reem lied to you. No doubt she had her reasons. Maybe she thought that if she lied you wouldn't go looking for her. Maybe she did not want you to be upset. It's understandable if you're right about what she's up to. She is pregnant. There was no other test, not at the hospital. There was only one. I am sure about that. I pulled her file the other day. Believe me. Reem is with child.'

Nessim had a name. That was all.

Katurian called him a taxi. Nick went back to his own flat, tore off his evil-smelling clothes, took a shower, and pulled on clean boxer shorts, jeans and shirt. He resisted the temptation to lie down on his bed because he knew he would not get up again.

'Talk to Ali,' Nessim had said. 'He plays the tenor sax. You'll know him when you see him – he's immensely tall and thin. He's a Shi'ite. Lost most of his family – his father to the PLO, his two brothers to our southern neighbours, an uncle and his own son to the Phalangists. He won't be there until late. Not before eleven. They take a break after about an hour. They have a smoke and something to drink. They break for maybe fifteen minutes. That's when you should try to get him on his own. I can't promise anything. But he knows where these OLCA people and others of their kind hang out. He's a communist himself. But as you'll discover, a man of few words.'

It was already 10.45.

Even if this Ali knew anything, there was no guarantee he would tell Nick.

And even if he took Nick along himself when The Blues finally closed down around 2.30 a.m., Nessim said, there was no way of knowing if they would let Nick in, let alone talk to him.

THIRTY-THREE

She was allowed out under cover of darkness.

The rest of the time, during daylight hours, she had to stay indoors. Reem could on no account be seen, not by the locals. The Ustaz warned her about overflights by reconnaissance aircraft, pilotless drones and remote sensors carried by invisible satellites, both US and Soviet.

She slept and read during the day, and went for walks with the Ustaz after dark, after they had eaten food prepared elsewhere and brought to the farmhouse by person or persons unknown.

Her arm gave her little trouble. It was getting stronger all the time, but it itched, especially in the heat of the day when she was confined to the two rooms they shared.

'You'll save many lives. Hundreds, perhaps; certainly scores. You knew that, didn't you?'

'No.'

'You alone will do what six infantry battalions and a Syrian armoured brigade can't do at Souk al-Gharb.'

She said nothing.

This was personal.

'But of course you won't be alone. We'll be with you all the way. Behind you, on either side of you. We'll be right with you. At this moment the engineers are working night and day to get your equipment ready. You don't know it, and they don't know it, but you have a back-up team of at least eighteen people all dedicated to getting you to your target at the right place and at the right time.'

They had crossed the wooden bridge, the field, climbed over a wooden stile, and made their way uphill along a track between two lines of conifers. It was a warm evening, and clouds of mosquitoes whined around them, seeking fresh blood.

Reem had borrowed a pair of rubber boots at least two sizes too big.

The Ustaz smoked to keep the insects at bay. Reem waved her hands at them, but she knew they were managing to feast on her exposed arms, her shoulders and neck. There was not much she could do about it.

'There won't be a battle, thanks to you. They'll have to pull back, rethink their strategy. You'll buy us time, Reem, and give us another chance.'

'I thought they were already fighting.'

'Skirmishing, probing attacks, aggressive patrols, artillery interdiction – it's a gradual stepping up of pressure. The enemy is testing our responses. If you succeed, there won't be a battle. You'll have decapitated the monster. He can't function in a coordinated fashion without a brain, without a head.'

'They'll soon find someone else. A new dictator . . .'

'It will take time.'

My life, Reem thought, and that of my unborn child will be the price.

'They'll react,' Reem said. 'They'll take their revenge.'

'They always do.'

He stopped, raised a hand.

The Ustaz put his head on one side. He was listening. Reem could not hear anything, but he stepped off the road into the wet, knee-high grass under the conifers and beckoned to her to follow. They waited a moment, then started walking again. Reem's trousers were drenched by the dew.

A dog barked somewhere off to their right.

She asked, 'That doesn't bother you – the retaliatory strikes?'

'We want to provoke them to overreact.'

The second night he drove Reem several miles south to another building where she practised with a variety of handguns and sub-machine guns in a basement range. The walls were sandbagged and the ceiling soundproofed. The Ustaz worked as her instructor. She stood on a little wooden stage at one end, while he stood next to her, controlling a projector that threw a film onto a big screen at the far end. The screen was a paper roll. It moved down while the film ran. When she fired, the film and the paper roll halted momentarily. The screen was backlit, so each round lit up clearly.

It was called instinctive shooting.

Look on it as a form of therapy, the Ustaz told her.

She uses both hands, left supporting the right by cupping it; both arms extended; feet slightly apart and left foot slightly ahead of the right, knees bent. A 9 mm Beretta is followed by a Browning Highpower, the 7.62 mm Makarov, a .38 Smith and Wesson.

The Ustaz loads the clips.

The targets include pedestrians on the street and passengers in vehicles, the cars stopping, the people getting out with guns. Reem fires steadily, double-tapping each target, taking out the driver through the windscreen as he pulls out a handgun while still sitting in his seat.

Not aiming but looking, both eyes open.

A woman pauses on a busy pavement, opens a handbag as if looking for a purse or make-up mirror. People pass between her and the camera. But she pulls out a pistol and brings it up. Without hesitation Reem fires twice.

The projector stops. Two pinpricks of light illuminate two neat holes, close together in the centre of the woman's forehead.

The film resumes.

The Ustaz nods approvingly. 'Good.'

Reem does not hear him. She is too busy shooting, utterly absorbed, adrenaline flowing, the detonations a rolling thunder even with the ear defenders clamped over her head. In another sequence, the video camera is in the front of a car, looking forward as it trundles down a country track. A man runs out of a stand of tall grass and proceeds to run ahead. As the car turns the corner, the man looks round. He holds a weapon. Reem double-taps, both rounds striking home. But there are several other men standing off to the left, all armed. Reem works left to right, two rounds per target.

She has two down, three to go when she runs out of ammunition.

The rest of the bunch drop their weapons and raise their hands.

Reem relaxes.

Mistake.

A gunman in blue T-shirt and white baseball cap appears in a doorway to her right. He is grinning at the camera. He holds a pump-action shotgun. He raises the weapon to his shoulder.

Reem's weapon fires on an empty chamber.

Click.

'Yal'an abouk . . .'

The gunman looses off both barrels at the camera before the Ustaz shuts down the projector.

The Ustaz chuckles. 'Always count your rounds,' he says, handing her a second clip. Reem reloads swiftly, her eyes never leaving the screen. She bounces on the balls of her feet. She enjoys it. The stench of the cordite is in her hair, her clothes.

She practises next with both an AKS rifle and an M-16, lying, kneeling, sitting and standing. Short bursts, this time, three or four rounds each.

After the expenditure of around two thousand rounds of ammunition, Reem is ready for sleep.

But the Ustaz is not finished.

She has to strip and clean the weapons.

Blindfold, down on her knees, she must reassemble them against the clock, the Ustaz standing over her with a stopwatch.

'Again,' he says. 'Do it again.'

Next door was a small, makeshift gymnasium with an exercise bicycle and treadmill. After an hour on her own he led her to a shower room and handed her soap and a clean towel.

'We'll do this every day, or something very like it,' he said.

He drove her back to the farmhouse at 3 a.m.

'How do you feel?'

'Better.'

'Tomorrow night we'll go for a five-kilometre run.'

Reem fell asleep on her cot as the sky turned pink above the hills to the east.

Nick seemed such a very long way off.

In another world.

A dream of things past.

THIRTY-FOUR

Ordinary life went on. There really was no alternative. It was impossible to be frightened all the time. People went to work, they fell sick, celebrated birthdays, went dancing, got drunk, lost money on cards, had their hair cut, flirted and gossiped in coffee shops, and on hot afternoons pulled down the blinds and made love or went to sleep. At the very least, the sensible stayed off Beirut's baking streets until the sun began its steep decline.

The workshop was not hard to find. Its dusty glass doors were wide open. A ginger cat slumbered in the shaded entrance. Two men played backgammon in the dark interior, a furious clicking of black and white counters on the board interspersed with a grunting – of impatience, satisfaction, anger – Nick could not tell which.

They took no notice of him.

There was sawdust underfoot, and a smell of wood, paint, turpentine, roasting coffee, and French cigarettes.

'Mr Sabri?'

He walked past the two carpenters in their shirtsleeves, down a channel between stacks of what initially appeared to be wooden boats. They were coffins, five or six in each stack, in varying stages of completion and piled up to the ceiling. Some were plain, little more than man-sized boxes. Others were highly polished or varnished, of dark and blonde wood, another painted a gleaming white with shining brass handles.

At the back was a glass booth. A man with cropped grey hair and a goatee watched Nick approach. He saw Nick looking at the coffins and run a finger along a shiny white lid.

He heaved himself out of his chair.

'Our only growth industry,' said the man with the goatee. He ushered Nick into an office crowded with junk; there were brushes and buckets, an enormous array of cold chisels on one wall, a battered carpentry bench, flagons of anonymous fluids, piles of yellowed newspapers and, hanging on the glass partition, a 1975 poster of a very blonde blonde in a yellow bikini, standing tall on high heels and arching her back at an impossible angle against a background of blue sky and green trees.

'The year it all started,' said Sabri, glancing up at the calendar.

They sat down, a dusty French table cluttered with what looked like invoices between them. Sabri studied Nick carefully.

'Ali sent you?'

'Yes.'

'Did you enjoy his music?'

'He's a great sax player.'

'We used to make violins and ouds. You know the oud? Your medieval lute is based on our instrument. Everything of value in the West is based on Arab civilization, whether it's music or astronomy or mathematics, even your knowledge of Plato and Aristotle. Regrettably, there is little market either for musical instruments or Plato right now. There is more money in coffins, thanks to cluster bombs and other wonders Washington sends us. You are British?'

'Yes.'

'Never mind. No one's perfect, Mr Lorimer.'

'Glad to hear it.'

'Do you mind if I ask you for some form of identification?'

'Not at all.' Nick pulled out his UN card and placed it on the table.

'Coffee?'

'Thank you.'

'I am Sabri,' he said, handing Nick a small, round, white cup with no handle.

Nick had to turn it constantly to avoid burning his fingers. As soon as it was empty, save for the thick slurry at the bottom, Sabri refilled it.

'Cigarette?'

'Have one of mine,' Nick said.

'Sure.'

'I hope you don't mind me asking, but what do they cost?'

'The caskets?' Sabri pursed his lips. 'We cater for all tastes. You can buy that white one – actually, it is made to order – for $11,000. Satin and silk interior, nine-carat gold furniture. Solid mahogany. Imported. Suitable for a patriarch of the Maronites – or an arms dealer. Or you can have the plain one you probably saw at the entrance for $350 – it's chipboard with a thin layer of beech.'

'None seems particularly cheap.'

'Death always seems too expensive to the living. To the dead it is an irrelevance. That is one thing to be said in its favour, I suppose.'

'These are for Christians?'

'Yes. A piano or a violin takes a long time to make. A coffin is much quicker. We have a high turnover, and the cash flow is good. I can't complain. For Muslims we make a sort of frame – see, in the corner – it's little more than a plank with a place for the head and the feet. The body, wrapped in muslin, is tied to the frame so it can be lowered quickly and efficiently into the grave. Speed is everything these days – the enemy has a way of opening fire at crowds of mourners, so most burials in the west take place at night.'

Nick gave an involuntary shiver.

'I wanted to ask about a friend of mine. Reem Najjar. I thought maybe—'

'She is not one of ours. I'm sorry. She is not a member of our organization.'

He shook his head. He seemed very sure of it. Emphatic. Nick must have looked disappointed, because Sabri leaned across the table and patted his arm. 'I checked after Ali spoke to me. He told me to expect you. I contacted our central committee. Believe me, Mr Lorimer, your friend is not a member. She never was. You were not told the truth. Maybe,' he paused, his eyes on Nick's troubled face, 'you were told for a reason. Whatever reason it was, it must be connected to the nature of whoever it was who told you.'

Major Dacre.

Nick felt his exhaustion catching up. He had a blinding headache. He could not look towards the entrance of the shop because of the brightness. His legs felt like lead. He could scarcely move.

He felt he had come to a dead end.

'We are a disciplined party, Mr Lorimer,' Sabri was saying. 'We do not let our people run unauthorized operations or take part in them. We are very strict. If you are not disciplined in this environment, you do not survive. And we are small. Easily crushed. Understand? There can be no – how do you say – freelance activities. If your friend is involved with the person they call the Ustaz, then rest assured it is nothing to do with us.'

If she was a member, would Sabri have said anything different?

Probably not.

'I am both glad and sorry that I could not be of assistance.'

'I understand.'

'Do you? It is not to say I do not sympathize with the young lady. Or with this Ustaz.'

Nick pushed himself painfully to his feet. He felt stiff, battered. He wanted to go to bed and sleep.

'I have taken up enough of your time, Mr Sabri.'

'It is nothing. But of course you have never seen me. We never spoke. You do not know my name and you have never been here. And I know nothing of you or of your interest in this lady. I do not know anyone who plays the tenor sax or anyone called Ali.'

'Of course.'

'Wait, Mr Lorimer. A moment. I want to show you something. Perhaps you can do us a favour one of these days.'

Sabri led the way. There was a back door, hidden behind some sacking. In the alley behind the row of shops – electrical supplies, furniture makers, a watchmaker's, an ironmonger – was a junk-yard.

'This way.'

They made their way past bathtubs, a broken-down tractor, several sections of an enormous pipe. They climbed a broad staircase of stone to what had once been a small Ottoman palace. Its roof had gone. The interior had been gutted. It was a shell of stonework, wrought-iron balconies, tall curved windows without glass now, but Nick could imagine how it must have been in its days of glory.

The place stank of cats and human faeces.

Sabri unlocked a metal door. He had to use his shoulder to push it open.

A single light bulb illuminated a storeroom.

'Our wood store,' Sabri said. He started moving planks of wood aside. Nick tried to help, but Sabri would have none of it.

'There.'

He was short of breath after his exertions.

It was a yellow forty-four-gallon metal drum, still tightly sealed.

'What do you see?'

There were faded labels on the side. Nick knelt down.

BAYARD IMPORT-EXPORT

PESTICIDE

Bugs can't fly from Spectracide

Nick stood up.

He did not understand.

'Bayard is one of el-Hami's companies. Liberian-registered. You have heard of el-Hami?'

'I've met him.'

'Sometimes, Mr Lorimer, we lose sight of why we are fighting. We forget what we are fighting for, and what we are fighting against.'

304

Sabri dragged the planks back in place, concealing the drum. He pulled the metal door shut and padlocked it. They descended the stairs together.

'Spectracide is perfectly legal,' Sabri said. 'It's available on the open market. The main compound of Spectracide is an organophosphate called Diazinon. You know what an organophosphate is, Mr Lorimer?'

Nick waited for Sabri to supply the answer to his own question.

'It's a molecule of carbon and hydrogen with an atom of phosphorous.'

They were outside the coffin-makers.

'What does that tell you?'

'Nothing, I'm afraid.'

'Have you heard of Soman?'

Nick shook his head.

'It was developed in Germany in 1944. Perhaps you have heard of VX, invented a decade later by your countrymen seeking a more effective pesticide. It's odourless, tasteless. It's like motor oil. Diazinon and Soman are very similar organophosphates, but as I said, Diazinon is available on the open market. Anyone can get hold of it, unfortunately.'

Sabri took him back through the shop.

The two men had stopped playing. They looked up as Nick walked past.

'You work for the United Nations, Mr Lorimer. Perhaps you will remember what I have shown you. Perhaps there will soon be a reason to remember. You will be able to stop what is happening, maybe. Six months ago there was a chemical spill in east Beirut, on premises at Hazmieh owned by el-Hami's associates. Six people were taken to hospital. The symptoms were headaches, nausea, dizziness and vomiting. Three of the patients lapsed into a coma. Two of them died. The third is there today – a vegetable, kept alive artificially. There was some speculation in the press it was a weapons laboratory.'

'Mr Sabri . . .'

'The antidote is called Diazepam. I hope neither of us will ever need it.'

'I hope so, too.'

'I hope you find your friend, Mr Lorimer.'

THIRTY-FIVE

Nicholas dearest,

*I'm writing this in a small room far away. A world away.
That's how it feels.*

*There is no power. For light I have something called a
pressure lamp. It has paraffin in the bottom, and a wick
under the glass and it is pumped up with a device like a
lever until it glows white hot. It is very bright. You are so
lucky, Nick. You have probably never heard of a pressure
lamp, let alone have had to use one. Or join queues for
water, or food handouts. But I am content. I am in a safe
place. It is comfortable. It is clean. The air is fresh, and it
is very quiet. There is no traffic here, no sound of private
generators, no shouting in the street outside. The only
shooting is a long, long way off. It sounds like a
thunderstorm and that is what I pretend it is.*

*I have plenty to eat. I sleep better than I can remember.
The nightmares are in abeyance. Maybe they're gone for
good, I don't know. I get plenty of exercise. I read lots of
books. I feel rested, at peace with the world, at peace with
myself. For the very first time I am not afraid. It surprises
me. I thought I would be racked by doubts and fears, but
these have fallen away from me. I have thrown them
aside like worn-out clothes.*

I thought I would miss the city. I don't miss it at all.

By the time you get this, Nick, I will have left this place.

307

My task will have been fulfilled. There are perhaps two or three days to go before I begin my final journey. Getting this letter to you will be my last request. Everyone in my position has the right. Some ask for new clothes, or a special dish, a film, a book, one of those portable cassette players. I just want to have this talk with you. A monologue, but it's the best I can do. I want you to understand, and if there is anything to forgive, for you to forgive me.

I do love you. I always will. I think I always did without knowing it. Loving you made me more happy than I can say. I do not have the words to express how I felt about you then or how I still feel about you.

For us, Nick, love will never be enough. Not in this life. It is not enough to take me away from here, it is not enough to make me forget. There are certain things, certain people, certain events I can never forget. I cannot allow myself to. Call it a sense of duty, a destiny.

Our love is very, very special. But it is not made of marriage, of rings and promises, of priestly ceremonies, of living together, of work, of forsaking my identity, or you yours.

I do not have any right to choose what you call a normal life.

We all make an exit, Nick. That is all death is. An exit. We leave behind the cage, the crate, the frame – this thing we call the body that imprisons us and which we fuss over and pamper and stare at in the mirror. It is a trap, a burden, a prison cell.

I choose the manner of my going, that is all.

I hear you – across oceans, time itself – ask how I can do this terrible thing. Like you I was taught as a child to love my neighbour. But I cannot love a neighbour who destroys everything I love, who steals everything of any worth, who takes my pride and self-worth, and still wants more than I can possibly give. I do not hate my neighbour. It is worse than that. I pity him. I strike at him for my own sake. To reclaim my self. To take back my dignity. To repossess what is mine.

They will call it a crime. They will call me a murderer. They will say I killed myself and the child I carry.

(I am continuing this at the same time as yesterday.)

I lied to you. I had to. I did not want you following me, trying to track me down. It would have been dangerous for all of us.

What future does this being in my womb have in my country? Among my people? What life would he or she have? Should I bear a child for our enemies to humiliate, to strip of his rights, his self-respect, his very soul?

Should I bear children only to take them away, to make them in your image, the image of those who did so much harm to the Arab nation, who bombed us, gassed our people, divided us, subjugated us, stole our land, offered us submission and slavery as survival, and in return exploited our resources and our labour to feed your shareholders' desire for profit?

Never.

I have chosen for both of us.

Pray for my soul, Nicholas.

I may have need of your prayers even if you do not believe. There will not be many who will include me in their prayers once I have left and the media have got hold of what they call a 'story'. For those news people that is all it is, an entertaining story and they will twist it to make it suit their purposes.

If there is a God, may he bless you, too.

Sleep well. I am beside you though you do not know it.

Sometimes I feel you right here, in this room, and I hear you speak to me, and I answer you. If only we could touch.

Until we meet,
Reem

'It is my last request.'

Reem held out the letter at breakfast. The Ustaz took it, turned it over and read the name on the front.

She said, 'I want you to make sure he gets it.'

'If that's what you really want.'

'I do. Afterwards.'

The Ustaz bowed his head in agreement.

Reem said, 'I know you will read it. You will steam it open and read it to make sure I have not compromised anyone's security. I can assure you I have not done so. There are no names of people or places. No clues, either. I was very careful. It's a love letter if you must know. Rather sentimental. I just hope you won't laugh at me behind my back and think me too foolish. But I do understand. I am not the first or the last. You have to protect yourself and your students from carelessness. All I ask is that you do not read it until my work is done, that you reseal the letter, place it in another envelope, and make sure he gets it. In person.'

'Sure.'

'You promise.'

'You have my word.'

'Thank you.'

'It's nothing.'

'On the contrary, Ustaz. It means everything to me.'

THIRTY-SIX

'My, this is a surprise. Nick Lorimer.'

'A not too unpleasant one, I hope.'

'Come in.'

Mona pulled the door wider and stood back.

Nick said, 'Your family . . .'

'I'm alone. You're quite safe.'

She wore silk, a simple shift of a dress, but it looked very expensive. It had a pattern of tiny printed squares. It was a rich brown colour. There was something about the way it hung, or perhaps the way it had been cut, that suited her figure and her skin. Her arms, shoulders, the upper slopes of her small breasts and the backs of her hands seemed to have been dusted by the sun, lightly tanned in a way that made her glow with health. Mona wore a little kohl, highlighting her large Arab eyes with a touch of purple, and her hair was cut short in a well trimmed bob.

'You look terrific.'

'Thank you.'

She was wary, but not unwelcoming. Surprised, cautious – and curious. She led the way into her family's opulent drawing room, stiff and heavy with gilt furniture, uncomfortable-looking sofas, Chinese lacquered cabinets, vast oil paintings that could have been old masters or simply copies.

'I need your help,' Nick said.

'Oh?' She looked at him over her shoulder, but did not slow down until they reached the balcony, which seemed to Nick almost as long as a tennis court. It ran the full length of the apartment, almost half a block.

Walking behind her, just three feet away, he could not help but stare at her legs.

He had almost forgotten her smooth, pampered skin, the muscular thighs toned by swimming and tennis at the smart country club she belonged to somewhere up in the Metn, above Bikfaya. For people like Mona, money surmounted all barricades. There was no east and no west. It was the poor who lived hemmed in by war, by ethnicity and faith. It was the poor who did the fighting and dying. It was always so, Nick thought.

The rich, especially old money, had their own rules.

'I was going to have a glass of champagne. Will you join me? They're at it again in our street, shooting at one another. It's amusing to sit out here on a warm evening and drink French champagne and listen to it.'

She did not mean it, surely.

When she had brought the bottle in an ice bucket and the tall champagne flutes, she sat down opposite him on a wicker arm-chair with plump floral cushions and started to peel off the gold foil around the cork. She sat upright, her narrow back very straight and her pointed knees pressed together.

'Well? What can I do, Nick?'

'I've fallen in love.'

'Not with me, I hope.'

'No danger of that.'

'Thank God. I'm in perpetual fear of men who cannot manage their feelings. Anyway, I am hardly the person to come to in a matter of the heart, Nick, as you know only too well. If you'd been afflicted with an antisocial disease I would have been able to point you in the right direction . . .'

She twisted the cork out in a single fluid movement. The action made a small pop, but no liquid was spilled. She was an expert.

'She's vanished. She's pregnant. It's my child.'

Nick had for reasons he could not comprehend always found

it easier to confide in women. Mona was someone who had secrets. He had agreed to keep her secret, and whatever else he knew of her affairs in the afternoons. He also knew her attention span was short, so he had decided to give it to her in headlines, without prologue or elaboration.

'Why me?'

'We have a secret. Or rather, we had a secret. I agreed to keep what I knew of your life strictly between us, and I have kept my word. Now I want to tell you my secret, and I want you not to divulge it to anyone. I suppose what I am saying is that I do feel I can trust you. You trusted me. I assume it works the other way, too.'

She raised her glass.

Nick picked up his.

'To secrets,' Mona said. 'Without them, life would be so drab.'

She made a noise of pleasure, mmmmm, as she drank.

His reply was lost in a burst of rifle fire from the street corner not a hundred metres away.

'The place to start is her home,' Mona said. 'You've been there since she went off without telling you where she was going?'

'No.'

'Why, Nick? It's the obvious place to begin looking. Her neighbours, the shopkeepers, the kids who deliver to her door . . .'

'I didn't think it would yield very much.'

'Is there someone else living there now?'

'I don't know.'

'Has she taken the furniture, the pictures with her? Did someone else take them?'

'I've no idea, I'm sorry.'

He could not imagine Reem being bothered about pictures.

'As soon as this squabble in the street stops, we'll head over there.'

Mona pursed her lips. Once she made up her mind, that was it.

313

'What, now?'

'Why not?'

'Are you sure you want to do this?'

'I'm fascinated. It beats getting drunk and being eaten by mosquitoes out here on the porch. I was beginning to get bored.'

'I'm sorry my company isn't up to scratch.'

'Silly boy – I meant before you arrived.'

'Are you still, you know . . .'

'Fucking in the afternoon, you mean?'

'Something like that.'

'Forget it, Nick. I never screw around here at home. I don't take men into my bed. You know that. Anyway, we're history, you and I. Didn't I tell you we'd get bored?'

'You did.'

'Wasn't I right?'

Nick shrugged, looked away.

'No need to be embarrassed, Nick. It's the truth. We had fun. It's over. But we're friends now. I hope we are. How many married couples in this town are friends? How many of those really trust each other? Oral sex seldom survives the honeymoon and it's downhill all the way thereafter. Let's finish the bottle and we'll go and have a look. What did you say her name was again?'

'Reem.'

'Reem Najjar.'

'That's right.'

As Mona got up to freshen her face, as she put it, she bent quickly next to Nick's chair and planted a sisterly kiss on his cheek.

'I'm glad you came over tonight, Nick. It's good to see you. Really.'

Mona's latest beau – post UN pilot – was the new Reuters man, not very experienced in bed, she added. Or perhaps unimaginative. At any rate, things had not got off to a promising start because a 155 mm howitzer shell, courtesy of the Lebanese Forces militia, had struck the roof of the building where he worked, penetrated down to the Reuters offices four floors below, and exploded in the middle of the newsroom. Her man was on his way out of the room at the time. The blast had blown him down the stairs, and he had broken both ankles.

Mona said a drunken Polish correspondent had been typing up a dispatch in the Reuters office at the time, and when the smoke and dust settled, there was no sign of him. He had simply vanished. There weren't any body parts, either. Not even so much as a toenail. His loss had plunged the entire foreign press corps into depression. His relatives back in Warsaw had been informed, and a memorial service organized by the Foreign Press Association in Beirut.

A week later, the Pole had turned up to send another dispatch. He was surprised by all the fuss. One office secretary had fainted at the sight of him, thinking he was a ghost. He was drunk once again, of course. He had not been harmed in the least, not even scratched, and, most curious of all, had absolutely no recall of what had happened.

'There wasn't a mark on him,' Mona said, manoeuvring her hatchback into a tiny space on the pavement outside Reem's old home.

'And your Reuters man?'

'Flat on his back and unable to move, and in a ward with twelve other patients. All of which somewhat limits the possibilities for watching videos.'

'I can imagine.'

'I don't think I've made a very good choice with him. Men are so strange. Englishmen especially. Is it true you British men prefer one another to your women? Mind you, I have seen English women at embassy receptions, so I can understand why so many of you are queer. Meanwhile, my pilot is engaged to a

Middle East Airlines stewardess. I've been invited to the wedding. It's next week and I am going to be one of the bridesmaids.'

The neighbours knew nothing. Reem had left, and that was it. No, they saw no one with her. They did not remember anything special. A nice girl. So sad – Reem had lost her folks. An orphan. From the south. Good people – Christians. The Najjars had lost everything during al-Nakba. Then again in '78 when the Israelis launched a big incursion. There was a nice man, her uncle, who paid her bills and had the place cleaned. No name, sorry. There was a Kurdish woman who did the housework, but no, they did not know her name or where she lived. She came two or three times a week, and she brought food, did the shopping and the cleaning and ironing. She had a limp.

Mona knocked on the apartment door. She hammered on it. She slapped it with the flat of her hands like a drum. She did not care if she woke the entire building, she told Nick. Better that way. People might talk just to get rid of them.

There was no one there.

She remained undaunted. She put on her sweetest smile and used her most persuasive voice, as if honey wouldn't dream of melting. She also palmed a sheaf of dollar bills, and that did the trick. One of the Daouk sons surreptitiously gave her the spare keys for thirty dollars. For just five minutes, you understand, m'mselle.

Had anyone else been round?

No.

Sure?

Just the cleaner.

Mona stalked around the flat first like a cat, breathing in the atmosphere. She found clothes in the built-in wardrobe of the main bedroom, all newly dry-cleaned and hung inside dust covers.

She stopped by the empty picture frames. Picked them up, set them down again, only upright this time, then went and sat down in an armchair.

'It's very dusty,' she said. 'No one's been to clean for at least a week.' And she ran a finger along the top of an occasional table and examined the labels on a row of empty bottles.

Back in the car, Mona asked Nick if he had a cigarette.

'Light it for me,' she said.

They sat together in the dark while Mona smoked, flicking the ash out of the window. She looked serious. Pensive.

'She has neither money nor taste. She's not interested in possessions, except for a few things that belonged to her family. She turned the flat into a sort of museum to their memory. She took a few clothes. Not many. Probably an overnight bag. She took family pictures. She's travelling light. She got rid of any papers or letters. She does not want people to know where she is. She does not want them to follow her. She planned this, Nick. It wasn't on the spur of the moment. She's not coming back.'

He said nothing. He waited.

Mona put her hand on his knee.

'I'm so sorry, my dear. But then you knew that, didn't you?'

Mona said he could put a notice in the papers.

But if his suspicions were accurate, she would not respond. Maybe she could not do so, even if she wanted to. She was probably hidden away somewhere. Her kind probably did not pop out to the shops for a paper and a packet of fags like normal people. Wherever she was, idling in a cafe over a coffee and a copy of *an-Nahar* or *L'Orient le Jour* was not on the list of recreations. She would be concealed in some ghastly basement in the southern suburbs. Somewhere where people kept their eyes averted and their mouths shut. Perhaps a Palestinian refugee camp where no law enforcement officers dared venture without an armoured brigade in support.

Mona drove Nick home. He kissed her chastely on both cheeks.

He thanked her and said goodnight. He climbed out of the hatch-back and shut the door.

'Nick . . .'

He peered down at her through the open window.

'Take some advice from an old trouper, Nicholas. Do something about that social conscience of yours. It's not very charming. It's going to turn you into a bore if you let it. Take some time off. Go somewhere different. Anywhere. Get away. Find a girl, preferably an odalisque. Try Cambodia. Get this Reem and this godforsaken country out of your system. And for fuck's sake, stop taking yourself so seriously.'

THIRTY-SEVEN

It rained during the night. The showers left a pungent smell of damp earth and vegetation.

There had been no outing under cover of darkness. The shooting practices had ended, and this time there was no trip to the exercise bike. Reem was advised to get as much rest as she could. She did not want rest. It was the last thing she wanted. She was ready, as ready as she would ever be, wound up tight like a spring, ready to leap. She spent the morning – her fourth in this secret place – studying her own enlarged photographs of the target area. Large-scale sketch maps had been pinned up on her wall. She familiarized herself with the sentry rotas, the position of the sandbagged emplacements on either side of the entrance to Karantina, the single roll of razor wire between the parking lot and the main headquarters building where the Protector had his offices.

She learned the distances by heart, the angles of approach marked out by the Ustaz in red felt-tip pen.

The wire would not hold her up.

There was a four-inch pipe that lay across the open ground.

That too, would not be more than a jolt at forty-five miles per hour, rising to sixty by the time she reached the inner sanctum.

She shut her eyes, seeing it unfold in her mind, and recited the details to the Ustaz.

Over and over, until she could do it in her sleep.

Her personal concerns had fallen away.

Even her nightmares had left her. She had butterflies in her stomach, but the queasiness she felt at the approach of the operation was not on her own account. She did not fear dying. It was rather anxiety that she should not fail. Reem knew that when push came to shove, soldiers do not fight for faith or country. Brass bands, medal parades and flag-waving are for the people back home. The truth is more prosaic; men and women fight for their mates, their section, their platoon. Individuals stay at their posts and do their best, enduring the unendurable, because they do not want to let the side down. It is a negative courage. It is pride in oneself, a self remade in the image of drill instructors the world over. Reem recognized that in herself. That was how she was now; part of a team and someone who wanted to keep up her end of it, the newest, youngest recruit who did not want to be the link in the chain that snapped.

How many times down the centuries had young men and women cheerfully set off on a mission, knowing their chances of survival were nil?

Three minutes, as it happened, would be the duration of her final run.

A lifetime, each second a universe. A straight line of 1,000 metres, a slow right-hand turn, decelerating for the thirty-metre approach to the entrance then the target, perfectly visible just over to the right at 150 metres.

An army checkpoint almost at the outset, and Lebanese Forces militia zealots on the gate itself, in Israeli body armour and helmets and carrying 5.56 mm M-16s or Galil assault rifles.

More of them inside.

She would see el-Hami's Mercedes just inside the compound, parked over on the left.

Reem helped the Ustaz take down the pictures and maps, pushing them into a large canvas bag. He said he would have them shredded, then burned. He would do it himself.

*

He was away a great deal. He came and went. He might be gone two hours, then four, then thirty minutes. There was no pattern, and the Ustaz offered no explanation.

He would stay for coffee or bring their meal and eat it with her.

The Ustaz said little. He seemed preoccupied.

He would raise his head, gaze at her for a moment as if suddenly recognizing her. 'All right, daughter?'

'Fine, uncle.'

He would nod and turn his attention back to his plate, eating quickly.

'Anything you want?'

'No.'

'Sure?'

'Sure I'm sure.'

He would push the plate away, take a last gulp of wine, perhaps grab an apple and get to his feet. Passing behind her, he would pause, place one hand on her shoulder and give it a gentle squeeze.

'I won't be long.' Without waiting for a response he would already be out of the door and Reem would hear his feet rattle down the stairs, crunch their way through the gravel and pound across the bridge.

Then silence would descend once more like a curtain, shutting out the world she had left behind.

She was tempted to ask if everything was all right, whether there was anything she could do to help. But she knew the answer to both questions. The best thing she could do was to wait, to be patient, and not ask anything.

They came for her at first light.

She was talking to whoever it was growing inside her.

Often she woke for no apparent reason and would talk quietly in the dark, whispering, her right hand on her abdomen where she imagined the tiny growth, the bud of a new human, to be. Did she have a soul? Did she think? Could she hear? Feel?

Reem would imagine how the child would be.

A girl, certainly.

Sweet face, big eyes, curly hair in pigtails.

Mischievous smile.

Herself replicated, repeated, returned.

'We will leave together, make our exit, you and I. Who knows? Perhaps we will come back to this world together . . . Perhaps we will know each other again, as mother and child in the next world, perhaps not. Perhaps this too will be a better time and place by the time we return. Who can say?'

At other times she would sing herself to sleep, crooning Fairuz quietly to the unborn.

Reem remembered Sabra and Shatila, the slaughter of the innocents. The baby Palestinian girl torn from her mother's womb, the mother dead, her throat cut, the newborn infant, umblilical cord still attached to the corpse, dying of starvation, thirst and exposure. And at Karantina, where the murdering Phalangists had used their bayonets on the pregnant, ripping the foetuses out of Kurd and Palestinian women alike, treating them like livestock. Worse. No slaughterhouse was ever like that.

It will never happen to a child of mine.

You will not be born into this nightmare not knowing who you are, fatherless, homeless, your soul adrift and without a past or a future to face these monstrosities.

We go to a better place, you and I.

Sanctuary.

'Do you hear me?'

Was that a kick? Surely not, it was far too early.

This time it was a truck that replied, its engine grumbling slowly down the avenue of firs.

Then the higher pitch of a motorbike.

Her watch showed 4.34 a.m.

'Reem.'

'Ustaz?'

She could smell him in the room, that male smell of tobacco, sweat and drink. He loomed over her, a darker shape than the darkness itself.

'You must get up, Reem. We are moving. Get your things together.'

She was always ready. She did not need to pack. Her bag was by the door. It was the way he had taught her. Just the book she was reading, the clothes she pulled on quickly, the comb she ran through her hair, shoes she pushed her feet into.

Reem found him out on the landing.

'Ready?'

'Yes.'

'Take this.'

He handed her two apples, a chunk of cheese and a plastic bottle of water.

'It will be some time before we eat again properly.'

He went down first, Reem following.

The birds were already singing, and there was a streak of pale light in the east. A low, pale mist shrouded the fields.

Reem felt immense relief, a heavy load lifted from her.

It was the end of the beginning.

For both of them.

THIRTY-EIGHT

Nick flew back to Beirut on Sunday, two days earlier than planned.

He had been gone barely three days in all. Fig Tree Bay had been a disappointment. He loathed every minute of it, and had not known what to do with himself. The beach out there was long and wide and of fine white sand. Perfect, in other words. The water was clear and clean. It reminded him of lemonade. It literally made his mouth water to look at it.

But that was all.

It was true what people said: there was Swedish wall-to-wall topless wherever he looked. But the tanned, blonde and well endowed Swedish girls who frequented the eastern resorts along with other Scandinavians and Germans did not speak much English, or perhaps they simply did not care to. They showed no interest in Nick, and they seemed to him so very much alike. They seemed to prefer the company of young Cypriot males. The bars were to be avoided; they were packed with pugnacious British squaddies, stocky youths covered with tattoos and with their heads shaved, projectile vomiting in the streets when they were not looking for a fight or a fuck. And after Lebanon the food seemed inedible, either raw or hopelessly overcooked, either way tasteless and devoid of garlic, olive oil or lemon – the way the northern Europeans seemed to want it.

He spent a restless first night in Nicosia's Holiday Inn. It was so quiet in the island capital that Nick could not sleep. The lack of gunfire and the empty streets made him nervous. The following morning, once he had paid his respects to the local UN representative, Nick hired a taxi for the drive east, through the one long extended building site into which the Greek Cypriots had turned their once exquisite island. Ranks of cheap concrete holiday homes in tower blocks were interspersed with seaside malls selling French fries, hot dogs and burgers along with 'English' pubs offering cold lager to busloads of scarlet-skinned, obese and skimpily dressed package tourists who had flown in on charter flights from Manchester, Luton, Stansted and Gatwick.

Cyprus had developed into the Mediterranean's prime processing plant for the tourist industry. To Nick, it had all the charm of a mechanized poultry factory. It was Magaluf all over again – except in Majorca it was still possible to bypass the worst bits and escape to parts almost uninfected by alien hordes.

In Fig Tree Bay, Nick tried to establish a simple routine, but it broke down before the end of the first day under the sheer weight of tedium. After an indifferent breakfast he pitched his towel on the beach, covered himself in suncream, smearing it on his face like warpaint, and settled down to read. He wore a white beach hat and sunglasses. He flung himself in the sea whenever the sun became unbearable.

By lunchtime he was bored.

That evening Nick hired a Suzuki convertible and drove west, the way he had come, stopping overnight at Limassol and moving on to the pebbly beaches favoured by British holidaymakers, to places such as Paphos and Pissouri, but here the tourists were older than the Scandinavians, mostly married couples and families.

It was Scunthorpe by the sea.

He called the airline, changed his flight.

He could not wait to get back. He drove to Larnaca and sat on a bench under an umbrella on the foreshore, his bag at his feet, waiting until it was time to make the ten-minute trip to the airport.

He knew there was nothing really wrong with any of the places he had visited. Not really.

It was entirely his problem, and it was this: Reem had been missing for eleven days.

Nick did not in the least mind the racket of west Beirut's streets, the intense heat, the logjam traffic, the fumes, the checkpoints, the stares – always the gaping at a foreigner. What was it Elias had said? Something to the effect that in Yemen the locals stare because they've knocked themselves out with their daily ritual of *qat*-chewing. In Beirut, it was because they were wondering to themselves why a foreigner was dumb enough, or mad enough, to hang around waiting to be kidnapped. It was Elias's idea of a joke.

It felt like home, nonetheless.

There was a lot of work that had backed up in his absence.

It would have to wait. Instead he riffled through the mounds of paper waiting on his desk, searching. The advertisements he had placed in *an-Nahar*, *as-Safir* and *L'Orient le Jour* headlined 'Missing – Reem Najjar' had brought but two responses, neither what he had hoped for.

No relatives or friends had come forward.

The first was simply a peremptory scrawl in Arabic, unsigned: 'Daoud would like to see you at your earliest convenience.'

The second was a sheet of grey notepaper with the embossed coat of arms and address of the British embassy. It too had been delivered by hand. The letter was brief, topped and bottomed in Dacre's distinctive handwriting: tidy, upright and very even.

Dear Nicholas,

We haven't seen you for ages. I noticed your advertisement vis-à-vis Miss Najjar. Your staff say you are in Cyprus. Do get in touch when you get back and let's have dinner and catch up. Sir H and Andrew both send their best wishes.

Yours,
Peregrine

Nick progressed no further with his in tray. There was an abrupt burst of gunfire directly in the street below, prompting a wilder fusillade in response.

Elias put his head round the door. He looked worried.

'This time it's Amal and Hizbollah . . .'

'Thanks, Elias. Get everyone away from the windows. What are they fighting over?'

Three rocket-propelled grenades detonated in swift succession, both men flinching at the impacts.

The staff scrambled to get into the passages and corridors, away from outside walls.

Elias came into Nick's office. There was barely room for the two of them and the desk. Elias was wearing a lightweight grey suit with a silver tie and matching foulard pocket hand-kerchief.

'It's the casino – you know the one, Nick, the entrance on the corner of the Commodore Hotel. It's in the basement. Hizbollah want to shut it down. It's long been an important source of revenue for the Amal commander in the area.'

Amal and Hizbollah were both overwhelmingly Shi'ite, the former with a founding charter based on the constitution of the United States, the latter an extensive social movement with backing from Iran and Syria, its small military wing trained by Iran's Revolutionary Guards. Hizbollah was disci-plined, organized, centralized and highly motivated. Amal had been around much longer, and had none of the zealotry of its rival.

Amal gunmen fought for fifty dollars a month.

Hizbollah's boys fought out of love and out of hate.

Love of Islam, love of country.

Hatred of foreign occupation, of Zionism.

Hizbollah was extending its grip street by street throughout west Beirut, and Amal was being squeezed out.

Nick went to the window and peered out.

'They're right outside,' Elias said. He was wringing his hands and looking sorrowful. This skirmishing was almost certainly going to spoil his lunch engagement.

They rang the bell first.

'Let them in.'

The staffer, Bashar, hesitated.

'I said let them in.'

There were five fighters. All about eighteen or nineteen, Nick thought, dressed in jeans and trainers and T-shirts. Two were clean-shaven, three had trim beards. Their hair was cut very short.

'*Salaam aleikum*.' Nick introduced himself as the boss, the *mudir* of the organization. 'I am sorry. You are very welcome, believe me, but we do not permit firearms in the UN office. It's the rule.'

He noticed they all had US-made M-16s.

They did not argue. Their leader ordered the rifles and spare magazines gathered up and taken out. Nick called for coffees all round and sent someone down to the cafe across the street to collect them. He invited the visitors to make themselves comfortable. They had the physical ease and alertness of trained soldiers. They were no longer individuals but parts of a whole, a unit, and one of the youngsters, himself no more than twenty, was clearly their commander. They deferred to him, and in this way were quite un-Lebanese. They sat quietly, looking about them, neither friendly nor hostile. Obedient to command. Polite. They had the professional soldier's capacity for waiting.

Without exception, they refused Nick's offer of cigarettes.

He knew joining Hizbollah was not easy. It involved a probationary period of several months in which recruits were encouraged to eschew cigarettes, swearing, crude talk of women and all bad habits. Personal cleanliness was insisted upon.

'We thought this was a media organization,' their leader said. 'Someone out there was taking photographs and we wanted a few copies for ourselves.'

Nick explained that the Yugoslav agency, Tanjug, was on the ground floor, the British television outfit Visnews was on the fourth, and there was the North American television network, CBS, on the sixth. Next door was AP along with NBC. Moscow's Novosti was also nearby.

They drank their coffee, thanked Nick gravely, shook hands with him and Elias, then collected their arms in the corridor where one of their number had kept watch.

The process had taken more than an hour of everyone's time.

The shooting was done, at least for now. Amal had been pushed back, losing an important source of local revenue. Hizbollah had advanced a couple of blocks more.

Nick wondered how long it would be before they took over Bliss Street and shut down Sammy's Bar.

The radios said two fighters were killed and seven wounded. Two civilians had been cut down in the crossfire. One was a deaf mute.

Nick returned to his office. He shut the door, his thoughts turning once again to Reem.

'She's left you, laddie, that's all there is to it.'

The waiter brought a second bottle of Ksara red to the table, turned the label to Dacre and on his nod of approval, started to uncork it.

'Thanks,' Nick said. 'That's a great help. Much appreciated.'

'Sorry, but I think it's all very simple. She's gone off, found someone else. Got herself a life. Beirut was dangerous. It damn near killed her. She needed to get out. I think the best thing you can do, Nick, is to put it down to experience and move on.'

'Easy for you to say. I asked her to marry me.'

Dacre looked up sharply.

'Then you've had a narrow escape.'

'There's one more thing you don't know. She's expecting my child.'

329

Dacre rubbed his face with one hand.

'So you see, Peregrine, I don't think she has, as you put it, just gone off, found someone else. Unless she's either had an abortion, or persuaded this other person the child is his and not mine. I asked her to marry me. I wanted to be a father. I still do. It's mine, too, you know. I offered to take her with me. I also said if she didn't want to leave, I was prepared to stay, even if it meant losing my job.'

'How did she take it?'

'She was pleased. She seemed pleased. Relieved. At least that was how it seemed to me at the time.'

'I'll say she must have been relieved. What changed?'

'I can't figure it out.'

Not entirely true, but Nick was not about to share his suspicions.

'That's all?'

'Then she said she'd made a mistake. There was no pregnancy. But I went to the hospital after she left, got hold of her doctor. She was lying. She was pregnant.'

'Have you heard from her at all since then?'

'She left me two messages. She said she loved me. She said she was sorry. She asked for my forgiveness. She hoped I would understand. That's all.'

'Understand what?'

'Leaving, I suppose.'

Nick knew it was not that straightforward.

It was one of Dacre's rare visits to the western sector, and he had invited Nick to the Spaghetteria for supper. The restaurant was a favourite of Nick's. The food was only so-so, but it looked out on the Corniche and the Mediterranean and he always got a warm welcome from the staff, even if they did serve up tinned peas. He was something of a regular in a city where to have regular habits at all was distinctly risky. Still, it was right below Nick's apartment block, a short run down a flight of stone steps to the seafront.

'I had no idea how strongly you felt, Nick. I am sorry.'

'As for OLCA, I checked it out. They say she's not a member, and never has been.'

'They would say that.'

Nick shrugged. 'It doesn't really help, though.'

'Ask yourself this, Nick. I know you feel badly. But do you think Reem would really have taken to life in merry England? The ruthlessness of life in the suburbs, the mortgage, the worn carpet, the damp, the endless utility bills, the street crime, the rain, the indigestible food, waiting for you to come home each day, the sheer loneliness . . .'

'To say nothing of the neighbours, the attitude towards foreigners.'

'Right.'

'Tell me, Perry. What is Diazinon?'

'Why?'

'Please answer the question.'

'It's a nerve agent.'

'Lethal?'

'Bloody hell, yes.'

'Did you know it was imported to Lebanon through a company called Bayard, a freight firm apparently connected to the Protector?'

'I've heard rumours.'

'That's all?'

'Why?'

'It took the form of a pesticide called Spectracide. I saw a yellow drum of the stuff the other day. It still had the Bayard shipping form and pesticide label. Bugs can't fly from Spectracide. Or was it Bugs can't abide Spectracide? I forget. I was told there was some sort of accident in the eastern sector some weeks ago. Several people were taken ill, some fell into a coma and two died. The premises were linked to the Protector. Ring any bells?'

'The communists told you this?'

'Maybe.'

'It's an old story, Nick. The fact is that things are very tense. They'll try anything on this side to stop el-Hami moving into Baabda palace, even if it's old stories to try to win over a young UN official.'

'I don't blame them, do you?'

'Maybe not. There's going to be a showdown. Everyone is reinforcing the front lines. Lebanon faces a choice. Is it an Arab and overwhelmingly Muslim country? Or is it a Christian-led ally of Israel and the United States, a right-wing Trojan Horse? Arms and ammunition are flowing into the illegal ports like never before. The Americans have mustered a carrier group offshore. The Protector's taking over in three days – four if you include today, Sunday.'

'So . . .'

Dacre drained his wine glass, picked up the bill and squinted at it. He nodded at someone over Nick's shoulder. Nick turned round in his chair to see a member of the embassy's close protection squad gesture to one of his comrades to fetch the diplomat's bullet-proof car and bring it up to the restaurant's front door.

'You should have stayed in Cyprus for another week or so, Nick. It would have been safer. I'm afraid no one is going to have time to spare worrying about this girlfriend of yours. I did warn you. There are bigger things at stake here right now. Shall we go?'

THIRTY-NINE

Reem liked the car. She liked the metallic grey paint and matching cloth upholstery in a darker shade of grey-blue. It was a manual four-door Honda saloon, just like the one Nick had rented on the east side. It smelled new, and looked impeccable inside and out.

She sat behind the wheel. It felt very comfortable. She found she could adjust the seat, and the angle of the backrest.

It had air conditioning.

'It's stolen?'

No answer.

The radio worked.

The Ustaz said, 'Don't touch the indicator switch.'

When she got out again, the Ustaz invited her to look in the boot, the wheel arches, and to use a little wheeled device with a mirror that was sometimes used by troops at the major checkpoints to look for bombs.

'What do you see?'

'Nothing. Nothing out of the ordinary.'

He helped her lift up the spare wheel in the boot, but there was nothing there, either.

'Come down here,' he said. She followed him into the well below the car.

He looked up and pointed a flashlight at the underside.

'See the wiring?'

He ran the light down the side where the wiring ran fore and aft, grouped together.

Reem nodded.

'Looks normal to you, does it?'

'Yes.'

They climbed out of the pit.

Whoever else was about – Reem assumed it was the mechanic and possibly the explosives people – they must have been told to steer clear, take a walk out the back. To avoid her. To avoid seeing her, or being seen.

In case she was taken alive.

She opened one of the rear doors, bent down and pulled up the rear seat. It took some doing in the heat, but she managed it with a final tug. There was nothing there, either.

'So, where is it?'

'Hidden.'

'All of it?'

'They'll never find it. They'd have to take it apart, piece by piece.'

Reem was impressed. She was meant to be.

'You'll take her for a test run. She's ready to go now, but I think it would be good to get used to the handling with the little extra weight.'

It was cleverly done, as the Ustaz explained. The fuel tank was now packed with C-4 plastic explosive. It looked normal. It was normal. Anyone taking off the petrol cap would smell petrol, and anyone probing around in there would find – petrol. The difference was that the fuel was now contained in a litre-sized heavy-duty plastic bag nestling within a cavity carved out of the packs of C-4. Like a colostomy bag only thicker, stronger, the Ustaz said. It contained enough four-star to take her and the car along with its secret load around the city a couple of times.

The wiring underneath – the set that linked up the electrics, particularly the indicator lights – was new, but it had been carefully 'stressed' to fit in with the rest of it.

The battery had been tested and was fully charged, the spark plugs had been changed, the carburettor cleaned, the oil and water topped up, the tyre pressures checked.

The Ustaz had thought of everything, but then of course this had been months in the planning.

There was only one question in Reem's mind.

She said, 'When?'

It was a garage, one of those anonymous places where the concrete forecourt and interior are steeped in decades of sticky, slippery petroleum spills. There was nothing to see out front except a ramp, a pile of worn-out tyres, an ancient air pump, a high-pressure hose and a couple of pre-war posters of Formula One cars, advertising products from Michelin and General Motors.

Inside it was crowded with vehicles, and parts of vehicles, wrecks most of them. Reem saw drums, acetylene gear, a step-ladder, a rack of soiled overalls, a workbench, a big toolbox, an overhead block and tackle, coils of hosing, a pile of rags and a selection of oil tins of various sizes and grades.

Junk, all of it.

A Pirelli calendar of a naked brunette hung up against the glass booth at the back – the glass panes cracked and covered with brown paper, presumably for privacy. Hardly the image of a way station on the path to martyrdom, but then that would be the point.

Dust everywhere, blowing up into tiny squalls.

All Reem knew was that this was in the port area, on the east side, and less than a mile by her reckoning from her final destination.

'You'll turn right,' the Ustaz said. 'That will take you to the end of the cul-de-sac, then left and you are on a straight east–west road – godowns, workshops and light industrial premises on either side. The port area is on your right. Karantina is half a mile ahead, also on your right. The road is straight. Almost immediately you will see an army checkpoint ahead of you. Slow down and come up to it gently. You are not turning right into the port so they won't be interested in you. They're only interested in people entering Beirut port. They'll look at you because you're a sight for sore eyes, and you've got a smart car. Play along with it. You have nothing to hide. Let them see your smile.'

She started the car, let it warm up in neutral while the Ustaz spoke. He was sitting directly behind her on the rear seat.

'Once you're through the army checkpoint, it's a clear run past Karantina. You'll see the two sandbag emplacements and the two soldiers on your right. They'll watch you go by but they won't try to stop you. If you're not going too fast, you can glance over to the entrance. You should see el-Hami's Merc parked in there. Keep going. Don't rush it. You'll see the red containers marking the start of the chicane ahead of the Green Line. The containers are a warning and they provide some cover from snipers lodged just across on the western side. The road dips, then rises again. Slow down, make an easy turn at the bottom of the dip just ahead of the containers and come back again. Clear so far?'

'Yes.'

'On the way back the army is not going to be interested in you. They may watch you because they're bored, but they won't interfere. Keep going. Keep going past this turn-off, too. When you get to the end of the road you'll see a couple of big gum trees on your left. Turn there. There's a cafe, and plenty of room to turn. There's more traffic there because it's a crossroads and the coastal highway is just beyond. Then come back to us. The doors will be open and we'll be waiting for you. Any questions?'

'No.'

'You will be followed and videoed all the way. The chase car and camera is for you, not us. You'll see the video later to assess your own driving skills and we can discuss how it went. Okay?'

'No problem.'

'Excellent.'

He put his right hand on the door handle.

'Now the most important thing, Reem – I have to remind you not to touch the indicator-light switch. If you do, you'll blow up yourself and everyone else within a hundred and fifty metres. This is your weapon, your hair trigger, and it's loaded and ready to fire.'

Reem felt that quick stab of nerves as he climbed out of the car. He shut the back door quietly and went past her up to the garage gates and started to drag them open. They rattled and shook, but they rolled back easily.

She felt her heartbeat rise.

Allegro vivace.

Reem had the antidote. She slipped a cassette into the player and jabbed the play button.

Mozart's Violin Concerto No. 5.

In A major.

She breathed in, slowly, as the first chords filled the car.

She eased off the brake.

Slipped into first gear, nudged the pedal.

Breathed out. Slowly.

The Ustaz stood aside and watched Reem drive out past him into the hard sunlight.

FORTY

'Nick? Nick, wake up for God's sake.'

'What?'

'Wake up, Nick.'

'Who is this?'

'It's Perry.'

'What's the time?'

'It's four fifty.'

'Fucking hell, major. It's still dark. What do you want?'

'You'd better get over here.'

'Where?'

'The crossings open in just over an hour. I need you over here.'

'What for? What is this?'

'They might not be open for very long. They're going to shut them before noon. You've got to move quickly.'

'What do you want?'

'Your Land-Rover was found on the road to Baabda. Apparently it was stuffed with explosives and various munitions, and wired up to an electrical detonator hidden under a culvert.'

Silence.

'You there, Nick?'

'Yes.'

'Your friend el-Hami has lodged a formal protest with the embassy, accusing both ourselves and the United Nations of a conspiracy to kill him tomorrow when he takes over the

338

presidency. He accuses you personally of actively assisting the would-be assassins. He says the embassy provided support. He's got all the television people over there, and he's brought in a US Navy demolition team. They plan to destroy your vehicle in a controlled explosion in front of the cameras. Several dozen residents have been evacuated from their homes. It's a media circus over here. He's making a meal of this. He's going to issue a statement to the press at noon. Sir Henry is apoplectic.'

'Bloody hell.'

'You and I are going to see el-Hami. He'll be at his office by seven. We have an appointment at seven thirty. We'll try to head him off. I'll do the grovelling. We'll try to get him to agree to get rid of the television crews and scrap the press statement in return for a promise of full cooperation in any investigation. You can explain as best you can about Reem.'

'Reem?'

'Reem Najjar. Isn't that her name? El-Hami says you actively helped her, introduced her into his circle, let her drive your UN vehicle around east Beirut without authorization, and that you provided the camera she used to photograph her potential victims. Is it true, Nick? He says her prints were found in your vehicle. He says she is a communist terrorist, trained by Syria and the man they call the Ustaz. El-Hami says his security services have scored a major coup against terrorism, but they are still searching for her. He says you were in cahoots with Syrian intelligence, and claims to have evidence of meetings between yourself and Colonel Daoud – both pictures and audio, apparently. It's all great for his political platform. He promises to bring law and order to Lebanon, to expel foreign forces – meaning the Syrians, not the Israelis – and eradicate terrorism. Nick, are you hearing any of this?'

'It's bollocks, all of it.'

'You've been declared persona non grata, by the way. You've got forty-eight hours to get out of the country or face deportation.

It doesn't mean much over in the western sector, no doubt, but your employers will probably pull you out anyway, if only for your safety.'

There were three Soviet-supplied Syrian army vehicles outside the drab structure where Daoud had his office: two GAZ-69s and a UAZ-469, both carrying Syrian airborne insignia. Pink Panthers – Syrian special forces soldiers in pink desert camouflage, wearing helmets and armed with Kalashnikovs and RPGs – squatted or lay in the street, smoking or sleeping, using their packs as cushions.

Nick took the stairs two at a time. No one stopped him. He found Daoud in his office, slippered feet up on the desk. He was reading the morning papers. He looked exhausted, unshaven. He wore a paisley dressing gown over rumpled shirt and trousers.

'Mr Lorimer. What a pleasant surprise.' Daoud did not look in the least surprised, nor did he seem particularly pleased. The colonel nodded to the empty chair opposite and pushed a packet of cigarettes towards Nick. He got up and shuffled to the door, put his head out into the corridor and shouted for coffee. He shut the door again and flopped down in his chair.

Nick helped himself to a cigarette, though he really did not want it. 'I'm apparently working with you in setting up el-Hami's assassination, and have been declared persona non grata. My UN vehicle has been found on the way to Baabda, rigged with explosives.'

Daoud put his papers aside.

'And?'

'My presence is required in the eastern sector. I'm going to see the Protector to try to explain. Of course, I'll deny everything, including any Syrian connection. It's all nonsense. He's about to put out a statement accusing me, British embassy staff and yourself of organizing and supporting an attempt on his life –

timed to coincide with his move tomorrow to the presidential palace for the inauguration ceremony.'

Daoud smiled. His face was puffy, his eyes red-rimmed. He looked as if he had been up all night.

'Why come to see me?'

'I wanted to assure you in person I had nothing to do with any of this. And I wanted to ask if there's anything – anything at all – that you can tell me.'

There was a knock at the door and a young Syrian brought in the coffee.

Daoud spoke to him briefly. Nick made out 'Najjar' and 'documents'.

'I have sent for her file.'

'Whose?' Nick pretended he had not understood.

'Reem Najjar. Your friend.'

'You knew?'

'I think I told you before, Mr Lorimer, that we know a great deal, but we don't necessarily have the means to do anything about what we know. It's in the nature of intelligence that we do not always know what it is we know, and our political masters prefer to know even less.'

'But you knew about Reem.'

The file arrived and was placed in front of the colonel. It was several inches thick, the grey cover held together with tape. Daoud carefully opened it up.

Daoud blew smoke at the ceiling, then looked down at the papers.

'Let me tell you a story, Mr Lorimer. One of my jobs here is to question suspects who are detained and brought here for investigation. One evening some people were brought in from the airport. They had come in on the last flight from Larnaca. One of them was a young woman, Reem Najjar.'

He paused, and sipped the coffee.

'This was about two months ago. Yes, I have the date here.' He glanced down. 'March six. I had instructions – I'm afraid I cannot tell you whose instructions – to question Miss Najjar and, if necessary, to use physical pressure. You understand?'

Nick was not sure he understood why anyone would give orders of that kind, and he was trying to grapple with the image of what Daoud might do to his prisoners.

'I was asked not to allow my people to mark the suspect, not to inflict any lasting damage, but to use my discretion.'

He finished his coffee and avoided looking at Nick.

'She resisted. She gave us nothing. She was defiant. She tried to fight back. I remember her very well. It was a most memorable evening. Or should I say morning. I was impressed, quite honestly. She was not intimidated. In the event, we let her go. No lasting damage was done. I received a telephone call ordering me to free her, but I did not inform the prisoner of that fact. One of my men drove her home. I think she lived in Verdun. Perhaps she told you . . .'

Reem had said nothing about this to Nick.

'What are you saying?'

'That this Reem Najjar was arrested by Syrian security forces on entering the country, was detained as a suspect, interrogated and, when nothing implicating her in criminal or subversive political activity was found, she was released. What else could we have done?' Daoud looked up and opened both hands. 'You may inform your British friends and the so-called Protector of these facts. I hope it's helpful.'

'In other words . . .'

'In other words, Mr Lorimer, Syria is as anxious to stamp out terrorist activity as the Western powers. We have all suffered enough from state terrorism at the hands of our southern neighbour. We have never been, and are not, involved in preparing bombs or trying to assassinate a future head of state in Lebanon or any other country.'

This time he did not see Nick to the door.

*

'Ready?'

Dacre looked at his watch. He had been waiting for almost an hour.

There were two Land-Rovers this time, both white, both carrying small Union Jacks on the front and rear. Five members of the embassy's close protection team were on hand, each armed with a pistol and carrying a sub-machine gun.

Dacre and Nick were in the lead vehicle with two bodyguards.

The major turned in his seat and looked at Nick sitting in the back. 'Well?'

'Well what?'

'Do you know where she is?'

'Reem? I've no idea.'

Nick did not care about Dacre. He did not care about Her Britannic Majesty's Government. He did not care about himself or his job. He wanted to find Reem. She was what mattered. He was tempted to jump out and make a mad dash down the street, find a taxi and head back to the western sector.

But what would he do then?

He had drawn a blank. He could not find her on his own.

The Royal Military Policeman sitting next to Nick – wearing a khaki waistcoat full of pockets and zips like a photographer's jacket and clutching a Sterling sub-machine gun – gave no sign of listening to what was said. He seemed to be watching the passing traffic, the windows and roofs as they passed. Nick could not see the soldier's eyes behind his Ray-Bans.

'You have to feed him something, Nicholas. You have to, if you want to get off the hook. Anything. If you know where she is, give her up for God's sake.'

Nick did not know where Reem was, but even if he had, he told himself, he would never have given her location away – not to Dacre, not to Daoud, certainly not to el-Hami. Not even if they used a thumbscrew.

He said nothing. They rolled down the hill from Hazmieh towards the port. All the windows were open. It was already very warm. Nick could see the cranes – rusting, unused – above the shell-pocked roofs of the port warehouses. He glimpsed one freighter lying on its side next to the quay, its funnel and masts almost at a right angle, parallel to the oily sea water.

Dacre turned again.

'When did you know?'

'I guessed a few days ago, while I was in the south. Everything seemed to fall into place. I had no idea, really.'

'That's not good enough.'

'What?'

'El-Hami wanted to take you when we brought you in. Have you detained and interrogated by his people and then tried on terrorism charges. Sir Henry stepped in. He said he would close down the mission on safety grounds if you were touched. He said he would make sure you left the country, but on no account were you to be arrested.'

'I'm grateful to Sir Henry.'

Nick had no wish to leave, not until he had found Reem.

'So do us all a favour, Nick. Earn your keep. Come clean. Don't hold anything back. Give them whatever you have, okay? El-Hami likes all things British, from Labradors to Purdeys. Remember that. We can use it, but don't hold out on him. He has a lousy temper.'

So this was what taking sides meant.

The street down by the port was straight. It ran east to west. There were warehouses and workshops on either side, most of them run down and shabby, still with the names of the firms above their doors. Tanourian and Sons – Importers and Exporters. Bassam Brothers Machine Tools. Ashur Shipping. Tripoli Freight Services.

Directly ahead was a Lebanese army checkpoint. The RMP driver slowed gently. They did not even have to stop. The soldiers waved the British on, smiling as they passed. Perhaps they recognized the flags as well as the young men in sunglasses with automatic weapons smiling back at them and giving them the thumbs up. It was all very cheery.

Nick looked to his right and saw the Lebanese soldiers were guarding one of the entrances to the port. He could see the ship he had spotted earlier, the freighter. This time he could see that the funnel was shot full of holes, and there was a gash several metres wide in the side of the vessel.

It looked as if it had caught fire when it was hit.

Dacre was sitting forward.

'Slow down. It's the next right.'

'Sir.'

The next bunch were not soldiers. They were Lebanese Forces. The only signs Nick saw suggesting they were not Israelis were the name tags. Instead of Hebrew, they were written in both Arabic and Latin script.

The Land-Rovers stopped. The gunman nearest the driver of the first vehicle collected all the documents and went through them.

Another, standing inside the sandbagged checkpoint by the white archway, spoke into a radio handset.

No smiles now.

The two Land-Rovers moved forward slowly, wheeling left into a parking lot. Nick spotted a big S-class Mercedes he assumed belonged to el-Hami.

'Over there,' Dacre said.

They parked, reversing into place, the two vehicles side by side, facing out.

They all climbed out, Dacre pulling at shirt and pants where they stuck to him.

'Stay around, Staff. Find some shade if you can. But you lads keep your eyes open and the vehicles in view. Be alert. I don't trust any of these people.' .

'Don't worry about us, sir.'

Dacre said, 'We'll be as quick as we can.'

There was a carpeted entrance, a receptionist with fake blonde hair and very long nails, a circular staircase up to the first floor and a chilly air-conditoned waiting room with leather sofas and armchairs, low tables and magazines. Like a dentist's waiting room, Nick thought. There were framed Tourism Ministry posters on the walls. Jbeil, the cedars, Baalbek. Beyond another glass door was an open-plan office where Nick assumed Sylvie worked among the various assistants and secretaries. He could see heads bent over typewriters, and occasionally a female shape would hurry past the door. He saw no sign of Sylvie. Maybe it was too early. At the far end of the open-plan area was a pair of double doors set in mock wood panelling.

El-Hami's office.

Dacre slumped in one of the waiting-room sofas. He was frowning, and occasionally he muttered to himself under his breath. He played with his regimental tie.

The tension was getting to Nick, too, but he stayed on his feet.

He glanced at his watch.

7.28.

He turned to the window, a narrow loophole that looked out on the Karantina parking lot and the archway.

He saw a grey car on the move. A four-door saloon. It was a Honda, he thought, and there was only one occupant.

It had stopped at the entrance, just before the sandbags.

God, these people started work early.

Maybe it was Sylvie.

Nick felt hungry and thirsty. He wanted his breakfast. He had a throbbing headache over his right eye. He told himself it was the cigarettes and coffee and the fact he had spent most of the night slouching around west Beirut.

Yes, about three months ago he would have felt ashamed. He

would have done what everyone asked of him. He would have tried to push it away from him, to wash his hands of it, to distance himself. From Reem, from Khaled, from all of it. Above all, he would have felt that so very middle class English emotion of embarrassment – embarrassment at being made a fool of, embarrassment at being involved, at becoming infected, at being committed. So he had been used. Sure he had. He had brought his office, his role, into disrepute. He had been careless, negligent even. Now it no longer mattered. Not to him. He did not feel guilty. Since he had stepped ashore at Jounieh, a stranger's brains all over his trainers, he had changed. He did not quite know how.

The woman driver had her side window down and was talking to the militiamen, gesticulating with one hand.

The gunman nearest to the driver was nodding and smiling.

The sentries seemed to know who it was.

The car started to move forward, picking up speed.

FORTY-ONE

07.20.

'Your papers.'

She took them from the Ustaz.

This was unexpected. There was a Canadian passport with a maple leaf on the cover, and an international driving licence.

'You're Fatima Hebden. You're twenty-five years old. Sylvie's friend. You met last year. You are of Lebanese origin, married to a Canadian national working in Beirut. Your maiden name is Darwish. You come from Montreal.'

Reem opened the passport. 'Fatima looks quite a lot like me.'

'She does, yes. She's taller, older and heavier, but it doesn't show in the photo.'

'And the real Fatima Hebden?'

'Asleep. Or perhaps eating her breakfast.'

'Has she reported the loss of her documents?'

'She doesn't know. She probably will know in an hour or two.'

'Is Sylvie at work?'

'She doesn't turn up, usually, until eight.'

'So?'

'You'll say you'll wait for her. If you're asked. Though it's highly unlikely anyone will ask.'

'Okay.'

'Anything else?'

Reem shook her head. She had not expected a last-minute change in identity. She knew there had to be a reason, and a good

348

one, but she was not going to ask. Not now. She guessed that her own cover must have been blown. What other reason could there be?

'Something to eat?'

'No, thanks. I feel a little queasy.'

It was not nerves. It was her first bout of morning sickness. She had thrown up what was left of her supper in the bathroom reserved for her use at the back of the garage, but no one saw or heard.

'Nothing at all?'

'I'd like to leave a few minutes early, go right rather than left and call in at the cafe at the end of the street and maybe get some water and a sandwich, then turn round and make the run. I'd rather do it that way if you don't mind.'

She saw no point in going down to the containers near the Green Line and turning round there. There was no logic to it.

The Ustaz hesitated, then nodded. 'Fine.'

There was more to it. She wanted the extra time and the visit to the cafe in case she felt ill again. She was already wearing her favourite dress. She was using her scarf as a wrap to cover the worst of the scars because her left would be nearest her side window. The wounds had almost entirely vanished, but there was a shadow of discoloration all the way round, starting at the elbow and running up to the left shoulder. The scar tissue was mostly on the inside and back of the upper arm, which helped.

Reem opened the car door and slipped in behind the wheel. She took the stolen documents and placed them next to her on the passenger seat to her right, along with her purse containing a few thousand lira, just enough for breakfast.

She checked herself in the mirror on the back of the sun visor and looked at her watch.

The Ustaz was opening the doors, pulling them back.

Reem slipped on her sunglasses.

It was going to be a scorcher of a day.

She turned the key in the ignition.

They had already agreed not to say goodbye.

07.23.

She turned in under the trees, halting in the shade.

A youth, wiping his hands on his apron, came out to her.

'Sabah al-khair.'

Reem replied, *'Sabah al-noor.'*

She ordered a Coke and *manaeesh*.

It took a matter of two minutes. Reem no longer felt nauseous. For no particular reason she felt hungry and thirsty. By the time the boy brought out the food and drink on a tray, Reem was salivating. She checked that the Coke was cold and asked him to open the bottle.

She handed over the money, and left the boy a tip.

'Shukrun.'

The way back was clear. The road was quite deserted.

She drank a little Coke and started on the sandwich, folding the paper down, careful not to drop oil on her clothing.

As she approached the narrow alley containing the garage, she slowed down. She did not glance left to see if the Ustaz was still there, watching, but she put her left hand out of the window and waved.

The soldiers looked at her out of curiosity more than anything else. Again, she slowed down. As she passed, she looked over at them, smiled and took a bite from the sandwich.

She held the Coke between her knees.

They waved her on and turned away.

Reem turned on the radio and found a music station.

07.28.

'Bonjour.'

She held the Coke in her right, the passport in the left.

'*Bonjour, m'mselle.*'

The Phalangist gunman took a step forward, reached for the passport, turned it around, opened it, glanced at it and handed it back.

'*Merci.*'

He stepped back. Now she had finished the Coke, she picked up the sandwich and took a huge bite. She nodded, looking a little embarrassed.

The gunman laughed at her awkwardness.

Both of them were grinning at her. They had pushed their helmets back. The man nearest her was sweating, and the sunlight caught the crucifix inside his shirt. His name tag read 'George Talat'.

Reem swallowed and smiled back at George.

She used the paper to wipe her fingers, then leaned forward and took a tissue from the glovebox. She touched her lips with it, wiped her hands and dropped it to the floor of the car near her feet.

By now they were waiting for her to move, not the other way round.

She was very deliberate. She kept her hands in view. She put the Honda into first, let off the brake, and rolled through the arch.

El-Hami's car was parked ahead, over on the left.

She saw the wire. The pipe.

The headquarters.

FORTY-TWO

The Honda speeded up.

Nick said, 'Major . . .'

The woman wore sunglasses. She had dark hair.

She was not going to park. She was headed straight for the offices.

She smiled.

Nick opened his mouth. He wanted to shout a warning. He could see at once it would be too late. That knowledge was immediately followed by recognition. It couldn't be Reem, but then again it was. Definitely. No doubt about it. He was not seeing things. It was her. The Honda was very close. Nick could not take his eyes off it. He saw every detail, the way the sunlight shifted across the polished curve of the roof, the way the chrome caught the light, winking back at him. Reem looked up – right at him, or so it seemed.

Her lips were parted.

The yellow dress.

His hands clawed at the window, hammered at the glass. There was no handle, no clasp. It would not open. It was not meant to. It was thick security glass. If only he could lean out, show himself.

Would she stop, even then?

He threw his shoulder against it, but it did not budge. In the corner of his eye he saw figures detach themselves from the car park. They moved towards the Honda. He heard the pop-popping of gunfire through the security glass. The British bodyguards. One had halted, was leaning towards the car. The car seemed to

352

hesitate. It trembled and shook like a dog emerging from water, only it was not water that flew up but fragments of glass. The man with the gun was still leaning forward, swivelling, his front leg bent, his back leg straight. He held a short black weapon into his shoulder.

Nick wanted to warn her.

Too late. The windows along both sides of the Honda flew outwards, then it was the turn of the windscreens front and back to collapse.

The shooting stopped, but the car came on, steady as before. Reem grasped the wheel with both hands. Nick could see her fingers quite clearly.

She showed no sign of having been hit.

They must have switched magazines and reloaded their weapons because they were shooting again, more bursts of three and four rounds, aiming low this time, trying to hit the tyres.

The bonnet of the Honda vanished from view. Followed by Reem. Nick's mouth was still open, the tongue still working to find the right sounds, his face pressed against the window. The warning shout was replaced by another word. The car was gone. It was right below. Nick knew, or rather sensed, what was about to happen. He also knew he could do nothing. There was recognition of another kind, a fleeting realization. His Land-Rover, left on the road to Baabda, was a diversion. So was he. Yes, so was he.

Reem's stalking horse.

Always had been.

Dacre was halfway to his feet behind him.

Voices reached Nick, among them el-Hami's.

The receptionist said, 'The president-designate will see you now.'

The president-designate.

All that Nick had seen and thought – the shooting, the Honda accelerating, Reem's face, the dress and her hands – all this had taken just long enough for Dacre to rise halfway from his seat.

He was shouting something, but Nick did not hear what it was. The single word that had formed in Nick's own mouth now escaped. It was the guttural sound of his own terror. It was a cry of disbelief at the sight of his own life ending right in front of his eyes. It was a shout of dismay that this was not the way it was supposed to be. It was the name of the woman he loved. It was all these things.

'Reem.'

It was the very last thing he heard.